THE
INNOCENT
WIFE

BOOKS BY LISA REGAN

THE
INNOCENT
WIFE

LISA REGAN

bookouture

Published by Bookouture in 2022

An imprint of Storyfire Ltd.
Carmelite House
50 Victoria Embankment
London EC4Y 0DZ

www.bookouture.com

ISBN: 978-1-80314-909-7
eBook ISBN: 978-1-80314-957-8

For Gemma Karim and all my amazing readers

PROLOGUE

DECEMBER

Josie's heart lurched into her throat as she watched a man on a bicycle fly along the sidewalk, headed directly toward seven-year-old Harris Quinn. She cursed herself for letting Harris run so far ahead, but it was almost Christmas and the storefronts lining Denton's central business district were awash in lights and the kind of person-sized decorations that no seven-year-old could resist touching—or sometimes climbing. In fact, it was a six-foot-tall lighted snowman that had caught his attention, its glow more pronounced in the waning daylight. Harris stood on the pavement, staring up at its top hat, his mouth agape, completely unaware of the cyclist coming at him.

Surely the cyclist was aware of Harris. But Josie couldn't see beneath the brim of his helmet. His head was lowered, body compact and pointed at Harris like a missile. An older woman stumbled to the side as he pedaled past her, nearly catching the sleeve of her coat with a handlebar. A tinsel-wrapped parking meter saved her from kissing concrete.

"Get off the sidewalk!" she shouted after the guy.

Josie picked up her pace, one hand waving, trying to catch

the attention of either Harris or the cyclist. "Har—" His name lodged in her throat.

The entire thing took seconds but felt like an eternity. Harris took a step backward, firmly in the center of the sidewalk, and turned to look at Josie.

Josie yelled, "Stop!"

Harris's face creased with confusion. The cyclist must not have heard her because he made no attempt to slow down. He was only a couple of feet from colliding with Harris. Josie's throat constricted. Why weren't her damn legs working? There was a flash of red as a woman sprinted from the street and onto the sidewalk, directly into the path of the cyclist. She seemed to come from nowhere. In one fluid movement, she closed the distance to Harris, scooped him up—no easy feat at his age—and stepped out of the way of the cyclist, bumping against the lighted snowman. For a second, it appeared they were going to make it out of the way unscathed. But then the cyclist's handlebar caught on a brown paper bag swinging from the woman's wrist. Like a dancer twirling away from her partner, she let go of Harris, who slid to the ground, and her arms flailed in the air as the impact of handlebar on bag spun her. The bag tore, its contents splaying all over the sidewalk. Glass shattered. The woman fell.

The cyclist kept going.

Josie ran after him, screaming obscenities, until she felt a small, familiar hand tugging at hers. Harris's face was flushed with cold and the excitement of what had just happened. "JoJo," he said. "That lady saved me. Did you see it?"

Trying to rein in her rage, Josie sucked in a deep breath. In through her nose for a four-count. Out through her mouth for another four-count. She did two more, but she still felt apoplectic. Stupid breathing exercises. They never worked for her. She should have tried to catch and arrest the guy. After all, she was a detective for the Denton Police Department. She was off duty, but she could have called dispatch and had a uniformed officer come take him into custody.

Nestled among the mountains of Central Pennsylvania, a great deal of the city spanned the rural areas on its edges. However, bicyclists were becoming more problematic in the central part of the city where the buildings were crowded closer together. The inconsistent weather—feeling like spring one day and winter the next, with more warm days than cold—meant that they were out in force even in December.

Harris pulled at her hand again, this time drawing her back to the scene of the incident. "JoJo, you have to put a whole bunch of dollars into the swear jar. Also, I think that lady needs help."

The woman—Josie's new hero—was still on her ass on the sidewalk, a broken high heel in her hand. Around her were fragments of something ceramic, a tan cashmere scarf with the tags still on, and a wooden box that had cracked open, golf balls and tees spilling out. Harris rushed over and dropped to his knees, gathering up the balls. A pair of women came out of the store. They offered to help but Josie waved them off and knelt beside Harris.

Pushing her long sandy hair out of her face, the woman smiled. Up close, Josie noticed how the corners of her eyes crinkled. Mid-forties, probably. She was dressed expensively in a pantsuit and a coat that probably cost more than Josie made in a month. She said, "Thank you."

Josie helped Harris get all the golf balls and tees back into the wooden box. "Please," she said. "I'm the one who should thank you. That was amazing."

Harris tried to close the lid, but it wouldn't sit right. One of the hinges was broken. Josie took it from him to see if there was any way for her to fix it.

The woman said, "I'm just glad I was in the right place at

the right time." Turning to Harris, she asked him, "Are you okay?"

He picked up the scarf, dusting it off. "I'm not hurt at all!"

"I'm so glad," she said, slowly getting to her feet. "That gave your mom a scare!"

Josie stood as well, holding the box closed with both hands. "Oh, I'm not his mom. I'm his—"

She broke off. There wasn't really a word for her relationship to Harris. Her first husband, Ray Quinn, had started seeing Harris's mother, Misty, after he and Josie separated. Both Josie and Ray had worked for the Denton Police Department. After Ray died in the line of duty, Misty gave birth to Harris. Josie had been helping Misty raise Harris. The two of them had started out rivals but their love for Harris had bonded them for life.

With a sigh, Harris said, "She's my aunt. Pretty much."

The woman laughed. "My name is Claudia... Claudia White."

Harris handed her the scarf. "My name is Harris Quinn, and this is my Aunt JoJo. Her last name is Quinn, too."

Josie held out the box. "I think it's broken. I'm so sorry. I'd love it if you'd let me replace it, together with whatever broke."

Claudia took the box from Josie, putting her broken heel on top of it. A large diamond ring sparkled on her left ring finger. The light from the standing snowman glanced off the huge emerald-cut center diamond, as well as the many smaller diamonds wrapping halfway around the band, sending reflective sparkles dancing across her face. Beneath the ring was a thinner band with even more diamonds. Josie tried not to gawk, but her mind was already calculating. That ring and band had probably cost more than her car. Claudia shifted her weight onto her stockinged foot and with her other heel, kicked the broken ceramic pieces behind the snowman. "It's fine, really," she said. "I was returning the mug anyway."

"JoJo, I'm freezing," Harris complained, grabbing her hand again.

With her free hand, Josie opened the door to the store and ushered Claudia inside. "Let's at least get out of the cold. Listen, they're not going to let you return any of this stuff. I'm happy to replace it for you. It's the least I can do."

The store was called Heartfelt Treasures, owned and operated by a local couple for the last fifty years. It was large and carried all kinds of merchandise, including some apparel. Mostly, they styled themselves as an upscale gift shop. Their slogan was *"Rare Finds for Discerning Minds."* Just inside was a park bench with a life-sized Santa figure seated on it. Claudia dropped down beside it.

Harris said, "JoJo, I bet we can find something for Uncle Noah in here! Can I look?"

Josie touched the top of his blond head. The swirl of hair at his scalp still made her breath catch, even after all these years. His father had had the exact same whorl. "Sure," she said. "But what's the rule?"

"I have to stay in your line of sight."

She nudged him away from her and he ran off, around the bench, past the Christmas items and toward the men's section, careful to look back and make sure he could still make eye contact with Josie.

Claudia turned her body and watched him go. When she turned back, her expression was wistful, almost pained. "He's very sweet. Very smart."

"Yes," Josie agreed. "He really is. Mrs. White, please let me do something for you."

Claudia took off her other heel and handed it to Josie. "Can you make this one match the broken one?"

Josie stared at it for a moment, uncomprehending.

"Please," Claudia said. "I've got to be able to walk back to my car. I can't do it with one shoe four inches higher than the other."

Josie would have rolled an ankle in four-inch heels. "This looks expensive."

Claudia sighed but her easy smile was still in place. "It is, but the other one is already ruined. I'd do it myself but..." She looked around, as if searching for something she could use to break the heel off. Her gaze landed on Josie's feet. "You've got boots on. Maybe...?"

Josie took the shoe from Claudia. Leaning down, she slid the heel under one of her boots.

Harris ran over, a tie in hand. "Look!" he exclaimed. "For Uncle Noah! He wears ties to work sometimes."

Josie eyed his selection. "I think he would like that."

With her other foot, she kicked twice, hard, and split the shoe from its heel. Harris's eyes went cartoon-wide. In a low, shocked voice, he said, "JoJo, you broke Claudia's shoe."

Claudia took it from Josie and slid it onto her foot. Then she put on the other one.

"It's okay, buddy. She gave me permission." Josie took the tie from Harris. "This can be from you."

Harris looked to Claudia, who stood up and took a few steps back and forth. Satisfied that she was fine with Josie breaking her shoe, he turned back to Josie. "I'll go look for something from you!"

"Oh well, I don't—" Josie started, but he was already off, weaving through the Christmas displays back to the men's section.

Claudia said, "Shopping for your husband?"

"Yeah. He's really tough to shop for." She ran a finger across the tie.

"Many men are," said Claudia. "What does he like?"

The answer came to her quickly and without thought. "Me."

Claudia laughed. "That's very good."

Josie said, "I didn't mean that to sound—well, he just—actually, he's really obsessed with astronomy. I was thinking of getting him a telescope. Taking him up to Cherry Springs state park in the spring. You can see the Milky Way from there, from what I hear."

"The telescope is great, but the experience is always a better way to go. Time with you under the stars?" She winked at Josie. "What gift could be better?"

Harris returned, a triumphant grin on his face. He held up a box of bandages in the shape of bacon strips. "This is the perfect gift!" he announced. "Uncle Noah loves bacon."

ONE

JANUARY

An icy drop of rain splashed onto the back of Margot's neck as she sprinted from her car, across the street, and toward the jewelry store. More drops followed, the sound of the rain going from an uneven patter to a steady roar as she pulled open the door to the shop. A gust of cold January air lifted the edges of her skirt and propelled her inside. Glass display cases formed a square in the center of the store. More glass countertops lined the walls. A white-haired man in a collared shirt stood inside the square helping a couple choose a diamond bracelet. Margot strode past them, her heels clicking against the white tile, and found a young female sales associate near the back of the store. Margot didn't wait for her to ask if she needed help. Instead, she announced, "I'm here to pick something up for Beau Collins."

The woman's fingers tugged lightly at her dark blue turtle-neck. She gave a tight smile. "Do you have a receipt?"

"He said he called ahead to make sure you would release the ring to me," Margot said but she already knew she wasn't getting the ring without producing the receipt. That was just the kind of day she was having. With a theatrical sigh, Margot plopped her large purse onto the glass counter between them and began riffling through it.

Voice smaller now, the sales associate added, "Sorry. Store policy."

The vibration of Margot's phone made her entire bag buzz. The glow of the screen illuminated the inside of the bag. Eve Bowers.

"Of course," Margot muttered. Literally nothing about this day was going right. She should be sitting at the bar at Sandman's Grill right now, white zinfandel in hand, chatting up the hot older guy from the TV station she'd been low-key seeing for the last few months. Things were heating up between them. Lately all she could think about were his hands.

"Miss?" said the sales associate.

Ignoring her, Margot sighed again and reached to the bottom of the bag, pressing Ignore. Eve would have to fend for herself. She'd only had one job today: help Claudia set up the anniversary dinner and make sure it was both television- and social media-worthy. How hard was that?

"Just a minute," Margot snapped, shuffling the contents of her purse once more. Her fingers closed over the crumpled receipt her boss had given her earlier that day. "Here it is!"

She passed it to the sales associate, who used both hands to smooth it out on the glass top. She must have been new because when she saw the price, her eyes widened. She made a quick recovery though, smiling brightly at Margot. "Is this for the Beau Collins on TV? Beau and Claudia Collins?"

Margot suppressed a scream of frustration as her phone buzzed again. Eve Bowers. Ignore. Plastering a smile on her face, she said, "Yes, that's right! He's my boss. I'm his personal assistant."

"I've seen their show," said the sales associate. "It's fun. My mom is obsessed with their book. She says it saved her and my dad's marriage."

Automatically, the words came from Margot's mouth. Beau's manager always wanted them to push the podcast with the younger demographic. "They've got a podcast, too. You should check it out."

"Maybe," mumbled the sales associate. She waved the receipt. "Let me go get this for you."

She disappeared into a back room. Margot's phone went off again. Eve Bowers. Plucking it from her purse, she made a noise of frustration loud enough for the other people in the store to hear. Ignoring their stares, she swiped Answer. "What is it?"

Eve's perpetually sunny voice asked, "Are you there yet?"

Margot's fingers tightened around the phone. "No, I'm— wait, you're not at the house? Eve—"

"I know," Eve interjected. "I'm really sorry. I don't think I can do this. Lately, I've been feeling like this job isn't right for me. I don't know if I should continue, and—"

Margot tried to shake off her surprise. Of all the people who worked for Beau and Claudia Collins, Eve was probably the most dedicated, hard-working, and enthusiastic. A team player, Beau always called her. Every single person on the staff adored her.

Margot tried to think of something to say. All she could come up with was, "You are Claudia's assistant. Literally your job is to assist her. Fine if you want to quit but don't do it today, of all days. Be professional. Claudia is good to you. She deserves the benefit of your two weeks' notice. At least."

"I know. But you don't understand. I—"

Margot cut her off again. "Eve, please. No one knows better than me how demeaning and frustrating this job can be. I get it, okay? But you have to pull it together for one night. Especially tonight. Get over there, help Claudia finish setting up, and then talk things over with her on Monday."

Eve was silent.

A beep interrupted the dead air. A text notification. "Eve," Margot said. "Just get over to the house, okay?"

"But I just talked to—"

Margot didn't let her finish. She swiped End Call and pulled up the text message. It was Beau. Texting to say he was going to be late for his own anniversary dinner. Could she let the video crew know? Could she go to the house and drop off the ring?

"You've got to be kidding me," Margot mumbled, seriously considering smashing her phone through the glass case.

"Here you go." The sales associate returned, holding out a small gift box, its top flipped open, as if she were proposing to Margot. Inside it, the thick, diamond-crusted band sparkled. It was far too ostentatious for Claudia, but what Claudia wanted wasn't the point. It was what their audience wanted. It was always about what the audience wanted.

Margot tossed her phone back into her purse and took the box, snapping it closed. "Yeah, that's it," she said. "Thanks."

In the car, clothes soaked and hair dripping from the freezing rain, Margot cranked up the heat and called Beau. He answered on the second ring and immediately started talking. "I know, I know. I'm sorry. I owe you."

He owed her from the last hundred favors that were outside of her remit. This job was supposed to be a nine-to-five thing, doing stuff like maintaining his calendar and running errands during business hours. Instead, she was his on-call minion. The workday never ended. Not to mention all the other things he owed her for. She hadn't been lying when she told Eve she understood not wanting to do the job anymore. Margot would bet her last measly paycheck Claudia treated Eve better than Beau treated Margot. Then again, it was Eve who always went the extra mile. Eve had taken the time to get to know every person who worked for Beau and Claudia. She knew all of their birthdays and brought in a pastry for the entire staff whenever someone turned a year older. She even knew that the audio-video guy had a nut allergy. For his birthday, she brought fresh fruit arranged to look like a bouquet of flowers.

"Margot, truly, I am sorry," Beau said, interrupting her thoughts. "I know you have your own life. It's unfair of me to put these responsibilities on you. Once this anniversary is in the books, we should sit down and discuss a more adequate compensation package for all the work you're doing that is above and beyond your job description. I know that's not really why you came here in the first place, but I do want you to know how much I value you—as a person and as my assistant."

There it was. The reason she stayed. He always seemed to read her mind and he knew just what to say, even if he didn't always follow through on his promises. This was the uncanny quality that had recently landed him and Claudia a deal that would launch their show from the local WYEP station in the small city of Denton to the national market.

She had to lock in her pay raise before that happened. There were lots of things she needed to do before that happened. Before his attention was even more difficult to get than it was now.

"How late will you be?" she asked.

She practically heard his grin. "That's my favorite girl! Not long. I promise. Are you headed there now?"

"Yes."

"I'll probably be five or ten minutes behind you, maybe not even that long. If you can just meet me there with the ring, that would be perfect." Margot was twenty minutes from the house, which meant he was almost thirty minutes from getting there—assuming there was no traffic.

"Beau, it's your anniversary!" Margot blurted. "What's so important—you know what? I don't want to know. I'll see you there."

She hung up and found a number for one of their camera

operators whose job it was to bring the video crew. Liam Flint answered, his voice tinged with annoyance. Without preamble, he said, "What is it?"

Margot resisted the urge to snap back at him. Beau insisted she be nice to everyone on the show, even though Liam tested her nerves on a regular basis. "Beau is going to be late," she said. "He wanted me to ask you to bring the crew at six thirty instead of five thirty."

There was a four-second silence, then a heavy sigh. "Beau Collins is going to be late for his own anniversary dinner? He couldn't even call me himself to let me know?"

Margot bit her lip to keep from defending Beau. It was a well-known fact among the staff that he was always late. Even his late was late, but Liam would have found fault with Beau even if he'd offered him a raise. She ignored his questions, asking her own instead. "Can you be there at six thirty instead of five thirty or not?"

"Has anyone told Claudia?" he asked pointedly.

Her irritation reached its flashpoint. "You know what? That's not my job, and I don't appreciate your tone. Just be at the house at six thirty."

Before he could respond, she swiped the End Call button, tossed her phone onto the passenger's seat and pulled into traffic. The Collinses' home was in a small but exclusive development that bordered the city park. There were only four other homes on their street, each one at the end of a long driveway and separated from their neighbors by dense clusters of trees. Margot wished her place afforded as much privacy, but she was still in a one-bedroom apartment in the center of Denton. She could have demanded so much more, but she had wanted to earn her own way. Maybe with a larger compensation package, she could finally buy her own house.

Eve's brand-new Nissan was parked outside the detached three-car garage. Margot parked next to it, jealousy flaring, making her stomach acids roil. She had never asked because she didn't think Eve would tell her, but she suspected that Claudia paid her a lot more than Beau paid Margot. She should find out before she renegotiated her salary with Beau. The Collinses were equal partners. They should pay their assistants the same.

Through the rain-splattered windshield, the golden glow of the floor-to-ceiling windows splayed across the front of the house were visible. Beau had told her how he and Claudia had the house custom-built almost ten years ago. The great room had twenty-four-foot vaulted ceilings. From the outside it looked like an enormous log cabin with more windows than logs. The three pitched rooftops were copper.

Cold rain pelted her as she stepped out of her car. A pair of headlights cut across the driveway. Margot paused at the bottom of the wide stone steps leading to the front doors and watched Beau climb out of his Lexus. He held his coat over his head. As he neared, he offered her shelter beneath it. This close, he smelled like expensive cologne and leather. Even in the dim light, the flush in his cheeks was evident when he smiled down at her. Margot felt some of her annoyance slip away.

She was about to tell him that she had called the video crew when the double doors at the top of the steps burst open. Eve stumbled out. Her hands were pressed against her cheeks. High-pitched screams tore from her body. Tucked under Beau's shoulder, Margot felt him tense. Eve rushed down the steps toward them.

"Eve," Beau said. "Are you okay? My God, is that blood?"

Eve fell into him, hand on his chest. A dark red streak slashed across her cheek. The coat flapped against the side of Margot's head.

"Ca—" Eve choked on the words. Coughed, swallowed, tried again. "Call 911. We have to call 911."

TWO
DIARY ENTRY, UNDATED

Today was the worst and best day of my life. How can that be? I'm still trying to process it. I did something terrible. Something unforgivable. Something I swore I would never do but when it happened, it felt so good. It felt right. That sounds awful. Maybe I'm not a good person. All I know is that I spent years trying to be a good person, a good partner, and it's never brought me anything but stress and heartache. Today I finally did something for myself and, even though I know it was wrong, it felt amazing. I feel amazing.

I just hope he doesn't find out. If he does, he'll make me pay.

THREE

The Chief's door had been closed for an inordinate amount of time. Detective Josie Quinn stood several feet away from it, hands on her hips, ears tuned to the voices coming from the other side. Behind her, the great room where the investigative team gathered at the Denton Police Department headquarters was silent except for a couple of her colleagues typing up reports. The room was large and open-concept. It held several desks, most of which were there for any of the uniformed officers to use for paperwork or phone calls or any other administrative work that needed to be done. The only permanent desks belonged to their press liaison, Amber Watts, and the four people who comprised the investigative division: Josie, her husband, Lieutenant Noah Fraley, Detective Finn Mettner, and Detective Gretchen Palmer.

"Can you hear anything?" asked Mettner.

"No," said Josie. She took a tentative step closer. "How long did you say he's been in here?"

The creak of a chair sounded behind her. Mettner said, "I came back from lunch around two and that's when I noticed it was closed."

Noah said, "It's after six o'clock now. Should we make sure he's still alive?"

"If the boss can hear voices, then he's still alive," Mettner said.

What seemed like an eternity ago, Josie had served as interim chief for a couple of years before the mayor had hired the current chief, Bob Chitwood, whose door she now stood before. Josie had taken the position after exposing a series of devastating instances of corruption from the lowest levels of city government to the highest. Her tenure was marked by a rebuilding of both the department and the trust of those who stayed on. Most of those people had taken to calling her "boss", and even after years under Chief Chitwood, they still said it. Josie had tried correcting people, but it didn't take.

Noah said, "Maybe he's talking to Daisy?"

"I don't think so," Josie said. "It sounds like two men's voices."

Daisy was the Chief's much younger half-sister that he had taken custody of six months earlier. No one had known of her existence before that. It was only after Josie's team cracked a case tied to the Chief's past that Daisy had come to light. Her upbringing had been bizarre, at best. A teenager being raised by an older half-sibling in his sixties was an unusual arrangement but so far, it worked. Since the Chief was single, he often brought Daisy with him to the stationhouse rather than leave her unsupervised. He had even set up a small desk in his office for her to do schoolwork while he worked.

Mettner said, "Daisy's with Gretchen and Paula today, remember?"

"Oh right," said Noah. "The concert."

Gretchen Palmer was the oldest and most experienced on their team, having come to Denton after a fifteen-year stint on Philadelphia's homicide unit. She and her adult daughter, Paula, who lived with Gretchen while she attended grad school, had started out helping the Chief look after Daisy, and now it seemed to have developed into a much more meaningful relationship. At sixteen, Daisy had never been to a concert before. When Paula found out, she'd made it her mission to remedy the situation. The result was a weekend trip for the three of them to Philadelphia to see Lizzo. Gretchen's absence was the only reason that Josie and Noah were working instead of attending Harris's basketball game at the rec center adjacent to the city park. He'd just taken up the sport and they tried to make as many games as possible.

"I guess I could just knock on the door," Josie said. "See if he wants coffee or something."

"He'll see right through that," said Mettner.

"So what?" said Josie. She walked toward the door, her hand outstretched, reaching for the knob when it suddenly swung inward.

Behind her, the typing stopped.

A large bloodhound sauntered out of the Chief's office. It stopped in front of Josie, tail wagging at the sight of her. Its adorable, saggy face looked up at her expectantly. It wore a black harness.

Mettner said, "Did a dog just open that door?"

Josie's stomach plummeted. She only knew one bloodhound, and in fact, he did know how to open doors. She adored that dog. It was the dog's owner that was the issue. Peering down at the sweet, eager face, she willed him not to be that dog.

She said, "Blue?"

His tail thumped more enthusiastically. Josie bent and scratched the top of his head. He nudged his wet nose into her palms, his tail now wagging at warp speed.

"Shit," she muttered.

Noah was beside her, smiling down at the dog. "You know this... dog?"

At that moment, Josie's former fiancé, Luke Creighton,

stepped into the doorway. His broad, six-foot-one body filled up the frame. He wore jeans and a polo shirt which stretched over his massive chest, muscles rippling beneath it as he stepped toward them. A full beard covered his angular face. He'd grown his brown hair long, almost to his shoulders. From beneath a hank of it, he looked from Blue to Josie and grinned. Josie felt Noah tense beside her. There was a charge in the air suddenly that hadn't been there before.

"Hey," said Luke. "Great to see you guys."

He addressed both of them, but kept his eyes on Josie, like they were old friends. While the last time they'd seen one another they'd parted on good terms, their history was a complicated one.

After Josie's first marriage failed, she had been engaged to Luke. At that time, he was a state trooper. When they met, he was someone who was very serious about the job and always did everything by the book. She should have known by the one small, harmless favor he'd done for her when she asked that he had the capacity to lie, but she had not seen it that way. That favor had almost gotten him killed. After spending the better part of two years nursing him back to health, Josie had watched the relationship disintegrate before her eyes. Luke not only betrayed his oath to uphold the law, but he'd deceived Josie as well. He had gotten caught up in a terrible situation that quickly spun out of control. Instead of coming to her for help, he'd tried and failed to handle it alone.

The fallout for his decisions had been brutal and the evidence of what he'd gone through was visible as he extended a hand to Noah to shake. During the case that had ended Luke's career and relationship with Josie and sent him to prison for six months, he'd been tortured. Both of his hands had been shattered. Surgeons had done their best to piece them back together but even now, seven years later, the silvered scars running along his fingers were bright lines across his skin. Two of the fingers on his right hand were flattened and misshapen. On his other hand, the pinky finger bent outward at an awkward angle.

If Noah noticed, he didn't let on. Shaking Luke's hand, he blurted, "What are you doing here?"

Luke's smile faltered for only a split second. He returned his gaze to Josie. "I'm here with Blue," he said, gesturing to the dog, as if that explained everything.

The Chief's voice boomed from behind Luke. "Don't give him a hard time, Quinn! I just hired this guy!"

Josie heard Mettner speak, his voice too low to reach Luke. "Well, this is awkward."

Noah said, "You can't hire him. He's got a criminal record."

The Chief appeared in the doorway, one white bushy eyebrow kinked. He stepped up next to Luke and patted Blue on the head. "Don't tell me what I can and can't do, Fraley. He's not a sworn officer or anything. He's a consultant."

Luke smiled down at Blue and then returned his gaze to Josie. She wished he would stop looking at her like she was the only person in the room. "Blue here helped on so many search and rescue operations after that Lucy Ross case here in Denton that I went and did the training with him. He's certified in live finds and cadaver. Blue and I started working with a nonprofit organization that provides search and rescue dogs to law enforcement for a nominal cost that covers some basic expenses. I know you guys have a need here."

Josie said, "You live here now?"

Luke had lived in Denton when they were together but had had to sell his house and move back home to Sullivan County to live with his sister, who ran their family farm. She knew he'd stayed there because he couldn't handle living alone. Had something changed? A girlfriend, maybe? Hopefully?

"I figure it's a good home base," he said. "Close to a bunch of major cities and rural departments that might need our help."

A phone rang. Mettner answered it. Josie heard him give a

few "yeps" and "got its" before the receiver clanked back into place. "That was a guy named Landan Clarke," he said. "He's got a farm in Southwest Denton. His six-year-old son wandered off two hours ago. He's pretty sure he's still on the property, but the whole family's a little shook up that they haven't found him yet. It's cold and raining."

Josie turned away from the Chief and their new K-9 consultants. She grabbed her coat from the back of her chair. "Let's go."

The Chief said, "Not so fast there, Quinn. This sounds like the perfect way to break in our new consultant."

Josie suppressed a groan. The last thing she wanted to do was be alone with Luke.

"Fraley," said the Chief. "You take this one. Luke and Blue can ride with you."

Josie chanced a glance back at her husband. No one else in the room would know it but she could tell by the way a tiny muscle in his jaw twitched that he wasn't happy. Still, he managed a smile. Through gritted teeth, he said, "Sure."

Once they were gone, the Chief retreated to his office. Josie sat at her desk, ignoring Mettner's stare. It was a relief when the phone on her desk rang. "Quinn," she barked.

A minute later, she let the receiver fall back into place, stood and put on her coat. "Let's go," she told Mettner.

"What is it?"

"A body."

FOUR

Josie flipped the windshield wipers to high as they rounded the city park, heading to its northwest end where a tiny smattering of houses bordered one of its running trails. She was familiar with the street that dispatch had mentioned. Having lived in the city her entire life, she remembered the many times developers had proposed building apartment complexes in that area. They would have towered over the park, offering stunning views for residents but making the park area congested and less accessible. Each time a new developer showed up at a city council meeting with a scale model and a pile of blueprints, they were sent packing. Eventually, the land in question was divvied up and sold to individuals who built their own homes.

"You get anything on the address?" she asked Mettner. She needed to talk about something, anything, that would keep her mind off the fact that her current husband was now out looking for a lost child with her former fiancé.

From the passenger's seat, his fingers flew across the screen of the Mobile Data Terminal. "The house belongs to Beau and Claudia Collins," he said. "He's forty-seven, she's forty-two. No criminal records. Driver's licenses in good standing. They bought the land twelve years ago and built on it. No prior calls to the address."

Josie slowed, searching for the turn she knew was ahead. January in Denton meant that evening fell fast and early. It was pitch-black, and here in this remote area, the streetlights offered little illumination. The name Claudia lingered in her thoughts. Memories of the woman who had saved Harris just a month ago flashed across her mind. But that woman had said her name was Claudia White, not Collins. Still, something in the back of Josie's brain clamored for her attention. She just wasn't sure what it was yet. "Why do those names sound familiar?"

From Mettner's direction came a heavy sigh. "Don't ask how I know this, okay?"

Josie found the cross street and made a right, navigating the car up a steep hill. She was relieved that the rain hadn't yet made the streets slick and slippery. "Now that's just not fair, Mett. You can't start out with a statement like that."

"You're not allowed to ask," he insisted.

Josie shrugged. Ahead, at the top of the hill, she could just make out the flash of emergency beacons. "That's fine. I'll infer. That's more fun."

He groaned. "I'm going to pretend you didn't say that. They're on TV. They're like this kind of famous couple who do relationship counseling."

"Kind of famous?" Josie asked.

"Yeah, around here. They're on WYEP. Their show is just local, but they've also got a book."

Josie slowed again as she approached the last driveway along the street. A Denton police cruiser sat next to its entrance, lights blazing. "What's the name of the book, Mett?"

"I don't—"

"And don't tell me you don't know. I know you do."

Another sigh. "Fine. It's called *Perfect Pursuit: Winning at Love.*"

"That sounds familiar."

"If you saw the cover, you'd recognize it. It was on the top of the *New York Times* bestseller list for like two years or something. Anyway, they were both marriage counselors and then they wrote this book, and it went viral. Then they started the show. I'm pretty sure they've got a podcast, too."

"So they give out relationship advice," Josie said.

"Yeah, pretty much, except I guess the idea is to make it fun or something. You've really never seen their show? A few of their clips have gone viral."

"I haven't had much time to watch TV the last..."

"Several years?" he filled in.

She laughed. "Yeah, that's about right."

A uniformed officer materialized from the darkness between the cruiser and the driveway, replete in drab gray rain gear. Josie cracked her window. After a brief conversation, the officer waved them along.

At the top of the driveway, a small triangular sign announced: *This Home is Protected by Summers Security*. Beyond that, asphalt gave way to a large expanse of cobblestone which surrounded the massive house. Several vehicles were crowded around a detached three-car garage: three civilian sedans, three police cruisers, an ambulance, and an SUV with the words "Denton Police Department Evidence Response Team" emblazoned across its side. Its hatch was open. Directly in front of it was a canvas pop-up tent. Beside that was a small white pickup truck that belonged to Denton's medical examiner, Dr. Anya Feist. Josie parked next to one of the cruisers and took a moment to study the windows at the front of the house, stretching from top to bottom and blazing with light. A crime scene tech in white Tyvek gear could be seen snapping photos.

"You ready?" asked Mettner.

They got out and jogged over to a set of wide stone steps presently guarded by another uniformed officer in rain gear. He took down their names and badge numbers on a clipboard he pulled from inside his rain jacket. On the landing at the top of the steps, someone on the team had erected another pop-up tent. Under it was a portable halogen light and several plastic bins marked "Property of Denton PD Evidence Response Team." Beside the bins, blocking the front door, was yet another uniformed officer. Josie recognized him without reading his nameplate. "Brennan," she said. "What've we got?"

He took out a notepad and flipped some pages, reading from his notes. "911 call came in at six thirteen p.m. from a woman named Margot Huff. She identified herself as the personal assistant of Beau Collins, one of the homeowners. She stated that someone was deceased in the home. We got here and found her, Mr. Collins, and another adult female who identified herself as Eve Bowers, assistant to Dr. Claudia Collins, waiting inside that Lexus over there." He pointed over their shoulders toward the civilian vehicles grouped around the garage. "The 911 operator instructed them to vacate the premises. It was raining, so they took cover in Mr. Collins's vehicle."

"Who found the deceased?" Josie asked.

Brennan said, "Miss Bowers. She arrived here around six p.m., she says, and went inside to assist Dr. Claudia Collins with party preparations. She relates that when she entered, she found blood in the kitchen and found Dr. Collins deceased in the dining room. She came out here just as Beau Collins and Margot Huff were pulling up."

"Did Beau Collins or Miss Huff go inside at all?" asked Mettner.

Brennan nodded. "Mr. Collins did, but all three of them say that he was not in there long. A minute, tops. He said he needed to see the body for himself. When we got here, we cleared the house, secured the scene and called in additional units. I got here around six forty-five. The ERT and Dr. Feist were already here. Dr. Feist waited here with me while the ERT got started. The three witnesses were placed in separate cruisers."

That accounted for the number of cruisers.

"You can send them to the station," Josie said. "I don't want them to have contact with one another, though. Separate interview rooms. Make sure they're comfortable. Get them something to eat and drink. We're going to be here a while."

Brennan nodded along with her words. Then he clicked the radio on his shoulder and dipped his chin to speak into it, giving orders to the officers parked in front of the garage.

Mettner said, "You don't want to talk with them first?"

"No," Josie said. "They'll be fine. I want to have a look at what we're dealing with before we sit down with them." Looking at Brennan, she said, "What else did you get from their initial statements?"

He flipped more pages in his notebook. "Today is the fifteenth wedding anniversary of the homeowners, Beau and Claudia Collins. As I said, Eve Bowers came to help Dr. Claudia Collins set up for dinner. Mr. Collins and Miss Huff were also here for the anniversary dinner. A video crew was also slated to appear."

"A video crew?" Josie said.

Brennan looked up from his notes. "Yeah. Apparently they've got some show on WYEP. Local celebrities."

"Mettner told me," Josie said. "But why a video crew for an anniversary dinner?"

"Ms. Huff said it was for their fans."

Mettner added, "Their whole schtick is about good relationships. They're like the models for it. They share a lot of personal stuff on the show and on their social media platforms."

Brennan continued, "Anyway, said video crew did show up after we arrived on scene. Two guys. They were pretty upset. We took their information down and sent them home. Also, neither Miss Bowers nor Mr. Collins took any life-saving measures after finding the decedent. Ms. Bowers stated that the deceased was 'definitely not coming back.'"

Unease uncurled in Josie's stomach like a coiled snake readying itself to strike. Near the garage, the sounds of engines revving battled the noise of the falling rain. The cruisers leaving to take Beau Collins, Margot Huff, and Eve Bowers to the Denton police station. From her periphery she saw a door on the side of the garage swing open, casting a dull glow on the cobblestones. Two members of the ERT, clad in white Tyvek suits, emerged. They moved through the night like ghosts. One carried a clipboard and pen. The other had a large camera. They disappeared behind the SUV.

"You cleared the garage," Josie said. "Find anything in there?"

Brennan shook his head. "No. Nothing looked disturbed. All the vehicles registered to this home are accounted for."

Josie asked, "When is the last time Beau, Margot Huff, and Eve Bowers spoke to Claudia Collins?"

"All three said they spoke with her earlier in the day at the studio which is located in the WYEP building across town."

Mettner motioned to the house. "Place like this, they've got to have a security system."

"They do," said Josie. "I saw the sign at the end of the driveway for Summers Security."

Brennan tapped his pen against the notepad. "You're right. They have it and it's active but there are no cameras."

"No cameras?" Mettner said. "You're kidding, right?"

Brennan shook his head slowly. "I confirmed it with Beau Collins."

Mettner said, "Their damn vehicles alone are worth a fortune! Not a single camera in this whole place? Inside or outside?"

"Nothing," Brennan confirmed.

"We can take this up with Beau Collins when we talk to him," Josie said.

Mettner said, "Do they have household staff?"

Brennan shook his head.

Josie asked, "What about passcodes? Do you need one to get in here? Did Claudia use it tonight? How many people have the codes?"

"The homeowners and both assistants have the codes. You have to enter them as soon as you walk into the foyer. If you don't, then the alarm company gets notified and then they, in turn, notify us that there's been an unauthorized entry. Eve Bowers related that the system was already disabled when she arrived, so she did not use a code. I'm not sure who else has them."

"We'll ask Mr. Collins when we interview him," Josie said. "Right now, I want to see the scene."

FIVE

There was blood everywhere. From the large foyer, through the massive great room, and into the kitchen—mostly full and partial footprints that appeared to be from a man and a woman —pointing both ways and overlapping. The majority of the blood spatter was in the kitchen. It cut a messy, mottled path across white granite tile into the dining room where a large oak table dominated the room. The body of Dr. Claudia Collins slumped in one of the chairs. Her long sandy hair obscured her face, but a cascade of blood was visible along her side. Dr. Feist stood on the other side of her, gloved hands probing at her forehead. With Mettner in tow, Josie rounded the table, drawing closer. Still-wet blood soaked Claudia's hair, dripping from its ends onto her khaki slacks and down her arm, which hung several inches above the tile. Rivulets ran down over her hand to her fingers and onto the floor.

Josie scanned the rest of the room. There was seating for a dozen people although there were only two place settings. Between the place settings, a bottle of champagne rested in an ice bucket that was now more water than ice. Beside it, a vase of fresh roses dripped petals across the white linen tablecloth. On either side of it candles flickered, their vanilla scent mixing with the scent of early decomposition and blood. Wall sconces shaped like lanterns dotted the walls. Each one was lit although collectively they did not look as though they gave off much light. Someone from the ERT had erected halogen lights on each side of the room so that they could work.

The head of their ERT, Officer Hummel, appeared in the kitchen doorway. "The candles were lit when we got here, as were the wall sconces."

Josie looked again from Claudia's hand to the doors leading to the kitchen. Droplets and more footprints. In this light it was easier to pick out the footprints that appeared to be from a woman's heeled shoe and another set that were larger, resembling a man's dress shoe. She and Mettner had been careful to avoid them, but they were everywhere, each one layered on top of another. "What a mess," Josie said.

Hummel followed her gaze. "Both Eve Bowers and Beau Collins stepped in the blood and tracked it all through the first floor. We've already taken their footwear into evidence. We'll match it up to what we've got here. Anything that doesn't match might belong to the killer. We didn't find any blood on Claudia's shoes, which, as you can see, are ballet flats."

Mettner said, "But whatever happened here clearly started in the kitchen."

"Which means someone carried her in here," Josie said. She pointed to the floor where, among the footsteps, was a trail of droplets, beginning—or ending—where Claudia's hand dangled. "The droplets coming from her hand are circular with no spines but the ones leading from the kitchen out here are elongated, oval-shaped, with spines—or cast-off marks, if you will."

"Right," Mettner said. "When blood gets flung rather than dripping straight down, once it impacts a surface, it has the elongated oval shape with an extension. You know when I learned about this, my instructor referred to the spine as an elephant's trunk."

Josie said, "I've heard that before."

Whether it was called a spine, a cast-off mark, or an elephant trunk, the measurement of the elongation and the exact shape of the oval were all dependent on the angle at which the blood hit a surface. However, passive drips, which were caused by gravity and not by force, and fell straight down, were circular with no cast-off marks.

Josie said, "Once she was in this chair, she didn't move."

Mettner followed the trail from the chair toward the kitchen. "These must be from her arm swinging while he carried her."

Hummel nodded and beckoned back into the kitchen, pointing out the trail as they walked. They had already passed through the room once on their way to the body, but now Josie took a closer look. Like the rest of the house, it was spacious. The tile was white granite, the cabinets oak. There was no island countertop, only a small, circular table with seating for two sat off to one side. Stacked high on top of it were a number of plastic takeout containers, covered with blood droplets. The faint scent of steak and salmon emanated from them. The stove and even the sink sparkled. Not a crumb or dirty dish in sight.

Except for the blood nearly everywhere, the room was pristine.

Across from the table, recessed into the wall was a small vestibule that led to sliding glass doors. Josie edged around more bloody footprints and droplets layered across the middle of the kitchen floor toward the doors. She pushed aside one of the hanging blinds. Exterior lights illuminated a large deck and beyond that, down a set of steps, an in-ground pool, now covered for winter.

"Were those doors locked?" she asked.

"Yes," Hummel said. "There is a keypad outside of the door, too, so to get in you need a passcode."

She moved to the table, again careful to keep her Tyvek booties out of the blood. No easy task. Mettner was already there, nudging one of the foam containers with a gloved finger. "Takeout food for their anniversary?"

Josie motioned to a large area of blood spatter on the wall over one of the chairs. More blood spilled across the table. "Is this where it started?"

Hummel pointed to a stained area of the wall that would have been about head level had Claudia been seated there. The blood droplets were small and scattered, indicating medium-velocity impact spatter, meaning someone had struck Claudia with something. Gravitational drips trailed down toward the floor. More blood pooled in several places at the base of the chair, thick and dark. Hummel said, "It was a head injury. I'm thinking blunt force trauma. Not sure with what. The doc maybe can help you with that. We haven't found anything here that could have been used as a weapon."

Mettner said, "Looks like she was sitting in the chair when it happened."

Hummel nodded. "I think so. She would have been facing away from the great room, so I think he came in the way we just did, from the front door, and snuck up on her. Hit her on the head before she even knew what was happening."

Josie looked from the door to the chair. "How many entrances to this place?"

Hummel said, "The front door and that one right there that leads to the pool."

Josie said, "She would have seen someone trying to come from the pool area. You're right. He had to come right through the front door. She left the alarm disabled, per Eve Bowers, probably because she was expecting people."

"What good fortune for the killer," Mettner said.

"Or he knew her schedule, knew she would be here and waited to catch her alone," Josie said. "Let's keep going."

Hummel pointed to the part of the table that was nearest the wall. "This is where her purse was sitting—we took it into evidence. Behind the takeout containers. It appears as though she came in here, put her things down, unpacked these, threw away the takeout bag—I found that in the trash bin—and plopped into this seat. She might have been on her phone—maybe that's why she didn't hear him? But her phone is not here."

"You're absolutely sure it's not here? Elsewhere in the house?" Josie said.

"Not in her purse or anywhere on the premises," Hummel said. "We've searched this entire place."

Josie said, "Did you have the husband call it? See if you could hear it ringing anywhere in the house?"

"Several times," Hummel said. "It's not here."

Mettner said, "We can get Brennan to call dispatch and get them to ping the number. See if we can find its location."

Hummel said, "You think this guy came in, killed her and just took her phone? There's a ton of jewelry upstairs—expensive stuff—and the electronics in this house would get a lot on the street."

"We don't know yet," Mettner said. "It's weird that it's not here. All right, he hits her in the head and carries her into the dining room."

"Yeah," Hummel said. "That's the weird part. I don't understand why he moved her."

The killer had made a point of depositing Claudia Collins into her seat at the anniversary dinner. What message was he trying to send? Josie asked, "Is it possible she was still alive at that point?"

Hummel said, "I don't know. Maybe the doc can tell you."

SIX

Again, they picked their way over the bloody tile and back into the dining room. Dr. Feist looked up from Claudia's head. She gave Josie and Mettner the same half-grimace, half-smile she always greeted them with at crime scenes. "You're back. I'm happy to see you two," she said. "But not over a dead body."

Mettner said, "I'm pretty sure that's the only way we ever meet."

Dr. Feist's head bent toward Claudia Collins's body again. "No, sometimes Detective Quinn and I have lunch. Or coffee."

"And talk about dead bodies," Josie sighed.

Dr. Feist did not argue, instead moving right into her assessment. "Your responding officers got an initial confirmation on her ID from the witnesses and her driver's license. Dr. Claudia Collins, age forty-two. She's only been dead two to three hours is my guess. She's not in rigor yet which, as you know, normally starts between two to three hours after death. I took her temperature under her arm. Under normal circumstances, I'd expect it to be about 97.6 degrees. Mrs. Collins's temp was 94.6 degrees. Typically, the body stays at its normal temperature for an hour after death—unless it's been left in very cold conditions. The thermostat in this house is set to seventy-two degrees so the cold isn't a factor. After that initial hour the body loses one and a half degrees per hour until it reaches the air temperature around it. I'll take her temp again from her liver when I get her on my table but for now, it looks like she's been dead a few hours."

Josie said, "What's your initial guess as to the cause of death? Blunt force trauma to the head?"

Dr. Feist pulled the curtain of hair back to reveal a gash in the woman's forehead, near her temple. It looked like a bloody, toothless mouth. "It appears that way from a cursory examination, but I really need to get her on the table. Make sure she doesn't have injuries that are not visible in situ."

Josie's heart did a double tap. Blood rushed in her ears. The sound of Dr. Feist's voice faded out. Her eyes were locked on the bloodied face of the woman she had met last month while Christmas shopping with Harris. The woman who had introduced herself to Josie and Harris as Claudia White.

Dr. Feist was still talking. "I'll get her cleaned up and take some x-rays. I need a much better look at this wound. I may be able to detect any patterned injuries, figure out what he hit her with. Maybe." She released Claudia's hair, letting it fall across her face, obscuring the horror of her savage death. "We'll also use the UV light to check her clothing and body for any DNA in addition to all this blood—semen, saliva, sweat—and we'll take swabs. Hopefully the killer left something behind."

"Boss?"

Mettner was looking at Josie, his brows knit with concern.

Hummel said, "Boss? You okay?"

"I met her," Josie blurted. "Last month. On the street. But she introduced herself as Claudia White. Not Dr. Claudia Collins."

Everyone stared at her for a beat. Then Dr. Feist said, "Maybe White is her maiden name?"

"Why use her maiden name, though?" said Hummel. "The Collinses are famous for basically being married."

Mettner said, "Maybe she didn't want to get into the whole celebrity thing? Maybe she was trying to fly under the radar?"

Josie sighed. "Could be, I guess." She took a step forward, closer to the body, trying to quell the feelings of dread rising up inside her, cloying and poisonous. Claudia's other hand lay palm up on her thigh. "Is she holding something?"

Dr. Feist stepped back so that they could get a better look. Seated in Claudia's open palm was a long, narrow wooden box —its top a light beige, its bottom red. Josie estimated it was approximately five inches by three inches and only two inches high. On top of it was a red gift bow crafted entirely from wood. The cold finger of foreboding poked at Josie's spine. The killer had dealt her a blow she would not survive, carried her into this room, and staged her body. He had wanted them to find her like this: sitting at her anniversary dinner with a gift box in her hand.

"That's not my department," Dr. Feist told them. "Hummel?"

Hummel stepped up beside Josie. "We took photos of everything already, but I wanted you to see it before they took it into evidence. No one has touched it."

Josie turned to Mettner. "Is this something from the Collinses' book?"

"It's a puzzle box," he replied. "They sell them on their website. It's symbolic more than anything. Beau Collins used it once on TV to demonstrate something and then people went nuts over it."

"Does it hold anything?" Josie asked.

He shook his head. "It can hold something. Like, it has a space inside. I've seen people on social media put different things into them." He waved a hand at the table. "It could be part of whatever they were setting up here to share on social media and the show."

Hummel left the room and returned with a paper evidence bag. He used a gloved hand to lift the box. He shook it gently while they all listened for any noise.

"Sounds like something is rattling," Josie said.

"It's a ball bearing," said Mettner. "It's attached to a magnet. It's actually what holds the box closed. If you try to just lift the box open, it won't open. The top slides open on an angle but in order to do that, you've got to find the corner that has the ball bearing in it and then try to knock it off the magnet. If you can do that, the top will slide open."

Hummel placed the box into the evidence bag. "I want to try to get prints from this before we start doing all that."

Josie said, "Mett, can you get it open easily?"

"No. I never opened one myself. I've only seen Beau Collins do it on TV about a dozen times."

"Take it," Josie told Hummel. "As soon as you have it processed for prints, I want it opened."

With a nod, he produced a marker and scribbled across the evidence bag. Josie stared at Claudia's open palm. It was coated in dried blood. Had she used it to try to hold the skin on her head together? Had she been lucid long enough to know what was happening to her, or had the blow rendered her too disoriented? The amount of blood might have terrified her. Sadness settled onto Josie's shoulders like a familiar cloak. She was good at her job but she hated it, too. She hated it because the lives of people like Claudia Collins were taken far too soon and with terrible violence.

Hummel went to the kitchen doors and called for a colleague. A moment later, Officer Jenny Chan appeared with a camera in hand. "Get some photos of her hand without the box," he told her.

They stepped back while Chan worked. Josie tried to quiet

her mind. The image of Claudia stepping onto the sidewalk and sweeping Harris out of the path of the bike with perfect ease kept replaying in her mind. She catalogued each detail of the encounter, searching for something. But what? That chance meeting had nothing to do with this. What was her brain trying to grasp at such a fever pitch?

"The rings!" Josie said. "Her rings are missing!"

Chan stopped snapping photos. Mettner said, "What rings?"

"She was wearing a very big, very expensive engagement ring and wedding band when I met her. I don't see them on either of her hands."

Hummel said, "I'll go double-check the bedroom where we found the jewelry."

Chan went back to her task. Dr. Feist snapped off her gloves and sighed. "I'll let you know what I find after autopsy and exam. I can have something for you by the morning as long as we don't get any more bodies tonight."

"Let's hope not," Josie said.

SEVEN

Josie's fingertips felt numb as she grabbed onto the door that led from the Denton Police Department municipal lot into the building. A blast of warmth hit them as she and Mettner entered on the ground floor and started up the stairs. Josie's cheeks were still stinging from the cold even after they got to the second-floor great room. Noah sat at his desk, typing at his computer. Josie looked around but there was no evidence of Luke or Blue. The Chief's door was ajar, but the lights were off inside.

"Did you find Landan Clarke's son?" Josie asked.

Noah kept typing. "Yep. Pretty quick, thank God." He heaved a sigh and looked up at her with a tight smile. "Honestly? Blue is a rock star. He found that kid in less than five minutes. It was awesome."

Mettner said, "What about Luke?"

Noah kept his gaze on Josie. She knew without him saying it that it had been awkward. The two hadn't ever been on bad terms—they hadn't really been on any terms at all—but everyone knew about Josie's history with Luke and what he had done to her. What only Noah knew was that there had been one night, long after Luke had finished his prison term and left Denton, that Josie had stayed over at Luke's house. He'd been helping her chase a lead; she and Noah had been on the outs; and they'd gotten drunk and fallen asleep together. Nothing had happened between them, but Josie was racked with guilt all the same. Afterward, Noah was understanding. He believed her and trusted that nothing had happened. They had never spoken of it again. They hadn't needed to. Luke was deep in the past.

Except now he wasn't.

Ignoring Mettner, Noah said, "Heard you guys caught a homicide. Pretty bad, huh?"

"It was weird," Mettner replied, taking the cue to let the subject of Luke go.

In her pocket, Josie's cell phone chirped. She took it out to read the text messages while Mettner brought Noah up to speed on what they already knew and what they'd discovered at the scene.

"Well," Noah said when Mettner was done. "I got back here about a half hour ago and the desk sergeant told me that Margot Huff was in the conference room, Eve Bowers is in Interview Room One and Beau Collins is in Interview Room Two."

"Guess we should get started," said Mettner. "I can take one of the assistants. Huff, maybe."

"Just a minute," Josie said. "Brennan texted me about Claudia Collins's phone. Dispatch was able to ping it. Last known location was the Collinses' home."

"Which means that it's still there and the ERT just didn't find it?" asked Mettner. "That place is huge, but I don't see Hummel's team screwing that up. They're pretty thorough."

Josie put her phone back into her pocket. "It could just be turned off. If the killer took the phone with him, all he would have to do is turn it off before he left their home and that would account for it still pinging there. We should get a warrant for Claudia's phone records, though."

"Agree," said Mettner. His phone was in his hands. He typed into the notes app, making a list. "I can get that prepared. You two talk to Collins. I've seen him on TV a ton of times. He's really personable, but I'd like for you to get a read on him. After I get the warrant ready, I'll start with one of the assistants."

Josie said, "Actually, I'd like to talk with Eve Bowers first, since she was the one who found Claudia. Also, we don't know if the killer drove right up the driveway and parked at the house, or if he was on foot."

Noah said, "If I'm going there to murder someone, I'm not going to drive right up to the house. What if someone pulled up after him?"

Mettner said, "Yeah, they had a lot of people coming and going this evening. Seems unwise to park in the driveway. He could have stashed his own vehicle along the road. It's secluded. The other houses are not even visible from the road. Even if they have security cameras, they wouldn't have caught anything from the street."

"True," Josie said. "There's another alternative. The Collinses' house backs up to the city park. The killer could have gotten to it that way. Lots of people walk, jog, and bike through the park, even in the winter. It wouldn't be suspicious. He could have just hopped off the trail that runs parallel to their street and made his way through the woods to their home. Let's draw up a geo-fence warrant that will incorporate their street and the city park."

A geo-fence was an excellent tool for law enforcement in cases like this. It was a location-based technology that allowed police to draw a virtual boundary around a specific geographic area—the city park, for example—and then track which smart devices like cell phones were inside that perimeter during a certain time period. Geo-fence warrants were first employed by law enforcement in 2016 and had been increasing ever since.

Some people in other states had raised privacy concerns but for now, it was a tool at their disposal and Josie was going to use it if she could.

Noah said, "That could net you a lot of numbers."

"True," Josie said. "But the geo-fence will just list phone numbers of people within the geographic boundaries. It won't give us any identifying information. We're only looking for cell phones that might have crossed out of the park and onto the Collinses' property, or gotten close enough to the property to have gone to the house. When we find out which numbers those are, we can ask for information for those numbers only. I think, based on what we already know and the scene, the judge will grant it."

Mettner was already at his computer. "On it."

"And check the LPRs in the area as well," Josie said.

LPRs were license plate readers. Three of Denton PD's patrol vehicles were outfitted with cameras that linked up to their mobile data terminals. They scanned the license plates of all moving and parked vehicles and alerted on any vehicles that had warrants out on them, had been stolen, or whose tags had been suspended. If any of the LPR devices had been near the Collinses' street or the city park in the time period during which Claudia Collins had been murdered, it would have picked up which vehicles were in the area at that time.

"You got it," Mettner said.

Noah said, "Let's go talk to Eve Bowers."

EIGHT

Interview Room One was the cleanest and least used of the department's interview rooms. Still, Eve Bowers looked out of place inside the cinderblock box, sitting at the scarred metal table. She had pulled her feet up onto the edge of her chair, hugging her legs to her chest. When Josie and Noah entered the room, big blue eyes, rimmed red from crying, peeked from behind her stocking-clad knees. Without shoes, her toes curled around the edge of the chair. Her head lifted, revealing a face full of freckles and a cupid's bow mouth. A smudge of dried blood flaked along the side of her nose.

Josie and Noah introduced themselves and sat down. "Sorry to keep you waiting so long," Josie said.

Eve stared at each of them for a beat and then lowered her feet to the floor, revealing a soft cream sweater dress that contrasted with her black stockings. Smudges of dried blood dotted the front of the sweater. Near her waist were three finger-shaped streaks. She had tried to wipe it off. "How is Beau —Mr. Collins?" she asked in a small voice.

Noah said, "We haven't spoken with him yet but as soon as

we're done getting all of your statements, you can talk with him."

"Okay," she said, leaning forward and resting her arms on the table.

Josie started with some simple baseline questions. "Eve, how long have you worked for Dr. Collins?"

"About three years," she answered softly.

Noah said, "You're her personal assistant?"

"Um, yeah. Claudia—Dr. Collins—always says I should call myself her 'executive assistant.' She says that makes it sound better. I guess for my resume or whatever."

"Were you looking for another job?"

Eve's gaze swept down toward her fingers. She picked at some chipped pink nail polish on one of her thumbs. "Um, I mean, not actively but I was—I mean—well, Claudia always said I was too smart to be her assistant forever. She thinks I can do bigger and better things. She says she won't be upset when I move on."

Noah said, "How was your working relationship with her?"

A pink speck of nail polish flew off her thumbnail and onto the table. "It was good. Fine. She's good to me." She corrected herself. "Was good to me."

Josie asked, "What kinds of things did you do for Dr. Collins?"

"Whatever she needed, but mostly maintaining her schedule and reminding her of things. Picking stuff up. Answering emails."

"What does your average workday look like?" asked Noah.

Eve worked the edge of her other thumbnail beneath what was left of the polish until more flaked off and scattered across the table. "I, uh, show up to the studio around seven in the morning and meet with her. We talk about the day. Claudia likes to do this thing where we set daily goals, which is basically her giving me a list of things she wants me to do or check on that day. Then I stay while she tapes the show with Beau. I snap some photos to send to Margot and Rafferty, the guy who manages the social media for the station, in case they can use anything."

"Why Margot?" asked Noah.

"She does social media for Beau and Claudia. They have profiles on just about every platform for their show. They used to have profiles for him, her, and the show, and they decided to just consolidate everything onto one set of profiles that revolves around the show, and Margot is responsible for that."

Josie nodded. "What time is the show over?"

"It airs from nine to nine thirty. There is usually a meeting after that to discuss the next day's show or any other issues that have come up. Everything is usually wrapped up by noon and then Claudia goes to her office and sees patients. I work from home the rest of the day."

"Is that the schedule you followed today?" asked Noah.

Eve began to dig at her cuticle. "Uh, yeah. Basically."

"Except that you were needed for the big anniversary dinner?" asked Josie.

Eve looked up from her hands and met Josie's eyes. "I was supposed to get some pictures we could use for social media and pass them along to Margot, yeah. I had offered to pick up the takeout, champagne, all that stuff, but Claudia wanted to do it herself."

"The last time you spoke with Claudia or saw her was when?" asked Noah.

"I saw her at the studio around noon," Eve said. "Which was the last time I physically spoke to her, but she sent me some photos before I got to her house." She reached behind her where a large purse hung from the back of the chair. Fishing her phone out, she punched in a code and then pulled up a text exchange between her and Claudia.

"May I?" Josie asked, taking the phone from her.

Eve shrugged. "If you think it will help you."

Josie scrolled back through a number of mundane exchanges having to do with scheduling, dry cleaning, and coffee. Then texts from that day beginning around two thirty in the afternoon.

Eve: *What time should I get there?*

Claudia: *Any time after five thirty, I guess. I'll have things set up by then.*

Eve: *K. Thx.*

The next text was from Claudia at 5:13 p.m., one hour before the 911 call came in. It said: *What do you think?* A series of photos followed. All of them were from the Collinses' dining room. One showed a bag of takeout from Cadeau. Another showed two place settings arranged on the table together with unlit candles. In the center there was a vase of roses and a champagne bottle resting in a bucket of ice. The last photo was a selfie of Claudia, smiling. She held the phone up high above her head so that it captured the dining room table behind her. This time the candles were lit. She gave a thumbs-up. The large diamond ring and matching band that Josie had seen when they met sparkled on her ring finger.

Josie added to the theory she'd been building since she saw the crime scene. The killer had most likely come in through the front door, since the security system was disabled. He'd approached Claudia from behind in the kitchen and struck her, causing severe blood loss. Then he had carried her into the dining room, put her into one of the chairs, and taken the rings from her fingers. Before he left, he'd put a puzzle box into her hand and left with her phone.

A terrible sense of foreboding made Josie's chest feel tight.

The last message was a text from Claudia received at 5:29 p.m. *Where is everyone? Thought we were doing this at 5:30. Food is getting cold!* As if to mitigate the tone of the message, she had added a smiley face emoji.

Eve had not answered.

Josie added another detail to her mental reconstruction of the evening. The killer had carried all of this out within a thirty-minute time period. Presumably, Claudia was still alive when she texted Eve at 5:29 p.m. Eve arrived approximately a half hour to forty-five minutes later and found Claudia dead—the scene staged—since the 911 call came in at 6:13 p.m.

Josie said, "May we have copies of these?"

Eve shrugged again. "Sure."

Josie handed the phone to Noah so that he could see the exchange. To Eve, she said, "Was the big dinner supposed to take place at five thirty?"

Eve nodded. She brought her thumb to her mouth and began chewing around the already irritated cuticle.

Josie said, "You didn't get there until when?"

From behind her hand, Eve muttered, "Six. I was late. We were all late."

She burst into tears then, her entire face crumpling. She splayed her fingers open and buried her eyes in her palm. Sobs racked her body. A high-pitched cry filled the room. Josie felt its vibration in her teeth. It was grief and guilt, pure and unadulterated. For a moment, Noah looked thrown, eyes widening as his gaze moved from the phone to Eve's shaking body. Josie lifted a hand from the table in a gesture meant to indicate that they should just give Eve a few minutes to compose herself.

"If we hadn't been late, maybe she would be alive," Eve cried, raking the sleeve of her sweater over her face. "We were all late. Every single one of us. If I had just gotten there when she told me, maybe it would have been okay. Claudia is a good person. She doesn't—she didn't deserve this. She's a great boss. The best. And the blood. There was so much blood. I stepped in it by accident, and it got everywhere. It's still on me!"

Eve was close to hyperventilating. Josie spoke calmly but

firmly. "Eve, look at me. I need you to take a few deep breaths. Can you do that for me?"

She nodded even as another sob shook her body. Josie could see in her eyes that she was fighting down the horror of what she had seen that evening. She took in a few shuddering breaths. Noah produced a box of tissues from the other end of the table and offered them to her. They let her blow her nose and dab at her eyes before continuing.

Josie said, "Eve, when you arrived at the Collinses' home, were there any other vehicles there? In the driveway? Any that you may have passed on your way up the street?"

Eve fisted the tissue and shook her head. "No. Nothing. Claudia always parks inside the garage, and I knew she was home but there were no cars in the driveway. I don't remember seeing any on my way up the street. Maybe I did, but I don't remember."

"Did anything strike you as unusual when you got there?" Noah asked.

"No. Not at all."

"You told one of our officers that you didn't need to use your passcode to get inside because Claudia had left the security system disabled," said Josie. "Did Claudia do that often?"

"Yeah. She did. If they were having a bunch of us over, Claudia disabled it so that we could all walk right in. It just made it easier."

"Would other people who came by regularly know this?" asked Josie.

"I'm not sure. I guess."

"Tell us about when you got to the house," Noah said in a gentle tone.

Eve resumed biting her cuticle. Her voice was muffled as her teeth worked. "I went inside. I called out for her. She didn't answer. I figured she was in the kitchen so I went right there. That's when I saw all this blood. On the table, the wall, the floor." She dropped her hands back onto the table and closed her eyes. "It was like a trail from the kitchen table into the dining room. I hoped that maybe she just cut herself. I know that sounds ridiculous but when I saw all that blood, my mind was just like, 'she cut herself, that's all.' I didn't want it to be any more serious than that. I wanted her to be okay. I thought, 'I'll go into the other room, and she'll just give me that big Claudia smile and make fun of herself for being so klutzy even though she is the least klutzy person I know. I'll take her to the ER and everything will be fine.' But then I saw her in the dining room."

Her eyes fluttered open, as if she didn't want to revisit the scene in her mind's eye. She held up her hands in front of her. There was more dried blood along the outer side of her right pinky. "I probably shouldn't have touched her, but I couldn't help it. I saw her like that, and I still didn't believe right away that she was really gone. I felt for a pulse in her neck. I probably, like, disturbed the scene, didn't I?"

Noah said, "It's fine. You did the right thing."

Eve didn't look convinced. She lowered her voice to a whisper. "She was so cold. Already. And just... not there, you know? Like, so still. It was so horrible. Oh God, poor Claudia."

Fresh sobs overtook her. This time she covered her face with both hands, crying a little more quietly than the last time. Josie and Noah waited for her tears to subside.

"Eve," Noah said. "Was Claudia having trouble with anyone lately? Was there anyone you can think of who might have wanted to harm her?"

Eve shook her head vigorously. "No. I don't think so."

"I think that's all we need right now," said Josie. "Thank you for speaking with us. We can have someone drive you back to your car."

Eve lowered her hands. "I think I'd rather wait until Beau and Margot are finished and go with them."

"Of course," said Josie. "Oh, just one last thing. Why were you late tonight? To Claudia's?"

Eve's blue eyes went wide. Her hands found each other, fingers lacing, twisting. "Oh, I, uh—" She broke off. Her shoulders slumped. Josie waited several seconds, hoping she would fill the silence. Eventually, she did. "This is going to sound terrible but sometimes, working for Beau and Claudia is hard. Not because of them. They're great people. It's because they've got it all, you know?"

Her eyes were pleading.

Noah said, "Sure. Successful careers, TV show, wealth."

"And their marriage," Eve said. "When you're single and nothing has worked out for you, sometimes it's hard to be around people who are so... committed to one another."

Josie said, "That's understandable."

More tears spilled down Eve's face. "So I didn't want to go. I wasn't going to go. I called Margot hoping she could take the stupid photos, but she talked me out of bailing on Claudia. Now Claudia is dead. If I wasn't so selfish, she might still be alive."

NINE

DIARY ENTRY, UNDATED

It's getting harder to keep things secret. The other day one of my coworkers said I looked happy for the first time since she's known me. She told me I was glowing. That's the word she used. I know that she's right. I've never felt this way before. I didn't know that being in love could feel this way. I know that I should end things, but I can't bring myself to do it. This is the only true happiness I've ever felt. But if a coworker can tell that something is going on, then I have to face the possibility that he'll be able to see it, too.

TEN

Down the hall from where Josie and Noah left Eve Bowers, exhausted and guilt-ridden, Beau Collins waited in Interview Room Two. Josie peeked inside the small, square window in the door to see him pacing the room in black dress socks, occasionally running both hands through his thick, dark hair. He had taken off his suit jacket and thrown it over the back of one of the chairs. His shirtsleeves were rolled up, revealing muscular forearms. Given his lean frame, Josie guessed he was a runner, or at the very least, he spent a lot of time at the gym. Every so often he stopped, picked his phone up from the table, checked something, and tossed it back. Someone had brought him coffee and some pastries from nearby Komorrah's Koffee, but everything had been pushed to the center of the table, untouched.

Josie felt the heat of Noah's body behind her. She motioned to the door. "Have you ever seen the Collinses' show?"

Noah shook his head.

"Read their book?"

"Nope."

"All right. Let's go."

Beau Collins stopped moving when they entered, frozen in

the midst of running his hands through his dense locks. It had the effect of making him look as though he was pulling his hair out. His face was splotchy and red from crying.

Noah gave him a sympathetic smile and extended a hand. "Mr. Collins. I'm Lieutenant Noah Fraley. This is my colleague, Detective Josie Quinn."

Beau slowly lowered his arms and shook Noah's hand. He held onto it for a beat too long, imploring Noah with his eyes. "Have you found anything?" he asked. "Did you catch who did this?"

Noah wrested his hand away and gestured for Beau to sit down at the table. "I'm sorry, Mr. Collins, but we're still investigating."

Beau turned toward the chair he'd strewn his jacket over and looked at it as if it were some object he had never seen before.

When he failed to move, Josie said, "Mr. Collins?"

Beau turned his gaze toward her, blue eyes squinting. "I'm sorry. I just—my Claudia. I keep seeing her there in the chair. I can't get the image out of my head."

Noah took his elbow and guided him down into the chair. "We're very sorry for your loss, Mr. Collins."

Beau nodded although Josie wasn't sure he had heard Noah or registered his words at all. His eyes grew moist with unshed tears. "My Claudia," he mumbled. "Do you know what happened to her? How it—was she shot?"

Josie said, "There was no evidence of that. She sustained a head injury. We'll know more once we hear from the medical examiner."

Beau's lower lip trembled. A deep frown appeared on his face. Although he looked tired and broken with a permanent worry line scoring his forehead, up close, he was an attractive man. In her mind, she tried to imagine him with Claudia—the Claudia she had met in December. They would have made a striking couple. Josie realized then that she hadn't seen any framed photos of Beau and Claudia in their home. She and Mettner hadn't explored the entire structure, but one would expect to find framed photos on the main floor. Her home was filled with photos, not just of herself and Noah but of all the people they loved: his late mother, her late grandmother, their siblings, his niece, their friend Misty and her son, Harris, their colleagues with whom they were very close friends outside of work.

"How long will that take?" he asked, voice husky. "For the medical examiner to... oh God, I'm sorry. I just can't believe this is happening. My God." He leaned forward, curling into himself, bent over in the chair. "I'm going to be sick."

Josie said, "I'm so sorry, Mr. Collins. I know this is difficult. We can give you a few minutes. I'm sure we can find some water or maybe ginger ale, if you'd like."

Noah walked back to the door. Josie turned to follow him, but Beau lunged forward and grabbed her wrist with both of his hands. His skin was warm and moist. "Please don't leave me alone," he begged. "Please. I'll just—I can do this. I can—" He loosened his grip and took in a deep breath. "You need to ask questions, right? That's what the police do when someone is... murdered. Talk to everyone who knew her, right? It will help you. Help find out who did this to my wife?"

"Yes," Josie said. "The first thing we need to do is get a feel for Claudia's routine and the people in her life."

He released her wrist. "I'm sorry. Did I hurt you? You'll have to forgive me. I'm not myself right now."

Josie took the chair beside him. "It's okay, Mr. Collins."

Slowly, Noah returned to the table and sat down as well.

Beau pushed his hands through his hair again and sat up straight, attempting to compose himself. Both his hands gripped the edge of the table. "Okay," he said. "I can do this. I can do this for Claudia. What do you need to know?"

Josie started with background. "Do you and Claudia have children?"

"No. It's just the two of us."

"First marriage for both of you?" Josie said.

Beau nodded.

"What about children from prior relationships?" she asked.

"No, no children."

"Where did the two of you meet?" asked Noah.

The hint of a smile pulled at Beau's mouth. "Grad school. I was laboring toward my masters in marriage and family counseling while Claudia was crushing everyone in her PhD program. She wasn't even interested in me. I had to work hard to win her over. But once I did, I wasn't letting her go. After school, I worked at a practice here in Denton. She came on part-time. Then the doctor who had hired us retired and we took over."

Josie said, "I understand you still have the practice."

"Oh yes, we do, but that is pretty much all Claudia now. Even after the book went big and the show started, she insisted on keeping her patients. I had to pull back. One of us had to focus on the show and the opportunities our book brought."

Talking about their background calmed him. His breathing evened out. The splotchiness on his face faded.

Finally, Josie moved the conversation in another direction. "Mr. Collins, can you take us through your day today?"

"My day? Sure. We, uh, taped our show like we do every weekday."

Josie said, "How did it go?"

"Great, I think. We were doing the anniversary special because tonight was our fifteenth wedding anniversary." Pain flashed through his eyes, as if the mention of their anniversary was a stab. His grip on the edge of the table tightened, turning his knuckles white.

Noah said, "At the studio this morning, was that the last time you saw your wife?"

"I—I believe so. Claudia usually leaves the studio around noon to see her patients. We were supposed to meet at home and tape the anniversary dinner."

Josie said, "Tape it? Not eat it? Celebrate fifteen years together?"

Nervous laughter erupted from his throat. Beau said, "That was all for the show, for our fans. We were going to celebrate privately after everyone had left. We have an anniversary tradition. It's personal." His voice grew scratchy, and he had to clear his throat several times before continuing. Tears gleamed in his eyes. "When we started doing the show, Claudia had a rule that there were some things between us that had to stay between us. She, uh, didn't want a three-way relationship, she said."

"Three-way?" said Josie.

"Her, me, and the audience."

Noah said, "What was the anniversary tradition?"

He swiped at a tear as it escaped his eye. "Canned noodle soup and peanut M&Ms."

Josie said, "That's oddly specific."

Beau gave a tremulous laugh and resumed his grip on the edge of the table. "We sit on the floor of our great room and eat from the coffee table. Our first wedding anniversary we were so broke. That was all we could afford, and we ate it on the floor of our first apartment together. We didn't even have furniture then. Claudia insists on recreating it each year. She doesn't want us to forget where we started. She said it was—" He stopped, his Adam's apple bobbing. When his voice returned, it was high-pitched and throaty. "It was the best meal we ever had because we were together."

ELEVEN

Neither Josie nor Noah spoke, giving Beau a moment to compose himself. His tears flowed silently. As she watched him cry, Josie couldn't help but think of her encounter with Claudia in December. When Josie thought he was ready, she asked, "What's Claudia's maiden name?"

Beau seemed surprised by the question, but he answered anyway. "White. Why is that—why do you ask?"

Instead of answering, Josie moved on to her next inquiry, keeping her tone bland. "Fifteen years of marriage is a long time. How were things between you two, privately?"

Beau tried to smile. "They were not bad, but not great. I'll be honest, we haven't had a lot of alone time together lately. We are both very busy. We've got a practice with patients. We've got the show every day. We've got the podcast each week. Our agent has been pushing us to write a new book. We just signed a huge new contract to take the show national."

"Things were strained?" asked Noah.

"I wouldn't go that far," said Beau. "I know what you're thinking—we talk the talk but don't walk the walk. I get it. Relationship gurus who don't practice what they preach. That's fair.

But—" Here, he stopped and craned his neck, looking at their hands. "I see you're both married. You must know that all marriages have ups and downs."

"Were you having a 'down'?" Josie asked.

This time, he managed a tight smile. "I wouldn't describe it that way."

"Would Claudia?" asked Noah.

Beau's fingers pressed into the table. "No, I don't think she would. But surely, you know how it is." He took on a pleading look when he turned his gaze to Noah. "You must have a very busy schedule, being a police officer. Surely, there have been times when you failed to make time for your wife and perhaps you drifted apart?"

Noah said, "My wife is my priority. I 'make time' for everything else. I'd quit this job in a heartbeat if it came between us."

The words hit Josie like a slap. It was the painful difference between them. She loved Noah, more deeply than she had loved anyone who came before him, but she wasn't sure she'd give up her career for him. Or for anyone. This job was difficult. The things they saw were unspeakable. Sometimes it made Josie question the point of existing at all. But it was hers and she was good at it. She had built her career with her own blood, sweat, and tears. Literally. Her success was hard-won and had come at an incalculable cost. She couldn't imagine not doing it. Even if Noah asked her to stop. Luckily, he hadn't. Here he was, by her side on the job, as he had been for years. Even before they got together.

Beau blinked. "Oh. Well, your wife must be very... demanding."

Josie wasn't sure if he was joking or not, but Noah simply smiled. "My wife is a formidable woman, an impressive woman, yes. Demanding? No. But even if she was, I'm not sure that's a bad thing. I like a woman who knows what she wants and makes that very clear. Was your wife demanding?"

Beau shifted in his seat, clearly uncomfortable with the direction that the conversation had taken. "I don't think I'm communicating clearly enough. My wife is—was an impressive woman as well, but we just became so busy that I think our marriage was pushed all the way to the bottom of our list of priorities. Plus, as I said, Claudia's primary focus is still the practice. Mine is the growing number of couples we're able to help through the show, the book, and the podcast. Anyway, it's something I had hoped to discuss with her after this anniversary dinner."

Josie brought the questioning back to that day. "So the last time you saw your wife was around noon today after you taped the show. What were the two of you doing for the rest of the day?"

She could practically feel Beau's relief. "Oh, like I said, Claudia had patients for the rest of the day. I had meetings."

Noah asked, "What kinds of meetings?"

"With our literary agent, the publisher, and then with some network people, my manager, our attorney. Like I said, we just closed a deal for the show to go national. We were also in talks to do two more books."

"Claudia didn't need to be involved in those meetings?" asked Josie.

"Claudia prioritizes her patients," he explained. "She trusts —trusted me to take care of the details when it comes to the show or the books."

Noah said, "Did you talk to her at all today after the show?"

"Briefly. After the meeting with the network people, I called her, and we discussed their terms. She was busy. We were going to talk more about it tonight."

Josie said, "Let's talk about tonight. What time were you supposed to get home?"

"Five thirty."

"But you were late," said Noah.

Beau swallowed. "Yes, I, uh, I got caught up at the studio. Lost track of time. I called Margot to see if she could pick up the anniversary band that I had ordered for Claudia and meet me at the house with it. When we got there, Eve came running outside. She was screaming and crying. I didn't believe her at first. I had to go inside and see for myself."

Josie said, "You weren't worried that the killer might still be inside?"

His eyes widened in surprise. Clearly, the possibility had not crossed his mind. He stammered, "I—I didn't—I guess I just didn't think... I only went inside for a few seconds, a minute, tops. I had to see for myself. There was so much blood. I came right back out."

"Mr. Collins," Josie went on. "You have a Summers Security system in your home but no cameras? Why is that?"

"Oh," he said, a slight blush staining his cheeks. "We just didn't think we needed them. In all these years we've never had an issue. It's just me and Claudia."

"And video crews," Josie pointed out. "And assistants. Do you have a company for lawn care and snow removal?"

"Sure, of course. The property is pretty large. We don't have the time or the skill to maintain it ourselves."

"Your home requires a code to enter it," said Noah. "You, Claudia, Eve and Margot have the codes. Is there anyone else?"

"I don't think so. Unless Claudia gave out the codes to someone, but I can't imagine who that would be."

Noah leaned in closer to Beau. "Is there anyone you can think of who might have wanted to harm Claudia?"

Beau shook his head vigorously. "No. No one. People loved her."

"Are you sure?" Noah said. "A former patient? Disgruntled former employee? Internet stalker?"

He shook his head no to each suggestion.

Josie's mind played back the pre-Christmas encounter. Had

Claudia given her maiden name because she didn't want to be recognized as a local celebrity? But why? What difference would it have made?

Carefully, Josie said, "I'm afraid we have to ask this. Is there any chance that Claudia was having an affair?"

Beau waved a hand in the air. "Oh no. Claudia would never."

Josie said, "Okay. Can you tell me, did Claudia still use her maiden name?"

Looking perplexed, Beau said, "No. She's been Collins for fifteen years. Her PhD is under her married name. She's always been proud of that. Dr. Collins. I didn't even get my doctorate!"

While he was still caught off guard, Josie asked, "Do you play golf?"

He looked to Noah for guidance. When none was forthcoming, he said, "Not regularly, no."

"Would you excuse me?" said Josie.

Without waiting for an answer, she left the room. In the great room, Mettner was already at his computer, typing away. "You done with Bowers and Collins?" he asked.

"Bowers," she said, booting up her own computer so she could get a photo from the newly minted Claudia Collins murder file to show Beau. "Still going with Collins. Where are you?"

"LPRs didn't turn up anything. I'm going to go get these warrants for the geo-fence and phone records signed. I talked with Beau Collins's assistant."

"What'd you get?"

Mettner recapped Margot Huff's statement which lined up exactly with what both Beau Collins and Eve Bowers had already told them. "How about you?"

Josie told him what they had learned so far from both Eve and Beau. Mettner gave a low whistle. "This guy was in and out of there quick."

"Violence does not require a great deal of time," Josie sighed. "Sometimes all it takes is seconds and then a person is gone forever."

She sent the photo to the printer. Across the room, it whirred lazily to life.

Mettner said, "He took big risks, too. That house should have been filled with people."

"It's awfully coincidental that none of the people who were supposed to be there were actually there," Josie said. "Beau was the one who set things in motion so that he, Margot, and the video crew were not there between five thirty and six. We should verify both Beau's and Margot's whereabouts prior to the 911 call."

"You think he had something to do with this? What about Eve? You just said she was having some kind of personal crisis over being single. I doubt Beau knew that. What he definitely would have known was that she was supposed to be at the house at five thirty."

Josie walked over to the printer and plucked the photo from its tray. "I don't know what to think at this point. This guy seems genuinely horrified by what happened. Also, from what he's told us, it doesn't benefit him at all for Claudia to be killed. They just signed a contract for the show to be broadcast nationally. They were in talks to write more books."

"Right," said Mettner. "Why sabotage all that? Yet, you're not entirely convinced that he's innocent in all this, are you?"

Josie sighed. "Like I said, Mett. I don't know what to think, but something about this case stinks to high heaven."

TWELVE

Josie slid the photo of the gift box across the table toward Beau. He leaned in to study it, the worry line on his forehead deepening. She said, "This is a gift box of some kind. Do you remember seeing it when you went inside the house to see Claudia's body for yourself?"

Horror stretched across Beau's face. "Wait. This was there? Is that—is that Claudia's hand? She was holding it?"

"Yes," said Josie. "You didn't see it?"

"I didn't—no, I didn't see. I was so focused on Claudia and the blood. I was just—"

"It's okay," Noah assured him. "In a highly emotional and adrenalized situation like that, it's not uncommon for a person to completely miss certain details. But yes, this was found in your wife's hand. Does that mean anything to you?"

Beau's brow furrowed. "Well, yes. It's a puzzle box. It's a tool we use in our practice and on our show. You can buy these on our website. It looks like it can't be opened, and it can't be, in a traditional way. A magnet actually holds it together inside. You have to hit it in the correct spot, with just the right amount of force to get it to open. The metaphor is that your partner is like this puzzle box—the puzzle box representing their most intimate inner self. If you can figure out how to open that, there is a gift inside. That gift is them."

Josie asked, "Can you think of any reason the killer would leave this in Claudia's hand?"

He shook his head vehemently. "No. Absolutely not. I don't understand what's happening here."

Noah said, "What's in the puzzle box when you use it in demonstrations?"

"Nothing," Beau said, his voice small. "That's the point. It's intangible. Your partner—"

Josie cut him off. "Who would do this? Who would want to hurt Claudia?"

"I have no idea. I'm telling you, I don't know."

Josie said, "Mr. Collins, what do you think is inside that box?"

He stared at it. "I don't know. Haven't you opened it yet?"

Noah said, "It's still being processed."

Beau continued, "I don't know what's in it. I wish I could help you. I do, of course. Claudia—" He hung his head, shoulders shaking a bit.

Evenly, Josie said, "Mr. Collins, does your wife have a life insurance policy?"

He looked up at her, wiping tears from his cheeks. "Of course. We both do. We took them out when it became apparent that we were going to accumulate some wealth. What's that got to do with anything?"

Josie said, "What's the payout?"

"Three million dollars," Beau answered easily. "But I don't see what this has to do with my wife's murder."

Noah quickly jumped in, tapping a finger against the photo of the puzzle box. "The killer took time to do this, to leave this box, for you, is my guess. You have no ideas at all why someone would do this?"

Noah pushed the photo closer to Beau. Helplessness flashed in Beau's eyes. "I'm sorry. I really don't."

Josie said, "You say you used puzzle boxes on your show. What else did you and Claudia incorporate into your show?"

A wobbly smile. "This may sound silly to you, but we use games."

He stopped, waiting for more questions. Clearly the killer was familiar with the show. Josie was not. "Tell us more," she urged.

"Okay. Well, the use of games and the concept of fun are a huge part of our message to couples. You see, most people don't know nearly as much about their partners as they think they do, even after many years together. It's a kind of intimacy when you know more about your partner than anyone else. From how they take their coffee to their deepest fear. Their favorite food to their deepest regret. We use games and the idea of play in general as a fun way for couples to deepen their bond and learn more about one another."

Noah asked, "What kinds of games?"

"Anything. We're still developing new ones."

Josie said, "What do you do most often—or encourage your audience to do?"

"I can tell you what's most popular, and those are our scavenger hunts and Five Familiar Facts quizzes. We feature the scavenger hunts on the show, but couples can take the Five Familiar Facts quiz right on our website. Then we encourage them to post the results on social media."

Josie said, "Do you ever use the puzzle boxes in the scavenger hunts?"

He pushed the photo away. Exhaustion tugged at his posture. Suddenly it seemed a great effort for him to sit upright without leaning his elbows on the table. "Do you believe that discussing my show will help further your investigation?"

She touched the photo of the puzzle box. "A killer used

something from your show to stage the scene of your wife's murder. Yes, I think this might help us track him down."

"Okay, okay. We have used the boxes in scavenger hunts before but typically, no, we don't. Usually, when we do the hunts, we give couples a list of things they have to find that are meaningful to them and then they compare their findings. They can gather the items if they want but they can also just take photos."

Noah said, "Things like what?"

Beau didn't need any time to think about it. "A movie neither of you has seen; an album you both like; an item that represents you as a couple—that's a really fun one—your favorite photo of one another; something your partner hates; something that represents a place your partner would love to visit. I could go on, but you get the idea. There are thousands of things we have couples look for. It brings them closer together and sometimes it exposes the gaps in their relationship, and they can work on bridging them."

Noah asked, "What's your most popular thing? The puzzle boxes? The scavenger hunts? Something else?"

By now, Beau was fully immersed in speaking about his work, the words coming easily, as if he'd said them a thousand times before, which he likely had. "Five Familiar Facts. It's a quiz. It's on our website, although we've been talking about rolling out an app of some kind. Our followers go on there and the idea is that a couple takes it together—answering five questions about their partner—and then they compare their answers. There are thousands of questions, and each quiz is different so you can take it over and over again and get a brand-new set of questions."

Noah said, "What kinds of questions?"

"That's the brilliant thing," said Beau. "It's five questions ranked according to different levels of intimacy. So you'll get an easy one like, 'what is your partner's favorite dessert?' and then each one after that gets a bit deeper until the final question, which is something like, 'what does your partner value most in life?' No couple ever gets all five correct. Well, it's rare. We encourage people to share their results on social media. We even have a hashtag they can use to share what they didn't know about their partner. It's #whatididntknow. You should check it out."

Josie asked, "Have you and Claudia ever done the quiz?"

"Of course. Many times."

"Have you ever gotten all five questions correct?" asked Noah.

"Most of the time, yes. We came up with the questions. Sometimes we do one on the show and intentionally miss something so we can demonstrate what happens when you don't know something. We want to show couples how to move forward from there, especially if it's a big question. It's playful and fun. That's the point. Getting deeper and closer doesn't have to be this painful therapeutic process. Sometimes you can get there the fun way."

Josie raised a brow. "Is that what you tell your patients?"

Beau waved a dismissive hand. "Of course not. There are some issues that need to be addressed via the therapeutic process. Our method is not a catch-all."

Noah said, "What's your book called? *Winning at Love?*"

"*Perfect Pursuit,*" said Beau. "The subtitle is *Winning at Love.* It's about always pursuing your partner as though you were still trying to win them over, like you were still dating. And, like I said, using play to grow closer and more intimate. You 'win' at love if you are always striving to be closer to your partner and maintain that intimacy."

He stopped talking and took a deep breath. Scanning the room, the earnestness that had lit up his face while talking about the show leaked away, replaced by sadness. His eyes grew glassy again. Blinking hard, he looked back toward Josie and Noah.

"Listen, officers. I'm exhausted. I've had the worst day of my life. I just want to go home. Well, not home, but somewhere to rest."

Josie said, "I think that's all for tonight anyway. We will need to meet with your staff at the WYEP studio though, the sooner, the better."

"Of course. I'm going to call an emergency meeting for tomorrow morning at the studio. You could come then if you'd like. Meet everyone, talk with them. Whatever you need to do."

He stood up and put on his jacket. His eyes were glued to the photo of the gift box. Fear flashed across his face.

Josie stood as well and handed him a business card. She said, "Mr. Collins, the killer went to great lengths to stage the scene. He left this box in Claudia's hand. We don't know why yet but there is a chance that he isn't finished."

Both of Beau's brows shot up. "Finished with what?"

"It's impossible for us to say." She leaned over so that she could reach the photo. She tapped her index finger against it, then met his eyes again. "He specifically referenced the puzzle box from your show. If he doesn't feel he's made his point with this, then he may try something else."

A look of horror stretched across Beau's face. "Like what?"

Noah said, "Playing a game."

THIRTEEN

Back in the great room, Mettner was gone but Hummel stood at Josie's desk, two paper evidence bags in his hands. "Boss," he said when she and Noah walked in. "I've got something for you."

Josie walked over and cleared a space on her desk. Noah stood next to her while Hummel snapped on some gloves and dumped the contents of the first bag. The splintered remains of the puzzle box tumbled out. Its oak and red wood was stained black with the remnants of fingerprint powder. Hummel caught the shiny ball bearing before it rolled off the table.

Noah peered down at it, one brow raised. "Couldn't get it open, could you?"

Hummel looked insulted. "You can clearly see that I did, in fact, get it open."

"With what?" Josie asked. "A hammer?"

Hummel scoffed. "You think I'm a barbarian? No. A rubber mallet."

Noah snorted.

Josie said. "Okay, what did you find?"

"Well, for one thing, I only got one usable print from the

bottom of it, but it didn't get any hits in AFIS." AFIS, or the Automated Fingerprint Identification System, was a database maintained by the FBI that held the prints of people with criminal records or people who had been arrested, as well as and prints from unknown persons found at crime scenes. "I did get elimination prints from Beau Collins since he is a resident in the house. The print did not belong to him."

He picked up the oak section of the box and ran his index finger along a rectangular compartment. It was no bigger than two inches across and one inch deep. "As you can see, there's a little room to hide something." He picked up the other bag and shook the contents out onto the desk. It was a six-inch by nine-inch piece of paper which Hummel had placed into a plastic sheet. It, too, was stained with fingerprint powder.

Noah said, "What is it?"

"A page from the Collinses' book," Josie said.

Hummel smiled. "Exactly."

He laid the page onto her desk and stepped aside so that she and Noah could read it. The page number said five but the chapter heading said one. Noah read the first line out loud. "*Welcome to your pursuit. If you're reading this, that means you're ready to perfect your quest for love. We're happy to guide you, whether you're single and looking for a partner or you've been married for years and are searching to reignite the spark in your relationship.*"

"Stop," Josie groaned.

"I'm just getting to the good part," Noah complained. "What if we need to reignite the spark in our relationship?"

She rolled her eyes. "I know you're not implying that our spark is gone. Besides, I'm not interested in anything this book says unless it helps us solve Claudia Collins's murder."

Hummel said, "I got three prints from this page but again, no hits in AFIS."

"How many of these books do you think are in print?" Josie asked.

"I checked," said Hummel. "Over two million copies."

Noah said, "Let's focus on what the killer is trying to tell us with this."

"Not us," said Josie. "Beau Collins. This is directed at him. I'm sure of it."

Noah leaned in closer to the page. *"These are the rules for your 'pursuit.' Communicate clearly and openly. Be honest. Be respectful. Trust your partner. Be supportive. Prioritize your partner."*

Hummel said, "Doesn't sound like the killer is playing by those rules."

"He's not," Josie agreed. "Why would he leave this page? Is he trying to set guidelines of some kind? For what?"

"It's a game to him," Noah said. "Or some sort of pursuit. Just like you told Beau Collins."

Josie said, "Right, and if that's the case, he's not finished."

"Exactly," Noah said. "Using things from the book, the show? He's clearly taunting Beau Collins. If this box contains the 'rules' then that implies there will be more contact."

"More murders," Josie corrected, the unease she'd been feeling since walking into the Collinses' home overwhelming now. "Let's put a unit on Beau Collins. This killer is just getting started."

FOURTEEN

Josie woke at seven the next morning to find her bed empty. Both Noah and their Boston terrier, Trout, were gone. There was only one reason Trout would leave both Josie and blankets. Sure enough, as she made her way to the bathroom, the smell of maple sausage wafted upstairs. At the top of the steps, she called down, "Don't give him any table food!"

Noah called back, "I'm not."

But Josie knew at least one morsel, maybe two, would "accidentally" fall onto the floor near Noah's seat.

Twenty minutes later, she was showered, dressed, and in the kitchen, watching Trout ignore her to sniff and lick every square inch of tile floor around Noah's chair. Noah was too engrossed watching something on his phone to notice. With a sigh, Josie walked to the counter, poured herself a cup of coffee, and took in the full extent of the damage. Three pans had been deposited into the sink. Two of their handles poked upright, crossing in the shape of an X, warning her not to get any closer. On the stove was another pan, its surface an abstract painting made with pancake batter. A pile of failed flapjacks sat on a paper plate on the countertop, leaning like a tower about to topple. Remnants of powder, broken eggshells, milk, and some sort of greasy substance covered nearly every inch of both stove and countertop.

She hated herself for it, but her thoughts went directly to Luke. She never thought of him anymore but yesterday, he'd been thrust back into her life. Looking at the disaster on her countertop and stove, she remembered what an excellent cook he was and how he could make a meal out of nothing and anything. How he'd made her breakfast in bed countless times. Plus, he had always been the neatest and most orderly person she'd ever met.

Noah broke through her thoughts. "I'll clean it up."

Pushing memories of her ex-fiancé out of her mind, Josie poked the stack of pancakes. They were cold and gooey. "What's the score this time?"

He sighed. "Pancakes, thirteen. Noah, nil." He pointed to a plate across from him piled high with scrambled eggs and two pieces of sausage. "You're having eggs."

She left the mess and sat at the table. "My high score is also zero, so we're still even."

In a culinary sense, they were a match made in hell. Josie could not cook at all, and Noah was only passable. Harris had stayed over a few weeks earlier. In the morning, he'd asked for pancakes. Josie had wanted to go to the Pancake Palace. Noah thought they could make pancakes at home from a box.

He was wrong.

After burning seven pancakes and setting off the smoke alarm, they had, in fact, eaten at the Pancake Palace, but Harris would not let them live down the pancake debacle. Since that day, they'd both tried perfecting the simple art of making a pancake. So far, they were failing miserably.

Josie sat down in front of the meal Noah had prepared for her and checked her phone before digging in. The only news was the results of Dr. Feist's autopsy, which confirmed what they had already surmised: Claudia Collins had died from a blow to the head. Dr. Feist was not able to determine what might have caused it. There were no signs of sexual assault. Manner of death was homicide. Dr. Feist had found DNA on her clothes which she'd swabbed and sent to the state police lab for analysis and comparison against all profiles in CODIS, the Combined DNA Index System. CODIS was a searchable database maintained by the FBI which collected DNA profiles from convicted criminals, people who had been arrested, and missing persons. The only issue was that the analysis itself could take weeks or months. It didn't help them now and it might not help them even when the results came in—unless it matched an existing profile. Josie doubted that would happen. They had already had no luck with AFIS. Their only hope once the results came in then would be matching them to a suspect, which they did not have. Yet.

Josie kept scrolling. The geo-fence results were a bust. The only phone at the Collinses' home at the time of Claudia's murder was Claudia's. Had the killer turned off his phone? Left it elsewhere? He must have known the police could use it to link him to the scene and locate him.

Dead ends.

Without looking up from his phone, Noah poked the empty pancake box in the middle of the table. "I don't understand. How hard can it be? I followed all the directions."

"Story of my life," Josie said, around a mouthful of eggs. "What are you watching?"

He didn't look up. "Couples' Corner With The Collinses. The one from yesterday. It's on the WYEP website."

He stood up and turned his phone toward her, pushing it across the table, together with one of his wireless earbuds. Josie pushed the earbud into one of her ears and pressed the play arrow. Under the table, Trout pressed his nose into the side of her leg. It was his way of letting her know that he knew she had sausage. Ignoring him, Josie turned the volume up.

"...anniversaries in the Collins house are always a huge event but this one is a big one," said Beau Collins. He was seated at a small white circular table. Beside him was Claudia. Both of them smiled brightly for the camera. Behind them was a large screen that flashed photos of them in a slide show. Some looked fairly recent, but others were clearly from when the two of them were much younger.

"Fifteen years!" Claudia exclaimed, clapping her hands together. Her eyes were locked straight ahead. "I can hardly believe it."

Beau looked over at her and then caught her hand in his. He gazed adoringly at her. A lot like Josie gazed at her coffee each morning. "Did you ever imagine, back when we were poor grad students, that we'd be together for fifteen years?"

Claudia laughed, long and loud, and then she covered his hand with her other one, making a pile between them. She turned to him, leaning in, and puckered her lips slightly, making him come in for the kiss. Keeping her eyes on him, she said, "I thought you would have dumped me long ago for someone far more interesting."

He kept his eyes locked on hers for another three-count. "Never, my dear," he said and then he turned back to the camera. "This brings up a great question, though. How do you stay interested in your partner after fifteen years?"

Josie pulled out the earbud. "I can't watch this. It's completely scripted. I can't believe people buy into this stuff."

Noah regarded her from across the room, his hip leaned against the counter. He sipped his coffee. "What stuff?"

Josie punched a finger against the screen. "This! That somehow marriage or a relationship is going to be perfect."

"Nothing is perfect," he said. "Well, except for the pancakes' record against us."

Josie laughed. She looked at the phone and exited out of the video. Using the internet browser, she searched for the Collinses' website. Its background was all soothing creams and pinks and graphics of hearts. The home page was filled with stock photos of couples. Each one showed a different pair posed artificially in front of an ocean or a forest or a cornfield, of all things. The biographies of Beau and Claudia were the only believable things on the website. Josie scrolled through the description of their book, with dozens of glowing reviews from colleagues and testimonials from readers. Next were hundreds of short clips from their show, each one captioned with something that made Josie cringe: Play to Win: Pursuing Your Perfect Partner; Sexy Scavenger Hunts to Bring the Spark Back; Pre-Gaming Your Marriage Goals; Solve the Puzzle of Your Partner's Innermost Desire.

Maybe Claudia had used her maiden name when she met Josie and Harris because she didn't want to be associated with this.

"Look at this website," Josie complained, turning the phone back toward him. He sat down again and scrolled through the site.

She said, "What are they trying to prove with all those hearts, anyway?"

Noah laughed. "I think you're missing the point."

"Am I?"

She leaned forward and touched the screen, stopping him from scrolling. On it was a photo of the Collinses, in profile, standing in front of a lake, a sunset in the background. Claudia's hair lifted flatteringly in the breeze. Her head tilted upward toward Beau, whose eyes drank her in hungrily. One of his hands rested on her hip. They looked as though they were about to kiss, like there was no one else in the world but them. It could have been the cover of a romance novel. "Real relationships don't look like that."

Noah put his hand over hers. "Are you saying I've never looked at you like that?"

Josie rolled her eyes. "Of course you have. That's not my point."

"What is?"

She pulled her hand away and stood up, heading back to the coffeemaker for a second cup. "Real relationships don't look like the cover of a romance novel. They look like... like standing next to one another while you bury a parent or grandparent. They look like being there for all the grief that comes after it, no matter how ugly and isolating it gets. They look like taking you to doctor's appointments. They look like helping you on and off the toilet after you break your leg. They look like being okay with not having any closet doors in your house because your spouse has childhood trauma. They look like being your worst self to someone and knowing they'll stay. They look like—" She gestured toward the mess on the counter. "Like making a thousand pancakes because you've become some kind of honorary uncle to your wife's dead first husband's kid and being totally okay with that."

Noah smiled. He had a lot of different smiles. Josie had learned all of them over the years. This was the sexy one that set her heart aflutter. He stood up and walked toward her, slowly. Trout paid no attention to either of them, still rooting around on the floor under the table in hopes of a sausage scrap. Noah took her mug out of her hand and set it on the counter between a batter-encrusted spatula and a powder-filmed measuring cup. He leaned his body into hers. The edge of the counter bit into her lower back but she didn't care. He was so close, his breath caressed her forehead. Josie felt everything between them all at once: electricity and comfort. Every muscle in her body loosened while every nerve ending on her skin buzzed with wanting him to touch her.

They'd never be the sunset photo, but damn if Josie didn't feel like they were in one.

"You're not helping," she whispered.

He kissed the thin scar that started at the bottom of her right ear and ended under her chin. "You left something out," he said. "Real relationships look like you seeing all your partner's scars and loving them."

Josie practically melted into the countertop. Still, one of her hands snaked upward, under his T-shirt to his right shoulder where a puckered circle of flesh ridged beneath her fingers. She had given him this scar when she shot him. It was long before they got together, and even though she had believed she was doing the right thing at the time, she still regretted it.

Noah caught her hand. He lifted his head so he could look her in the eye. With a smile, he said, "They look like forgiving your spouse after she's shot you."

Josie wanted to kiss him. She wanted them to make far better use of the kitchen right now than ruining pancakes. But her brain wouldn't let her. It was back in the interrogation room with Beau Collins.

"Noah," she said softly as he kissed the tips of her fingers.

His head dipped down, tongue finding the hollow of her throat, arms wrapping her up. Involuntarily, she moaned. Getting her bearings again, she said, "What you said to Collins yesterday, about giving up the job for me, did you mean it?"

His tongue stopped only long enough for him to mumble against her skin, "You really want to talk about this now? We have to be at WYEP in an hour. Let's use the time well."

She thought about the lesson that all her relationships had taught her. It was an awful thing, probably because it never went the way you hoped it would. It was that you could never know who a person truly was until they were tested. You thought that the boy you fell in love with at nine years old would grow up to be someone brave, courageous, and with enough integrity and backbone to stand up to corruption. But when he was tested, he wasn't that person at all. You thought that the fiancé you fell in love with after him was honest and loyal, that he would never push you away or cheat on you, especially after you nursed him back to health from a near-fatal injury for over a year. But when he was tested, he failed.

There were all kinds of ways that people were tested—in and out of relationships—and there were ways that relationships themselves were tested. You never knew how strong your relationship was until it was challenged because you never knew anyone—not really—until they were put to the test.

Noah lifted her off her feet, pulling her legs around his waist. Josie's body adhered to his without thought, her physical need for him overtaking all else. Only the sound of her phone ringing stopped them from going back to bed. It took everything in her to peel herself away from Noah. He clung to her, talking into her neck. "Don't answer that."

"I have to," she said. "At least let me see who it is."

With a sigh, she extricated herself, walked back to the table, and picked up her phone. The number was local but she didn't recognize it. Still, she swiped answer. "This is Detective Quinn."

A woman's hushed voice said, "Detective? This is Margot Huff. From last night? I think we need your help."

Josie heard shouts and crying in the background. "Where are you, Margot?"

In a whisper, she said, "At the studio. Please hurry. I think Eve is missing."

FIFTEEN

WYEP, Denton's local television station, was located on top of a mountain in the northwest quadrant of the city. It was a blocky, two-story building that could have been any office building in the city except for the news vans lined up side by side in the parking lot. It had been less than twenty-four hours since Claudia was murdered, but Josie wondered if anyone from the local news had found out yet. It would be a huge story and difficult to contain, seeing that the Collinses taped their show in the same building as the WYEP news.

Josie and Noah flashed their credentials at a security guard who buzzed them through a vestibule into a large hallway. A sign hung on the wall, listing all the main attractions on the first floor with arrows pointing either left or right, depending on their location. The main studio was to the left. Studio One, which was where the Collinses taped their show, was to the right. At least the reporters were on the opposite end of the building.

Voices could be heard from behind the door to Studio One before Josie pushed it open. As she and Noah entered the small, dark space, a man shouted, "—you shut up, you hag! You never cared about Claudia either!"

In the center of the room, illuminated by a circle of bright light, the set held the white couch and coffee table from which the Collinses did their show. Several people were gathered around the table, including the man who had just shouted. He pointed a finger at a tall woman on the other side of the table.

"Shut up, Liam!" she snapped. "I'm raising a legitimate concern. Whether any of you like it or not, we still have to decide what to do about this show."

Breathing heavily, Liam curled his hands into fists. "Who cares about this stupid show? Claudia was murdered! None of you even care."

Someone else said, "That's not true!"

Beau, who had been sitting on the couch, stood and tried to put an arm around Liam's shoulder.

"Don't touch me," Liam said, shrugging him off. "This is all your fault."

Beau looked stricken. The room fell silent except for someone sobbing quietly. Slowly, he walked away from the group. The tall woman said, "Beau, please. I don't mean any disrespect. I'm just trying to be practical. I'm a producer. That's my job."

"Kathy, please," he mumbled, walking away from her. He headed toward a darkened control room. Two other women followed. Josie and Noah picked their way past lighting equipment and three cameras. Everyone had backed away from Liam. Kathy turned toward him and said, "You should watch yourself. You're just a camera operator. We could replace you within the hour."

Liam lunged toward her and the other people by the couch and coffee table surged between them. Kathy's hand shot between the shoulders of the two men pulling him away from her and yanked at Liam's beard. He cried out and twisted his head away from her. Long nails raked down his face, knocking his glasses onto the floor and leaving three welts on his forehead.

"Bitch!" Liam cried as he was dragged away and off to the side of the room. One of the women in the room picked up his glasses. She shot Kathy a dirty look before walking over to where Liam was now, assuring the men he would stay calm.

Josie didn't miss the producer's satisfied smile. She kept her tone low so that only Noah could hear. "Gretchen should be on shift now. Text her and ask her to get over here. We're going to need statements from all these people about their relationship with Claudia, when they last saw her, and where they were last night."

Noah's fingers flew across his phone screen. "You got it."

Margot stood behind the couch, her eyes wide with horror. Her hair was greasy, her face pale. She looked as though she hadn't slept at all the night before. Josie didn't blame her. Behind her stood a tall man with a dark, neatly trimmed goatee. He wore khakis and a white polo shirt with WYEP embroidered on the upper left side of his chest. Over it, a name had been stitched in black: Raffy. One of his hands rested on Margot's shoulder. Soulful brown eyes gazed down at her as she looked on at the spectacle, bewildered. When Raffy noticed Josie and Noah, he leaned closer to Margot and spoke softly. Josie read his lips. *The police are here. Tell them.*

With that, he nudged her gently forward. Clutching her phone to her chest, she maneuvered around the couch and past the knot of people now staring at Josie and Noah. "Thank you for coming," she said.

"Who are these people?" said Kathy.

Josie and Noah introduced themselves, providing their credentials for everyone to see. Beau reappeared, suddenly the gracious host, introducing them to the staff, including Liam, who kept his distance. The other people present included two other camera operators: Sean House and Jim Fogle; the person responsible for lighting: Jewell Cartwright; an audio-video technician: Kyle Schwarber; a floor director: Marissa Parker; and two stylists: Cindy Stamm and Stephanie Horvat.

"I'm sorry for what you just witnessed," Beau said. He sent a sympathetic look in Liam's direction. "I had the staff come in for an emergency meeting so I could tell them about Claudia myself. As you can see, not all of us are handling it that well. Anyway, I know you two needed to speak to the staff, so feel free—"

Josie looked past him to Margot. "Where's Eve?"

Beau looked confused. Slowly, he scanned the room. Margot looked at Raffy, who gave her an encouraging smile, and then she stepped forward. "She's not here."

Beau shook his head. "No, that's not right. She was supposed to get coffee and bagels."

Margot said, "That was hours ago, Beau."

"No. That's not possible."

"Yes it is! She left my apartment around five this morning. You were there!"

There were a couple of murmurs from the rest of the staff. Margot rolled her eyes and addressed the group. "We were freaked out, okay? I mean, Eve and Beau saw Claudia's body." She put emphasis on the word *body* as she panned the faces in the room. From the corner, Liam made a small noise, something between a gasp and a choking sound. Cindy Stamm, the stylist who had picked up his glasses, patted his shoulder.

Beau waved his hands up and down, signaling for his staff to bring down the tension in the room. "I know it sounds odd," he said. "But we were all very, very upset and traumatized. Eve was a wreck. Margot told her she could stay at her place. I was going to go to a hotel—I don't know how I can ever go back to that house." He shuddered, eyes closing briefly before refocusing on everyone surrounding him. "Margot and Eve were kind enough to let me stay as well. I don't think any of us slept a wink."

Noah tried to get the conversation back on track. "Was that the last time you two saw Eve? At Margot's apartment?"

Margot nodded. "She was still awake at five this morning. She said she was going to drive back to her place to shower and get changed. She had already made all the calls to everyone here the night before, letting them know to be here by eight. She said she was going to get bagels and coffee. Not that any of us can eat. I guess it just felt like something to do."

Josie said, "But she never showed up. No one here has seen her today?"

Some murmured no and others shook their heads.

Josie said, "Does she live alone?"

Margot nodded.

Noah said, "Is she dating anyone? Does she have close friends nearby? Anyone whose house she might have gone to?"

"I don't know," Margot said. "I don't think so."

Kathy said, "She's dating someone."

All heads turned toward her. Beau said, "How do you know?"

Kathy shrugged. "I've seen her on her phone when she thinks no one is paying attention, texting away with this smile on her face. That is the look of a woman in love."

Josie looked around at the stunned faces. "Does anyone know who Eve is seeing?"

Silence.

Noah said, "Did any of you try calling or texting her?"

Margot thrust her phone toward Josie. "I did. Starting around seven, after we got here at six thirty. We called and texted. No answers at all. Not everyone was here yet, so I went over to her apartment. Her car wasn't there, but she keeps a spare key under the potted plant outside her door and I used it."

Josie said, "You know where her spare key is, Margot. Do you know of anyone she might be with now?"

Margot shook her head. "No. If I did, I would have called them! That's why I went to her apartment. I know it's intrusive to go inside, but I was really worried. I didn't touch anything. I only wanted to make sure she was okay, but she wasn't there."

Josie said, "How did the apartment look? Did it appear as if anything had been disturbed?"

Margot shook her head, pulling her phone back to her chest and hugging it.

Beau stared at Josie with dawning horror. "What do you mean, 'disturbed'?"

Josie ignored him.

"I went to the bagel place," added Margot. "But they said they hadn't seen her at all. Or at least no one remembered seeing her today."

"When you were at her house," Josie said, "did you look in the bathroom?"

Beau touched Margot's shoulder, but she shrugged him off. Raffy watched warily. Margot said, "What?"

Josie said, "You said that Eve told you she was going home to get a shower. Did you look inside her bathroom? Was the inside of the shower wet?"

Margot's lower lip trembled. "I don't know."

Beau clamped a hand over Margot's shoulder. "Why didn't you tell me?"

Raffy's eyes were locked on Beau's hand. He took a step forward and reached out, as if he were going to intervene, but then Margot stepped out of Beau's reach. Raffy quickly wrapped a protective arm across Margot's shoulders.

Beau gave Raffy a puzzled look, as if he had only just registered his presence. It lasted a beat too long, stretching the moment into awkwardness. Had the two never met before? Or was Beau just so busy and self-absorbed he simply hadn't noticed the obvious affection between Raffy and Margot? Finally, Beau blinked and turned his attention back to Margot. "Why? Why didn't you say something about Eve?"

"Because I kept thinking she was just going to show up. Maybe she was having some kind of meltdown or personal crisis. Yesterday she was talking about quitting."

Beau looked as if she had slapped him. "What?"

Margot ignored him, instead looking down at her phone. She punched something into it and then swiped a few times before turning it toward Josie and Noah. "But the reason I called you was this."

Josie moved closer. Margot thrust the phone at her until Josie took it. The screen showed text messages between Eve Bowers and Margot.

Margot's started at six that morning and continued on for an hour and a half.

Where are you?

Is everything okay?

Are you all right?

Are you coming in? If you don't want to come, I understand. I'll tell Beau.

No one will be mad. Just let me know you're okay.

Eve, you're starting to freak me out. Please answer.

Are you okay?

I'm coming over to your apartment.

There was a thirty-minute gap.

Eve, seriously. Please answer me.

Then, at seven forty-three there was a reply. *Tell your boss he doesn't get to dictate the rules. I do. THE GAME IS ON.*

SIXTEEN

Josie used a gloved hand to pull back the shower curtain in Eve Bowers's tiny bathroom. Inside, drops of water clung to the tile and the bottom of the tub. A laundry bin in the corner of the room was full to the brim with clothes. On top was the crumpled cream sweater dress Eve had been wearing the night before at the stationhouse. A quick pass through the clothes in the basket revealed that they were all the same size and similar in style—so likely all belonging to Eve. The head of her toothbrush was still damp. She had made it home from Margot Huff's apartment. She'd had time to shower and change. Josie hadn't found any evidence of another person in the apartment. No extra toothbrush. No photos other than Eve with two people Josie assumed were her parents, given their age and resemblance. If she was dating someone, it was not yet serious enough for the other person to leave evidence of themselves in her home.

Noah's voice came from somewhere else in the apartment. "Josie?"

She left the bathroom and walked down a short hallway to the living room. A stack of books rested on the coffee table next to a half-filled bottle of water. "Eve Bowers was here this morning."

Noah stood just inside the front door. "I know. I just talked to a neighbor who saw her get into her car and drive off at six fifteen."

"Alone?"

He nodded. "I had the super of the building pull security footage. She definitely left alone."

Josie studied the pile of books. There were six in all. They were a mix of pop psychology and relationship advice, including the Collinses' book. She bent over and pulled it from the bottom of the pile, flipping through the pages. Several of them were dog-eared. Many passages were underlined.

Noah walked over. "Do you think she was practicing the principles of her boss's book on the person she was supposedly dating? Assuming that producer was right about her?"

"I don't know," Josie replied. "She told us she was single. Maybe she was highlighting these passages for when she met someone. Maybe she was dating someone and had recently broken up with them."

A white paper fluttered from the pages of the book and onto the floor. Josie put the book back on the table and picked up the paper, turning it over in her hands. Not a paper, an unopened envelope. "What is it?" asked Noah.

Josie showed him the front of the envelope. It was addressed to Claudia Collins from a local nonprofit. The postage mark was from mid-December. Josie had received an identical envelope a month ago during their big holiday push for fundraising.

Noah said, "Junk mail?"

"I wouldn't call it junk mail," she replied. "But I doubt it's crucial or personal."

"What's on the back?"

She flipped it over. In a small, cramped hand, someone had written a name. Josie read it aloud. "Archie Gamble."

"The boyfriend, maybe?" Noah suggested.

"I don't know. This is addressed to Claudia. I'm not sure if this handwriting belongs to her or to Eve."

They looked around, searching for anything in plain view that might have Eve's handwriting on it, but there was nothing. Noah said, "Take a photo. We'll check it out later. Right now, we need to keep moving."

Josie snapped a picture with her phone and then put the book back as she had found it. Noah motioned for her to follow him outside. Eve's apartment building had exterior entrances along the first floor with parking spots directly in front of each unit. She put the spare key back where they'd found it. They hadn't taken the time to get a warrant, but the landlord had given them permission to enter the property for a welfare check.

Josie looked up and down the street. "Which way did she go?"

Noah pointed in the direction of the bagel place that Margot had told them Eve frequented. "Let's head to the bagel place next," she said.

Josie drove while Noah checked his phone for updates. They had left Gretchen and a couple of uniformed officers at the WYEP studio to take statements from everyone who worked on the Collinses' show. They'd roused Mettner from his much-deserved rest to have him try to find out whether or not Eve's Nissan had a navigation system that could be used to track her whereabouts. With every minute that passed, Josie's dread grew bigger. The coffee she had had that morning burned a hole in her stomach.

Noah said, "Dispatch pinged her phone. Last known location was the city park."

Josie glanced at him. "The city park is between here and the bagel place, assuming she took Squillace Road over to Greiner Avenue. Let's just go there."

"That would be the quickest way with the least traffic,"

Noah said. "Although that early in the morning in January, on a Saturday? I don't know that there would be that much traffic."

"Did they get a specific location within the park?"

"Near the main entrance."

"What are the odds she's just hanging out there by the main entrance?" Josie muttered. "Call in some units in case we need to search the park."

Noah made the call. It took ten minutes to get to the city park. Josie scanned the vehicles lined up on the sidewalk along the street near the park's main entrance, but she didn't see a Nissan. There were already units on hand. Josie instructed them to circle the entire park and drive up to Beau and Claudia Collinses' home again, just to make sure Eve hadn't decided to go there for some strange reason. She and Noah drove on and checked the parking lots inside the city park. They found nothing.

Back at the main entrance, Josie parked her SUV. She and Noah got out and started walking toward the handful of patrol officers standing just inside the park, awaiting further instructions.

Noah said, "You want to send these guys out to look for Eve Bowers's car?"

Josie sighed. "Mett's checking on the navigation system. There's already a BOLO out so someone might see it, and if it turns up on any of the LPRs, we'll know."

"We might find it faster if we send more units out to search."

They passed through a wide break in a row of shrubbery that separated the park from the sidewalk. In a cobblestone clearing, a sign that said "Welcome to Denton's City Park" greeted them. Next to it was another sign that listed the rules of the park. There were many. Benches were scattered around the space. There were four different paths leading away from the area, each one marked by a sign that indicated which park attractions citizens could find along the way. Playground, carousel, band shell, softball fields, gazebo, pond, jogging and biking trails, community picnic areas. The uniformed officers were gathered in a tight knot beside the trail that led to the playground and carousel.

Noah touched Josie's arm. She turned toward him, but he wasn't there. He'd stopped near the path that led to the jogging and biking trails. "What is it?" she asked.

He strode over to one of the benches and circled behind it, squatting down. Josie followed and watched as he took out his phone and snapped photos of some object lodged between two cobblestones. Next, he fished a pair of gloves from his coat pocket and snapped them on. He lifted the object and held it up so that Josie could see. Her heart gave a small flutter before speeding up. Staring back at her from a Pennsylvania's driver's license was the face of Eve Bowers.

"She was inside the park," Josie said.

A few of the uniformed officers had jogged over. One of them offered to get an evidence bag and ran off to his car.

"Or the killer took her and tossed her driver's license here to throw us off."

Josie walked up the path a bit, to where the cobblestone ended and both sides of the path were grass, dirt, and dead vegetation. The other officers had already spread out across the clearing, eyes searching the ground for more clues.

Josie said, "It doesn't matter, does it? We can't take the chance of not searching the park because if she is here, and there is even the smallest chance he hasn't killed her yet, we need to find her."

"If she's here, he's here," Noah said. The uniformed officer who'd offered to get an evidence bag from his car returned. Noah deposited Eve Bowers's license into the paper bag and the officer took custody of it, using a marker he'd brought with him to properly label the bag.

"I don't think he's here," Josie said. "He wouldn't stick around."

"Then he took her in her car," said Noah. "And planted the license here so we would split our resources in the search. We need to be looking for the car."

Josie couldn't disagree. What evidence they had told them that Eve Bowers had left her apartment alone in her own vehicle. Then her phone had pinged outside the city park entrance. That was the last place they could put her. But she wasn't here and neither was her vehicle. It was a lot harder to hide a vehicle than a person. Splitting the police resources to give the killer more time made sense. He had turned off Claudia Collins's phone when he left her home. Somehow, he'd encountered Eve Bowers here, used her phone to text Margot, and then most likely turned it off. He knew enough about police procedure to ensure that he couldn't be tracked by phone, which meant he probably knew that Eve's vehicle, a fairly recent model, likely had a navigation system in it. It was only a matter of time before the police located it. Making it look like Eve was inside the park was a good distraction.

"What if she's here?" Josie said.

Noah followed her partway up the path. "Josie, her vehicle's not here."

The words from the killer's text came back to her. *THE GAME IS ON.*

"He will want her to be found," Josie said. "I think there is a reasonable chance that he left her here."

"And what? Drove off in her car?" Noah said. "How would that work? He would have to leave his own vehicle nearby. He may want us to find her, but I'm pretty sure he's not too eager to get caught."

Again, Josie couldn't argue with his logic. "Fine," she said. "You leave me with a few people here and we'll search the park. Send a couple of units out to check the tags of all vehicles parked nearby. Everyone else looks for Eve's car until it's found either by them or through the navigation system that Mett is running down."

"Josie, this park is huge."

"But if you're right about him trying to throw us off, then you'll find Eve's car pretty quickly and we can call off the search here. Anyway, there are still people inside the park just going about their days. We've already dodged the press on this for the last eighteen hours. It's probably best if we don't attract attention by flooding this park with police officers unless we absolutely have to do so."

As if on cue, a jogger and another man walking his dog came from one of the trails, staring at the police officers as they exited the park.

"We should call Luke," Noah said. "We can get something from Eve's apartment for Blue to scent. If she is here, the dog will find her in minutes."

Pulling the collar of her coat up around her cheeks, Josie said, "I'm not sure we have time." She pictured Claudia's head wound. If the killer attacked Eve the way he'd attacked Claudia, she might bleed out before they found her, if she hadn't already. Whether Eve was somewhere in the park or halfway across town in her own car, she needed to be located as soon as possible.

Noah took out his phone. "I'll call him and see how fast they can get here."

Josie said, "I'll go get our radios from the car. Then I'll start here. I'll work my way across the park."

Noah nodded. "I'll get everything else coordinated. Be careful."

SEVENTEEN

Once she had her radio affixed to the back of her pants, Josie took off at a run, her breath coming out in puffs as she headed up the path leading to the jogging and biking trails. She reached another clearing, this one asphalt, where the path diverged into six different trails. Josie chose the trail that ran along the outermost edge of the eastern side of the park. She'd gone a few feet when something along the side caught her eye. It was nestled among the branches of an unruly hawthorn bush. At first, she thought it was merely a dried leaf but as she drew closer, she saw that it was dark blue. Leaning in for a better look, Josie's breath caught in her throat.

It was a credit card. Eve Bowers's credit card.

She took out her phone and snapped several photos of it. She radioed the rest of the team and then returned to the trail, picking up her pace as it meandered through a couple of grassy areas with benches and one knoll with a small fountain that had been turned off for winter. Two walkers and a runner passed her, giving her curious glances. Trees began to close in on either side of the trail. They were barren, giving her a relatively unobstructed view into the forested areas around her. A quarter of a mile from where she'd found the credit card, deep in the brush, Josie found a woman's purse. It lay on its side, its contents spilled out of its open top. Josie snapped a few more photos and then used the edge of a stick to poke around inside it until she found a wallet with more credit cards belonging to Eve Bowers.

No car keys or fob. No phone.

She searched the surrounding area for any sign of Eve or evidence of a struggle but found none. Leaving the purse as it was, she returned to the trail, radioing the team once more. As she continued on, her mind worked through a possible scenario. Eve Bowers had left her apartment alone, driving off in her Nissan. She had stopped or somehow been stopped at the main entrance to the city park. She had to have known the killer if she had stopped for him. Unless he had called her ahead of time and arranged to meet her there. Clearly, she'd gotten out of her car. She had either chosen to follow him deeper into the park, likely not seeing him as a threat, or he'd forced or coerced her. But she must have realized very quickly that she was in trouble because she'd tossed her license onto the ground very close to the park entrance.

Then she had attempted to leave a trail.

Josie was impressed by Eve's quick thinking and ingenuity. Unfortunately, the clues ended with the purse. The killer must have realized what she was trying to do. Had he dragged Eve back out of the park at that point? To her car?

Her radio squawked. All units were heading in her direction.

She kept going. Her calves burned as rolling green areas turned to a wooded hill. Near the top was an opening in the trees. A sign next to it announced: Lovers' Cave. Below the name was a short summary of the lore that had grown up around the cave. *In the late 1800s, two skeletons were found inside Lovers' Cave, lying side by side, holding hands. Their identities remain a mystery to this day.*

Josie peered down the dirt path that led to the cave. It was covered in decaying leaves, tamped down by foot traffic. A few years earlier, the city council had taken pains to make the Lovers' Cave area a proper tourist attraction rather than just a creepy spot in the park that drew the interest of teenagers looking for a place to get drunk. They cleaned the area up and installed several picnic tables outside of the cave. In fact, before a case they were working on went sideways, Noah had planned to bring Josie here for a picnic to propose. She texted Noah once more and turned onto the path. Sunlight streamed through the branches overhead. In spite of that, and the fact that she was sweating from exertion, Josie felt a chill seep into her bones.

The tables were empty. The only sounds in the clearing were the angry caws of a couple of crows perched in the tree-tops. At the mouth of the cave, a waist-level plexiglass turnstile door had been installed along with a sign that read: DO NOT ENTER. It seemed like the least effective deterrent possible. When Josie was a teenager, her classmates had dared one another to go inside Lovers' Cave. She had never gone in. She didn't do well in dark, enclosed spaces. Smudged fingerprints and even some handprints covered the plexiglass. Josie nudged it with her hip, and it swung in toward the opening of the cave.

The entrance was short and misshapen, although wide enough for the average person to pass through if they ducked their head. Josie stared into the blackness, feeling the blood rush to her head. As an infant, Josie had been abducted by a woman she could only conclude was Satan incarnate. From the age of six until she was fourteen, Josie had been solely in her abductor's custody. That time had been marked by trauma, including hours spent locked inside a small, dark closet. No amount of therapy or forcing herself to go into dark enclosed spaces as an adult with a gun had mitigated the physical terror that overcame her whenever she faced something like this. The infinite darkness of caves was particularly harrowing.

She could wait for back-up, she decided. Send in a couple of the uniformed officers. She didn't even know if Eve Bowers was inside the cave.

She took a step back. The plexiglass door followed, its bottom brushing the dead leaves on the ground. A tiny speck of pink emerged, a pinpoint of warm color in a vast landscape of brown. With growing dread, Josie knelt to have a better look at it. The roar in her head got worse.

The tip of a fingernail, covered in pale pink chipped nail polish, lay in the dirt.

Eve Bowers had scraped this very same color nail polish off her fingernails in the interview room the evening before. Josie did not think this was a coincidence.

She stood and straightened her spine. Without thought, her hands found her radio and her mouth spoke into it, giving brief details of her location; what she'd found; and advising that she was going to look inside the cave. Voices burst back at her, urging her to wait. She turned the radio down and then she flicked on her phone's flashlight app. Her right hand unsnapped the gun holster at her side and slid her service weapon out. Holding her phone's flashlight outward with her left hand and her gun pointed in the same direction with the other, Josie stepped past the plexiglass door.

And stopped.

The nine-year-old inside her wailed. Her own heartbeat thundered in her ears like a thousand horses galloping. She could wait. Should wait. Every other time she'd gone into spaces like Lovers' Cave, Noah had been with her, his presence keeping her demons at bay, just barely. Surely even a uniformed officer going in with her would be preferable to going in alone. Her arms began to lower but then, somehow, a noise broke through the panic building inside her. A rustling from within the cave.

Josie had always promised herself that she would never let

her own trauma keep her from doing her job. She would not let her abductor win. She would never put innocent civilians at risk because of her personal issues. Her arms lifted again, straight out in front of her, the flashlight barely piercing the darkness ahead.

Ducking her head, she stepped into the blackness. Her frenzied mind tried to do one of the breathing exercises her therapist had taught her. It was no use. Her chest heaved with each breath, making the light and her pistol unsteady. She barely registered the cold which was deeper and more penetrating in the bowels of the cave, or the smell, foul and earthy. The flashlight illuminated stone walls with dark things growing along them. Dirt and rocks underfoot. Josie stayed crouched until she realized the ceiling had raised. Panning upward with the flashlight, she saw dozens of bats hanging like sacs suspended from above. Her stomach pitched, sending a wave of nauseated panic through her body.

Her feet hurried her beyond the chamber to where the ceiling lowered again about a foot above her head. She tried to listen for the rustling noise she had heard earlier, but the sound of her heartbeat was far too loud. The walls closed in. The hands of fear squeezed her rib cage until each step forward became physically painful. Josie opened her mouth to identify herself and call out for Eve, but the only sound that came from her throat was a strangled wheeze.

She tried to find the rational part of herself, the adult inside her mind, who understood that her fear was based on something that had happened long ago.

The rustling came again. Josie swept the flashlight from side to side. Her entire body froze when two glowing eyes peered at her from the darkness. Her lips twitched, trying to form words, to make any sound. Nothing happened. The hands crushed her ribs. Breathing was impossible.

The eyes blinked and then they were gone. Josie willed her

arms to move, to follow with the flashlight, but her body rebelled, stuck in place. There was a louder rustling now, only feet away.

Then came a moan that loosened Josie's bowels. It was definitely human. Close.

She tried to say "Eve", to say *anything*, but she was still paralyzed.

The eyes reappeared, now in triplicate. Three sets of glowing eyes at various heights but close to the ground. It wasn't until they all rushed toward her that a scream broke free from her throat, filling up the cave, and reverberating off the stone so hard, it felt as though her teeth were rattling. Heavy creatures, about the size of her dog, scuttled over her feet and through her legs, knocking her off balance. She managed to hold onto her pistol, but her phone flew through the air. As she fell onto her rear end, the light from her phone tumbled, illuminating the fat, furry tail of a raccoon hauling ass in the direction Josie had come from.

There was no time for relief. The moan she'd heard echoed through her head. On her knees, she scrambled across the dirt floor and snatched her phone up, whipping around, searching for the source of the unholy noise. The beam landed on a foot, clad in a stylish gray boot, its bottom streaked with mud.

Now came words. "Eve!" Josie cried.

She stood and sprinted toward the foot, closing the distance quickly. Her trembling hand passed the flashlight over the body until it landed briefly on Eve's face. Josie holstered her pistol and tried to find a pulse but there was nothing. Eve's skin was ice-cold.

But the moan.

Eve was propped against a wall, canted awkwardly to her left, arms and legs slack, like a doll that had been tossed aside. Josie put her phone on the ground, light pointed upward, and lowered Eve until she was flat. Josie started chest compressions, counting off in her head. The familiarity of the act, of the trained police officer inside her taking over, loosened fear's steel grip around her ribs. Still, when she bent to administer rescue breaths, it was difficult to take in a full breath.

Eve's lips tasted like ice and death.

Josie kept going until the cave was lit with the torches of a half dozen other officers. She kept going until one of them picked her up and carried her away.

EIGHTEEN
DIARY ENTRY, UNDATED

I can't take this much longer. I want to make a clean break. As clean as it can be with him. I can't take the lying and the sneaking around anymore. It's ruining the purest and most profound joy I've ever experienced. I don't want our future to be tainted by betrayal. I want to be free to shout it from the rooftops that I'm in love—that we're in love. I know we'll both be hated for a long time, maybe always. But we'll have each other and that's all that matters. We won't have to lie and cheat any longer. That's what matters. But every time I imagine the two of us sitting down to tell him, I can't breathe. He will never understand or accept this.

I am afraid neither of us will survive him.

NINETEEN

Two hours later, Josie sat on top of a picnic table outside of Lovers' Cave, staring at its opening which now glowed with light. The clearing was filled with people and equipment. Uniformed officers stood sentry around the perimeter, waving off any park visitors who stopped to gawk or speculate on what was happening. It hadn't been possible to get an ambulance this close to the cave, but paramedics had wheeled two gurneys with body bags on top of them into the clearing. One of them had offered Josie a blanket, but she'd turned it down. The cold she felt had little to do with the January weather. The ERT had wheeled their equipment up the trails in collapsible wagons. They'd set up enough halogen lights inside the cave to disturb the bats. That had caused quite a commotion but hadn't stopped Hummel and his team from continuing to process the scene.

Dr. Feist arrived while they were inside the cave. She took one look at Josie and snatched the blanket from a nearby gurney. She strode over, snapping the blanket like a bullfighter, and then wrapping it tightly around Josie's shoulders.

"Doc," Josie said.

"Shut up." Dr. Feist placed the back of her hand against Josie's forehead, then her cheek. Somehow, between the folds of the blanket and Josie's coat, she found her wrist and pressed two fingers against the inside of it.

"I'm fine," Josie said.

Dr. Feist ignored her. When she was satisfied with the rate of Josie's pulse, she disappeared and reappeared seconds later with a bottle of water. "Drink this."

Josie knew the doctor well enough by now not to argue. She took a long swig and put the bottle on the table next to her.

Dr. Feist said, "Where's Noah?"

"Trying to find Eve Bowers's car," Josie said. "We think the killer drove off in it."

Dr. Feist bent her knees, leaning in to get a better look at Josie's face. "Are you all right?"

Josie managed a weak smile. It certainly wasn't the first time she'd had to go into a dark, enclosed space in the line of duty, or the first time she'd tried to save someone but failed. But it always cost her something. She said, "Would I tell you if I wasn't?"

Dr. Feist held her gaze for a moment. Her face softened. "You could, you know. Tell me. We can talk about things besides bodies."

Josie sighed and pulled the blanket tighter around her shoulders. "If it's all the same to you, I think I'd rather stick with bodies. At least for today."

Dr. Feist nodded. "Then tell me what we've got."

Josie recapped the events inside the cave. Dr. Feist asked a few questions. Then they waited until Hummel emerged from the cave to give the doctor the go-ahead to take a look at the body. Dr. Feist found a Tyvek suit, complete with skull cap, gloves, and booties nearby and pulled it on. "Care to join me?" she asked Josie.

Josie looked at the light shining from the maw of the cave. It seemed even brighter as the sun sank lower on the horizon. "No," she said. "I'll wait."

Dr. Feist went in. The afternoon wore on. What seemed like an eternity later, the doctor came back out. She snapped off her gloves and beckoned to two paramedics. After a brief conversation, they rummaged through their equipment for a backboard and disappeared into the cave.

Tugging off her skull cap, she walked over to Josie. "If you're flogging yourself for not being able to save that young woman, you can stop."

Josie hopped down from the table. "What are you talking about?"

"She's been dead for hours, Josie. She went into rigor while the scene was being processed. Based on her body temperature and the temperature in the cave, my initial estimate is that she was killed sometime between seven and nine a.m."

"But I found her sometime around ten," Josie said. "I heard her moan. There was rustling and then a moan. I heard it."

Dr. Feist gave a pained smile. "You said there were at least three raccoons in there with her, didn't you? That was probably the rustling you heard. Hummel found all kinds of wrappers in there. Half-eaten food. It seems they brought stuff inside the cave to eat it."

"But the moan," Josie said. "I've dealt with raccoons before. They don't make that kind of noise. Not like what I heard. It was human. She was alive."

Now the smile turned to a full grimace. "I know you've seen a lot of dead bodies, Josie, but you haven't spent as much time around them as I have. Bodies still moan, groan, and sometimes even squeak after death."

Josie stared at her.

"Air gets trapped in the lungs. Not often, but occasionally, and then when they're moved, the air is expelled, and it can sound like a moan. The most likely scenario is the raccoons nudged her and moved her out of position and the air escaped her lungs. That was the moan you heard."

Josie blinked. A sinking feeling settled into her stomach. "I destroyed the scene," she said. "When I gave her CPR, I destroyed the scene."

Dr. Feist sighed. Behind her, the paramedics struggled out of the cave, trying to keep the backboard level. They'd secured Eve inside a body bag. Josie watched as they transferred her from the backboard onto one of the gurneys and strapped her down. Hummel and another member of the ERT came next, carrying evidence bags and lights. Dr. Feist motioned for Josie to follow her and together, they walked over to the gurney. The paramedics backed away and let Dr. Feist unzip the bag and spread it apart.

Up close, Eve Bowers's beautiful face had been transformed into a thing of horror. Dr. Feist pulled a penlight from one of her pockets and clicked it on. She held it in one hand, shining it into Eve's eyes. They bulged, grotesquely, pinpoint petechiae dotting the sclera. Her lips were swollen. Around her neck were angry red ligature marks.

"He strangled her," Josie said.

"Yes," said Dr. Feist. "Possibly with a belt. A cursory look tells me there is a patterned injury there, but I'll know more after my exam."

Patterned injuries occurred when the source of the injury sustained by a victim was reproduced on their skin. Sometimes the injury was a mirror image of the object used to kill the victim.

Dr. Feist zipped the bag back up and signaled to the paramedics that they could take Eve. "I'll have the autopsy results as quick as I can."

Hummel walked up next to Josie. He held a digital camera in his hands, the display aglow. "We're finished here, but before you go, there's something you're going to want to see."

He angled the camera so that Josie could see the photo. For the first time in several hours her heartbeat ticked upward again. Less than a foot from Eve's body, along one of the cave walls was a rectangular wooden gift box in the shape of a wrapped present. It had probably been in her hand when the killer left her inside the cave. Either the raccoons or Josie had dislodged it.

Josie said, "The moment you get that thing open, I want to know what's inside it. How about her phone? Did you find that in the cave?"

"Sorry, but no." Hummel clicked through more photos. "One last thing."

He turned the digital display toward her again. It was a close-up of one of Eve's delicate hands. Jammed over the first knuckle of her ring finger were Claudia Collins's engagement ring and wedding band.

Hummel said, "That looks like the jewelry missing from the scene from last night?"

"Yes," Josie said. "It does."

Before she could consider what it meant, a figure appeared along the path back out to the park. Josie's knees nearly gave way when she saw her husband. She resisted the urge to run over to him and fall into his arms. She could tell by the look on his face they weren't nearly done for the day.

Hummel said, "Fraley. What is it?"

Noah gave Josie a once-over, his brow kinking just slightly as he silently asked her if she was okay. After she gave him a barely perceptible nod, he replied. "We found Eve Bowers's car."

TWENTY

Josie kept the heat in the car on full blast as Noah weaved through the streets of Denton. At nearly six p.m. the evening in South Denton was pitch-black. Only a sliver of moon punctuated the sky. Not enough to give off any significant light. Unlike the steep hills and rising mountains of the rest of Denton, the southern part of the city was flatter, giving way to rolling hills, farmland, and a smattering of stores. A branch of the Susquehanna that ran through East Denton curled along the southern border of the city. Ahead of them, Noah kept Mettner's taillights in sight as he navigated the vehicle over the narrow south bridge and into a more remote part of South Denton. Gretchen had been sent home to rest.

They'd spent the first ten minutes of the drive catching each other up on the developments so far, with Josie doing most of the talking. She expected Noah to rib her about the raccoons, but then she realized he knew how difficult it had been for her to even go into the cave in the first place. She waited for him to admonish her for not waiting for back-up, but he said nothing.

She loved him more for his silence.

She turned the conversation to Eve Bowers's car. "Where did they find it? We're getting pretty close to Lenore County. Is it even in our jurisdiction?"

"I'm told it is still Denton," Noah said. "Well, it's actually on state gameland, but since there's no body inside it, the state police are happy to let us handle it."

Blue and red lights strobed ahead, lighting up the night. All Josie could see was a narrow two-lane road, two Denton PD cruisers, and lots of barren trees, their dark, spindly branches reaching in every direction. Mettner parked behind one of the cruisers. Noah pulled in after him. He put the vehicle in park and took his phone out, pulling up a map of the area. He pointed to what seemed like a random road. "We're right here." He used his index finger to shift the map. A red pin icon appeared off to the side of the road, in a wooded area. "The car is here."

Josie took his phone and studied the map. She pinched her thumb and index finger together and then spread them apart to zoom out. There was hardly anything but forest for miles. She pointed to the wooded area across the road from where the car had been located and traced a line around a large tract of property that stretched from the road they were on to another road west of them that ran parallel to it. "What is this?"

Noah smiled. "That is where things get really interesting. That is private property that belongs to a man named..." He hesitated for dramatic effect before delivering the surprise. "Archie Gamble."

Josie turned her attention back to the phone, zooming in and out to try to get a better sense of the property. "That's the second time I've heard that name in a matter of hours," she said. "You know what that means."

Noah reached across and powered up the Mobile Data Terminal. "I'm way ahead of you," he said. A moment later, a driver's license photo of Archie Gamble appeared on the screen. It was not at all what Josie had expected. Not that she had known what to expect. Maybe the elusive boyfriend of Eve Bowers? Then again, did women cryptically write the names of their boyfriends on the back of their boss's junk mail and leave it inside a book about relationships? Josie couldn't say, but she would be surprised if Gamble had been the person to give Eve the "glow of a woman in love." The man was in his fifties, grizzled, with hard, flinty eyes, long salt-and-pepper hair, and an unruly beard to match.

"Record?" Josie asked.

"Believe it or not, no," said Noah. "He's clean."

"As far as anyone knows," Josie said. "Let's go."

Outside the car, her breath made tiny clouds that floated up and away into the darkness. The night brought a deeper cold which sent a shiver up and down her body. She pulled her coat more tightly around her. Near one of the cruisers, Mett gathered with two uniformed officers, talking in low tones.

Josie recognized one of the officers as Dougherty. He pointed behind them, to the shoulder of the road and beyond. All she could see was blackness. "We took a walk into the clearing about fifty or sixty feet from the road to make sure it was the vehicle everyone's looking for. It's a Nissan Rogue. Tag is registered to Eve Bowers. VIN is a match. Minimal damage to the car, no skid marks on the road that we could see, so it doesn't look like this is a crash. You probably know we've got permission to remove the vehicle since it's on state gameland. But we figured you'd want the ERT out here to have a look at it before they impound it, so we didn't touch or disturb anything."

"Good call," Josie said. "But the ERT is going to be a while. They're packing up at another scene."

Dougherty nodded. "No problem. We'll wait."

Mettner gave a long sigh. "So that's it? We sit out here for a few more hours?"

"No," Josie said. "There's something else we can do."

Noah brought Mettner up to speed on the discovery of Archie Gamble's name inside Eve's apartment as well as the fact that he owned the property adjacent to the state gameland where Eve Bowers's car had been found.

Mettner grinned. "Well, hell. Let's go talk to him."

TWENTY-ONE

They left the uniformed officers to guard the scene while they drove around the wooded area to the front of the property. A rusted metal mailbox teetered on a post next to a dirt driveway. Josie bounced in her seat as she turned the SUV into the driveway. Headlights illuminated dead grass and barren trees on either side of them. It felt like she'd been driving for an hour before a small house came into view. As the headlights landed on the white siding, something fluffy and gray scurried along the side of the house and ran into the darkness. It looked very much like a cat. Gamble's abode was a single-story, low-slung rectangle. Off to their right, an awning was visible. The small porch beneath it was a black hole. No lights came from the windows or anywhere on the exterior of the house. Josie parked next to a small black pickup truck.

Mettner said, "Leave your headlights on. Can't see shit out here."

She left them on although the light didn't reach past the pickup and didn't illuminate the front porch. As they piled out of the vehicle and carefully made their way closer to the house, she blinked a few times to adjust her vision to the darkness. On the other side of the pickup, the first few slabs of a concrete walkway were visible. They followed it until it made a sharp turn toward the porch.

Before them, an orange circle glowed, disembodied. Then the scent of cigarette smoke reached Josie's nostrils. The three of them froze. Josie's fingers twitched, wanting to reach for her service weapon but not yet having any clear indication that a threat was imminent. They had found a murder victim's car on the property next to Gamble's—which was bisected by a road. That didn't give them the right to enter his property. The only justification for their presence was that they'd found his name in Eve Bowers's apartment, which gave them the right to attempt to question him. It was possible he had nothing at all to do with Eve's murder, or Claudia's, and that his name turning up twice in one day in the course of their investigation was simply a coincidence. Except that Josie didn't believe in coincidences. Her stomach clenched. She squeezed her hand into a fist. Noah's breath tickled the back of her neck. Something in front of them creaked.

"Mr. Gamble?" Josie called out. "Archie Gamble?"

A low, raspy voice spoke from somewhere in the darkness. "Three of you all coming here around evening time dressed like that—you must be cops."

Noah called out each one of their names. "We're here from the Denton Police Department."

"Whatcha all want with me then?" came the voice.

Josie blinked again, willing her eyes to adjust more quickly to the darkness. When he took another drag of his cigarette, Archie's face came into relief for a second. He looked even more grizzled than in his driver's license photo. Unkempt hair, sunken eyes with pouches of wrinkles under them, unruly eyebrows, a long beard.

Mettner said, "We're sorry to disturb you, sir, especially in the evening. We found a vehicle near the backside of your property where it butts up against Wertz Road."

"You say you found a vehicle on my property?"

"No," Noah said. "Across Wertz Road from your property."

"That's state gameland, son. Got nothing to do with me."

Josie said, "That vehicle belonged to a woman who was murdered today. We found your name among her personal items. We'd like to ask you some questions."

The orange circle flared and then sailed through the night, leaving a trail of sparks that quickly faded. Something landed at their feet. Another creak. Archie said, "I'm gonna turn on this here flashlight I've got so we can see each other properly, but I'm gonna tell you right now I've got a pellet gun in my lap. I'm not aimin' to harm anyone with it, so don't you all shoot me."

Before any of them could answer, the light snapped on. It was a battery-powered lantern rather than a handheld flashlight. It rested on a small circular wrought-iron plant stand beside an ashtray which was overflowing with cigarette butts. Archie sat straight-backed in a wingback chair whose upholstery had seen better days. His jeans were faded and torn, a hairy knee poking from one worn pantleg. His black T-shirt read: *You Sound Better With Your Mouth Shut*. The aforementioned pellet gun lay untouched across his lap. He held his hands aloft so they could see them, and Josie felt a small trickle of relief.

Mettner said, "May I ask what you're trying to shoot with that?"

Archie smiled, the corners of his eyes crinkling. "Son, you may ask whatever you like."

Several seconds ticked by. It became evident that he had no intention of answering the question. Josie said, "Any chance you're shooting feral cats?"

Archie ignored this question as well. "You all mind if I put my hands down now?"

Mettner said, "If you wouldn't mind just putting the pellet gun on the ground, we'd appreciate it."

The chair groaned beneath him as Archie slowly placed the pellet gun on the floor of the porch and nudged it aside with his boot.

Josie said, "I know someone at Precious Paws Rescue who would be happy to come collect any feral cats on your property and take them off your hands."

Archie leaned forward, capturing her gaze. His lips twitched in what was almost a smile. "I'm not too keen on people running around my property unsupervised, but thank you just the same."

Josie didn't push the issue. If she was right, and he was shooting pellets at feral cats, even on his own property, it was illegal. She could deal with the cat situation later, but right now, they needed to ask him how he knew Eve Bowers. The sooner the better. She said, "We won't take up too much of your time. Do you know a woman named Eve Bowers?"

He lit another cigarette. "Nope. I sure don't."

Josie took out her phone and pulled up Eve's driver's license photo. She showed it to Archie Gamble. "You don't know this woman?"

Without hesitation, he answered, "Nope."

Mettner said, "Do you have any idea why your name would be among her personal effects?"

"I do not."

The envelope had been addressed to Claudia. They hadn't had a chance yet to verify the handwriting. "How about Claudia Collins?" asked Josie.

One of Gamble's brows kinked. The cigarette between his lips bobbed a couple of times before he pinched it with two fingers and took it out of his mouth. "That sure sounds familiar." He took two more puffs. "She on TV or somethin'?"

Josie said, "She hosts a television show on WYEP in the late mornings. Weekdays. With her husband, Beau Collins."

He let out a slow chuckle. "Oh right. The one about relationships. What a bunch of horseshit. So what happened? That douchebag husband of hers get into some kind of trouble? Get some young lady involved?"

Mettner opened his mouth to speak, but Josie nudged him silent with a discreet elbow to the ribs. She said, "Why do you think he's a douchebag?"

He took his time answering, which Josie realized now was just his way. Whether it was purposeful or not, it had the effect of making them hang on his every word. Her feet were getting cold. Archie said, "I know people, that's why."

"What do you know about Beau Collins?" asked Josie.

He winked at her. "You're a smart one, aren't you? I know he's on TV on a stupid show about stupid things with a stupid wife who's probably not worth the space she takes up."

Josie felt the barb against Claudia as if they were old friends even though they'd only met once. She wondered if he'd call her stupid if he knew she had been murdered, and decided he probably would.

"You ever meet his wife?" asked Mettner.

"Nope."

Josie said, "Why do you think he got into trouble?"

Another long drag on the cigarette, the orange circle flaring. "Seems like the type."

Josie asked, "Have you ever met Beau Collins?"

"Not officially, no," Archie replied. "Ran into him at the DMV once. He cut in the line in front of me. I told him about this thing: it's called manners. He didn't know about it. Didn't want to talk much to me after that. Went to the back of the line."

"How did you know who he was?" asked Mettner.

"The women in the line were fawning all over that jackass, that's how."

Noah changed the subject. "Are you married?"

The raspy chuckle came again. "Son, I wouldn't get married if someone was gonna pay me to do it. People never hate anyone more than they hate their spouses. Now, are you three about done?"

"Almost," said Josie. "We have a couple more questions. Have you been home all day?"

Archie sighed. "Nope, I surely wasn't, but if you're looking to make sure I wasn't involved in whatever you got going on here, I was at Leo's bar from about five till eleven."

Noah said, "Before that, where were you? This morning between six and ten?"

"I was here, son. This is where I live."

Josie asked, "What about last night? Starting around five?"

"Leo's. Over on Stott Street. I go there every Friday after work and weekends, too."

"Where do you work?" asked Mettner.

"I'm a carpenter, son. Don't have a shop right now but I'm in the union. I go where they tell me when they can get me work."

Josie said, "Do you live alone?"

"Sure do."

Noah said, "When you were home today, did you hear anything?"

"You mean like if a woman crashes her car in the woods and no one's there to hear it, did it really happen? Son, I've got twenty acres that span from that road there over to the next one. Like I told you, the vehicle you're asking after is on state game-land. It don't concern me, but since you're asking, I don't hear nothing but what's right here in front of this house."

Mettner said, "Are there any paths from here to that area

that go through to the other side of the property? Over to Wertz Road?"

"You askin' if I walked over to the state gameland? To this car you're worried about? Or if I walked from the car to here?"

"Both," said Mettner.

Archie smiled at him but there was a hint of menace in the way his eyes narrowed. "You askin' if I had anything to do with... what'd you say earlier? A murder victim?"

Mettner answered, "Yes."

"The answer's no. I didn't know a thing about any murder victim or cars on land that don't belong to me until you all just showed up now to tell me about it. Now, you go on and handle your business over on the state land and get off my property."

Josie stepped forward and handed him a business card which he took, squinting at it. "Quinn," he read. "Seen you on TV, too."

"Call us if you remember anything about Eve Bowers," she told him.

He tucked the card into the crease of the chair where his other possessions apparently lived. Then he reached over and snapped off the lantern. As they turned to go, something pinged off the back of Josie's calf. The cigarette butt. She stopped and looked down at it, watching its glow die.

Archie's voice floated through the darkness. "You all be careful out there. Never know what can happen."

TWENTY-TWO

Josie clapped her gloved hands together and then rubbed them as fast as she could, hoping to get some of her circulation back. Standing outside on the shoulder of the road for two hours in temperatures flirting with below freezing had numbed every part of her body. But she wasn't leaving until Eve Bowers's car had been put on the flatbed tow truck and transported to the police impound lot. Along the horizon, the sky was a deep cobalt. Stars glittered like jewels. The thick clouds that had brought rain the evening before now left a clear and unblemished dome overhead. Josie was grateful. Few things were more damaging to a crime scene than inclement weather.

Noah emerged from their vehicle, phone in hand. His cheeks were bright pink. "Why don't you get in here for a few minutes? I'm telling you, it helps."

Josie ignored him and looked back at the wide opening between one copse of trees and another through which a killer had driven Eve Bowers's car. Through bare, gnarled branches, the bright white of an ERT member's Tyvek suit flashed every now and then. One of them had put up lights around the perimeter of the scene and she could even see a small slice of the car's silver paint. The killer would have had to walk out of there. Where did he go? There wasn't anything for miles.

Except Archie Gamble's house.

She felt Noah sidle up to her. His physical presence had become like a magnet. If he was within reach, it seemed like every cell in her body yawned open toward him. "What is it?" he said. "Gamble?"

The back of her calf still prickled where his last cigarette butt had bounced. It hadn't hurt her. There wasn't even a stain on her jeans. But something about the man had thrown her hackles up.

As if reading her mind, Noah said, "I get it. My alarm bells were going off too, but I couldn't find a damn thing to connect him to Eve Bowers or the Collinses. I checked multiple databases, social media, cross-referenced known addresses and employers. Nothing comes up."

"He could be Claudia's patient," Josie suggested. "That wouldn't come up in any search, not with the strict privacy laws in place."

"Gamble's not married—doesn't sound like he ever was—and he denied knowing her at all. But it won't hurt to check out that angle, I suppose. I'll add it to the list. Maybe Gamble and Claudia were having an affair."

It was hard to imagine the kind and vivacious Claudia that Josie had met in December with the tetchy man they'd just met who was very likely shooting cats on his property. Josie didn't like to make assumptions—doing so could be the difference between life and death in their line of work—but her gut told her an affair was not the connection between Gamble and Claudia. "I doubt that very much," she said.

He sighed. "Me too. Just trying to consider every possibility, especially with a case so thin on leads."

Josie looked over at him. Dark stubble ran the length of his jaw. No one was around, so she lifted a finger and ran it along his jaw. "We should be in bed right now," she said.

He captured her hand and gave it a squeeze before releasing it. "Don't remind me."

They had sent Mettner home to get some sleep. The department was already stretched thin as it was with two murders in less than twenty-four hours. None of them wanted to go home, not while such a huge case was going on, but they needed sleep if they were going to solve this thing.

"I'm calling Precious Paws Rescue as soon as they open," Josie said.

"You're going to piss this guy off," said Noah.

"I hope so," Josie answered.

His chuckle faded as Hummel emerged from the gap in the trees, his breath clouding in front of him. Dirt and dead leaves streaked the knees of his suit. Brittle twigs crunched under his feet. "We're ready to get it out of here."

"Did you get anything?" asked Noah.

"A phone," Hummel said. "Presumably belonging to Eve Bowers."

"It would make this a lot easier if it was the killer's phone," Noah pointed out.

Josie said, "Figure out the number. We'll draw up a warrant for the phone so we can access its contents as soon as possible."

"Sure thing," Hummel said.

He made no move to return to the car.

Josie said, "What is it, Hummel?"

"Listen, we didn't really find anything useful in this car. I mean, I've still got to process it for prints, but other than that? So far, all we found were a couple of short, dark hairs. None with roots. Regardless, those could belong to anyone Eve Bowers had in her car. We'll go over the entire car once we get it to the impound lot, but it doesn't look promising."

"What are you getting at?" Noah said.

Hummel said, "If he came here in her car, this guy had to be on foot, right?"

"That's what I thought," said Josie.

"I hear we've got a new K-9 officer," Hummel said.

"News travels fast around here," Josie said.

"He's not an officer," Noah said. "He's a consultant, and yeah, we've got one." He looked at Josie. Tension knotted her shoulders. There was no question that a search dog might be useful in this scenario. The killer had been inside the car. There would be a scent trail. Maybe he had gotten into another vehicle that he'd stashed nearby. Maybe he'd walked all the way home. Maybe he was Archie Gamble. But they couldn't explore those possibilities unless they got the dog out here to search. Even if the trail disappeared, following it might yield important clues.

Josie said, "Okay. Hold off on impounding the car. I'll call Luke."

TWENTY-THREE

By dawn, Josie and Noah were exhausted and no closer to finding the killer. Luke and Blue had shown up ready to work but Blue was only able to follow the killer's scent from Eve's car out to the road and then about a half-mile south, which led Josie to believe that he'd stashed another vehicle out there for the purpose of leaving once he'd killed Eve. How he had gotten from the stashed vehicle to the park was another matter. On foot? Bicycle? By some other means? Had someone helped him? Josie shuddered to think a killer this ruthless had help. There was also the possibility that he'd used a ride-sharing service. She had prepared a warrant for all the area ride-share services to see if anyone had picked up or dropped off a passenger in that area in the relevant time period. They would have to wait for those results. Josie hoped it would not take more than a day.

When Blue's search turned up nothing, they scrutinized the evidence available to them after Hummel and the ERT processed the scene and car. None of the prints found inside or out of the vehicle were in AFIS. The puzzle box found near Eve Bowers's body was empty. Josie had no idea what kind of game the killer was playing but she knew that whatever it was,

Beau Collins was the center of it. The killer had killed his wife and her assistant, leaving puzzle boxes from Beau and Claudia's show at the scenes. In one of those boxes he'd left a page from their book. He'd gone to the trouble of removing Claudia's engagement and wedding rings and putting them on Eve's finger. The text to Margot from Eve's phone was directed toward Beau.

Once Josie and Noah got access to Eve Bowers's phone, it became clear that Beau had not been honest with them from the start.

As the sun rose over the ridges of the mountains surrounding Denton, Josie and Noah stood outside the door to Margot Huff's apartment. Unlike Eve Bowers's spacious first-floor unit with its small front walk and parking space, Margot's place was deep inside a blocky, three-story building that boasted over fifty units. Threadbare brown carpet crunched beneath Josie's feet as she pounded on the door for the third time. They hadn't called ahead. A unit had been assigned to Beau Collins. Josie had only needed to call them to find out Beau had arrived at Margot's place shortly after the scene at the studio the day before and had not left.

"Mr. Collins, Ms. Huff!" Josie said loudly. "It's Denton PD."

Down the hallway, a woman in a shower cap poked her head out her door. Josie managed a tight smile for her, and she retreated into her apartment.

Margot's door swung open. Beau Collins stood before them in a white T-shirt and pair of dark blue pajama pants. He squinted against the harsh hallway lights. His hair was in disarray. A patchy beard covered his face. "What's going on?" he said.

Noah said, "Mr. Collins, we need to talk."

Wordlessly, he moved out of the way and let them inside. The living room was tiny, not much bigger than the interview rooms at the stationhouse. Beau had to edge around them, nearly touching them both, to get to the couch. He bent to move a bedroom pillow and blanket out of his way before sitting down. He hooked a thumb over his shoulder. A kitchen and two other doors stood in semi-darkness. The only light in the entire place came from the fixture over the sink.

"Margot's asleep," Beau mumbled.

"Not anymore," came a sleepy voice from the semi-darkness. Margot stepped out from behind one of the doors, pulling a hooded sweatshirt around her. "What's going on?"

"Sit," Josie told her.

Margot perched on the edge of the couch, leaving two feet between her and Beau. She stared up at Josie and Noah with apprehension. Her voice squeaked when she asked, "Did you find Eve?"

Josie was a firm believer in giving bad news as quickly and directly as possible without dragging it out. Best to rip off the bandage and be done with it. "Her body was found about late morning yesterday. She was murdered. Our county medical examiner contacted the medical examiner where Eve's parents live. They were notified about a half hour ago."

Margot pressed a palm over her mouth. Her body rocked back and forth.

Beau blinked away any remaining exhaustion. "What?" he said. "You can't be serious. I don't understand. I just saw Eve—we were all here in this apartment Friday night. She was fine. Why would he kill her? Why her?"

Noah said, "We're very sorry for your loss."

"What did he do to her?" Beau demanded, voice stronger now.

"We're not at liberty to give out those details," Josie said. "I'm sorry."

"But you think it's the same guy?" Beau pressed. "The same monster who killed my wife?"

Noah said, "Yes, we do."

Margot cried softly. Her hands curled into the sleeves of her sweatshirt, and she used them to wipe her tears. Beau looked over at her, as if he was considering trying to offer her comfort, but decided not to, returning his attention to Josie and Noah.

Josie took out her phone and pulled up a photo of Claudia's rings. She showed it to Beau. "Are these your wife's rings?"

Beau stared at it, uncomprehending. "Y-yes," he stammered. "I don't understand what this—"

"The killer took them from Claudia on Friday. After he killed Eve, he put them on her hand," Noah said.

Beau pushed his hands through his hair. "I don't understand."

Josie said, "Neither do we. We were hoping you could explain to us why the killer would do this."

"Me? How the hell would I know?"

"Mr. Collins," said Noah. "We know you haven't been truthful with us."

His voice went up an octave. "Me? What are you talking about?"

Josie reached into her back pocket and pulled out a folded sheaf of papers. She spread them across the narrow coffee table. "Please look at these."

Beau looked as if it physically hurt him to view the blown-up text messages that Denton PD had gotten from Eve's phone. Josie said, "The killer left Eve's phone behind. We were able to access its contents. These only go back three months, but I think they are sufficient."

Margot lowered her hands from her face and leaned in, eyeing the pages.

When Beau didn't respond, Josie picked one up and read it out loud. "On December third at seven fourteen p.m., Eve texted: 'I miss you so much. Seeing you only twice a week isn't enough. I need more. It's been a whole year. When are we going to be together? For real?' Five minutes later, you responded, 'I know. I want to see you more, too, but it's just not possible. I don't want Claudia to get suspicious.' Eve replied: 'Claudia won't even notice or care. You can't possibly love her anymore. Not if you love me, too. Tell me you're only doing this for the show.' You replied: 'All I can think about is you. I'll see if I can find more time for us to be together.'"

Josie let the last statement hang in the air. Margot stared at the side of Beau's face, her mouth hanging open. There was only silence. All that could be heard was the hiss of the heating vents and a television playing somewhere.

Beau's voice shook. "I love my wife. I don't know what you're trying to do here, but—"

Noah said, "Having an affair with her assistant is a funny way of showing your love, Mr. Collins."

Beau shot to his feet. His hands balled into fists at his sides. "Eve was fixated on me. She was young and beautiful and yes, I had a lapse in judgment, nothing more. I was trying to find a way to end it with her."

Josie shook the page she had just read. "This doesn't sound that way."

He turned to Noah. "I fail to see how this helps find the killer. Who cares if I had a lapse in judgment? I didn't kill anyone. This—this monster did! You should be looking for him, talking to him, questioning him."

Josie said, "If you were not truthful about this affair, it begs the question: what else did you lie about?"

"Nothing!" he said. "I swear to you. Nothing."

Josie reached down and shuffled the pages again until she found a call log from Friday. She pointed to the call she'd highlighted before they arrived. "This is a phone call received by Eve from your cell phone on Friday afternoon."

Beau didn't look at the log but Margot did.

Noah said, "You talked to Eve at four in the afternoon. Not long before your wife was murdered in your home while she was there alone."

Beau looked from Noah to Josie and back helplessly. "So what? Now you know we were having an affair. You just read those intimate texts. What's so special about a phone call?"

Ignoring the question, Josie asked, "What did you talk about?"

"I was trying to break things off. Again. It was my fifteenth wedding anniversary, for crying out loud! Eve was going to be there for the taping—in our home, with me and my wife—it felt wrong. Before that happened, I wanted to be clear with Eve that it was over between us."

"Did you tell Eve not to come to the anniversary dinner?" asked Noah.

Beau's brow furrowed. "What? No. She's—she was—Claudia's assistant. I wouldn't do that. It would have raised too many questions—"

"My God," Margot spat.

Beau's head snapped in her direction. "What?"

Her lip curled. "Do you even hear yourself? You're so disgusting!"

"Margot, please—"

Josie interrupted them. "When you finished this twenty-three-minute phone call with Eve, you fully expected to see her at your home by five thirty for the anniversary dinner and taping?"

"Of course," Beau said, looking at Josie and Noah once more. "She wasn't happy with me, but she promised she'd still be there."

"On time?" asked Noah pointedly.

Beau threw both hands in the air and let them fall to his lap.

"Yes! What is this all about? Stop making this about me and start making it about the killer! I beg you!"

Changing tack, Noah asked, "Does the name Archie Gamble mean anything to you?"

Beau's fists clenched. "Who?"

Josie tossed the printout back onto the table and took out her phone, pulling up Archie Gamble's driver's license photo. "Who is this man?"

He stared at the photo, his face trying on several different expressions before finally settling on consternation. "I don't know. Why? Is he the one who killed Claudia and Eve?"

"We're not sure," said Noah.

Josie showed the photo to Margot, but she shook her head. "I've never seen him before."

"I'm going to ask you again," Josie told Beau. "Who is this man?"

Beau's nostrils flared. He didn't answer.

Noah said, "You've never met this man? Not ever?"

"No. Of course not! I'm telling you the truth."

Margot had inched slowly away from him until her body was pressed against the opposite side of the couch. Her hands gripped the arm as if it were a lifeline. She stared at him with open disgust. "How can we be sure? How can anyone be sure of anything you say anymore?"

Beau turned to her, eyes pleading. "Margot, please."

He reached for her but she slapped his hand away. "Don't touch me!"

"Margot!" he said, his tone switching rapidly to annoyance. "You can't possibly be angry with me. You never even told me about that man you've been seeing from the station."

"That is none of your business!"

"You've been keeping things from me!"

Margot opened her mouth and sucked in a big breath. As if sensing that she was about to explode on Beau, Noah quickly said, "Archie Gamble's name was found written down among Eve's things."

Margot's mouth clamped shut, her expression morphing from anger to confusion. For the first time, Josie saw a true crack in Beau's television personality veneer. For a fleeting second, his expression of earnest indignation, exhaustion, and stress slipped and in its place was naked fear. A vein in his temple bulged, the tiny pulse vibrating so hard it was visible. He said, "Eve—wait, did Eve know him?"

"You tell us," said Noah.

"How would I—how would—how would I know that?" he stammered.

Josie said, "Archie Gamble's name was written on the back of a piece of mail addressed to your wife. It's possible that Claudia wrote his name down and Eve took it. We would need handwriting samples to clarify."

The pulsing vein slowed incrementally. "I can do that. I can get those for you. Today, in fact."

"Great," said Noah. "How about your wife? Did she know Archie Gamble?"

"No. I don't think so. I wouldn't know. Is he a patient of hers, or maybe he had been in the past? I can talk to Claudia's secretary. Her name is Trudy Dawson. You may still need a warrant, given the privacy laws, but she'll be able to help you with anything having to do with Claudia's practice."

"That would be great," said Noah. "It's unlikely that Mr. Gamble is or was a patient of your wife's, but we'll look into it. Is it possible that Gamble and Claudia were having an affair?"

A noise of incredulity came from deep in Beau's throat. "No, no," he spluttered. "That's not possible."

Margot narrowed her eyes at him. "How would you know?"

Beau threw his hands in the air. "Because Claudia would never have an affair! She just wouldn't! If she had, even with... a person like that, I would have noticed. Seen him lurking around or something, but I've never met the man before. Never even seen him until just now!"

He had met Archie Gamble at the DMV if Gamble was to be believed. Was it possible he simply didn't remember? What reason would he have for lying about something like that?

Josie brought up the photo of Gamble once more and turned it toward Beau. "In the meantime, I want you to take a moment. Look at his photo again. Tell us, truthfully, that you've never met this man in your life."

With a sigh, Beau took the phone from her and studied Gamble's photo. It looked more like a mugshot the way that Gamble stared down the camera, all menace. Josie counted off ten seconds before Beau handed back the phone. "I swear to you that I do not know this man. I've never met him. I'm not sure what else you want me to say or what you want me to do. My wife is dead. Eve is dead. My entire life is falling apart. You should be out there doing your jobs instead of here interrogating me like I'm some kind of criminal, because I am not."

Noah said, "We are doing our jobs, Mr. Collins. Someone is killing people around you. Taunting you. You must have some idea who would want to do this."

Beau unclenched his fists, shaking his fingers. "I don't know. That is the truth." He turned to Margot. "Margot, tell them. You're my assistant. You see practically everything that goes on behind the scenes. Everyone in my life. You know that I'm being honest. Tell them."

Margot gazed up at him with a mixture of hurt and fury. "I didn't even know about Eve."

"Eve was a mistake!" he insisted.

Margot stood, folding her arms across her chest. "How could you? I can't even believe I thought you were— You know what? It doesn't matter. I'm over this whole thing."

"Margot, please," he began, but she spun on her heel and left the room. A door slammed behind her.

Beau trained his gaze on Josie. "Are you happy now? You're blowing up my entire life!"

"Not me," said Josie. "Someone who very much wants to watch you suffer. You must have some idea who that person could be. Tell us."

"I don't know!" he yelled, spit flying from his mouth. He began to pace the tiny area between the couch and coffee table. "I honestly don't know what I could have done to anyone to make them want to kill Claudia—or Eve—no one even knew about us."

But someone had. The killer had even made a point to put Claudia's rings onto Eve's hand and to leave Eve in Lovers' Cave, an aptly named place to leave someone's mistress. Whether Beau was lying about having enemies or not, someone was targeting him and using those around him to make their point.

"Mr. Collins," she said, making her tone conciliatory. "We're not trying to blow up your life or expose your 'lapses in judgment.' We are trying to prevent more murders."

He froze, the worry line on his forehead deepening. "More? Why would there be more?"

"Because," Josie said, "this killer thinks he's playing a game and he's not going to stop until he thinks he's won. The question is: how many more people does he have to kill before he feels as though he's won? Who are those people?"

Noah lifted his chin in the direction of Margot's bedroom door. "Miss Huff?"

Beau looked stricken. "Margot? No. She's just my assistant. That's all."

"Who else?" Josie asked. "Who else is important enough to you for this killer to target?"

He hung his head. "Detectives," he said. "There was only one person who was important to me and that was my wife. Anyone who knows me knows that. For fifteen years, she has been absolutely everything to me. Whoever this monster is, he can't hurt me more than he already has by taking my Claudia away from me."

Tears leaked from his eyes. He sat back down, sobbing into his hands. "I'm sorry," he said. "I honestly don't know who is doing this."

TWENTY-FOUR

Eight hours later, after some tumultuous sleep, Josie and Noah returned to the stationhouse where Mettner and Gretchen sat behind their computers, typing away, looking haggard and exhausted. They didn't even look up when Josie and Noah entered. Not until Josie crinkled the plastic bag filled with takeout food between two fingers. Gretchen stopped typing. From over her reading glasses, she eyed the bag. "It's been a long, tedious day with not many leads," she said. "If that's not dinner for us, I'm going to have to ask you to leave."

Without looking up from his computer, Mettner said, "Palmer, if they leave, we're stuck here for another shift."

Josie laughed as she reached into the bag and lifted out plastic containers—one for Gretchen and one for Mettner. She handed them off to Noah, who distributed them. "Your favorites," he told them.

Josie plopped into her desk chair. "Not many leads," she said. "Just what every detective wants to hear."

The room went silent as Mettner and Gretchen dug into their dinners. Across the room sat their press liaison, Amber Watts, at her desk. A cell phone was trapped between her ear and shoulder while she typed on her laptop. Every so often she spoke into the phone, but Josie couldn't make out the words.

Mettner glanced at Amber and then back at Josie and Noah. "Chief wants her to keep the press off these murders."

Noah laughed. "Yeah, right."

Amber offered them a strained smile and went back to typing and talking.

"Seriously," Mettner said. "She's been holding them off all day by telling them we'll hold a press conference soon."

"Great," Noah said. "That'll be fun."

Josie logged into her computer and found the Eve Bowers and Claudia Collins files, scrolling through the reports that had been uploaded by various members of the team.

Noah said, "You guys didn't get anywhere today?"

Mettner sighed. "Nowhere that helps us find this guy sooner rather than later."

Gretchen said, "By the way, we've gone through the list of employees of the Collinses' show. I interviewed them yesterday. I ran background checks. Then I moved on to station employees from WYEP—since they're all in the same building. We've been running background checks on them as well. So far, no one throws up any red flags, but we'll keep working at it."

"A couple of people with criminal records," Mettner added. "But not for violent crimes."

"Yesterday when I was at WYEP, I spoke with Raffy, who is the social media manager for the station," Gretchen said.

"He and Margot Huff are dating," Josie said.

"Yes," Gretchen replied. "He mentioned that. We were looking for internet trolls. Anyone who might have been blocked by the station or the Collinses for posting or messaging inappropriate or hateful things about Beau and Claudia. He said he was going to see Margot today and the two of them would have a comprehensive list for us this afternoon. He's going to email it to us. We're waiting on that."

Josie thought of the way Margot had looked at Beau that morning when she found out about his affair with Eve. The way Beau, even at the station the morning before, was always trying to touch her even though she clearly did not want any physical contact. The way he'd quickly become accusatory about the fact that she was dating Raffy. Was there something more between them? Maybe not now but in the past? She asked, "You weren't going to meet with them?"

Gretchen raised a brow. "I didn't see a need, unless you think one of us should."

All eyes were on Josie. "I'd just like to talk to Margot when she's not with Beau."

Mettner said, "I talked to her Friday night without Beau Collins. You think she's hiding something?"

"I'm not sure," Josie said. "But her level of disappointment with Beau when she found out about the affair with Eve was..."

"Strange," Noah filled in. "He's just her boss. Why does she care so much how he acts morally or ethically?"

"Besides," Josie said. "I don't think we're looking for an internet troll. Obviously, we have to look at that angle, but I think this killer is more likely someone in Beau and Claudia's inner circle. Someone with enough access to the Collinses to know their schedules and figure out what was happening between Beau and Eve."

"But you said Beau's own assistant didn't even know about him and Eve," Mettner pointed out. "The killer could just as easily be a stalker of some kind. If he's been following the Collinses, he might have seen Eve and Beau together. If he was watching them, he might have just seen his opportunity to attack Claudia and gone for it."

"That's pretty risky," said Gretchen. "Traipsing into her house without knowing when or whether anyone else was going to show up while he was mid-murder."

Josie said, "I still say inner circle. Eve knew the killer. I don't think she would have stopped for him otherwise. There's nothing on her phone to indicate he contacted her before she went to the park yesterday. I think he was waiting for her to pass by."

Gretchen said, "Then we take a closer look at the inner circle—again. Starting with everyone who was supposed to be at the Collinses' house on Friday night. We can take another look at the video crew."

Noah said, "That Liam is a hothead, and he doesn't seem to like Beau very much."

"Right," said Gretchen. "Of everyone I spoke with at the studio, he was the most broken up over Claudia's death. I'm not sure that makes him a killer, but we can certainly speak with him again."

Noah said, "Someone should talk to the producer again. Her name's Kathy."

Mettner said, "You think she's the killer?"

Noah shrugged. "She seemed to enjoy antagonizing Liam Flint. Not that that makes her a suspect. I just think that she knows things. She was the only person on the staff who knew that Eve Bowers was seeing someone. No one else even noticed."

"Let's add her to the list then," Josie said. "But I'd like to start with Margot."

Gretchen smiled. "You got it, boss. Let me make some calls and see if I can pin her down and then you guys can go speak to her." She picked up her phone. "Mett, tell them about Dr. Feist's findings."

"Right," said Mettner. "The doc gave us her preliminary findings on Eve Bowers. No sign of sexual assault. Time of death was likely between seven a.m. and nine a.m."

"Which aligns with what she told me yesterday at the scene," Josie said. "He killed her immediately."

"Looks that way," Mettner agreed. "The doc was able to get

some DNA from her clothes. It's been sent to the state police lab. Because this is our second murder in two days by the same killer, the Chief has asked that the DNA analysis from both crime scenes be expedited."

Noah said, "That's great, but we could still be waiting days."

"Days is better than weeks, Fraley," Gretchen reminded him. "Or months."

Mettner looked back and forth between them. Once satisfied that they were finished speaking, he continued his review of Dr. Feist's autopsy findings. "Eve Bowers's cause of death was strangulation with ligature. You have the file up? You'll want to see the photos."

Josie clicked through various documents until she found the photos of Eve's throat that Dr. Feist had taken on exam. Noah came around the desks and stood behind her, leaning over her shoulder to get a better look. Under the harsh lights of the morgue, the red ligature marks were in stark contrast to Eve's otherwise unblemished, youthful skin.

"Two inches wide," Noah read. "What did he use? A belt?"

"I don't think so," said Josie. "Look at this." She pointed to the top of the ligature mark where a minuscule pattern emerged. Tiny, uniform grooves almost like a dense webbing. "Whatever he used, it was tightly woven."

"Rope?" said Noah.

"I don't think so," said Josie.

"Too wide to be a piece of rope," Mettner said. "The weaving is too tight, I think."

Mettner added, "We were thinking some kind of cloth women's belt? Dr. Feist found fibers under two of Eve's fingernails."

Noah said, "A leash of some kind, maybe?"

"Too wide, I think," Mettner said. "But yeah, the pattern looks similar, doesn't it?"

Josie felt a surge of hope. This was something. It might not help them identify or locate the killer today, but it was more than they'd had yesterday. Between this and the DNA samples found at each crime scene being expedited, the case might move more quickly. She kept clicking through the file until she found the images of the fibers which were so small, they had to be viewed under a microscope. Tan-colored.

Mettner said, "Hummel was able to analyze them in-house. Polyester. Oh, and I almost forgot—Beau Collins sent over those handwriting samples for Eve and Claudia. The writing on the back of the envelope belonged to Claudia."

"Did you upload them to the file?" asked Josie, clicking furiously. She found what she was looking for and pulled up photos of each sample. She put them side by side with the photo she'd taken of the envelope. Noah leaned in to study them. Josie caught a whiff of his aftershave.

"Yeah, that's definitely Claudia's writing," he said. "Look at the difference."

Eve's handwriting was a series of hurried slashes, whereas Claudia's handwriting was small and neat, matching the envelope Josie had found in the pages of the Collinses' book. "Why would Claudia write down Archie Gamble's name?"

Mettner shrugged. "Why would Eve take the envelope?"

Noah stepped away and moved back to his own desk. "Neither of them is here to elaborate, unfortunately. All we've got is Beau, who has already insisted that neither he nor Claudia knew Gamble."

Mettner said, "She wrote it on the back of a piece of junk mail, though. You don't write down the names of people you know on your junk mail. She was jotting this down for some other reason. Then, somehow, the envelope ended up inside the book and in Eve's apartment."

Josie sighed. "You're right, and this doesn't really get us anywhere, but now we know that Archie Gamble—for whatever reason—was on Claudia's radar before she died. The postage mark on the envelope was mid-December, so at some point in the last month, she became aware of him. Aware enough that she wrote his name down. What if she gave it to Eve to check out?"

"That's possible," Noah said. "Listen, all we can accurately say is that there is a very high probability that the handwriting is Claudia's. Everything else is just speculation, and I'm not sure it's going to get us anywhere."

Josie nodded. "Let's move on then."

Noah looked over at Mettner. "Did you hear anything from the ride-share companies?"

"Yeah. No passengers were picked up or dropped off near the city park around the time of Eve's murder or where her car was found."

"Speaking of where the car was found," Gretchen said, pulling the cell phone away from her ear, "Precious Paws Rescue was over at Archie Gamble's house today gathering up feral cats. He's got a burn barrel behind his house. The ash at the bottom of it was still warm."

A collective groan went up around the room. Burn barrels were not uncommon in Central Pennsylvania. Many people with large properties burned their trash rather than pay for waste removal. Or they burned remnants of leaves and downed trees. But for Archie Gamble to be burning things inside his barrel right after two murders—and immediately after the vehicle of one of those victims was found close to his property—was not a good sign.

Then again, it could mean nothing. That was the infuriating thing about murder investigations. Sometimes you didn't know what was important until it was important.

"I don't suppose we can get a warrant for the remains inside the barrel," Noah said.

"We tried," Gretchen said as she dialed another number on

her phone. "Not enough probable cause. Not a strong enough connection between Eve's murder and his burn barrel."

Josie swore. Dead end after dead end.

"Let's talk about alibis," said Noah.

"Gretchen and I looked at the show staff and station staff today," Mettner said. "Including Beau. The security guard at the station told us that he was there until five forty-five on Friday night. The guy saw him leave. Then he was with Margot on Saturday, as you know. In terms of the other staff, some have alibis for one murder but not the other. The only person who really doesn't have an alibi for either is the camera operator, Liam Flint. His background check didn't turn up anything worrisome. We looked at Gamble, since his name has come up now. He's got no alibi for the time of Eve's murder but the bartender at Leo's says he's there every Friday night from five p.m. until about eleven."

Josie said, "But did the bartender see him there between five and six p.m. the night that Claudia was killed?"

Mettner raised a brow. He took out his phone and looked at his notes. "He did not specifically say. Every time I asked he just said, 'Gamble's always here at five on Fridays.' Other regular patrons said the same."

Josie trusted the word of the crowd at Leo's about as much as she would trust a shark not to eat bloody chum. "I'd say that's shaky, at best. Would any of them testify in court?"

Noah laughed. "I doubt that."

Gretchen tossed her cell phone onto the desk. "Margot and Raffy will be at WYEP in one hour if you want to meet them to get the list of internet trolls and talk with Margot."

"Perfect," Josie said. "In the meantime, there's someone else we need to talk with—someone who's had access to the Collinses' lives for longer than anyone else on their staff."

Gretchen said, "The practice secretary?"

"Yeah," Josie said. "She was the last person to see Claudia alive."

Gretchen consulted a notepad on her desk. "Already on it. Her name is Trudy Dawson." She rattled off an address in East Denton. "We stopped at her house earlier, but she was out. There was a nurse there. Evidently, Trudy lives with her elderly mother who needs a lot of care. She was out getting groceries. The nurse said to stop back, but we didn't get a chance. She ought to be home."

"Well," said Josie, standing up. "Let's go talk with her. Secretaries know all the dirt."

TWENTY-FIVE

Trudy Dawson lived in a small one-story bungalow in a quiet neighborhood in East Denton. Her front walk was lined with solar-powered path lights that glowed in the dusk. An overhead light was centered over her front porch. Before Josie or Noah could knock on the door, it swung open. A woman stood before them, dressed in a pair of jeans and a blue sweater. Her brown hair was cut in a shaggy bob and shot through with gray. Dark brown eyes gazed at them over a thick pair of reading glasses.

"You're the police," she said, waving off their proffered credentials. "Beau called me yesterday to tell me the awful news. Then again this morning to give me more bad news. He asked me to look something up for you, too. The day nurse told me you'd been here earlier, but I was out."

She stepped aside and ushered them into the house. Hot air enveloped them, slapping at Josie like she was standing in front of an oven turned up to broil. Immediately, sweat beaded along her upper lip. The front door opened directly into a small living room with a recliner and a saggy brown couch. Both were pointed toward a television tuned to the evening news on WYEP. A glance told Josie that in spite of the Collinses being part of the WYEP line-up, the news division still hadn't caught wind of Claudia's or Eve's murders. They were instead reporting on a "heavy police presence in the city park" the day before—thanks to the machinations of Amber. It was only a matter of time before they found someone else—from the Collinses' camp or WYEP—to go on the record about the two murders.

"Have a seat," Trudy told them, pointing to the couch. Josie and Noah edged their way around a small circular coffee table and sat. Josie tugged off her coat. Noah pulled at his collar but left his on.

"I'm sorry about the heat," said Trudy. She sat on the edge of the recliner. From the small end table beside it, she took a remote control and pressed one of its buttons. The chair emitted a whirring noise and lifted Trudy slightly upward. "It's my mom," she continued. "Early onset Alzheimer's. She forgets to eat. Forgets how to eat. She's skin and bones now, so she's always freezing. I can open a window if you'd like."

Josie wanted to jump at the offer, but Noah smiled and said, "That's fine. We won't take up too much of your time."

Trudy fiddled with the chair remote again until she found a comfortable place. She sniffed and used her free hand to wipe away tears as they slid down her cheeks. "I'm still having trouble processing this. It doesn't seem real. Poor Claudia. Have you made any progress?"

"Our investigation is ongoing," said Noah.

Trudy set the chair remote aside and swiped at her cheeks again. "I'm sorry. I thought I was all cried out yesterday, but I guess not."

Josie said, "Miss Dawson, we can come back another time if you'd like."

"No, no. Please. The least I can do is answer your questions. Oh, I'm supposed to tell you this. There was a man, Archie Gamble. Beau asked me to check to see if he was a patient. I'm really not supposed to reveal patient names, but Beau was very convincing. He promised me I would not get in any trouble. At any rate, I don't suppose it matters since we've never had a patient by that name."

"Thank you," Josie said. She took out her phone and pulled up the driver's license photo of Gamble. Turning it toward Trudy, she asked, "Have you ever seen him before?"

Trudy studied his face. "I'm sorry, no. I haven't."

Josie asked, "Did Claudia ever mention him?"

"No. Never."

Noah said, "How long have you worked for Beau and Claudia?"

Trudy gave a watery smile. "Since before they were Beau and Claudia. I worked for the doctor who had the practice before Beau took over. Beau came into the practice right after grad school. Then the other doctor retired, and Beau was flying solo. Claudia started on a permanent basis when it became obvious he was running the entire thing into the ground. She saved it. She's saved that practice—and my job—more than once over the years."

With the back of her hand, Josie wiped at the sweat forming on her brow. "What do you mean?"

"I just mean that, well, Beau? God love him. He's not that hard on the eyes and he's got good intentions, but he never seemed to do well in private practice. He'd get complaints. Lose clients."

"What kinds of complaints?" asked Noah.

"How many kinds are there?" Trudy laughed weakly at her own joke and then thumbed away more tears. Taking in a long breath, she held up a hand and wiggled her fingers. One by one, she pushed the fingers down using her other hand. "Missed appointments. Being late. Billing incorrectly. Not seeming interested in the patients. Seeming *too* interested in the patients. I just don't think he ever liked doing it, and so he didn't take it all that seriously." She dropped her hands into her lap and sighed.

Josie said, "What do you mean, 'seeming too interested' in some patients?"

Trudy shook her head. "There were just some misunderstandings over the years. Sometimes a couple would come in and I can tell you that ninety-five percent of the time, husbands do not want to be there so they're already hostile. Then they would see Beau being kind to their wives, really listening to them for the first time in their lives, and they didn't like that at all. They'd accuse him of playing favorites or flirting and we'd never see them again."

"Was he flirting?" asked Noah.

"Goodness, no. Like I said, some of these wives were so starved for attention that their natural reaction to someone finally wanting to hear what they had to say was pure joy. They'd hang on his every word, look forward to returning."

Josie said, "You weren't in the sessions, though, right?"

"Of course not, no. All of that is private and protected by HIPAA laws. I'm only telling you what I observed in the waiting room before and after appointments. What I overheard in the waiting room when Beau wasn't there, or what the husbands told me when they called to cancel all future appointments."

"Did Beau ever cross the line?" Josie caught a drop of sweat with her forefinger before it rolled down her nose. "Was he ever inappropriate?"

"I don't think so," said Trudy. "If he was, I never saw that."

Noah asked, "Did he ever have any contact with patients or former patients outside of therapy? That you're aware of?"

Trudy narrowed her eyes at Noah. "Are you asking me if he ever had an affair with a patient?"

"Did he?" Noah coaxed.

Trudy's face loosened. A faraway look flashed across her

eyes. Something over their heads caught her attention. She stood up, arm extended. "Mom!" she said. "Where is your walker?"

Josie and Noah turned their heads to see an elderly woman with short, thinning white hair approaching them from the doorway of another room. She was just as thin as Trudy had suggested. A purple sweatshirt hung on her birdlike frame. Spindly fingers grabbed at furniture to help her advance. As she moved deeper into the living room, her gait wobbled. Trudy closed the distance between them and expertly slid an arm around her waist before she fell. "Mom. You need your walker so you don't fall."

"Who are these kids?" she said, pointing at Josie and Noah.

"Those are not kids, Mom. They're here to talk to me about my boss."

Her mother tried to push Trudy away, slapping at the arm around her thin waist. Her attention was still on Josie and Noah. "You better send them to the office. If you catch them out here in the hall without a pass, it's right to the office!"

"Mom, come on. Let me help you. I have to hold on so you don't fall." Trudy kept one arm firmly around her mother's waist, steering her away from Josie and Noah, and guiding her down the hall. She returned a few minutes later, an apologetic grimace on her face. "I'm so sorry about that."

Josie smiled. "Was she a teacher?"

Trudy returned the smile as she settled back into the recliner. "Yes. Thirty-seven years. Elementary school. Now, where were we?"

Josie said, "We wanted to know if Beau had ever had an affair with a patient?"

"Right," said Trudy. "I don't think so. If he did, I certainly didn't know about it."

"But you're not sure," said Josie.

Trudy didn't answer, her attention suddenly focused on a frayed thread on the arm of the chair.

Softly, Noah said, "Mrs. Dawson, I understand if this feels awkward, but these are questions we have to ask in cases like these. What we're looking for is anyone who might have held a grudge against Beau or Claudia Collins. Anyone who might be angry with one of them, with Beau in particular. Anyone who might wish him or Claudia harm."

Trudy tugged at the thread and then wrapped it around her index finger.

When it was clear she wasn't going to reveal what she knew, Josie said, "You mentioned that some of the husbands Beau Collins treated became dissatisfied. Angry, even. Are there any of those men, or any patients—former or current—that you can think of who might target the Collinses?"

The thread left small red indents in Trudy's fingertip. "I honestly can't think of any, although I couldn't tell you even if I did. You should know that. HIPAA laws prevent me from disclosing anything at all, even names."

Noah said, "In this case, if you believe that a particular patient is a threat, I think you would be allowed to tell us their name."

"But that's just it," Trudy said. "There were patients who were unhappy with Beau, but I can't think of anyone who seemed threatening. I'm not comfortable telling you the names of the patients who were dissatisfied or who left the practice. With Claudia gone, I have to find a new job." She motioned to the doorway across the room. "I've got my mother to think about. I have to provide for her, and I want to keep her home with me as long as possible. For that, I need income. If I violate privacy laws, I'll never find another job like this one."

Josie said, "I get that, Trudy, I do. But Claudia's killer is still a threat. We're not asking to see a chart, here. We're asking for a name."

With a sigh, Trudy met Josie's eyes again. "I'm sorry. Even if I could think of one, which I can't, I'm not comfortable disclosing it. There really is no one I believe would harm Claudia or Beau. That's the truth. Beau doesn't actually see patients anymore. He stopped seeing them a long time ago. It's just Claudia, and her patients adore her. They did adore her. My God. I guess I have to start making phone calls tomorrow. Break the news."

She stopped as more tears slid down her face. "Claudia is the only reason the practice was even still alive. Like I said, if it weren't for her, I would have been out of a job a long time ago. With my mom being as sick as she has all these years, I needed this job. I don't even know how I'll make it until I find something else. Maybe I can cut out the home nurse for a bit. I'll have to talk to Beau. My brother lives in Virginia and he travels for his job. I'm all Mom has left. She's confused enough already—"

Josie's heart ached for the woman. She remembered when her grandmother, Lisette, had finally had to go into a skilled nursing facility. Josie had kept Lisette home with her and Ray as long as she could. She had hated moving Lisette to a facility even though it was for the best and even though Lisette insisted on it. Josie reached over and touched Trudy's hand. "We're the ones who are sorry. We didn't mean to upset you. We just want to find the person who did this. You were the last person to see Claudia alive. How did she seem to you?"

Trudy took a steadying breath. "She seemed fine. She's always her best self when she is treating patients. That's what she really loves—loved. All this book and TV stuff," she flapped her hands in the air. "That's all Beau. She went along with it to humor him. The money didn't hurt either, I'm sure."

Noah asked, "Did she mention whether she'd been having trouble with anyone lately? Maybe not a patient, but anyone else? Maybe someone at the studio? A neighbor? A friend?"

"No," said Trudy. "There was nothing like that. Claudia was a sweet person, though. I've never known anyone to get upset with her."

Josie said, "To your knowledge, was Claudia having an affair?"

Trudy's eyes darkened. She tried a smile but it didn't hold. After a brief hesitation, she said, "Not to my knowledge, no. She was long-suffering, certainly. Beau can be a lot with all his grand ideas, always adding more and more to their plates, but she loves him—loved him. I don't think she would cheat. I mean, I don't think—" She broke off.

"What is it?" asked Josie.

Trudy looked at the floor and waved a dismissive hand in the air. "It's nothing. I'm overthinking, and with Claudia dead, it wouldn't be fair to say."

"Say what?" asked Noah.

Tears leaked from her eyes again. "I just don't want to—to besmirch her character in any way. She really was the most lovely person."

Josie softened her voice. "Trudy, I promise you that telling the truth will not besmirch Claudia's character. It might bring us closer to finding her killer."

"But I don't know the truth," Trudy said. "I just know…"

She looked away, the nail of her index finger digging into the arm of the chair. "I don't want to start something. Rumors. They never lead to anything good."

Noah said, "Then just tell us what you know. Exactly what you know. Nothing more, nothing less."

Trudy drew in a shuddering breath. "In the months before her death, maybe even a year, she left the office for lunch."

Josie and Noah exchanged a look. This was the scandalous secret that Trudy didn't want to disclose?

"I don't understand," Noah said.

Trudy dug out another thread from the chair's fabric and

pinched it between her thumb and forefinger. "In all the years that I knew Claudia, she loved her work—the practice, not the other stuff—more than anything in the world. Once she was at the office, she didn't leave until the last patient of the day had gone. If she ate at all, it was at her desk. Something light. Often, Beau tried to get her to join him for lunch but she wouldn't go. Then one day, she started going out for lunch. Just like that. Not quick ones, either. Some days she was gone for over an hour. Several times I had to push back her patients because she ran late."

Josie said, "Did she ever tell you where she was going?"

"No," Trudy said. "She just said she was going out and would be back before her next patient. She always used that time for charts before. It was very strange."

"Did you ask her about it?" said Noah.

Trudy shook her head. "It didn't feel right. It wasn't my business. Plus, she always came back looking so... refreshed. Whatever she was doing, it made her happy. I hadn't seen her like that in a long time. Not since early in her marriage to Beau."

Noah asked, "Do you think she was having an affair?"

Trudy pursed her lips. The thread pulled away from the upholstery, lengthening. "I don't know. It just seems so unlike her to do something like that."

"Lots of people have affairs," said Josie. "Even people who seem unlikely to do so."

"Yes, but Claudia just... Maybe you're right, but it seems very out of character for her."

"Do you have any idea who she was having lunch with?" asked Noah.

"No, and I'm embarrassed to admit this, but I did look at her personal calendar once and there wasn't anything on it at all. Maybe she wasn't having lunch with anyone. Maybe she was getting a massage or taking a yoga class. This is why I didn't want to discuss this because I really don't know what she was doing during those times. I'm sorry I can't be of more help."

Josie stood up and felt sweat sluice down her spine. Her hand was clammy as she fished through her pocket for a business card. Handing it to Trudy, she gave her the standard spiel about calling them if she thought of anything they should know. Anything at all.

In the car, Josie told Noah, "We need to see if we can get Claudia's phone records expedited. Maybe there's something in them that will shed some light on this—text messages or voice-mails. Something."

"I'll make a call to the provider's legal department," Noah said. "Rattle some cages. In the meantime, let's go see Margot Huff."

TWENTY-SIX

The halls of WYEP were oddly quiet for a television station. The news was being broadcast live in the main studio. The Collinses' area of the station was deserted. No Margot anywhere to be found, even in the small row of offices belonging to the Couples' Corner With The Collinses staff. Kathy, however, the producer, was alone in her office, staring at her computer screen. She jumped up from her desk when Josie knocked on the half-open door.

"I'm sorry to bother you," Josie said.

She smoothed her dark hair and offered a smile. When she saw Noah standing behind Josie, she looked down at her white blouse and tan slacks, running her palms over the wrinkles. Up close, Josie estimated that she was in her mid-fifties. Behind her, the walls of the small office were filled with photos of Kathy with various celebrities.

Noah nudged Josie across the threshold and extended a hand to Kathy. She took it, her smile widening but still nervous, judging by the tiny quiver at the corners of her mouth. Nervous because she found Noah attractive, or because she was hiding something?

"I hope you don't mind us dropping in," Noah told her. "We just had a few questions."

"Of course," said Kathy. "I, uh, heard the awful news about Eve. Very sad. Tragic. She was so young."

"Yes," Noah agreed. "It's been a very difficult forty-eight hours for your team and ours, really, trying to figure out who's behind all this. We know you spoke with our colleagues and gave them some background—you've worked on Beau and Claudia's show from the beginning. You came over from the WYEP news department where you'd worked for years."

Kathy nodded along, keeping her eyes glued to Noah's face.

He put the next part delicately. "You also maintain that your relationship with Beau Collins and everyone else on the show staff has always been completely professional."

"Yes, that's right," Kathy said.

Josie said, "We wanted to talk to you because out of everyone on the staff, you were the only one with a keen enough eye to realize that Eve was in love."

Kathy turned her gaze to Josie, a genuine smile now spreading across her face. "Thank you. I didn't realize it was important. I was just noting what I'd observed."

Noah said, "It was very helpful. We were wondering if there were any other things you'd observed or overheard or noticed in the last few months, maybe even a year, that you could share with us."

"Oh, well, I told your colleagues everything I know."

Josie took out her phone and pulled up the photo of Archie Gamble. She turned it toward Kathy, but she showed no signs of recognition. "Who's that?"

Noah said, "We were hoping you could tell us."

Kathy shook her head. "I've never seen him."

"His name is Archie Gamble," Josie said. "Does that ring a bell?"

Another blank look, another shake of her head.

Noah said, "You do know Liam Flint though, don't you?"

Kathy's expression darkened. "I'm sorry about that scene on set the other day, but honestly, that guy is an arrogant jerk. He really does think he's better than everyone else. Full disclosure? No one likes him. We all just tolerate him."

Josie said, "Are you aware of any grudges he has against Beau or Claudia?"

Kathy laughed, the sound high and unexpected. "Maybe Beau. He's never made a secret of the fact that he hates Beau, but listen, Liam's got a grudge against the world."

Noah said, "In your observations, have you ever noticed anyone you think might want to harm the Collinses or even kill Claudia? Or Eve?"

The last vestiges of Kathy's laughter leaked away as she considered the gravity of the question. She took a long moment. Then she said, "I can't think of anyone. Not here. Not that I've noticed. They get a lot of hate on the internet though. You should talk to Margot about that. She does the social media."

"Will do." Noah smiled at her. A dazzling smile. Josie had seen him use it on witnesses dozens of times. He handed her a business card. "Thank you, Kathy," he said. "You've been a big help. Please call us if you think of anything else."

Kathy stared down at the card as Josie and Noah started to exit the office. They were in the hallway when she called, "Wait!"

She joined them in the middle of the empty hallway, looking around to make sure no one was near before lowering her voice to a near whisper. "I didn't tell you or your colleagues this because I figured that Eve must have told you before she died, but maybe she didn't."

"Tell us what?" asked Josie.

Kathy tucked the business card into her pants pocket. She brushed her hands through her hair again. "About a month ago, maybe between Thanksgiving and Christmas, I overheard Eve and Claudia talking. They were in Claudia's office. The door was ajar. I had gone to ask Claudia for something but I heard them talking when I reached the door so I stopped and... I'm ashamed to say I listened. Just for a few seconds. Claudia was telling Eve that she thought someone was following her."

"Did she say what made her think that?" asked Noah.

Kathy shook her head. "I came in right at the end of the conversation. I just heard her saying something to Eve like, 'it's just a feeling I have lately like someone is watching me everywhere I go.' Then Eve said she was a celebrity and in the public eye all the time and maybe it was just that. Then they heard me outside the door and stopped talking altogether."

Josie asked, "Did you say anything to either of them?"

Kathy put a hand to her chest. "Oh no, of course not. I didn't want them to think that I was eavesdropping. If Claudia thought someone was following her, really following her, I figured she would go to the police. Or she could have hired a private investigator or a bodyguard or something. Claudia and Beau are wealthy enough to do that. I never heard anything about it again, so I figured either it was resolved or Eve was right —it was all in Claudia's head."

TWENTY-SEVEN

Josie and Noah thanked Kathy for her time and went back to the security desk to get directions to Raffy Sullivan's office. The door stood open. Behind a tiny desk in a windowless room that was easily a quarter the size of Kathy's office, Raffy sat, scrolling through WYEP's Facebook page on a laptop. Two cell phones lay next to his computer. Crammed into the small space was another office chair next to the one he occupied. A woman's purse hung from the back of it.

"Oh, hey," Raffy said when Josie knocked on the doorframe. "I'd say come in, but there's not much room."

Josie managed to squeeze inside. Noah stayed at the threshold.

"As you can see, they started converting closets into 'offices,'" Raffy added, using air quotes for the word offices. "Margot's in the bathroom, but I've got that list your colleague asked for if you want to take it." One of the phones on the desk buzzed. Raffy quickly covered it with his hand, dragging it toward him and deftly dismissing the call. Tossing it back onto the desk, he lifted a stack of pages from the other side of his laptop and handed them to Josie. She flipped through them while Noah asked questions.

"These are people who have been blocked from both the WYEP platforms and the Collinses' platforms?"

"Yeah, exactly," Raffy said. "Margot and I figured we'd combine forces. As you can see, most of the trolls target the Collinses directly. But every now and then we get some who also troll them on the station's social media. Some come over to the WYEP pages after Margot blocks them on the show page."

The list was long. Names, profile photos, and any information that could be gleaned from their profiles. It was mostly men.

Noah said, "You've had to block them for trolling the Collinses. What kinds of things have they said? Is there anyone who seems to have a personal vendetta against either of them?"

Raffy stroked his goatee thoughtfully. The buzz of his cell phone sounded again. With a frown, he looked at the screen. This time, Josie saw a name flash across the screen. Brooke. Raffy swiped dismiss and looked back at Noah. "A vendetta? That's a strong word. What we've got is mostly just a bunch of really mean people who hate the Collinses for various reasons: their hair, their voices, something they said one time on one show. One woman started trolling them because she tried one of their exercises on her husband and he called her stupid. Then there are the women who are obsessed with Mr. Collins and think he should leave Claudia." He pointed to the pages in Josie's hand. "Those two are on page ten, I think. There are screenshots of whatever content got them banned after each profile."

Josie flipped to page ten and read over the profiles and then the comments and messages the women had left.

I know we're meant to be together. I know you know it, too, deep down. You have to work up the nerve to leave her once and for all.

Beau, baby, you're all I can think about day and night. Please come to me.

Claudia is a dumb bitch who will never satisfy you. Let me show you what a real woman can do.

It makes me sick watching you pretend with her every day on TV. I know you hate her. I am the only one who can make you happy.

The tone of what they'd posted bordered on psychosis, but was it enough for either of them to try to ruin Beau's life? Would their delusions allow them to plan so carefully? Did they even live in the area? A thorough background check was in order for later.

"Any threats?" Josie asked.

"That depends," said Raffy. "There were a few things I sent to my boss because I thought maybe we should get the police involved, but his feeling was that 'I hope you die' is not a direct threat."

"Really?" said Josie. "Which one of these people said that?"

"Page fourteen," Raffy told her. "But what you're looking for is on page twenty-one."

Josie bypassed fourteen and flipped to twenty-one to a profile of a man called Ron Abbott. His profile photo showed a man likely in his thirties with a thick head of blond hair and a moon face. As she paged through screenshots of his messages and comments, Raffy narrated.

"Like, five years ago, after the Collinses' book went viral or whatever, and about a year after that, they started doing the show at the studio, this guy was trolling the station social media hard. He was nasty. Really nasty. Saying all kinds of things about Mr. Collins. Made it sound like Mr. Collins had done something to him personally. At that time, I was just starting to manage the social media platforms, so I was the go-to guy for stuff like that. Margot hadn't started yet. I kept blocking him, but he always came back under some dumb, fake username. I kept taking the stuff to my boss but again, either it wasn't anything he felt 'rose to the level of a threat,' or he promised to just 'pass it along to Beau and let him deal with it.' One day, Abbott just stopped. I figured, great. I'm done with that, finally."

"But he wasn't done," Josie said. Skimming over Abbott's words, she felt the cold fingers of foreboding trail up her spine.

I hope you die a horrible, slow death.

You and your bitch wife deserve to be tortured.

Someone should hack you into pieces and make your dumb wife watch.

Raffy's cell phone began buzzing once more. Brooke again. He heaved a sigh and dismissed the call for the third time. Then he set the phone to silent. "I'm sorry," he said. "Ex-girlfriend. She can't let go. Anyway, what were you saying?"

"That Ron Abbott wasn't finished with his hate campaign," Josie said.

"No, not at all," Raffy replied. "He'd just found another way in. That was when the Collinses shut down their personal platforms and created single accounts for the show. Then they put Margot in charge. Apparently, Beau and Claudia had been blocking him on their personal accounts for ages. But when the new profiles were created, Abbott went right for them. That's how Margot and I met, actually. Over this Abbott guy. He kept coming back under different names, but you could always tell it was him by the language. Anyway, I don't think she was prepared for him. Like, at all."

"Well," said Josie, pointing to a screenshot. "Here he suggests that Beau Collins deserves to have his genitalia violently removed and then used to do some pretty disgusting things to his own person."

Noah leaned over for a look. He gave a low whistle.

Raffy said, "That's not even the worst of it. If you keep going, you'll see."

"But he words it so that it doesn't sound like a threat," Josie said. "He isn't saying he's going to do this, he's only saying it should happen."

"Right," said Raffy.

Josie's stomach dropped when she got to the screenshots of what Claudia deserved. *Someone should take hot pokers to both of her eyes. She deserves to suffer just as much as her piece of garbage husband.*

"These may not be direct threats," Josie said. "But they're certainly enough to justify a restraining order. Did you ever find out why neither Beau nor Claudia went to the police?"

Raffy stood up and stepped between Josie and Noah, poking his head into the hallway. He scanned one way and then the other before turning back to them. "I probably shouldn't tell you this. I only know about it because I overheard Beau talking with my boss, but this Abbott guy? He was a patient."

"A patient of whose?" asked Noah.

Raffy sat back down in his chair and laced his hands behind his head. "I'm not sure, but probably Beau's, since most of his ire was directed toward Beau. I think they were just trying to keep it quiet, especially with the show just starting to gain traction."

Josie flipped to the end of the packet, to the last of the fake accounts that Ron Abbott had ostensibly created to terrorize the Collinses. "These stopped last year. Do you know why?"

He shook his head. "On my end, monitoring just the WYEP content, they stopped long before that. You can ask Margot, but sometimes these people just stop showing up on social media and we never know why."

TWENTY-EIGHT

DIARY ENTRY, UNDATED

He knows. I'm not sure what tipped him off. Maybe a thousand little things that I can no longer control. All my careful planning for how to tell him was for nothing. I wanted us to do it together, and I wanted to be able to leave this terrible home right after we told him so he couldn't hurt me. Somehow, he just knew. He was cruel and angry. He did hurt me but it wasn't anything he hasn't done to me before. Part of me is relieved. The worst is over. I hope. Maybe it will be okay. I keep telling myself that even after what I've done, I don't deserve this. My lover tells me all the time that I deserve more and better than this. A real life with true love. I can't even bring myself to write his name down. Even now.

I'm going to meet him now and tell him the news. We don't have to hide anymore.

TWENTY-NINE

Josie handed the packet over to Noah and left him with Raffy. They'd been speaking to him for several minutes, and Margot had not yet returned from the restroom. Either she was in some kind of distress, or she was actively avoiding them. The nearest ladies' room was at the end of the hall. Josie pushed through the door and began checking stalls. All of them were empty except for the last one. Two delicate feet in black ballet flats quickly disappeared upward the moment Josie approached the stall.

"Miss Huff," Josie said. "I know you're in there."

Silence.

Josie waited a few beats and tried again. "Margot, please. I just have a few more questions for you. I know you've been under a tremendous amount of stress this weekend with all that's happened. I'm not looking to make things worse for you. I promise it won't take long."

A creaking sounded from behind the door. Then came Margot's voice, small and squeaky. "I already talked to someone on Friday after Claudia—after Eve found Claudia. I told that guy everything."

"Yes," Josie said. "I know. We appreciated your cooperation, especially at such a difficult time, but on Friday we didn't know all the things we know now, so my colleague couldn't have known to ask you the questions I'd like to ask you now."

"I didn't know about Beau and Eve. I swear to you."

"I believe you," said Josie. "Margot, you're not in trouble. I want you to know that. Really, I just want to talk. Give me five minutes. You can set a timer if you like."

Another creak. "I left my phone in Raffy's office."

"I've got mine," Josie said. She took it out, punched in her passcode and pulled up the timer app. She set it for five minutes. Then she squatted down and placed her phone, screen up, onto the floor. Slowly, she pushed it under the stall. "I'm hitting start right now."

As she tapped the start button, one of Margot's feet descended from the toilet seat. "Okay," she said.

Josie would have preferred to see her face, but she'd work with this. "What can you tell me about Ron Abbott?"

"The internet troll? Everything I know is in the packet that Raffy and I made. Didn't he give it to you?"

"Yes," Josie said. "But Raffy didn't know why Abbott suddenly stopped trying to terrorize Beau and Claudia last year. I wondered if you did."

"No. I'm sorry. I have no idea. One day he just stopped."

"What do you know about him?"

"Only that he was a complete psychopath. A sick, sick psychopath. I told Beau he should talk to you guys, but he said that the guy would get tired of being ignored eventually and just go away. He was right."

"Margot, don't take this the wrong way. I have to ask. Did anything romantic or sexual ever happen between you and Beau Collins?"

There was a beat of silence, then a rustling and the loud clank of the toilet seat slamming down on the rim. The stall door flew open. Margot stood before Josie, chest heaving, face lobster red. "Are you kidding me? That is so gross. No. Never. The other guy asked me that, too. Why do you all think that me and Beau..." She looked up at the ceiling and shuddered. "It's too gross to even think about."

"Fair enough," Josie said, bending to retrieve her phone from between Margot's feet.

"Just because he was sleeping with Eve doesn't mean that I would. Blech." Her mouth twisted in disgust.

"You seem to know him really well," Josie said. "The two of you have a level of intimacy that seems rare for a boss and employee."

Margot strode past Josie to the sinks and studied her face in the mirror. Her eyes widened when she saw the deep flush of her cheeks. She turned on the nearest faucet and used her hands to dab her face with cold water. "I guess you're right," she said. "But it's only because Beau is a really nice guy. This is my first real job. I graduated from Denton University with a degree in communications. I wanted to stay here but I couldn't find work. Then I completely flubbed my interview with Beau, but he was so kind and so gracious. I wouldn't have given me the job, but he did. He's always been nice and not ever in a creepy way, if that's what you're thinking."

She met Josie's eyes in the mirror. Josie said nothing.

"So yeah, maybe it seems like we're... I don't know... informal or something, but that's Beau. He's always been a good guy—I mean, I thought so but now that I know about Eve, I'm rethinking every interaction I ever had with him. Everything he ever said, everything I ever saw him do, everything I ever overheard. Like this one time—"

She stopped talking and turned the faucet off. Her flush had reduced to a healthy pink. Josie surreptitiously checked the timer on her phone. One minute and thirty-seven seconds.

"This one time what?" she prompted.

According to the timer, she took seven seconds to think it

over. "I guess it doesn't matter now," she said finally. "This one time a few months ago, I overheard Beau and Claudia fighting. It was here in the studio. In his office. He had sent me to get him lunch and when I came back, his door was closed but they were loud enough that I could hear a lot of what they were saying. I didn't catch all of it but from what I could gather, he found loads of cash in her briefcase. Like, tons. He was completely beside himself. He kept saying how could she do this without even consulting him, stuff like that. Then that stupid producer, Kathy, came down the hall. She's always ratting everyone out over everything, and I didn't want to get in trouble, so I went back to the studio and waited for him to call me."

"Did you ever ask him about it?" Josie said.

"I wasn't going to, but he was so off for the next couple of days that finally, I just blurted out that I'd overheard them. I wanted to make sure everything was okay. I mean, I need this job."

Less than thirty seconds. Josie said, "What did he say?"

"That Claudia had liquidated a very large account of theirs because she wanted to make a cash donation to the new women's center. She wanted it to be in cash because she didn't want the donation coming back to them. She didn't want it to look like they were trying to get good press by making such a large donation. He said he was angry that she didn't consult him at all—not that he would have stopped her, but just that it was such a large amount of cash, in both their names, and she should have come to him first."

"How much cash?" Josie asked.

Margot pressed her fingers to her cheeks. "I'm not sure. Beau never told me. He only said it was tens of thousands of dollars."

"When was this?"

Thankfully, Margot didn't waste too many precious seconds trying to remember. "Early October, I think."

"Did you believe him? About the money? Where it came from and what it was intended for?"

The timer beeped, echoing in the tiled bathroom.

Margot jumped slightly. She watched as Josie dismissed the alarm.

Josie looked back at her to see if she'd answer the final question. She turned around to face Josie. "I used to, but now I'm not so sure."

THIRTY

Noah was still lingering in the doorway of Raffy's office when Josie emerged from the bathroom. She'd left Margot inside to compose herself, although she was certain that Margot had no intention of coming out until Josie and Noah had left. As she got closer to the office, Raffy's voice carried into the hallway. "... just not a believer in all this relationship stuff. I mean, it's cool, and I know a lot of people get something out of it, but I tried it on my ex and it did not work at all."

"Playing games as a way to foster intimacy didn't work?" Noah said.

Raffy laughed. "No way, man. All it did was make us realize we wanted different things, and once that happened, it was over."

"When was this?" Noah asked.

"I don't know," Raffy said. "A few years ago. But we always kept in touch. It didn't end on bad terms, it just ended. Look at this, man. Six calls from her in the last half hour. She gets drunk every now and then and pulls this shit and then in the morning, she doesn't even remember."

"You think you'll ever get back together?"

A sigh. "I don't know, man. Maybe."

"You ever think about asking Beau Collins for relationship advice? One on one? Or Claudia?"

Raffy's laughter was louder this time. "You're kidding me, right? No way. I like this job and I want to keep it, but between me and you, they're a joke. They're getting trolled for a reason, man. Think about it. Why would a former patient say those things that Abbott said? There's something there. No way am I taking relationship advice from people whose patients think they should be tortured."

"Margot seems to take her job pretty seriously. Does she know how you feel about them?"

A chuckle. "Oh, man. Listen, Margot and I are a thing, but it's not serious. I don't really care what she thinks. It's never going to go anywhere with her."

Noah said, "Beau Collins seems worried that it might be."

A long exhale. "I bet he does. That dude is something else."

"What do you mean?"

Raffy lowered his voice and Josie tiptoed closer to the door to hear him. "There's no way he's not banging everything that moves when his wife isn't looking. Margot told me about Eve. I'm not surprised at all. She never said but he was probably banging her, too."

"Margot?" said Noah.

"Hell, yeah. All the time those two spend together. The way they talk to one another. They had to. I'm not about to go the distance with that dude's scraps."

Josie had had enough. She walked up behind Noah. "You ready?"

Raffy startled at the sight of her. "Oh hey, you talk to Margot?"

"Yes," Josie said.

She didn't bother with saying goodbye, instead striding away with Noah in tow. Once they were outside, she said, "The best thing that will ever happen to Margot will be breaking up with that douche."

"Agreed," Noah said.

They climbed into the car and Josie headed back to the stationhouse. She caught him up on everything Margot had said.

"Do you think Margot is telling the truth about not having any kind of affair with Beau?" asked Noah.

"She's lying about something," Josie said. "But not that. Beau's wife and his mistress were just murdered. If I were Margot and I'd been having some kind of affair with him—past or present—I would tell. It's self-preservation."

"Agree. What about the money Claudia supposedly donated? What do you make of that?"

"I'm not sure," said Josie. "The point of that story was that Margot was afraid Beau had lied about the entire thing."

"Still, it's a helluva story. Claudia Collins takes tens of thousands of dollars out of their bank accounts without even discussing it with him? There's got to be something there. Then you've got Kathy saying that Claudia thought she was being followed. We're barely scratching the surface of whatever the hell was going on with these people."

"I get the same feeling," Josie agreed. "But what do we do with this information? We can't prove Claudia was being followed—or who was doing it—and the money? Assuming she really didn't donate it, can we connect it to the murders?"

Noah thought for a moment. "I'm not sure a judge would grant a warrant for the Collinses' financial records at this point. It's odd, but it doesn't connect to either murder. Unless Beau was lying, and the money was for something else, but again, we'd have to be able to demonstrate a clear connection to the murders."

"We can check with the women's center and find out if they received a large, anonymous cash donation during the month of October. I'll call first thing tomorrow," Josie said. "We'll also ask Beau about the money, but before we do, I want to do a little research into Ron Abbott."

Back at the stationhouse, it took only minutes to connect the profiles that Raffy and Margot had shared with them to a Ron Abbott who lived in Lenore County, south of Denton. Josie discovered pretty quickly why he had abruptly stopped trolling the Collinses online. Staring at her screen, her stomach acids went into overdrive. "Noah," she said. "Come look at this."

He wheeled his chair around their collective desks until he was next to her. As he read the news article dated nine months earlier from the *Fairfield Review*, a small local newspaper based in Lenore County, he muttered, "Holy shit."

LENORE COUNTY SHERIFF'S DEPUTIES RESPOND TO MURDER-SUICIDE

Fairfield, PA – The Lenore County Sheriff's Department responded to 911 calls from neighbors along rural route 714 last night. Many residents reported hearing gunshots from the direction of a residence owned by Ron and Casey Abbott. One neighbor reportedly heard shouting coming from the residence prior to the gunshots. When Lenore County Sheriff's deputies arrived on scene, they found the homeowners, Ronald Abbott, thirty-four, and his wife, Casey Abbott, thirty-three, deceased in an apparent murder-suicide.

"The investigation into this horrific tragedy is ongoing," said a representative from the sheriff's office.

Neighbors and friends of the couple report that the Abbotts had been having marital trouble for years.

"It wasn't a good situation," said one of Casey Abbott's coworkers, who asked to remain anonymous. "They were always arguing. He was controlling and he only got worse as time went on. I think they might have tried counseling once but it didn't do any good. I don't know why she stayed, to be honest. I always worried he would do something like this but Casey wouldn't hear of it."

Ronald Abbott's brother tells a very different tale of the couple's marriage. "My brother was a good man and a devoted husband. I don't know what went on behind closed doors. I haven't talked with my brother in years—I've been away with the military—but I know he wasn't a violent man. Whatever happened in that house, Casey drove him to it."

Funeral arrangements for the couple will be private.

Josie printed the article and then clicked out of it. She pulled up the WYEP website and entered a number of search terms pertaining to Ron and Casey Abbott as well as murder-suicide and "Lenore County couple." Nothing came up. "WYEP didn't cover this."

"But it's in their backyard," said Noah. "You think the Collinses killed it?"

"There's one way to find out," Josie said. "We've got a whole list of things to discuss with Beau Collins."

"We should also probably ask Trudy Dawson about the Abbotts as well."

"I don't think she'll tell us unless Beau gives her permission first. We should just prepare a warrant."

"For the Abbotts' records? No judge will grant it. The Abbotts are dead. They can't possibly be connected to these murders."

Josie swore. "You're right."

"Why don't I call the unit we put on Beau and see where he is?"

"Okay," Josie said, "but first I want to check out a few more of these internet trolls to make sure we're not missing anything else."

"I'll split the packet with you. We're going to need more coffee."

THIRTY-ONE

Josie reached into one of her desk drawers and fished around until her hand closed on a bottle of ibuprofen. She twisted it open and shook out three pills, then swallowed them dry. Between the case, lack of sleep, and staring at the computer screen the last two hours, a headache had formed across her forehead. She picked up the Komorrah's cup on her desk and drained what little was left of it. Across from her, at his own desk, Noah dozed in his chair. Josie didn't have the heart to wake him. He'd already worked through his half of the list of internet haters. She didn't begrudge him a ten-minute catnap.

Josie finished up the last of her searches. More dead ends. None of the other people who'd been banned from the Collinses' and WYEP's social media platforms lived in Denton. Only one of them—one of the women obsessed with Beau— lived within driving distance.

It had to be someone local. Someone familiar with the city park and the areas of the city with the fewest cameras where LPRs were least likely to be. As much as Josie detested Raffy, he'd made a good point about the Collinses' former patients. Trudy had denied any issues with past patients, but Josie had a feeling that she would do anything to keep her job, even covering for Beau. If he didn't want the subject of these patients coming up, Trudy would hold her tongue. But if what Raffy had overheard was correct and the Abbotts were former patients, it stood to reason they weren't the only ones who took issue with Beau Collins.

Josie brought up her internet browser and searched for the Collinses' marriage counseling practice. It took a while to find anything that pertained specifically to the practice since the first thirteen pages of search results had to do with their book, show or podcast. Finally, she found what she was looking for: reviews. There were some on Yelp, mostly favorable. The two- and three-star reviews had to do with Beau's lateness to appointments several years earlier. There were even fewer Google reviews. Those were all favorable, more recent, and discussed only Claudia—in glowing terms. Josie found a third site specific to Denton called Citizen Review. There were many more reviews than the other sites. Josie bypassed the good reviews and clicked right on the one-star reviews. There was only one. It had been posted by a user simply listed as 'Anonymous' over four years ago.

> *Beau Collins is a lecherous liar who cannot be trusted. He is not a real therapist. He's not there to help you. He's there to steal your wife. He should not be allowed to counsel couples. Watch out for him. He will turn your wife against you. Flirt with her right in front of you and then laugh when you tell him to knock it the hell off. He will call your wife and have private conversations with her that you don't know about. He is a fraud and a cheat. He will ruin your marriage and your life. Don't pay him to steal your wife! STAY AWAY FROM HIM. He is a horrible person who deserves to feel the wrath of all the husbands whose wives he screwed. I hope one day this bastard gets what he deserves.*

Had Ron Abbott written this review? Or someone else?

They'd add it to the list of questions for Beau Collins.

Josie prepared a warrant for Citizen Review to see if they could find out who had written the review. She could wait until the morning to have it signed and then email it to Citizen Review. Noah startled awake just as she was finishing up. He blinked and swiped his hands over his face. "Why'd you let me sleep?"

"You weren't out that long," Josie said. "Why don't you call the unit assigned to Beau and find out where he is while I print something out? I want you to see this."

While Noah made the call, Josie printed the review.

Noah said, "Beau's staying at the Eudora."

The name of the hotel sent an instant wave of dread through Josie. A recent case had uncovered several unsavory activities happening at the hotel—although without the knowledge of its manager. While the Eudora was the oldest, largest and most upscale hotel in the city, the reminders of that case were unavoidable. If Josie never set foot in the place again, she'd be fine with it. "Of course he is," she said, standing up. She circled her desk and handed the review to Noah. "I'll drive. I want you to read this on the way over there."

They found Beau Collins at the bar inside Bastian's, the restaurant just off the hotel lobby. He sat alone at the end of the bar, staring into a glass of amber liquid. Bourbon, from what Josie could tell as they got closer and the smell of it reached her nostrils. Something inside her twisted in yearning. A sense memory of Wild Turkey burning a satisfying trail from the back of her throat to her stomach made her feel momentarily heady. She'd given up drinking years ago. After the last time she saw Luke Creighton, when she realized that getting blackout drunk, as good as it felt while doing it, led to poor choices and even worse consequences—and did absolutely nothing to dispel her psychic pain.

Beau Collins had no such compunction.

He slugged down the bourbon and signaled the bartender for another. The man gave Beau the once-over, taking in his sad, uneven stubble, his uncombed hair, wrinkled shirt buttoned crooked, and his slumped posture. He poured Beau another but qualified it with, "Last one."

Beau didn't argue. Instead, he stared deep into the glass. Josie wondered if it was speaking to him.

Noah nudged her with an elbow. "He may be too drunk to talk."

"Only one way to find out," Josie said. "He may be drunk, but we've got two murders to solve."

As they reached him, Josie clapped a hand on the back of his shoulder. The alcohol had slowed his reflexes. It took a second for his head to swivel in her direction, his blank expression filling with annoyance. "Detective Quinn. Are you following me?"

"You know we are," she answered, taking the barstool next to him. "We're trying to keep you safe."

His gaze returned to the bourbon in front of him. Noah moved around to his other side. "How many of those have you had?"

Beau picked up the glass and swished the liquid around. "Not enough to forget that my life, as I know it, is over."

Josie bit back the words: *you're still here. Claudia and Eve are not.* She needed answers from this man.

Beau put the glass back down and looked from Noah to Josie. "Let me guess: more questions."

Josie nodded. "Let's start with Claudia. A few months ago, she took a large amount of cash out of one of your accounts. Or so you told Margot."

"Jesus," Beau muttered. "That kid—is nothing sacred? That was private. A private matter between my wife and me."

Noah said, "So she did take out cash from one of your accounts without consulting you?"

"Yes. It was for a cash donation to some charity she was into."

Josie asked, "How much cash are we talking?"

"Thirty thousand dollars."

Noah said, "What was the charity?"

Beau shrugged. "I don't know. Something to do with women. Probably domestic violence or something. Why?"

"You don't know which charity your wife gave thirty thousand dollars of your money to?" Josie said.

"Claudia did what Claudia wanted, okay? I never cared about the donation, only that she didn't talk to me first. She wanted it so that it wouldn't be traced back to us. I don't understand what this has to do with her murder."

Josie changed the subject. "Did you know that Claudia was leaving the practice office to go to lunch almost daily for the last year? Sometimes for more than an hour. Sometimes so long she had to push her patients back?"

Surprise washed over Beau's face. "No," he said. "I didn't know that. Who was she having lunch with?"

Noah said, "We were hoping you could tell us."

Beau sighed. He pushed the heels of his hands into his eyes and rubbed. "I have no idea," he said. "You'd have to ask Trudy."

"We did," said Josie. "She doesn't know who Claudia was seeing."

"I can't help you with that," said Beau.

Noah said, "Claudia told Eve she thought she was being followed. Back in October. Did you know about that? Did Claudia ever say anything like that to you?"

Beau blinked slowly. "What? No, no, no. I never—she never

—she thought she was being followed? She never said a word. I can't help you there either."

Josie said, "Then tell us about Ron Abbott."

Beau shook his head and then squeezed the bridge of his nose between his thumb and forefinger. "He's dead."

"We know," said Noah. "He killed his wife and then turned the gun on himself."

"Tragic."

"Was he your patient?" asked Josie.

"Why are you asking me about a dead man? A dead man didn't kill my wife, didn't kill Eve."

Noah said, "No, but someone who knew him, who cared for him, might have."

Josie repeated, "Was he your patient?"

Beau studied the bourbon glass again. "Yes. For a very short time. Ron was obsessive, controlling, cruel. He was never going to benefit from counseling. I tried my best, but as predicted, he bailed after only a month."

"Because you were having an affair with Casey Abbott?" Josie asked.

Beau chuckled. "You just think I have affairs with everyone now, don't you? Because of Eve."

Noah said, "Did you sleep with Casey Abbott?"

"No. I most certainly did not," Beau answered. "But even if I had, what difference does it make? She's dead. Her husband's dead. Everyone's dead! Except the killer that you two don't seem very motivated to find."

"The Abbott murder-suicide made the local news in Fairfield, Lenore County but WYEP didn't pick it up. Did you have it killed?" Josie asked.

Beau hung his head. "I'm not proud of this but yes, I spoke to the WYEP news director and asked him not to run the story. He did it as a favor to me."

The ease with which he admitted this made it sound like

the most truthful thing he had told them since his wife was murdered.

He added, "Will you leave me in peace now?"

Josie found the review in her pocket and took it out, smoothing out the creases on the bar. She pushed it over to Beau. "Did Ron Abbott write this?"

Beau read over the review with glassy eyes. "I have no idea."

"Were you aware of this review?" asked Noah.

Silence.

"Mr. Collins?" Josie said.

He picked up the bourbon and knocked it back in one gulp. He smacked his lips together and then wiped his face with the cuff of his sleeve. "Yes. I was aware of the review when it was posted several years ago. I don't know if Ron Abbott wrote it."

"Who made you aware of it?" asked Josie.

Beau's tone was laced with fatigue. "Claudia. She was upset. She took it quite seriously. But as I told her then, and as I am telling you now, I don't know who wrote it or why. After it was posted, I reviewed the files of all clients who had recently left the practice. There was no one I believed might have reason to write that review. I have never been inappropriate with a client. I have never had any flirtatious, romantic, or sexual relationship with any client, past or present."

"Not even with Casey Abbott?" asked Josie.

Beau didn't answer.

Noah said, "Then why would someone write this review?"

Beau stared longingly at the bottom of the empty glass. "Detectives, you're wasting your time with this. I don't know why someone I don't know would write a review like that. I always thought that the person who wrote that had me mixed up with a different marriage counselor, or maybe they just wanted nothing but to embarrass me and damage my reputation. Certainly, that was accomplished since it caused quite a bit of difficulty between me and Claudia."

Josie said, "If you were worried about damage to your reputation, why didn't you track the guy down and sue him for libel? Or at least request to have the review removed?"

"Have you tried getting in touch with Citizen Review yet?"

"Not yet," said Josie. "We wanted to hear from you first."

"Well then. I'll leave you to that. You'll quickly see why I was not able to do either of those things. Believe me, that stupid review is a stain. Thank God now that it's been so many years, it's not as prevalent when you pull up our reviews. For a while, it was a very big issue."

Josie said, "We would like you to provide us with the names of all patients who stopped receiving counseling from you around this time."

"I cannot possibly disclose something like that. You must know that. Without a very specific threat, I cannot give you names. Even though my intention is to close the practice now that Claudia is gone, it could still be an issue with my licensing should any of the former patients whose names I gave you take issue with it, which they might. If you want names, I have to ask for a warrant although, even with my limited legal knowledge, I'm pretty sure that it is extremely unlikely that a judge would sign a warrant for a blanket request."

Josie met Noah's eyes. They both knew that Beau was right. They could certainly prepare a warrant, but with no way to draw a connection between any names they might get from Beau's files and the imminent threat posed by the killer, no judge would grant it.

Beau continued, "Also, bear in mind that this person, whoever he or she may be, chose to post their complaints anonymously, on a site that is unreliable at best. These are pretty serious accusations and yet, no formal complaints were ever lodged against me with the state licensing board. You can check that for yourselves. Trust me when I tell you that this was someone playing a cruel game and the object was to ruin my reputation. Ultimately, it did not work."

Noah said, "I just want to be clear: you are absolutely sure that this review was not written by a former patient."

Beau hesitated before answering. "Unless Ron Abbott wrote that, in which case, I've already told you it's all lies, then yes, I'm sure. Now please. Leave me alone."

They did as he asked. Josie was relieved to be out of the hotel and back in her car. She turned the ignition and pulled out of the Eudora parking lot. "He's lying," she said. "He had an affair with Casey Abbott."

"Yes," Noah agreed. "We can call the Lenore County Sheriff's office and talk to whoever worked the Abbott case. See if they turned up anything. Maybe contact her coworkers, the neighbors, his brother. Someone has to know something."

"But that doesn't get us any closer to the killer," Josie said. "Collins is right. A dead man did not kill Claudia or Eve. I just cannot figure this guy out. Why lie about the Abbotts? It doesn't matter anymore."

"Because if he admits to having one affair with a patient, he's got to admit to having others?" Noah suggested.

"Sure," Josie said. "But what if the stuff he's not telling us is the key to cracking this entire case? There has to be something he knows that he's not telling us. He must have some idea who is behind all this. His wife and his mistress are dead. His practice, his show, book deals, everything he has is now on the line. Does he even have those things without Claudia? Their success is a result of them putting themselves out there as some kind of perfect couple—whether that was true or not."

"If he loved his wife as much as he claims," Noah said, "none of that other stuff would matter. If anything ever happened to you, I'd burn this entire city down finding the person who hurt you."

THIRTY-TWO

Beau Collins was right about the Citizen Review website. After getting the warrant signed, Josie and Noah spent the rest of Sunday night just trying to track down where to send the warrant for information about the site—to no avail. Every email address they tried was defunct. When they finally found a name associated with the site, it was so generic that they had no way of narrowing where to find the owner. By early Monday morning, the entire team sat at their desks, each down their own internet rabbit hole trying to find more information about the site and how they could access personal information about reviewers.

Another dead end.

Josie momentarily gave up on Citizen Review and called the women's center to verify the anonymous thirty-thousand-dollar donation from October. But they had not received it. Not in October or any other month in the last year. In fact, Josie's contact at the women's center laughed so hard and so long at the suggestion that the rest of the team heard her through the phone receiver. Josie hung up and briefed the team. They were discussing what might have happened to the money when the

Chief strode out of his office and across the great room. He walked over to the television affixed to the wall, found the remote control, and clicked to power the TV on. Then he turned the channel to WYEP. Beau Collins's face filled the screen. He was clean-shaven but his face looked sallow and sunken, even with the copious amounts of make-up that had obviously been caked on his skin.

The Chief turned to them. "This bastard is live, on the air, right now." His acne-scarred face flushed bright red. With each word, his voice grew louder, until he was shouting. "His wife was violently murdered in his home on their wedding anniversary, then her assistant—his damn mistress—was murdered, and this jackass is doing a show about relationships right now. Did any of you know about this?"

They all shook their heads. Josie leaned back in her chair and folded her arms across her chest. "We never discussed whether or not he would move forward with the show."

Gretchen said, "I just assumed he wouldn't be stupid enough to do live shows this week."

The Chief pointed the remote over his shoulder at the screen. "Amber's been working her ass off to keep the press out of this as long as possible so we could control how and when they found out. She worked so hard I gave her the morning off! This guy is going to blurt it out. Then we could have a nightmare on our hands."

Gretchen stood and walked over to the Chief. She took the remote from his hand and pointed it at the television. "Or it could bring the kind of attention that makes it much harder for the killer to operate without getting caught."

"I think this killer wants the attention," said Noah. "What better way to punish Beau Collins—which seems to be the goal —than to bring him low in front of the public?"

The Chief shouted at the screen as if it were Beau himself.

"Take a hiatus! Go off the air for a few weeks like a normal person!"

Josie said, "It would have gotten out soon anyway, Chief, even with Amber's efforts. Trudy Dawson, the practice secretary, was planning to start calling Claudia's patients today to inform them."

Gretchen clicked a button on the remote and the volume increased. Beau's voice was nowhere near as confident as it had been in the previous videos that Josie had seen.

"Faithful viewers, I know you're all wondering, after Friday's show, how the big anniversary dinner went! Maybe you were online this weekend, expecting to see photos or videos. Believe me, we were prepared to bring you what you wanted. Unfortunately—" His voice cracked. He lowered his chin to his chest for a long, agonizing moment. Then he sucked in a breath and looked at the camera once more. Tears glistened in his eyes. When he next spoke, his voice was husky, "Dearest viewers, friends, colleagues, I'm devastated to tell you that, over the weekend, I lost my beloved Claudia. She passed away unexpectedly. I can't even believe I'm saying these words." A tear slid from the corner of his eye and rolled down the side of his nose. He took another moment to compose himself. Still, his voice was unsteady. "I don't know how I will go on without my partner, the love of my life. I don't know what life is without Claudia. She was everything to me. She made me better in every way. You saw—you all saw how she brought out the best in me on this very show. We had so much planned for the future. Our future, the future of this show. We hoped to help so many couples know the deep, unshakeable connection that Claudia and I spent our lives building and refining."

He paused. The camera was still tight on his face, close enough for them to see one of his eyelids twitch. More tears came and he wiped them away with a tissue that someone off-camera handed him. With another tremulous breath, he went on, "All that planning right down the drain. Sometimes life does that to you. Sometimes no matter how carefully you plan or how hard you try, things just happen. Sometimes it's an unexpected external force." He cleared his throat, swallowed twice. "Like an unimaginable tragedy."

Josie was on her feet, moving over to Gretchen's side as the camera panned out, away from Beau's face, giving him time to shift in his seat. Then he looked to another camera and went on. "And sometimes it's your own failure. We don't always talk about failure on this show because we want all of you to succeed! But failure—it, um, it's real and everyone goes through it. My, uh, wife, for example. You know, I think she would tell you—" He stopped and leaned forward, lifting a coffee mug to his lips. His hand shook as he took a generous swig and then used his sleeve to wipe his upper lip.

"My wife, Claudia," Beau continued. "Would have told you that her greatest failure was not getting this position she wanted so badly when we were very young. She was a few years out of her PhD program. She wanted so badly to work with victims of domestic violence."

Noah and Mettner now stood behind Josie, Gretchen, and the Chief. Noah said, "What is this guy doing?"

Mettner added, "His wife was just murdered and he's on TV talking about her biggest failure? Is he for real?"

Josie held up a hand to silence them as Beau kept talking. "No one was better qualified than Claudia for that position. Maybe I'm biased"—weak smile—"but she deserved it, and she would have been a great asset to that program. Sadly, they went another way. Claudia didn't get the position. To say she was devastated is putting it mildly. Of course, now we know that it was for the best. We went into practice together, eventually wrote a book, and we were lucky and privileged to spend the last few years with all of you!"

"I've seen enough," said the Chief.

Josie went to her desk and snatched her coat from the back of her chair. "Let's go," she said. "We have to get over there."

Everyone looked at her. "Right now?" said Mettner.

Josie said, "His wife's greatest failure? What does that sound like to you?" She looked at Noah.

"A question from their Five Familiar Facts game," he said. "Holy shit. The killer contacted him."

Gretchen muted the television. "And told him to go on air today and answer that question."

The Chief hollered so loud, it startled all of them. "Don't stand here talking about it! Get your asses over to that studio!"

THIRTY-THREE

For the first time since the investigation started, Beau Collins looked frightened. Seated in a large leather executive chair behind the desk in his office at the WYEP studio, he also looked small. His gaze darted around the room, which had grown very crowded in the last few minutes. Josie was practically shoulder to shoulder with Noah and Margot Huff. Behind them were Kathy, the producer, and Marissa Parker, the floor director. Lingering at the doorway to the office were a couple of other people Josie remembered from Saturday.

Josie said, "Everyone except Mr. Collins, if you would, please go out into the studio and wait."

When they were alone with Beau, Josie closed the door and advanced on him, leaning over the desk. She said, "Mr. Collins, did the killer contact you directly?"

He said nothing, glancing at the closed door. "Yes."

Noah sighed. "Why didn't you call us as soon as you heard from him?"

Beau held up his hands and shrugged. "What was I supposed to do? There wasn't time!"

Noah said, "You had enough time to script that show. You could have called us."

Josie said, "How did he contact you?"

He picked up his phone, punched in a passcode and then handed it to Josie. "From Claudia's phone."

On the screen was a series of text messages between Beau and the contact he had named "Beautiful Claudia" with three heart emojis after it. Scrolling back, Josie saw several messages between husband and wife about the anniversary dinner and scores of other scheduling issues. There was nothing at all unusual in them unless you counted the lack of emotion or playfulness in their exchanges. Even Josie and Noah sent each other heart and kissing emojis now and then. She went back to the most recent exchange. A message had come in from Claudia's phone at seven thirty that morning. Two full hours before the show aired. Josie set aside her fury for the moment and read:

> *Play my game and no one else has to die. Go on air today. Tell them the answer to this question: what is my wife's greatest failure? Get it right or pay the price. If you don't go on air at all, there will be consequences.*

After that was a series of texts from Beau, each one more and more desperate.

> *Who is this? What do you want?*

> *Why are you doing this?*

> *Are you still there? Hello? Please answer.*

> *ANSWER ME! WHY ARE YOU DOING THIS TO ME?*

There was no response.

Josie scrolled back up to the time period before Claudia's murder and studied the messages. "You and Claudia have the same model phone?"

He nodded. "We got a deal on them."

Josie said, "You can tell when she's read your messages."

Beau nodded eagerly and pointed to the phone. "Yes! That's right. You can see from the older messages, it says 'read' under them. None of the new messages say that. I don't understand what happened. What does it mean?"

Josie handed the phone to Noah so that he could look at it. A moment later, he said, "I'll call dispatch, see if I can get them to ping Claudia's phone again."

He slid the phone back across the desk to Beau and left the room. Josie said, "It means that the killer turned off her phone as soon as he knew you'd read his text. He knows enough to leave it turned off most of the time. Otherwise, we would be able to locate him pretty quickly."

Beau grabbed the phone excitedly and waved it in the air. "But it was on this morning! You can see where he was then, can't you?"

"That's what my colleague is checking on right now, yes," said Josie. Somehow, she didn't think that it would lead anywhere. So far, the killer had been several steps ahead of them. He was savvy, sophisticated, and seemed to know a fair amount about the ways in which police used technology to track criminals—or at least enough to have eluded them thus far.

"Then we can find him!" Beau said, the naked hope in his voice so childlike and desperate that Josie actually felt badly for him.

"It's not that simple," she told him.

"But it is! You ping this, or whatever you do to figure out where it was this morning. You go there. You arrest him and this nightmare is over."

Josie said, "Mr. Collins, if this guy knows enough to turn

her phone on and off so we can't locate him, I don't think he would be stupid enough to stay in the place he last turned it on. But we will certainly search the area where it was last turned on for any clues."

"I did what he said," Beau said. "I played by his rules. That means he'll stop, right?"

Josie's stomach burned. "Mr. Collins, why would this killer want you to go on television and talk about your wife's greatest failure?"

Beau looked everywhere but at Josie. A framed photo of him and Claudia in front of the Eiffel Tower sat next to his laptop. He picked it up and turned it toward her. "I always wanted to go to Paris," he said.

Josie wondered where he was going with this. Had he cracked under the stress?

"I grew up on fishing boats in Maine. What did I know about Paris? It seemed like the height of sophistication to me." He chuckled. "Silly, I know. When we sold the first million copies of our book, Claudia surprised me with a trip to Paris. Look at us. We were so happy."

Josie took another glance at the photo. It had been taken during the day. Sunlight cascaded over Claudia's long blonde hair, making it almost as sparkly as her giant smile. Beau stood behind her, his arms circling her waist. His cheek was pressed into her temple as he, too, grinned for the camera. They did, in fact, look happy and very much in love.

Beau said, "That was before... all this. Before we even got our first big royalty check. She actually dipped into our savings to finance that trip, knowing we'd have money from the sale of the book coming after. We were just two broke marriage counselors then." He laughed. "Feeling like we'd just hit the lottery."

"Mr. Collins?" Josie said.

Beau blinked several times. His eyes were glassy with fresh tears. "We have money now. A lot of money. But none of it means anything without Claudia. Why would he keep torturing me if he's already taken away the most important person in my life?"

The door swooshed open. Noah stood with his cell phone in hand. "Last ping was at the city park—well inside of it. It was a couple of hours ago, but we should probably take a look."

Josie reached over the desk and pressed a hand over Beau Collins's. "We have to go. If the killer makes any further contact with you, you need to call us immediately. Or take your phone out to the officer we have watching you. If you tell him the killer has just messaged, he can call dispatch and have them ping Claudia's phone right then and there. It may be the only way we can find this guy—and put a stop to all of this."

THIRTY-FOUR

Josie huffed, watching her breath dissipate before her, as she climbed one of the more remote hiking trails in the city park. It was almost at the opposite end of the park from Lovers' Cave, for which Josie was grateful. She had no desire to revisit that scene any time soon, with or without her team. On either side of them, trees rose toward the sky, their trunks like tall, dark sentries stretching off as far as the eye could see. Josie's calves burned and in spite of the fact that the weather had dropped below freezing, sweat gathered along the back of her neck. She unzipped her coat and kept trudging. Behind her, the footsteps of the rest of the team crunched over the dirt. Heavy breathing could also be heard. Gretchen mumbled, "I should not be this out of shape."

"Too many pecan croissants?" Mettner teased.

"I'm not too out of shape to kick your ass, Mett. Just remember that."

Noah laughed. "I'd actually pay to see that."

Josie was too focused on the path ahead to join in the banter. She looked at the map on her phone and stopped. "I think this is it," she said.

Turning in a circle, her heart sank. They were in the middle of a trail that hardly anyone used, mostly due to the steep incline that snaked around the northernmost part of the park, near where Denton University bordered it. Sometimes students used the path to access the park.

Mettner said, "There's nothing here. What's so special about this spot?"

"Nothing," said Noah. "That's why he chose it."

Gretchen looked back down from the direction they'd come. "This comes up from the main area of the park and what? Loops back down?"

"Yeah," said Noah. "The other end of it comes out where the softball fields are but it's so steep not that many people use it."

"But enough people do for him to blend in," said Mettner. "This park is still pretty active, even for January, especially during the day."

As if proving his point, two women power-walked up behind them, shooting dirty looks at the detectives as they edged their way around them.

"Shit," said Josie once they were out of earshot. "There are three access points to this trail, assuming he didn't cut through the woods."

"And it's been almost four hours since he was here," said Mettner. "Another dead end."

"No," Josie said. "It doesn't have to be. We can get another geo-fence—"

"Which is going to show what?" said Mettner. "Nothing. This guy is too smart."

"But even the smart ones mess up from time to time," said Josie. "It's worth a try. We run through the license plate readers near the park."

"'Cause that worked out so well for us last time," Mettner groused.

"Hey," Noah said, his tone a warning. "We've got to try everything. You saw what this guy is capable of."

Gretchen sighed. "It's worth a try. He's obviously still in the area. I think we should also use the dog."

All eyes turned toward Josie. A long, pregnant moment unfurled itself between her and the rest of them. When the silence was too uncomfortable for her to bear, she snapped, "What?"

No one spoke.

Josie tried to take the edge off her tone. "Listen, I get that this is awkward. Luke and I used to be engaged. Luke..." She trailed off.

Noah filled in, "Betrayed you in every possible way?"

"Ouch," Mettner said under his breath.

Gretchen grimaced. "Not just you, boss. All of us."

Josie opened her mouth to defend Luke but then clamped it shut. Noah and Gretchen were right. So why did she feel the urge to speak up for him? Was it because he'd paid a horrible price for all the poor choices he'd made? She didn't remember much from the night they'd spent together five years ago but she did remember the conversation they'd had afterward, when he and Blue had come to Denton to help police find a missing seven-year-old girl. The Luke she'd talked to that day was not the man who had betrayed her and all of their colleagues. His experiences had humbled him—broken him, even. For years, he had hidden on his sister's farm where he could have safely remained for the rest of his days, in seclusion. Instead, he was trying to rebuild. To find lost souls. To help people.

Josie sighed. "All of that is in the past. Really. It's been years. He served his time. He'll never wear the uniform again. But he's here whether we like it or not. The Chief hired him as a consultant, so I'm going to tell you the same thing the Chief would: we need to view Luke as just another resource. A resource this department needs badly. That is it. That is all."

"His dog is incredible," Noah conceded.

"Okay," Mettner said. "We call in the dog. But what are we going to use to scent him?"

"Eve Bowers's car," said Gretchen. "We need to do it. We can get the car towed here, get Luke to meet us with the dog. We have nothing else."

They went quiet as a man jogged up the path, running past them without so much as a glance.

Once he was out of sight, Mettner said, "It's true. We've got nothing else."

Noah stomped his feet and shoved his hands into his coat pockets. "All right, well, we need to come up with some kind of plan instead of standing around here freezing our asses off all day. I can do the geo-fence."

Mettner said, "I'll run the LPRs and see if we can get anything from surveillance in this area, residential and commercial."

Gretchen added, "I'll stay on Citizen Review and see if we can track down the angry reviewer."

Josie sighed. "I'll call Luke."

THIRTY-FIVE

An hour later, Josie sat in her blessedly warm vehicle in the city park lot closest to its main entrance watching a flatbed tow truck pull in with Eve Bowers's Nissan on it. Hummel followed in an SUV. Luke and Blue weren't far behind. She waited until everyone else was out of their vehicles before she joined them. Blue thumped his tail a few times when she approached. Josie knelt and gave him a few good pets behind his ears. Luke grinned at her. Returning a tight smile, Josie explained what they needed. She was relieved to see his face morph from a playful smile to all business. Moments later, the tow truck driver had lowered the back of the flatbed enough for Blue to lumber up onto it and sniff the driver's seat.

Hummel stood next to Josie, watching Luke give Blue instructions. "You sure this is gonna work?"

Josie sighed. "I don't know, but we're running out of leads to chase."

Seconds later, Blue scrambled down the back of the flatbed and trotted off toward the trail that Josie and the team had been on earlier. As he passed her and Hummel, Luke said, "He's got it."

The next few hours passed in a blur. Josie was glad that she and Noah had made running a regular part of their exercise routine. Blue kept both her and Luke at a steady jog, leading them with confidence and only stopping when Luke made him. He took them on the full loop around the park and then out of it, circling the central part of the city and heading south.

"When he finds the scent, he loses track of everything else," Luke said the first time he made Blue stop. He used a bottle of water and collapsible rubber bowl that he carried in a backpack to give the dog a drink.

Warm and flushed from exertion, Josie paced along the pavement, looking back in the direction from which they'd come. If this was the route the killer had traveled on foot, he'd taken pains to avoid the more congested areas of the city. Here it was still residential, but the homes were further apart and set back a good distance from the road. Even if any of the houses had cameras, they likely wouldn't pick up a man walking, and yet, there was enough foot traffic that he probably had not stood out to anyone. "I can call for a unit," she told Luke. "Have them meet us here. Blue can take a rest and get warm in the back before we continue."

Luke shook his head. "Nah, he's good for now." Blue was already tugging at the lead, nose working furiously. "I'll let you know when we need that unit, though."

They resumed the search with Blue in the lead, Luke behind him murmuring encouragement and Josie in the rear. She lost track of time. There was no chance to check her phone or watch. There was only the search. When they stopped again, they were in South Denton, and she estimated that they'd traveled nearly four miles from the city park. Luke made sure Blue was hydrated and then Josie called in a unit. After a short rest, Blue was ready to go again. Josie's mouth was dry, and she wondered just how far the killer had walked—or run? She wanted to ask Luke how long he thought Blue could reasonably keep searching, but she didn't dare break their concentration.

It was only when she saw Blue turn into a gravel driveway marked with a beat-up mailbox that she allowed hope to surge through her. A familiar house with a familiar truck came into view at the end of the driveway. Blue was about five feet from the truck when he made his passive alert, sitting obediently and regarding Luke with solemn eyes.

"This is it," Luke said.

"This is—" Josie's words were cut off by the sound of a man's grizzled voice.

"You all better stop right where you are, turn your asses around, and get off my property or there'll be hell to pay."

Archie Gamble stepped from behind the truck, a crossbow in his hands.

Blue shot to his feet and began barking at him.

In quick succession, Gamble waved the crossbow at each of them before settling it in the direction of Blue. Luke immediately put himself between Gamble and the dog. He threw his hands up and said, "We don't want any trouble. Just stop pointing that at my dog."

Josie's service pistol was in her hands. She took on a shooter's stance and angled herself so that if she had to fire, she would not risk injuring Luke or Blue. "Mr. Gamble, lower that weapon right now."

He turned it toward Josie. "You're on private property, miss."

"I'm also a detective with the Denton Police Department, and I am instructing you to lower that weapon right now."

Luke gave Blue a command and the dog stopped barking. A low growl emanated from his throat as he peered between Luke's legs at Gamble.

A humorless laugh erupted from Gamble's throat. The bow

wobbled in his grip. Josie's eyes were glued to the bolt, loaded, ready to be fired. Its broadhead had three blades. Gamble said, "You gonna shoot me? On my own property?"

"Not if you put that down," Josie said.

Luke said, "Sir, we're really sorry. We were conducting a search. The dog led us onto your property. We meant no harm. We're happy to leave if you'll lower your weapon."

Archie glanced over at Luke, whose hands were still up. Getting a good look at them now, he froze, then turned his body in Luke's direction, lowering the bow somewhat. "What the hell happened to your hands?"

Luke glanced at Josie. She gave him a slight nod, indicating he could continue to engage with Gamble. He already had the man's attention, and the bow wasn't pointed at any of them for now.

"It's a long story," Luke told him. "I'd be happy to tell you about it sometime, but maybe over a beer and not a crossbow."

As if just realizing the bow was in his hands, Archie looked down at it. He laughed and let it fall to his side. Looking over at Josie, he scowled. "Guess you won't be happy till I'm not holding this, huh?"

Josie nodded at him. He turned and put the crossbow into the bed of his pickup. Once he had taken a few steps away from it, Josie holstered her weapon. He took a closer look at her. "You," he said. "You were here the other night."

"Yes."

"'Bout some lady and a car."

"That's right," said Josie.

"You sent those damn animal rights people over here. Trying to collect the cats. You got some nerve, you know that?"

Josie said nothing.

The crunch of gravel sounded from behind her. She chanced a look over her shoulder. Relief flooded her. The cruiser that had been on-call most of the afternoon for when

Blue needed to rest and get warm had just pulled into the driveway. Two uniformed officers got out. Josie signaled them to wait.

Archie scowled. "What's the problem now?"

"Our search dog followed the scent of the suspect in two homicides to right here in your driveway. What can you tell us about that?"

One of Gamble's bushy brows rose. "I'll tell you this. You better get you a warrant and me a lawyer before you say another word. Now get the hell off my property."

"I'll do that," Josie said. "While I do, my colleagues are going to hold the property."

"Hold it?" Gamble said. "What in the hell does that mean?"

One of the uniformed officers stepped forward. "Come with me, sir," he instructed Gamble.

"The hell I will!" Gamble snarled.

The other officer approached. "Is there anyone else here with you?"

"No, now get off my property!"

"We can't do that, sir," said the first officer.

Josie let them handle the situation. They'd make sure that Gamble didn't go back inside his home and tamper with any potential evidence before the warrant could be served. They'd also clear the premises to make sure there was no one else there.

Keeping her eyes on the three men, Josie waved Luke and Blue toward the road. She followed with her back to them, watching as Gamble argued heatedly with the men.

Once out by the road, several feet from Gamble's driveway, Luke let out a long breath. Josie didn't notice just how badly he was trembling until Blue whined. Luke dropped to his knees and the dog licked at his cheeks. "It's okay, boy. It's okay."

He lifted his mangled hands to touch Blue's face, but they were quivering too badly for him to pet the dog.

"Luke," Josie said.

He curled into himself, head on his knees. Blue whined again and nuzzled the back of Luke's neck.

Josie had seen him like this once before. He'd helped her locate a witness but when they found the guy, he had been murdered. The crime scene had brought back a great deal of trauma for Luke. His voice was muffled. "It's okay. It's okay."

Josie got onto her knees next to him and slung an arm across his back. She brought her face to his ear. He smelled like blood-hound and aftershave. "Luke, look at me."

He shook his head. Blue yelped. Patting the dog's head, she assured him, "Everything's okay, boy."

She riffled through Luke's backpack until she found a bottle of water. "Luke, sit up and drink this."

Slowly, he lifted his head. His face was ashen. He reached for the bottle, but his hands were still too shaky. Josie put the bottle down and grabbed his hands with hers. "Look at me," she told him. "You're fine. You're safe."

In her grip, his hands felt odd, not like hands at all, but like two badly restructured mounds of gnarled bone, metal plates, and lumpy flesh. How did it not bother him? Resisting the urge to look at each one up close, Josie held his gaze until the panic fled his blue eyes and was replaced by something close to relief. He was coming back to himself. Next to them, Blue's tail wagged. He snuffled at Luke's shoulder.

Luke pulled his hands away and swiped them down the front of his jacket. "You should call about that warrant," he mumbled.

Josie didn't move. "Luke—"

He stood up, inhaling a shaky breath, and turned away from her. "I'm okay," he said. "I— You should get your warrant. Do what you need to do."

He wouldn't look at her, but he seemed to be functioning a hell of a lot better than he had been moments ago. Leaning over, he rubbed Blue's sides and was rewarded with slobbery kisses to his face.

Josie took her cell phone from her pocket and called the team.

THIRTY-SIX
DIARY ENTRY, UNDATED

There was an accident. That's what he tells me. He says he's my husband, but I don't remember him. I don't remember this house. My life. This man is cruel. It doesn't seem like I would be married to someone like him. Then again, I didn't know who I was before until I found this diary. Now I know that I betrayed my husband in the most terrible way. Now I understand why he treats me so badly. I try hard every day to bring back the past. It won't come. There are only flashes from the accident. I can't make sense of them yet. Mostly, I am just plagued with the feeling that there is something crucially important I'm supposed to recall, and I simply can't.

I wish I could remember the man I fell in love with, the object of my betrayal. If he loved me so much, where has he gone?

THIRTY-SEVEN

Josie felt the force of Archie Gamble's glare as he walked from the cruiser parked in his driveway to the road where Josie, Noah, and Mettner stood, waiting to enter the property. Two uniformed officers flanked him. They'd amassed enough police cruisers along the road, with headlights on, to fight off the darkness falling all around them. It was dinner time but no one was interested in eating. Because Gamble was not exactly thrilled about them being there, they'd decided to escort him to a different cruiser, parked on the roadside, where he couldn't watch and protest their every move, at least until Josie, Noah, and Mettner had completed the search. As Archie passed them on his way toward it, a deep, phlegmy noise came from his throat. He turned and spit over his shoulder, a glob of yellow-brown mucus landing on Josie's boot. She ignored it, instead staring him down, unblinking, until he looked away first. Next to her, Noah muttered, "I'd really like to punch that guy in the face."

"Get in line," said Mettner. He pulled a pair of latex gloves from his coat pocket and put them on.

Josie stared down at the spit globule. "I'm going to need one of you to bag this."

Noah said, "What?"

She looked over to see that Archie Gamble was now arguing with one of the uniformed officers, gesticulating wildly, an unlit cigarette in his mouth. He would not be allowed to smoke in the cruiser. "My boot. The spit. Bag it. It's a DNA sample."

Mettner walked over and looked down at it as well. "You're kidding, right?"

"Not even a little bit," Josie said. "We're not on his property. This is discarded spit."

Mettner stared at her.

Noah said, "We can get DNA from inside the house. The warrant is broad enough for us to collect DNA from the premises. This guy's got discarded cigarette butts everywhere."

Josie smiled. "We barely had enough probable cause to get that warrant signed in the first place. Any defense attorney worth their salt will move to suppress the DNA gathered from those cigarette butts found on his property. We can collect them, but I also want this sample."

Mettner sighed, "I'll get an evidence bag."

"Just a minute," said Noah. "We keep changes of clothes in the backs of our cars. I'll grab your back-up boots."

Gamble glowered at Noah as he ran past the cruiser, down the road to their vehicle. When he returned carrying a pair of boots, a slow grin spread across Gamble's face. He turned toward Josie, teeth gleaming, looking very satisfied with himself. Josie met his leer head-on and grinned right back at him until his smile faltered and the expression on his face turned to uncertainty. The uniformed officer said something, drawing Gamble's attention away from her. Gamble didn't look back again.

Once the sample had been stowed and Josie outfitted with a clean pair of boots, she and Noah also put on gloves and walked onto the property. While Mettner began searching the truck, using a flashlight, Josie and Noah went inside the house. Gretchen had gone home to sleep. The smell hit Josie first, an eye-watering combination of nicotine, sweat, and spoiled food. Behind her, Noah gagged. "Good God," he said.

Josie wrinkled her nose. "Let's get through this as quickly as possible."

"It won't be fast enough. Look at this place."

The living and dining room areas were contained in one large, open room. Along one wall was a doorway that appeared to lead to a hall. Toward the back of the house, Josie could see a portion of the kitchen. Every surface, including most of the floors, was covered with stuff. Her mind tried to process it, but she didn't know where to look first. To one side was a couch-shaped pile of pillows, clothes, and magazines. As Josie walked closer, she saw they were all pornographic magazines. Naked women in all manner of poses were splayed before her on the open pages. A small area in one corner of the couch about the size of Archie Gamble's rear end was free from any detritus. Ashtrays, beer cans, empty, crushed cigarette packs, and old food containers covered the coffee table. Three televisions leaned against one wall. Only one of them was plugged in. Coffee cans filled with bolts, nails, washers, and drill bits littered the floor. Josie catalogued other items that seemed to be randomly strewn about: a bike seat, a bent lawn chair, a cane, a tackle box, a bowling ball, and a dresser drawer filled with Allen wrenches. Everywhere she looked was more of the same.

Noah said, "This guy is a hoarder. I mean, look at this." He pointed to a long table in the dining area filled with more stuff that seemed completely random: a microwave, a metal bedpan filled with remote controls, a pile of worn leather work gloves, an old neon sign advertising Black Label beer, and a plastic lawn decoration in the shape of a snowman. "How the hell are we supposed to find anything in here?"

The front door squealed. Mettner appeared. His eyes widened. "You've got to be kidding me."

"I wish we were," said Josie.

"The smell," Mettner complained. "That's why this guy was on his porch at night. Who could sleep in here?"

Noah picked his way toward the hall. "Maybe the bedrooms aren't so bad."

"Doubtful," Mettner mumbled. "How are we even going to do this?"

"Thoroughly," Josie said. "You start in here. I'll start in the kitchen and Noah will take... whatever rooms are back there."

The smell in the kitchen was stronger. A tower of dirty dishes in the sink threatened to topple. Half-eaten, moldy microwave meals were strewn across the countertop. More empty cans of beer and ashtrays brimming with crushed cigarette butts covered the small Formica table. More magazines featuring naked women were spread across the rest of it. A couple of folded newspapers peeked from beneath them. The only clear surface in the room was a chair tucked under the table. Its vinyl seat was pristine. Josie stood behind it and took a photo to preserve exactly how she had found the table. Then she carefully moved the magazines and newspapers aside. She found a fork crusted over with some substance. Another full ashtray. A lighter. A pair of glasses. A pen.

A small, lined notebook with handwritten notes taken in careful block letters.

The top of the first page bore the initials "C.C." Beneath it were columns headed with dates. Beneath each date were times and what appeared to be locations. The entries started a more than a month earlier. The first date was 11/13 and under it the notations read:

7a studio (alone)

1030a office

1p the grotto

213p office

5p home (alone)

The combination of the initials C.C. and the notations about "studio" and "office" were enough to convince Josie that Archie Gamble had been following Claudia Collins for at least the two months before her murder. He had even noted when she was alone.

"Noah? Mett?" she called.

She flipped more pages. It was more and more of the same, documenting where C.C. was at any given time of day, when she arrived and left, and whether she traveled alone. Some of the notations were strange combinations of numbers and letters: 4342SSRD appeared twice, but Josie couldn't figure out what it meant. She snapped some photos and called for Noah and Mettner again. "I think I've got something!"

Mettner appeared in the entrance to the kitchen. Noah followed a few seconds later. Josie showed them what she had found.

"We need to comb every last inch of the rest of this place," Noah said. "And take Gamble in for questioning."

THIRTY-EIGHT

Hours later, after midnight, Archie Gamble strolled out of Denton Police headquarters, whistling a jaunty tune and smiling at anyone who glanced at him, including the crush of reporters surrounding the building, hungry for any news on the murder of Claudia Collins. He ignored them as he got into his truck and drove away. The moment Gamble had been taken into custody for questioning, he had demanded to contact an attorney. Shortly after that, Denton's premier criminal defense attorney, Andrew Bowen, arrived to represent Gamble. Josie and Bowen went back several years, and it was not a pleasant history. He shot daggers at her while she explained the situation as well as what they had found on Gamble's property. Unfortunately for the Denton PD, Claudia Collins and Eve Bowers, the only evidence they had retrieved was the notebook. Despite an exhaustive search, Claudia's phone was not located. The contents of the burn barrel would take days, if not weeks, to process. In addition, among the myriad possessions in Archie Gamble's home, they didn't find anything that might have been used to strangle Eve Bowers.

Bowen advised Gamble not to speak to them at all. Without

verification that the book belonged to Gamble or that it was his handwriting in it or irrefutable proof that C.C. was Claudia Collins, and without any other evidence pertaining to Claudia Collins found anywhere on his property, they had to let him go. A notebook with the initials C.C. written inside with a schedule that was suspiciously close to Claudia's would not be enough to charge Gamble with the murder of Claudia Collins. They had even less to justify charging him with the murder of Eve Bowers. Other than finding his name written down in her home, there was no discernible connection between them. They didn't have enough to charge him with anything.

Bowen knew it. Gamble knew it. Josie and the team knew it.

They were at an impasse.

When Gretchen came back in for the night shift, Josie, Noah and Mettner briefed her, and went home. On autopilot, Josie showered and changed, microwaved herself and Noah something for dinner, and fed, walked, and played with Trout. Once the three of them were nestled in bed together, Josie's mind went into overdrive.

Was Archie Gamble the killer? Had he gleaned all the personal information the killer seemed to know about the Collinses from stalking Claudia? Was he the person Claudia believed had been following her? Had she somehow caught onto him and figured out his name? Written it down on a piece of junk mail that had somehow ended up in Eve's possession? Kathy had said that she'd overheard Claudia telling Eve she thought she was being followed. Had Claudia given Eve the envelope with Gamble's name on it so that Eve could look into him? If that was the case, why hadn't Eve mentioned it the night of Claudia's murder?

Then there was Gamble. If he was the killer, where was he hiding Claudia's phone? Had he destroyed evidence from her murder in his burn barrel? But if that was the case, why wouldn't he destroy all of it? Why leave the notebook laying around? Or had he simply forgotten about it? Lost track of it in the mess that was his home? If he had been careful enough to burn physical evidence, why take other risks? Like drawing attention to himself by ditching Eve's car so close to his property? Unless he hadn't ever thought that it would lead to him. He had no idea that Eve had written his name down until they told him.

The killer's text to Beau Collins kept coming back to her:

Play my game and no one else has to die. Go on air today. Tell them the answer to this question: what is my wife's greatest failure? Get it right or pay the price. If you don't go on air at all, there will be consequences.

Beau had done as the killer asked. Did that mean he was finished killing? Would there be more messages? Josie had difficulty believing this killer would be able to stop. She looked over at Noah. He lay on his back, bare-chested, one hand folded behind his head, the other pointing the remote control at the television. Josie looked at the screen, but he was flipping through the guide so quickly, she could barely make out any of the names of shows. He wouldn't pick something. He hardly ever did. It had driven her crazy for years until she figured out that he wasn't looking for a show that would help him unwind. It was the act of searching that helped him relax.

For her, any show about restaurants or cooking or anything even remotely related to food would put her to sleep in seconds.

When he reached the limit of the channels available to them, he started over. Josie climbed over a snoring Trout and stretched out beside Noah, laying her head against his chest.

"You're doing all the thinking, aren't you?" he whispered into her hair.

Josie put a hand over his heart, its steady beat reassuring.

"Do you think Beau Collins answered the killer's question correctly?"

"I don't know," said Noah. "But I don't think this guy is done. He says it's a game but as vicious as this guy is? I don't see him letting Beau win it. Although if Gamble's our guy, we've just made it a hell of a lot harder for him to continue playing."

"True," Josie said. "The Chief put a unit outside his house."

"I don't know. He could easily sneak out the back, disappear on those twenty acres he's got, and come out somewhere no one would know to look for him. Where do we even go from here?"

"I think we need to consider former patients, people like the Abbotts," Josie said.

"But we can't do that if no one will tell us who these patients are," Noah reminded her. "Beau Collins is definitely not going to give up the names of any patients—not for anything."

"But Trudy might," Josie said. "I know it's a long shot, but I think we need to talk to her again. Confront her with what we know about the Abbotts and the review. She knows something she's not telling us."

"Then tomorrow we go talk to her again." Noah brought his arm down from behind his head and wrapped it around her. "How were things with Luke today?"

She hoped he didn't feel her stiffen. "Fine," she said. "I just —I think it's going to take him a while to adjust to being back out in the field."

"I guess we know what his greatest failure was," Noah muttered.

"Hey," said Josie, again seized by the compulsion to defend Luke.

"I'm sorry," Noah said, brushing his lips over her forehead. "I'm being mean. You were right about what you said earlier, about him facing the consequences of his actions and serving his time. He didn't have to come back out into the world and start working alongside law enforcement again. He's got to know people hate him, but he's trying to do a good thing and that should mean something."

Josie thought of Luke on his knees, his mutilated hands in hers, the panic running through him like a current of electricity. She didn't want to talk about him anymore. "How do you think you and I would do on a Familiar Five quiz?" she blurted.

Noah laughed. "I thought you didn't believe in that stuff."

"I don't," she said, tracing her fingers over the muscles of his abdomen. "But there's a big difference between not knowing how your partner takes their coffee and not knowing what they think their greatest failure is."

He squeezed her. "It's the same for us both. The failure thing."

"What do you mean?"

"You think your greatest failure is not saving your grandmother."

Josie's breath caught. She had failed at a lot of things in life. Stopping the woman posing as her mother from hurting people, herself included; being married; being engaged; saving her late husband; saving people she had sworn to protect and serve; solving cases. But if she had to choose her greatest failure of all, then yes, it was not being able to save her grandmother's life. She felt the uncharacteristic sting of tears behind her eyes. Her therapist had been working with her on trying to "emote" but Josie still hated it, and always resisted crying at all costs.

Swallowing over the lump in her throat, she said, "And you think your greatest failure is not getting to your mom's house ten minutes earlier."

Noah's body tensed. His voice was husky when he replied, "I guess we know each other pretty well then."

"No matter how many times we tell each other that those things weren't our fault," Josie said. "We'll never believe one another, will we?"

For both of them, the self-blame would always be there, rooted in their psyches. Immutable truths.

His fingers tangled in her hair. "Unfortunately. But you know, if you asked me what my wife's greatest failure was, that's not what I would say."

She shifted so she could look up at him. "Really? What do you think is my greatest failure?"

He smiled. Dropping the remote, he traced the scar on her face again. "It was not marrying me sooner."

THIRTY-NINE

By Tuesday morning, the number of reporters outside the police station had grown exponentially. With assurances from Chief Chitwood that he and Amber would handle the press, Josie and Noah headed out to speak with Trudy Dawson again. Heavy gray clouds filled the horizon by the time they got to the squat, single-story flat-roofed building in South Denton's commercial district that served as the Collinses' practice. It sat on its own parcel of land with a small asphalt parking lot. Only one car was parked in the spot nearest the front door. Josie parked next to it.

The office door was unlocked. Noah pushed it open and held it for Josie. She took two steps inside and found a scene eerily familiar to the one they'd found in the Collinses' dining room just three days earlier. There was no blood, but the other parallels were unmistakable.

She said, "Noah."

Her service weapon was in her hands. Behind her, she heard Noah's holster unsnap, then the sound his gun made when he slid it out of its holster. Her breathing slowed. Quietly, he said, "Let's clear it and then we'll call in the cavalry."

Josie nodded. The front door of the office opened directly

into a huge reception area. The walls were painted mauve, decorated with close-up photographs of flowers. Together, they moved past two rows of chairs bracketing a narrow coffee table toward a massive reception desk. Behind it sat Trudy Dawson, slumped in the chair, her chin against her chest. To the side of the desk, a dark hallway gaped. Noah kept his pistol trained on it while Josie reached beneath Trudy's curtain of hair and pressed two fingers to her throat. The moment she felt the perfect stillness of Trudy's body, she knew she wouldn't find a pulse.

She looked at Noah and shook her head. He nodded and signaled toward the hallway. Together, they worked their way through it, clearing each room as they came to it: two offices, a file room, bathroom, breakroom, and two closets. Finally, a rear entrance, locked. There was no one there. Nothing even looked amiss.

Except poor Trudy.

They holstered their weapons and returned to the parking lot, careful not to disturb any more of the scene than they already had. Josie took a slow walk around the building while Noah called dispatch. Outside, everything looked untouched, except the surveillance cameras. There were four in all, one on each side of the building. All of their lenses had been covered with black spray paint. Snowflakes began to fall lightly. When she returned to the car, Noah held open the door. "Get in," he said. "Stay warm. It's going to be hours before we can go back in."

Josie's breakfast churned in her stomach as she watched vehicles arrive one by one and pack the small parking lot. Two cruisers, the ERT SUV, an ambulance, Dr. Feist's small pickup truck and finally, Gretchen in an unmarked car. She got out and walked over to Josie and Noah's vehicle, climbing into the back seat. "Mett caught another call. Unattended death. What do you have?"

Josie and Noah brought her up to speed. When they finished, Gretchen sighed. "All right. We'll have to try to get the footage from the practice cameras to see if we can see the person who spray-painted them."

"I doubt we'll get anything," said Noah. "But we can try."

"I'll go ahead and collect surveillance footage from the other businesses along this road to see if anything turns up." A creak came from the back seat. Gretchen tapped a pen against Josie's shoulder. "We'll get him, boss. It's what we do."

"Thanks, Gretchen," Noah said. Once she exited the car, he took out his phone. Josie listened as he called the officer tasked with sitting outside of Archie Gamble's house. In the confines of the car, she could hear the officer's tinny voice. Gamble hadn't so much as poked his head outside since he returned home the night before. After he hung up, they sat in silence, watching ERT members come in and out of the office.

Josie thought about Trudy's mother. The ache in her heart that had started when she discovered Trudy slumped behind the desk worsened. Trudy had been so devoted to her mother. Alzheimer's was a horrible, ruthless disease. Josie had admired Trudy's determination to care for her mother at home. Now what would happen to the poor woman? If Trudy's brother didn't take the reins, she would have to go into a facility. Either way, life as she knew it was over. Josie said, "We need someone to go to Trudy's house. Her mother has Alzheimer's and can't be left alone, remember? There's a day nurse, but—"

Noah covered her hand with his. "Let me make some calls. I'll take care of it."

He must have sensed that she wanted to be alone because he got out of the car to make the calls. Finally, the ERT gave them the go-ahead to enter the building. They found crime scene equipment in the back of Hummel's SUV and suited up. Inside, Dr. Feist was already at Trudy's side, using gloved hands to gingerly lift Trudy's chin. Noah stood in front of the desk while Josie rounded it. "Same type of ligature marks," Dr. Feist said, pointing to the purplish-red striations circling Trudy's throat.

Dr. Feist continued, "It's almost identical to the injuries found on Eve Bowers's body. Looks like he used the same type of ligature."

Noah said, "Any guesses as to time of death?"

"She hasn't been dead very long, I can tell you that. She's only now starting to go into rigor. Based on my initial findings of her temperature and the temperature of this room, I'd say she was probably killed around eight or eight thirty this morning."

Noah said, "The day nurse at her home said she left at seven thirty this morning."

Josie said, "She would have gotten here by eight at the latest."

They had found her around nine fifteen. It was now after eleven.

Josie turned her attention to the items on the desk. The laptop screen was dark. The phone's receiver rested in its cradle. The photographs on the desk showed Trudy Dawson with an older woman and a younger man. Her mother and brother, no doubt.

Dr. Feist moved to the other side of Trudy Dawson's body and for the first time, Josie had an unobstructed view of Trudy's lap. One hand rested on her thigh, palm up, holding a wooden puzzle box shaped like a gift.

Acid burned in Josie's stomach. "Noah," she said.

He walked around the desk for a closer look.

Hummel emerged from the hallway. "Hey," he said. "I left it because I wanted you guys to see it. I'll get it processed and opened as soon as I can."

Josie said, "Thanks. If there is anything inside, I'd like to know as soon as possible. What about Trudy's phone? Is that here, or did he take it?"

Hummel said, "You mean, is this guy a collector of phones? No. It's here. So is her purse. The whole place looks pretty undisturbed."

Josie walked back to the front door and surveyed the room again without the rush of adrenaline that accompanied finding a dead body and without her anger. Her eyes traveled from the desk to the hallway. All Trudy would have had to do was stand up and walk four or five steps to get from her chair to the hall. The rear door was at the end of it.

Noah raised a brow in Josie's direction. Then he glanced down the hall and back to her. Following her thoughts before she voiced them, as he often did, Noah said, "She had a clear line of sight to the back door. It would have taken her seconds to get there."

Josie looked around at the chairs and the table. All of them looked perfectly in place. "There couldn't have been any appointments today. Beau announced on air yesterday that Claudia had passed away. Trudy would have come in to contact any patients who might not know."

Josie went back to the door and then walked slowly toward the desk. "Did she know him? He got close enough to kill her. She didn't run."

Noah said, "Maybe she didn't have time to run."

Josie looked all around the desk, bending over to look beneath it. "She didn't fight. Or if she did, he covered up the evidence. Put everything back into place."

Dr. Feist said, "From this cursory exam, I don't see any evidence of any other injuries, but I'll let you know once I've finished the autopsy."

Noah said, "If we could make the case that she knew him, we might be able to convince a judge to sign a warrant allowing us to see the names of some of the patients."

Josie shook her head. "They'd probably only let us see the names of the patients who had appointments for today that had been scheduled prior to Claudia's death. We should get a warrant for those. We need to talk to them, make sure none of them were here today."

Hummel said, "They weren't. Nobody was except for Trudy and the killer. Her computer screen was on when we got here. The security system app is on her desktop. It was open."

Noah said, "She was checking the cameras when this guy showed up?"

"Don't know," Hummel said. "All I can tell you is that the program was open. I did a quick review of the footage. Someone was here around seven forty-five although you can't see them. But it was around that time that the nozzle of a can of spray paint appears in the field of view of each camera. Each camera was spray-painted. The killer was careful enough not to be caught by any of them before or during."

"Great," Josie sighed. "Just great."

Noah said, "That's why Gretchen went to canvass the other businesses along this road. If we can't get anyone on film here, maybe one of the cameras from a nearby business caught something. A vehicle, maybe."

"I've seen enough," said Josie. "Hummel, let me know if you get any hits on any prints you've pulled. I need to know what's in the box as soon as possible."

"You got it, boss," he said.

The front door swung open. Officer Brennan's voice carried across the threshold. "Detective? Lieutenant? Detective Palmer's back. She says she's got something."

FORTY

Josie smoothed her hair back as she and Noah crowded behind Gretchen around a small laptop screen behind the counter of a rental car company. Prime Car Rental was situated across from the Collinses' building, and while it did not line up directly, their cameras had caught a sliver of the practice parking lot entrance. The manager sat directly in front of the computer, queuing up the footage for the second time.

Noah said, "Are you sure about this?"

"Yes," Gretchen said. "Watch again."

The manager pressed play. The screen filled with the parking lot just outside the front doors where several cars were parked. Beyond that was the road and on the other side of the road was the rise of a curb and then the smooth surface of blacktop where the entrance to the Collinses' parking lot began. The view only showed part of it. Josie knew that from this vantage point, facing the Collinses' office from across the street, the half of the entrance they were able to see was the side to the south of Denton proper. The timestamp on the bottom right of the screen read 8:28 a.m. As they watched, a car passed along the road, then a van, both traveling northbound, toward the city.

Several more cars flew past moving in the other direction, away from the city.

"Here it comes," said Gretchen. "Keep your eyes on the entrance to the Collinses' parking lot."

Another couple of seconds ticked by and then something blurry blipped across the screen, appearing for a second in the part of the entrance visible to the camera. Then it was gone.

"What are we looking at?" asked Noah.

Gretchen made a noise of frustration. She reached past the manager and after some manipulation, rewound the footage and paused it when the object appeared. "This is not a car," she said.

Josie leaned in closer, trying to make it out. "But it looks like a wheel. Sort of."

"Because it's a bike!" Gretchen said triumphantly. With her index finger, she traced the lines that reached out to the edges of the blurred half-circle. "These are the spokes. This is part of the tire. That—that square thing—it's a foot or a pedal, I think."

Noah said, "This is a bike leaving the parking lot of the Collinses' office. That's what you're telling us."

Gretchen's face was flushed with excitement. She ran a hand through her spiky gray-brown hair. "Yes! It would explain why we're getting nowhere with the damn license plate readers."

"It would explain how the search dog was able to follow the killer's scent for over five miles," Josie added. "From the city park to Archie Gamble's house."

Gretchen said, "Did you find a bike on Archie Gamble's property?"

"A few," Josie answered. "In the garage. I'm not sure whether any of them were in good enough shape to be riding all over the city, but I didn't look very closely. I didn't know it was important."

Gretchen said, "We'll get another warrant for them."

"And what?" said Josie. "Prove that Archie Gamble owns a bicycle? Probably the majority of people in this city own one."

"But are they riding them around in January?" asked Noah.

Josie shrugged. "Some people are—the weather's been inconsistent. Even if I can get a judge to sign a warrant to take Archie Gamble's bicycles into evidence, we can't prove that he was at either crime scene. We've got an officer sitting outside his house."

"He could have gone out the back," Gretchen suggested.

"Sure," Josie said, "but we can't prove anything. We'll spend hours and manpower on this and all we'll have is a couple of bikes and still no leads. We need to find this guy, or if Gamble is somehow behind this, we need to gather enough proof to charge him. This killer is smart. Way smarter than your average criminal. He leaves no prints, no DNA. He's not on camera anywhere. Even here!"

Noah said, "Can we follow the surveillance cameras of nearby businesses? Try to follow his path? See if we can get a better picture of him? Of the bike? Or maybe we get Luke and Blue back out here and see if we can get them to follow the scent of the killer from here to wherever he went."

Josie said, "I'm not sure about them. They might need a rest. We could call in the sheriff's K-9 unit."

Noah said, "Luke was on the job once. He understands how important this is. He knows we wouldn't ask if the killer wasn't moving so quickly. He's had a day of rest. Besides, he's nearby. He can be here way faster than the sheriff's unit. Call him. Gretchen and I will handle the cameras."

Josie felt Luke's mutilated hands tremble in her own again. Archie Gamble had nearly unraveled him. What would happen if they came face to face with the murderer—whether it was Gamble or someone else?

"Josie," Noah said, pulling her from her thoughts. "Did you hear me?"

"Yeah, yeah. I'll call Luke."

FORTY-ONE

By late evening, the excitement of potentially viable leads was gone, slipping away like a camera flash fading to black. Noah and Gretchen had found grainy footage of what looked like a man on a bicycle—too indistinct to tell if it was Gamble or someone else—and tracked him via seven different businesses to a section of Denton that Gretchen called a "dead zone." It was the same zone that Josie and Luke had passed through between the park and Archie Gamble's place the day before. Spread out residences, no cameras. They couldn't pick him up after that in any direction.

Luke had been happy to get back out on the search with Blue, who had picked up the killer's scent at the Collinses' office but then lost it in the middle of one of the dead zone streets. Josie had talked to every resident on the block, but no one remembered seeing a man on a bicycle or a man putting a bicycle into a vehicle and driving off—which Josie was pretty sure was what was happening. License plate readers were not in use in this area of Denton or anywhere close enough to warrant searching them. They wouldn't know what vehicle they were looking for anyway.

Now, seated at their desks in the stationhouse, they worked silently at their computers. No one had the energy or optimism for banter. Mettner came in to relieve Gretchen and spent several minutes catching up on the new developments in the case. Gretchen was about to leave when the stairwell door whooshed open and Hummel stepped through it, two paper evidence bags in hand.

Josie stood up and immediately cleared off her desk. He snapped on a pair of gloves before he dumped the first bag. It was the remnants of the puzzle box that had been found at the Trudy Dawson scene. Two splintered sides, one with the wooden bow on it and the other with the long, rectangular compartment. This time, he expertly caught the ball bearing as it rolled toward the edge of Josie's desk. "Same thing," he said.

Noah and Mettner walked over and crowded behind them. "You still can't get it open?" asked Mettner.

Hummel rolled his eyes. "Unlike this bastard, I don't have time for games. We dusted it. Got some partials, one full print, but no hits in AFIS."

"What was inside it?" asked Josie.

Hummel held up the other evidence bag which was larger than the first. Inside was some sort of envelope, creased where it had been folded several times. Hummel handed the bag to Josie. Then he gathered up the pieces of the puzzle box and deposited them back into their bag. Once he finished, Josie handed him back the bag with the envelope. He shook it loose and smoothed it out on the desk. Its creamy surface was gray and smudged with fingerprint dust. "Again," he told them. "The prints were a bust. We were able to eliminate some as Trudy Dawson's. Dr. Feist gave us a set of elimination prints from her. As you know, I also have some for Beau Collins. Other than that? Lots of prints and partial prints, no hits in AFIS."

Josie peered down at the return address on the envelope. It was Claudia Collins's practice. It was addressed to the Pennsylvania Women's Alliance for Refuge and Assistance. No postage had been put on the envelope. Gingerly, Hummel removed the envelope's contents—also covered with fingerprint dust—and laid them out on the desk, smoothing the creases as he went. There were four pages. The first one was letterhead with Claudia Collins's name emblazoned across the top. The date was fourteen years earlier. "This is a cover letter," Josie said. "Enclosing her résumé for Director of Services."

Noah said, "Beau Collins went on television yesterday and told the viewers that Claudia didn't get this job."

"Of course she didn't get it," Mettner said, pointing to the envelope. "Her application wasn't mailed."

"Why would Trudy Dawson have this?" asked Noah.

"We know why," Josie said. "When we talked to her, she said how important—no, how critical—it was for her to keep the job as the practice secretary. Without that job, she couldn't take care of her mom. Beau said that as a result of Claudia not getting that position, she stayed in practice with him."

Mettner said, "Beau wouldn't have kept Trudy on as secretary if Claudia left?"

"It's not that," said Noah. "Beau would have run the practice into the ground. It would not have survived without Claudia. That's what Trudy said."

Mettner pointed at the application. "You're saying the secretary sabotaged Claudia's career?"

"I don't know," said Josie. "Would Trudy have even known what this was? Is it something Claudia would have mailed from the practice where Trudy might have seen it and taken it?"

Hummel interjected. "Trudy's prints are on it. Not the contents but the envelope."

Trudy Dawson had been truly devastated that Claudia had been murdered. Was it all simply to do with keeping her job? Had her mother even been diagnosed all those years ago when

Claudia put the résumé together? Would Trudy have had reason to act so desperately then?

"I think we need to talk with Beau," Josie said. "About a lot of things."

FORTY-TWO

Josie marched over to the Eudora with Noah by her side and once again, found Beau at Bastian's bar. Her heart sank when she saw how glassy and empty his eyes looked. "Oh, hey there, detecshives."

"You're drunk," Noah said. It wasn't a question.

Beau waved an arm in the air and nearly toppled off his barstool. Josie caught him, sliding an arm around his waist, and guiding him upright again.

"Thanks," Beau said. He signaled to the bartender but was ignored.

Josie said, "Mr. Collins, we have some questions for you."

"Queshions, queshions," he muttered. "Always with queshions. I told you errything I know."

Noah bumped shoulders with Josie. "He's in no condition to answer any questions right now."

Anger seared the lining of Josie's stomach. Every moment he was drunk to being nearly incapacitated was a moment he slowed their investigation. She said, "Mr. Collins, do you know about Trudy Dawson?"

His face fell. One hand clutched the empty glass on the bar, searching its depths for more. "Why do you think I'm drunk? One of your offishers told me when he ashed me for permission to review the offish surveillansh footage."

Beau started to cry. Sobs shook him so hard that he started to slide off the stool. Both his hands gripped the edge of the bar. The bartender shook his head, snatched the empty glass away and walked to the end of the bar, where he made a phone call.

Noah stepped in and lifted Beau to standing. "I think you're getting tossed out of here. Why don't you let us get you up to your room?"

Beau nodded wordlessly. His splotchy red face was swollen and wet from crying. Josie positioned herself under his other arm. They started toward the exit. Several patrons stopped speaking and eating to stare. Josie saw one or two of them with their cell phones up. It would be on the internet in no time, she thought, and yet, Beau Collins would find a way to spin it. His grief over Claudia was so bad that he lost control and got so smashed, he had to be carried to his room by officers.

The manager of the hotel, John W. Brown, met them in the hotel lobby. He had been cooperative and fair during their investigation into people connected to the hotel, and had somehow weathered the scandal that broke as a result of that case. However, Josie knew that his priority was always the reputation of the hotel.

"Detectives," he said, regarding them with a pained smile. "Mr. Collins."

Beau didn't look at him. Instead, he continued sobbing quietly. Even his tears smelled of bourbon.

Josie said, "We're accompanying Mr. Collins to his room."

Brown gave Beau a once-over. "Yes, I gathered that. I understand that you've been through a horrible ordeal, Mr. Collins. I do think Detective Quinn is correct in thinking that the proper place for you right now is in the comfort of your suite. However," he turned his attention to Josie and Noah, "having a high-profile guest who is obviously in great distress carried from the bar by police is not a good look—for any of us concerned. How about if my staff assists Mr. Collins from here. I'll be sure to call you directly if any other issues arise?"

As if on cue, two male members of the hotel staff appeared behind Brown. Noah gave them a nod and they stepped in to take Beau. As they struggled with him down the hall toward a staff elevator, Josie looked back at Brown. "As you know, we've got a uniformed officer outside to keep an eye on Mr. Collins, should he decide to leave the hotel."

Brown smiled tightly. "Yes, your Chief contacted me directly about that. I've made no issue of it."

Noah said, "But there are many ways to exit the hotel, and as drunk as Collins is—"

Brown raised a hand to silence Noah. "Say no more. I'll have the staff discreetly keep an eye on him for the duration of his stay. I doubt he can go anywhere tonight in his condition, but I'm happy to do what I can to assist you in securing his safety."

"Thank you," said Josie. "We'll speak with Mr. Collins tomorrow when he's sober."

There was nothing more they could do but wait until the next day.

Unlike Beau, Josie spent the night wide awake and seething while Noah and Trout snored beside her. Studying Noah's face in the half-light from the moon, her anger turned to bewilderment. His words from the other day came back to her.

"If anything ever happened to you, I'd burn this entire city down finding the person who hurt you."

She knew this was true. He would move heaven and earth. He would not rest. She would do the same for him. That was better than them knowing Five Familiar Facts about one another any day. Josie had grown up in a toxic environment, raised until age fourteen by a woman whose definition of a good relationship was one in which she literally got away with murdering her partner. Or disfiguring them. Josie's best friend and first love, Ray Quinn, had come from an almost equally toxic family. His father had been an alcoholic who beat his mother—and him—until one day he abandoned them altogether. Neither Josie nor Ray knew what a "good" relationship entailed. They just knew they wanted to stop pain from being inflicted on one another. They'd tried and failed at marriage. Miserably. Josie had tried and failed in her engagement to Luke. Miserably. Noah was quick to blame Luke, but the truth was that Josie had withheld so much of herself from him, he hadn't had much to work with.

Still.

Even with her deep psychic wounds, literal scars, and toxic relationship examples, Josie loved fiercely enough to fight for both Ray and Luke. It hadn't been enough, but she had tried.

Beau seemed more concerned about his own status than losing Claudia. He was falling to pieces when they needed him most to catch her killer. A killer he might be able to lead them to if only he'd stop lying. He said that Claudia had meant everything to him, but given a chance to identify any potential killers, he clammed up. Why? Had the distance between them grown so big that it had become impossible to bridge? Had there ever been any real affection between Beau and Claudia Collins? The photo from Paris made it seem as though they'd once been deeply in love. But had they really?

A warm palm touched Josie's hand, squeezing and then traveling up and down her arm in smooth, even strokes. Her body relaxed. In a sleep-drenched voice, Noah said, "You need to get some sleep. Beau Collins will still be there in the morning, and I promise you, he'll be every bit as much of an asshole as he was the last time you saw him."

He was right, but it didn't help her sleep.

. . .

The next morning, the unit assigned to Beau advised Josie and Noah that he'd gone to WYEP. Shortly after that, they stood in the middle of the Collinses' set, staring down at Beau Collins, who was seated on the white couch being primped by one of the stylists. No cameras were rolling. They still had over an hour before Beau went live, but several of the staff strode about, making preparations for that morning's show, including Liam Flint, who seemed to be doing a very poor job pretending to fix some imaginary knob on the camera's side while he eavesdropped on the conversation. Just off stage in the other direction, Margot Huff lingered, hugging a tablet to her chest and watching them warily. A make-up artist carrying a small pouch walked up to Beau but he waved her off.

Josie said, "Mr. Collins, maybe we should go into your office."

He looked back up at Josie and Noah, his face full of genuine distress. He swallowed hard, Adam's apple bobbing in his throat. His voice was husky. "If this is about Trudy, I will reach out to her brother. I want to cover the funeral costs, and of course, I'll do anything I can to help with her mother's care."

"Were you and Trudy close?" asked Josie.

Beau said, "She was the practice secretary for over twenty years—before we even took it over."

Noah said, "But you hadn't practiced in a long time."

"Sure, but Trudy was still a vital part of our work. She single-handedly ran that practice."

"She had a lot of responsibility," said Josie.

He nodded.

Noah added, "You could trust her with anything."

"Yes," Beau whispered. "Anything."

Josie moved around the small coffee table between them, insinuating herself between it and the couch. She perched on the edge, almost knee to knee with Beau. She leaned in close to him. He still smelled faintly of bourbon. "If there was some important document that needed to be retrieved, you could ask her to do that, couldn't you?"

Beau said, "Of course."

Josie said, "Even if that document was supposed to be mailed. You could ask her to get her hands on it and hold it, couldn't you?"

Beau's brow furrowed in confusion. "I don't understand."

From inside his jacket, Noah pulled a sheaf of papers. They were copies of Claudia's job application packet. Noah handed them to Josie, and she spread them carefully across the table, scooting over a bit to make room. As Beau studied them, his body stiffened.

"I still don't understand," he said. "Is this... this looks like Claudia's résumé. What relevance does this have to your investigation into her murder? What are you trying to tell me? That my wife was actively looking to close her practice and move on to this place?" He reached out and pulled the copy of the cover letter toward him. "This— Wait. The date on this—"

Noah interjected. "Is fourteen years ago. What do you know about this, Mr. Collins?"

Beau took a long moment to study each document. Then he tapped a tremulous finger against the page. "I told you what I know about that. I told this entire city what I know on the air yesterday. I don't know what you're trying to accomplish here, but—"

Josie said, "We think that you got the answer wrong."

Beau looked stricken. "What?"

"The answer to the killer's question," said Noah. "'What is my wife's greatest failure?' You answered it incorrectly. We believe that may be why the killer targeted Trudy."

Josie said, "The killer put this inside one of your puzzle boxes and then left it in her hand after he killed her. He staged it so that we would find it and know that it was significant."

From her periphery, Josie was aware of Liam Flint moving

closer, not even bothering to pretend to fiddle with his camera any longer.

Beau shook his head vehemently. "I did not get the answer wrong! What I said was correct. That was the right answer. I don't know what you're saying."

Josie pointed to the cover letter. "The Pennsylvania Women's Alliance for Refuge and Assistance didn't 'go another way,' did they? Claudia didn't get the job because they never received her application. Trudy took it. Held onto it. Since Trudy was the practice secretary, Claudia probably asked her to call and confirm that they'd received it. It would have been easy enough for Trudy to lie and say she had called and was told they had gotten Claudia's application."

"I don't—I don't understand what you're saying or where you're going with this," said Beau. "Trudy was a loyal, steadfast employee. I don't appreciate your impugning her character like this."

Josie said, "Did Trudy do this on her own or did you tell her to do it?"

Beau wouldn't look at them. "I don't know what you're talking about. I don't know what any of this has to do with my wife's murder."

Noah said, "It has something to do with it or the killer would not have brought it to our attention."

Beau took one more horrified look at the pages on the table and then he stood and stomped off. Margot hurried after him, her heels clacking. Josie looked over toward the camera, but Liam Flint was gone. They were as alone as one could be on a television set.

FORTY-THREE

In the hall, WYEP employees gave Josie and Noah curious glances. It was the third time they'd been to the station in five days. They were halfway to the doors that led back out to the lobby and security desk when Liam Flint emerged from an unmarked door. He didn't see them. He was in a hurry as he walked away from them, head down, a backpack and bike helmet clutched against his chest. Around his neck was a tan cashmere scarf.

Josie's heartbeat ticked upward. "Noah, look," she whispered. "He's got a bike helmet."

Something else struck her as well, but she couldn't put her finger on it.

"Mr. Flint," Noah called.

The sudden hitch in his shoulders told Josie that Liam had heard Noah, but he didn't turn around. Instead, he hurried his pace, bypassing the doors to the lobby and swinging a left down another hallway.

Josie and Noah followed. "Mr. Flint," she said loudly when he came back into view. "Please stop. We'd like to talk with you."

He stopped this time but didn't turn around, instead waiting for Josie and Noah to catch up with him. Without looking at them, he asked, "What do you want?"

Josie said, "Where are you going? Isn't the show about to start?"

Liam looked down at the backpack and helmet in his hands. He lifted one hand and adjusted the scarf. Again, Josie felt there was something important right in front of her—besides the bike helmet—if only she could key in on it. Liam said, "I can't be a part of that show anymore. I'll give Beau my resignation some other time. I just can't be in there."

"Because of Claudia?" Josie asked softly.

Finally, Liam looked over at her. Tears spilled down his cheeks. With one hand, he used the end of the scarf to dab under his eyes. "There is no show without Claudia."

That was when it hit Josie. The clue staring her right in the face.

"She was important to you, wasn't she?"

He didn't answer.

Josie pointed to his scarf. "That's a very nice scarf, Mr. Flint. Where did you get it?"

Behind his glasses, his eyes bulged. "It was a gift."

"From Claudia?" she asked, even though she already knew. The day Claudia had saved Harris from a bike-on-pedestrian accident, one of the items in her bag was a tan cashmere scarf exactly like the one Liam now wore.

He stared at them for a few seconds, letting go of the scarf. "I really have to go," he said.

"Claudia gave you that scarf, didn't she?" Josie pressed. "For Christmas."

He said nothing, slowly inching away from them. For a moment, she wondered if he was going to run. At the end of the hall was a door marked EXIT.

"You like to play golf, don't you?" she asked.

Confusion lined his face at the sudden change in subject. "I, uh, I—yes, but how did you know that?"

Liam gave the exit door a furtive glance. Josie kept pushing. "Claudia also gave you a set of golf balls and tees for Christmas, didn't she?"

"It's not what you think," he blurted out.

Noah said, "You've taken Claudia's murder hardest of anyone on the show. You clearly haven't been forthcoming with our team in terms of your relationship with Claudia. Mr. Flint, it kind of looks like you and Claudia were having an affair."

Liam looked stricken. "That's not true. We absolutely were not."

"But obviously Claudia was very special to you," Josie said.

He hung his head. "She was, yes. I was in love with her, but we weren't having an affair. It wasn't like that."

Noah said, "It sounds like it was."

Liam shook his head. "It wasn't. I swear to you. It's not what you think. Believe me, I wanted to consummate our attraction, but Claudia would never do that. Not while she was married to Beau."

"There was something between you," said Josie. "Did Claudia feel the same way about you?"

"I believe she did, but we never crossed the line." They must have looked unconvinced because he added, "I don't expect you to understand."

Josie let the silence do the work, waiting to see what Liam Flint would say when he felt compelled to fill it. Finally, he whispered, "He did it, you know."

Before Josie or Noah could respond, a woman came striding around the corner and down the hall toward them. Josie didn't recognize her, but she barely gave them a glance, passing them with a curt nod and disappearing into a room near the end of the hallway.

Once the door closed behind her, Josie said, "Who did what?"

Liam kept his voice low. "Beau Collins made his secretary take that job application out of a stack of outgoing mail so that Claudia wouldn't be considered for that job."

Noah asked, "How do you know that?"

Liam took a deep breath. "Claudia told me."

Josie said, "Claudia knew about the application?"

"She always suspected that Beau had sabotaged her application, but she could never prove it. Then, a few months ago, Trudy confessed to it."

Josie said, "What happened a few months ago?"

"They got their first offer to go national with the show," Liam said. "Apparently, Trudy was worried about her job. She told Claudia she was afraid that if the show got any bigger, Claudia would have to close the practice. Claudia said she would never do that. That's her favorite part of the work. That was always the rule between her and Beau. They could do whatever he wanted—a book, a show, a podcast—but she would maintain her practice no matter what. That's when Trudy said that Beau would get what he wanted no matter what he had to do. Claudia asked her what she meant by that and after some discussion, the whole thing came pouring out. At the time that Trudy took the application, Claudia was only part-time at the practice. Everyone knew she had no intention of staying and that she wanted to work with domestic violence survivors. She put the application package into the outgoing mail bin. Beau convinced Trudy to take it and destroy it."

Josie said, "Trudy just went along with this?"

Liam shrugged. "Haven't you guys seen Beau on television? He can be pretty convincing. Besides, Trudy got a raise and job security out of it."

"How did Claudia respond to this revelation?" asked Noah.

"In the only way Claudia ever responded to things: compassionately. She was angry and hurt, of course, but it also validated something she had suspected for a long time. Things always go Beau's way. It was starting to feel suspect to her. Anyway, Trudy told her it was okay if Claudia fired her because she had felt terrible about it all these years, but Claudia kept her on. I always say to Claudia that she's too kind for her own good."

"Was he lying when he said not getting that job was Claudia's greatest failure?"

Liam wiped his nose with the sleeve of his shirt. "No. She did think that for a long time. She told me that that position was one of the only things she ever wanted and one of the only things she ever failed at. In a way, she was glad when Trudy told her the truth."

"Do you know if she ever confronted Beau about it?" asked Josie.

"I don't think she did."

Josie said, "Did you and Claudia spend a lot of time together?"

"Whenever we could. Usually, we met for late lunch. After she tapes the show, she sees patients until one or two. By that time, I'm usually done here so I bike over that way and meet her. There's this little place in South Denton that serves lunch and dinner. The Grotto."

Archie Gamble had mentioned the restaurant several times in his notes. Mettner had been the one to follow up with the restaurant. Workers there remembered Claudia coming to lunch frequently and meeting a man, but no one remembered what he looked like or how old he was or much of anything except that he was male. The Grotto's surveillance footage was erased every twenty-four hours unless there was an incident.

"I've heard of that restaurant." Noah motioned to the

bicycle helmet in Liam's arms. "You ride your bike a lot? Even in January?"

Liam nodded. "As long as it's not snowing or icy, I do. Trying to save the environment and all that. It's good exercise, too."

"Do you own a motor vehicle?"

"Yeah, but if I can ride my bike, I always prefer to do that."

Josie gave Noah a look and he nodded almost imperceptibly. They'd do a much deeper dive into Liam Flint's background as soon as they could but for now, they needed to know what he knew and how he knew it.

She said, "You and Claudia were meeting for lunch at The Grotto. Claudia wasn't worried about the two of you being seen together?"

"Why would she be? Like I said, nothing ever happened between us. Not physically."

"But other people wouldn't know that," said Josie.

Noah asked, "Does Beau know about your... friendship?"

"No. No one does. We didn't keep our lunch meetings secret, but we didn't broadcast them either. When we were here, it was all business. Casual hellos, friendly goodbyes. That was it. But Claudia was never really herself when she was here anyway," he added wistfully.

Josie said, "How long has this been going on between the two of you?"

"About a year," said Liam, swiping at a tear that slid down his cheek and into his beard. "I, uh, found her outside in the parking lot last year, sobbing her eyes out. She was mortified but I told her there was no need to be. We talked. It grew from there."

Noah said, "Does your partner have a problem with this relationship?"

"I'm single."

"What was Claudia crying about?" Josie asked.

"She said she was tired of lying."

"Lying about what?" Noah said.

Liam looked again at the exit door. His expression switched from longing to resignation. With a heavy sigh, he turned back to them. "A lot of things."

FORTY-FOUR

Josie pointed toward the end of the hallway where the exit door waited. "Is your bike out there? Maybe we should step outside before we discuss this any further. Less chance of one of your coworkers rounding the bend and hearing us."

She also wanted to get a look at his bicycle.

Liam nodded and led them down the hall and out into a small alcove at the back of the building. A small concrete landing held a bench with an ashtray next to it and a bike rack off to the side. Only one bike was chained to it. Liam walked over and hung his helmet on one of the handlebars but made no move to unchain it. Josie studied it, trying to figure out if it matched the bike that they'd found on surveillance after Trudy Dawson's murder. While Noah took up the questioning again, she surreptitiously took a few photographs of it and texted them to Gretchen.

"What was Claudia lying about, Mr. Flint?" said Noah.

"Most of it was to do with the show. She lied a lot on the show."

"Because her marriage to Beau was a sham?" asked Noah.

Liam's face darkened. "No. That's not true. I wish it were.

That would mean Claudia and I could be together. But she loved him. She genuinely loved him." The words were uttered with part disgust and part disbelief. "But a lot of the stuff they did on the show was made up."

"Like what?" asked Josie.

"For example, she didn't like tiramisu. She hated it, in fact. But Beau said she liked it on a show once and then she was always getting tiramisu from viewers, readers, fans, and even patients. She even had to eat it on camera sometimes."

Josie said, "She couldn't have just corrected him? If they were playing Five Familiar Facts, couldn't she have just corrected him and have him tweet out the hashtag whatididntknow?"

Liam laughed. "Then Beau would spend all his life tweeting and he would have looked like the ass he is on television."

Josie said, "You're saying he didn't really know anything about his wife?"

"I'm saying he didn't see her. He never really saw her. I guess he used to pay attention to her but once the book started selling and all these other opportunities came up, he stopped."

Noah said, "She didn't bring that up with him in private?"

"I don't think that was the dynamic of their relationship. I don't know. Maybe she did but even if she had, Beau Collins is not the kind of man who will ever take responsibility for something that is even mildly unflattering to him. It's almost pathological. He does not like blame."

This rang true to Josie. Even when presented with clear evidence of his affair with Eve Bowers, he had downplayed it, describing it as a lapse of judgment and turning the conversation back to his anniversary again and again. "Did Claudia know about his affair with Eve?"

Sadness washed over Liam's face. "If she did, she never told me. I doubt it, though. She loved Eve."

"Did you know about it?" asked Noah.

"No. I don't think anyone did, honestly. Maybe Margot? There was never any talk about it, that's for sure. I definitely would have told Claudia if I had heard something like that."

"When was the last time you spoke with Claudia?" asked Josie.

"Friday after the show. We talked about how awkward it was going to be with me being part of the crew taping the big anniversary dinner."

Noah said, "Before that, when was the last time you saw her privately?"

"Wednesday."

"Did the two of you keep in contact by phone or text?" asked Josie.

"Yes. I texted her Friday night to tell her that Margot had called me because everyone was running late."

They would have known this if Claudia's cell phone carrier had been willing to expedite their warrant for her phone records. Josie pushed her frustration aside and kept her focus on Liam. "Did she answer you?"

His eyes grew moist. Huskily, he said, "No. But she was gone by then. I didn't know until later when we arrived to do the job and the police were there."

Noah said, "When our colleagues interviewed you the other day, you didn't mention any of this. Why not?"

Liam looked at his feet. His voice was thick with unshed tears. "I'm sorry. It's private. Claudia wanted it kept private, always. I was trying to respect her wishes. I didn't want to risk tarnishing her reputation. People wouldn't understand. They would think the wrong thing—just like you did. They'd make assumptions. She's not here to defend herself anymore. Also, you probably think I'm a suspect now, don't you?"

"It certainly undermines your credibility," Josie said.

"Where were you on Friday afternoon before you arrived at Claudia and Beau's house for the shoot?"

He lifted his gaze to the sky, avoiding eye contact. "I was home."

"Does anyone live with you who might be able to verify that?" asked Noah.

Liam shook his head.

Josie said, "What about Saturday morning between six and eight?"

"Home until seven thirty. That's when I left for the studio."

Noah said, "Yesterday. Between seven forty-five and nine a.m.?"

"I was home until eight fifteen. I was supposed to leave the house at seven thirty, like always, but I was upset and frustrated. I considered not coming in at all. I was late. I got here at eight forty-five-ish."

Josie said, "Did Claudia ever mention a man named Archie Gamble?"

"No," Liam replied easily.

On her phone, Josie pulled up the driver's license photo of Gamble and showed it to Liam. "Have you ever seen or met this man?"

Liam took a few seconds to study the photo before answering, "No. Who is he?"

Josie ignored his question and pocketed her phone. "Did Claudia ever tell you that she thought someone was following her?"

His eyes widened. "What? No. Was she?"

"We believe so," Noah. "Mr. Flint, you said that Claudia was lying about a lot of things. Was there anything else besides show-related things?"

He turned away from them, pacing slowly in a small circle. When he made no move to answer the question, Noah said, "I know you're concerned about Claudia's reputation. That's admirable, but I can assure you that no damage to her reputation is worth someone's life. Her killer is still out there. He's taken three lives already within five days. If you know anything that might help us, even if you're not sure whether or not it will help, we need to hear it."

Liam stopped walking. His eyes stayed glued to his feet. "The thing is, I don't know what the lie was—Claudia would never tell me—but whatever it was, it was huge."

"What do you mean?" Josie said.

Finally, he looked at her. "Claudia was hiding something. A few months ago, after the Trudy thing, I noticed she was upset about something. At our lunches, she was distracted. A few times here at the studio, I noticed her getting teared up and trying to keep it from Beau and the staff, although that wasn't hard since no one really paid attention to her. I asked her what was bothering her a few times. She denied anything but I told her, 'denial might work with Beau, but I know you. Just tell me what's wrong.'"

Noah said, "What did she tell you?"

He adjusted his glasses. "She broke down crying. She said that she couldn't ever tell me. I told her she could tell me anything and I would always love her. No matter what. All she would say was that years ago, she'd done something terrible and only recently did she realize the harm it had caused. I tried to console her, but she said that what she had done was unforgivable. I told her it was hard for me to imagine her doing something terrible. She was genuinely the best person I ever knew. She said she wished she could take it back and that no one could ever know about it. It would destroy her life."

"But she wouldn't tell you what it was?" asked Josie.

He shook his head. "I tried and tried. I thought if she just told me, she'd feel better. Or maybe we could work through it together. After a while, she asked me to drop it. She said she had made her peace with it. I had to let it go. But I think it haunted her."

Noah said, "Do you have any idea what it was? Could you speculate?"

"I have no idea," Liam answered. "I spent weeks trying to come up with a theory. I couldn't. There's literally nothing I can imagine her doing that would be so bad. I just can't imagine what would be unforgivable in her mind."

Josie asked, "Did you ever ask her if Beau knew about it?"

"She'd never give me a straight answer. She would just say, 'I don't want to talk about this anymore.' I respected her wishes. I honestly thought that one day she would feel comfortable talking about it. But months passed and her mood returned to normal and since she was happy, I didn't push the issue. I planned to ask her again one day but then she was murdered."

A few months ago, the Collinses had signed a huge contract to take their show national. A few months ago, Claudia had found out that her husband had sabotaged her career goals. A few months ago, she had taken thirty thousand dollars in cash out of a bank account to donate to a charity—a charity that had no record of such a donation. A few months ago, Archie Gamble had started following her.

None of these things seemed related to one another at all.

Before she could ask Liam more questions, Josie's phone rang. She fished it out of her pocket. It was Beau Collins.

Liam's face paled. "You don't think her murder is related to whatever she was hiding, do you?"

Josie swiped answer. "Quinn."

Beau Collins's voice announced, "I need you to come back to the studio right now."

"What's going on?" she asked.

"Please come as fast as you can. I got another text from the killer."

FORTY-FIVE

Back in the studio, a knot of people gathered around the couch where Beau now sat, cradling his cell phone in his hands. Everyone who worked on the show was there. Margot stood behind the couch, just over Beau's shoulder. The crowd parted as Josie and Noah approached with Liam Flint in tow. Josie held out a hand for Beau's phone. His hands trembled as he gave it to her. The screen showed a new text message from Beautiful Claudia with three heart emojis. It had come in six minutes earlier.

Noah was already on the phone with dispatch requesting that they ping Claudia's phone again. Excitement surged through Josie. They might have a chance to catch the guy before he slipped away again. She looked at the message on Beau's phone.

> Let's try this again. Go on air today and answer this question: what is my wife's deepest regret? If you're not on today or don't get it right this time, you know what happens.

This time, Beau had not answered. Noah hung up. "Dispatch is pinging it now. Could take up to a half hour though."

Josie turned the phone toward him so he could read the message. "Shit," he said.

Beau's skin was bone white. "What do I do?"

"We need to stall," said Josie. "If dispatch can find the phone, we can send units and get this guy."

Margot stepped forward. "The show starts in fifteen minutes. He is supposed to go live."

"We have no time," said Beau. "I have to do this."

Noah said, "Can you cancel the show for today? Have WYEP claim technical difficulties?"

"Not in fifteen minutes," said someone behind them. The producer, Kathy, stepped forward. "He has to go on. I don't care what he does, but there has to be a show. We've got sponsors to worry about."

"Fine," said Josie. "Do the show."

"But do I answer his question?"

She made a number of split-second calculations in her head. To their knowledge, there was no harm in Beau going on air or even in him answering the question. The audience had no idea what was going on. They knew that Claudia was dead, but the only people who knew about the game were the killer and the people in this room. While Josie would never advocate for playing directly into the hands of a brutal killer, the potential benefits seemed to outweigh the cost. The killer had made it clear: if he didn't go on air, there would be consequences. If he answered the question incorrectly, there would be consequences. The last time, Beau had answered incorrectly, and Trudy Dawson was murdered. It was safe to assume that if Beau failed to go live or answered the question wrong, someone else would die.

The only issue was that they didn't know who the killer would target now if Beau answered incorrectly.

In Josie's ear, Noah whispered, "He has to answer. We can't tell him not to answer knowing that someone might die. Our best shot at avoiding another murder is having him do this."

In spite of how cool the studio was kept, sweat gathered along the nape of Josie's neck. "Mr. Collins, what's the answer to the question?"

Beau looked momentarily stunned. "What?"

"You're going to do the show and you're going to talk to the audience about Claudia's deepest regret. What is it?"

Kathy added, "Yeah, we need to know so we can write some copy before you get on there."

Josie resisted the urge to elbow the woman.

Beau seemed confused. "Her deepest regret? It's the same as yesterday. Not getting that job. She wanted to work with domestic violence survivors. She never had the chance. I told her with our new status and financial security, she could probably start doing it. She could open her own damn shelter if she wanted."

Josie did not point out to him that Denton already had an excellent women's shelter. Instead, she said, "Are you absolutely sure?"

"Yes," he insisted.

Noah said, "If Claudia were standing here right in front of us and we asked her the question, that's what she would say?"

"Yes!"

"No," said Liam Flint.

He stepped into the group. All heads swiveled toward him. Beau said, "Who the hell are you?"

"He's a camera operator," Margot mumbled.

"What?" said Beau. "I've never seen him before."

Margot said, "He got into a physical altercation with Kathy right in front of you on Saturday. You don't remember that?"

Beau turned and looked up at her, fury flashing in his eyes.

"Well, excuse me for not noticing every little thing. My wife has just been murdered!"

Kathy said, "People, we don't have time for this. We've got seven minutes."

Liam's hands fisted at his sides again. Under his beard, his face flushed. "I've worked here since the show started, you jackass, and you're wrong. Not doing the work she wanted isn't Claudia's deepest regret. It's that she never had children."

Beau looked as if he'd been slapped. There were a few seconds of perfect, shocked silence.

"It's true and you know it," Liam said. "She wanted children."

"But I—I can't. She knew that. She knew I couldn't... you know."

Liam shot back, "But you could have adopted, and you refused."

"How the hell do you even know this? You're nobody!"

Liam's voice shook. "How dare you?"

"Four minutes, people!" shouted Marissa, the floor director. "Get off my set! Let's go, let's go, let's go!"

Noah gently pushed Liam back, away from the set. Everyone else except Beau and the make-up technician retreated to the outer edges of the studio. Someone darted over and made sure that Beau's microphone was working. Then he was alone on the couch, and someone was counting down: "Live in three, two," the one was silent, marked only with a hand signal. As soon as he saw it, some automatic process in Beau's body seemed to take over. A smile perfect for the grimness of the situation spread across his face. He started talking, smoothly and confidently but also with an air of solemnity. It took Josie a few seconds to find the teleprompter. He took a moment to welcome viewers and thank them for tuning in. "I've received such an outpouring of support from all of you at home over Claudia's death. It may seem strange for me to be here, talking to you, when my wife has just been taken from me, but I've always been honest with all of you. As you've taken comfort in our show, I take comfort in you, the audience. You knew my beloved Claudia almost as well as I did. Who better to grieve with than the people who loved her most?"

Then his smile faltered. He hesitated, blinking at the teleprompter. With far less confidence, he said, "You lovely folks out there have always said how much Claudia and I helped you get through all kinds of rough patches in your life. I come to you today asking you to help me in my darkest hour. I ask you to sit with me for this next half hour and remember the incredible woman who used to sit right here by my side."

He patted the seat next to him. From where she stood, Josie could see that his fingers were shaking. The print on the teleprompter disappeared. That was as far as Kathy had gotten. It was all Beau now. She sent up a silent prayer that whatever he said was the correct answer. She still wasn't sure who she trusted more—Beau or Liam. Perhaps neither of them knew Claudia as well as they thought they did.

Beau looked around the set, as if searching for someone. Then he looked at his lap. Airtime ticked by. Kathy hissed something into her headset. Finally, he looked up. "Claudia and I were slated to do an edition of Five Familiar Facts on the air today. I just wanted to take a few moments to really talk about that particular segment. As you all know, the quiz is available on our website. Claudia and I always thought it was a fun and easy way to grow more emotional intimacy between you and your partner. Claudia loved it. She loved the way it started with easy questions and then ended with a very profound question. She used to say that was where the gold was—in those serious questions— because they're hard to answer and they're difficult for your partner to confirm or deny. I'll tell you—" He broke off and pointed toward someone off camera, his confident but appropriately somber smile flickering back into place. "Can I get the last question for today?"

No one outside of the camera's view moved but Beau nodded anyway and said, "Thank you." Addressing the viewers once more, he said, "Claudia and I did not know these questions ahead of time. That's cheating, isn't it?"

For a moment, he looked confused and then he gave the camera a nervous smile. "Well," he said. "I'm not sure what happened here. We were supposed to do the anniversary edition, but it looks like this is just a regular question." He waved a hand at no one. "No, no, it's fine. I'll just go with this." Smiling at the center camera again, he added, "We have to be flexible in life, don't we? And learn to adapt."

Josie was impressed by how easily he had adapted to having no script in a high-stakes situation, all while pretending everything had been prearranged and that the staff was in on it.

"Okay, here is the question we were supposed to answer at the end of today's show." He pretended to read: "What is my wife's deepest regret?"

"What do you think he's going to say?" Noah whispered.

"No idea," she said under her breath.

Beau looked at his lap and then back at the camera, his face all soft, sympathetic lines. "Folks, if you had asked me this a few years ago, I would have told you that it was the fact that Claudia never got to work with domestic violence survivors. This was a cause near and dear to her heart. Life kind of got away from us. Our practice got busy. Then we wrote the book and, well, you know the rest." Big smile. "But once Claudia and I got a bit older, some... windows of opportunity passed us by... I will tell you the painful truth. My wife's deepest regret is that we never had children."

"He gave both answers," Noah said.

It was brilliant, although Josie would never tell Beau Collins that. She let out a small breath of relief. Surely the killer had to give him "credit" for getting the answer right. Unless, of course, both answers were wrong. A headache started to throb in Josie's temple.

Beau continued, "Claudia and I were always so focused on our careers and on helping people like you that we never even discussed it until we were both approaching forty. Then it seemed that it might be biologically impossible for us to have children. We thought long and hard about adopting and in the end, decided that if we were going to do that, to bring a child into our home and into our lives, that child deserved our complete attention. We had to make a decision: keep our work going full throttle and help as many couples as possible, or scale back, adopt, and focus on helping only one person?"

Josie resisted the urge to roll her eyes.

Noah said, "Is this guy really trying to make being an asshole sound noble?"

"It appears that way," Josie muttered.

Beau stopped for a commercial break. Noah checked his phone. "The phone pinged on the state gameland about a mile away from Archie Gamble's property. Mett and Gretchen are already en route with back-up units."

Someone gave Beau another countdown. He started talking again, this time discussing his own deepest regret, which was not being there when his mother was getting treatment for cancer. As he went on to make a bunch of excuses, Josie turned to Noah. "Let's go."

FORTY-SIX

It was late afternoon by the time Josie and the team returned to the stationhouse. Her entire body was stiff and chilled to the bone from being outside for so many hours. The Chief had called in officers who were off to assist with a massive search of the state gameland adjacent to Archie Gamble's land. The officer assigned to watch Gamble's home reported that Gamble hadn't left all day but Josie knew he could have easily slipped out the back, walked through the woods, crossed Wertz Road, and sent the text to Beau. They hadn't found Claudia's phone during their search but that didn't mean he didn't have it. It could be stashed somewhere. Regardless, they'd found nothing.

The killer had eluded them again.

Now Chief Chitwood stood in front of their collective desks, arms crossed over his thin chest. "You're telling me this guy was on state gameland near Wertz Road at eight thirty-five this morning just long enough to text Beau Collins one of these asinine questions, and that in spite of the fact that a dozen police officers got there under a half hour later, we've got nothing?"

No one answered.

"Quinn!" he barked. "What's the next step?"

Exhaustion pulled at every inch of her body. She tried to settle her thoughts, bring them back into focus. "Maybe we try another geo-fence."

Mettner said, "'Cause that's your new answer to everything?"

"Watch it, Mett," said Noah.

"Both of you shut up," the Chief said.

"We look at the location where Claudia's phone last pinged today and we expand the fence out from there in every direction for the hour after the text was sent," Josie said.

"That's broad," Gretchen said. "Very broad. It could be hundreds and hundreds of numbers to sift through. Besides, this guy has to be shutting his own phone off before he gets to wherever he's decided to turn Claudia's phone on and text Beau. If he's been smart enough to keep Claudia's phone off except when he needs it, then he probably won't show up on the geo-fence."

"But he may not even know about geo-fences," said Josie. "What if he turns his own phone off while he's still in the geo-fence? How far is he from the location of the ping when he turns it off? What if he's already there, in the geo-fence, but we're not seeing him because he seems too far away from where Claudia's phone was last pinged? What if he's right there and we haven't seen him because we're not even looking for him?"

Mettner said, "You're the one who said you think this guy is in the Collinses' inner circle. The inner circle was there today, at the studio."

"The killer could have help," Noah said. "It could be more than one person."

"True," Josie said. "What if we've been too focused in on the inner circle to look elsewhere?"

Gretchen said, "We have looked elsewhere. Archie Gamble."

"Quinn, you can only go where the evidence takes you," said Chief Chitwood.

She booted up her computer, mostly because she didn't know what else to do. "What if we've missed something in the evidence? What if this guy was within the geo-fences when he turned his phone off, but we didn't notice his number because it doesn't show up close to where Claudia's phone last pinged?"

The Chief, Noah, and Mettner looked confused. Gretchen said, "There's an easy way to figure out if he's been under our nose the whole time and we've just missed him. We could cross-reference the two geo-fences we already have and see if the same number shows up both times."

The Chief sighed. "Might as well. This guy would have no way of knowing how big the geo-fences were or even that we'd use them. Now, let's talk about the killer's next target. You have any idea who it might be?"

Josie pulled up the results of the two geo-fence warrants and began examining the numbers again, starting with the most recent results from the park the day Eve was killed.

Noah said, "No idea. Beau claims he has no idea either. I called him from the field and drilled him on this. He says there is no one left to target."

"Has to be Margot Huff," said Gretchen. "She makes the most sense. She's with him all the time. Some people think they either had or are having an affair, despite her denials. Maybe Beau won't admit that he'd be devastated if she was murdered, but he would."

The Chief made a noise of agreement. "Let's put a unit on her. Now. Have them make contact with her and let her know they'll be with her until we've got this mess straightened out."

Gretchen picked up her desk phone to make arrangements.

Mettner said, "I guess this killer isn't going to care whether or not Beau answered his question correctly or not. Which answer do you think was the right one for today?"

"The not having kids thing," said Gretchen, hanging up. "It's definitely that."

"Why?" asked Noah. "Because she's a woman? Not all women want children."

"No," said Gretchen. "Not because she's a woman. Because a regret implies something that can't be undone. Like what Beau Collins said about not being present during his mother's cancer treatments. You can't get that back. That's what makes it a regret. But if you had wanted children and then you find your-self in a marriage where your husband either can't have or defi-nitely doesn't want children, then yeah, you might have regrets."

"That makes sense," Noah said. "Although technically he did get the first question right. According to Liam Flint. So why did this guy murder Trudy Dawson?"

Josie looked up from her computer screen and said, "This killer is playing by rules we don't even know about."

The Chief said, "Or he's just a cold, batshit-crazy psychopath. I don't care why he's doing any of this, I just want him caught. Caught! Do you hear me?"

Gretchen said, "Chief, we're working our asses off, and trying, to some degree, to figure out why this guy is doing things the way he does could generate leads."

Chitwood pointed at her. "Well, come up with some fast, Palmer. I don't want this jerk killing people in my city anymore."

With that, he stomped off to his office and slammed the door closed.

"So much for a new, more user-friendly Chitwood," muttered Mettner.

Noah said, "That *is* the new, more user-friendly Chitwood."

Gretchen laughed.

Josie turned back to her computer and moved on to the next set of geo-fence results, from the night that Claudia was murdered.

Mettner said, "Does anyone think these questions are weird? Why is this guy making Beau Collins go on television and talk about his wife's innermost secrets? What is he trying to accomplish?"

Noah said, "Maybe he's trying to expose Beau for how little he really paid attention to Claudia. Make him look like a fraud."

"If that's the case," said Mettner. "We need to take a much closer look at Liam Flint. From what you told us about your interview with him this morning, he not only had it bad for Claudia, but he hates Beau."

"The problem with that is that he was with us today when that text came in," said Noah.

Josie glanced up at Mettner long enough to read the disappointment and frustration in his face.

Gretchen said, "Like Fraley said, Flint could have help."

Mettner walked over and stood next to Josie's chair. "Boss, you see Flint's number on those geo-fences?"

Josie said, "I don't see Flint's number on here." But there were two numbers that caught her eye. Familiar numbers. She picked up her cell phone and scrolled through her contacts. People never dialed numbers anymore. Instead, everyone you knew was listed in your phone under their name or photograph and all you had to do was press or swipe call.

"Just a second," she told Mettner. "I need to check something."

She confirmed that the first number she recognized belonged to Misty DeRossi, which made sense. The night of Claudia's murder, Misty had taken Harris to one of his basketball games at the new rec center next to the city park. Josie and Noah would have been there with her if they hadn't had to work.

She moved on to the second number, looking it up first in her phone and then double-checking it in a database. "Son of a bitch," she muttered.

"What is it?" asked Mettner, leaning in closer and peering at the computer screen.

Josie used her phone to find Misty's Facebook page and scrolled until she found the photos from Harris's game. Misty had not posted any; she never shared photos of Harris online, but she had been tagged by the basketball coach, along with about a dozen other parents, in a number of photos of the children playing. Josie clicked through them. None of them captured Harris, but she wasn't looking at the kids.

Mettner's voice was suddenly very close to her ear. "Boss, I don't think it will go over very well if new, user-friendly Chief sees you scrolling on Facebook when we've got a major case going on."

Josie found what she was looking for and zoomed in on the corner of the photo. Excitedly, she thrust the screen at Mettner's face. "This is a basketball game that took place the afternoon of Claudia's murder at the rec center by the park. This is a crowd of onlookers."

She pointed to a man. He was hanging back, arms crossed, and his head was down.

Chairs creaked as Noah and Gretchen stood and walked around to stand with Mettner behind her chair. "That can't be right," said Noah.

"He said he was at the WYEP studio," Mettner added. "We have evidence!"

Gretchen said, "Not evidence. Just a statement from the security guard. He could have lied. He was probably paid to lie.

It's obvious that Beau Collins wanted to keep his presence at that game a secret."

Noah said, "But why? What the hell was Beau Collins doing at a basketball game for kids in the first place?"

"I have my suspicions," Josie said. "But we won't know for sure until we talk to him. Let's go."

FORTY-SEVEN

Beau Collins answered the door to his hotel room looking like someone had beaten him up. His hair stuck up in three different directions. Dark circles smudged the skin beneath his eyes. A five o'clock shadow dappled his face. Gone was the sharply cut suit he'd worn at the studio. Now he wore sweatpants and a T-shirt that bore some sort of unidentifiable stain. His shoulders sagged. He seemed to be shoring himself up for bad news when he saw Josie and Noah. The smell of bourbon wafted off his breath when he spoke. "Is someone else dead?"

"Mr. Collins, can we come inside?" asked Josie.

He looked behind him. Josie and Noah had already been inside his suite, which offered a living area and a bedroom. The bedroom had been a mess of discarded clothing, but the parlor area hadn't been too bad. Josie said, "We don't care about a mess."

With a sigh, Beau said, "It's not that. Margot is here, and it's not because I'm sleeping with her. She's here to offer support."

Noah said, "We're aware. Our Chief has a unit assigned to her. That officer is out front. We spoke to him when we arrived."

Josie added, "As long as you don't mind answering more questions in front of her."

Beau gave a dry laugh. "She's already heard every deep, dark secret I didn't want anyone to know in the last few days. What's one more?"

When Josie didn't respond to that, worry flashed across his face. Still, he stepped aside to admit them. In the living room area, Margot was walking around with a trash bag, scooping up takeout containers. With no make-up, dressed casually in jeans and a long-sleeved black shirt, she looked more her age. In fact, she looked very young, and there was something vaguely familiar in the look of surprise that she gave Josie and Noah. She dropped the bag onto the floor and wiped her hands on her jeans. "I can go," she said. "I'll leave this for housekeeping, but Beau, you have to let them come in tomorrow."

From behind them, Beau said, "No. Please stay, Margot. I would feel better if you stayed."

She looked toward the doors that led to the bathroom and bedroom. "I'll just use the restroom."

Beau watched her go and plopped onto the long, overstuffed couch. "Tell me," he said gravely. "Don't spare me any details."

Noah said, "No one's dead. Yet."

Beau looked momentarily confused. "What?" A tremulous smile appeared on his face. "That's a good thing!"

"Yeah," Noah said, exchanging a glance at Josie. "It is."

"But you have news."

"We have questions," Josie said. "First of all, a member of your show's staff told us earlier today that Claudia was keeping some kind of secret. Were you aware of that?"

His brow furrowed. "No. I am not aware of Claudia keeping secrets. Who told you that?"

"It doesn't matter," Josie said. "What matters is that it was a secret that Claudia believed could destroy her life."

Beau laughed. "That's absurd. I don't know who said that

but they're just plain wrong. My wife was a good person. A kind, caring, woman. An honest woman."

"Can't say the same about you though," said Josie.

"What does that mean?" Beau said.

"You also lied about the donation that Claudia made," Noah pointed out.

Beau's mouth fell open. Josie counted two beats before he clamped it shut. His lips worked before any words came out. "I did no such thing."

"The women's center never received a cash donation for thirty thousand dollars," Josie said.

Beau blinked. "What are you saying?"

"Claudia didn't donate that money. What did she do with it?"

"I don't know. How would I know?"

"You never asked her for a receipt?" Noah asked. "For tax purposes?"

"I—I didn't think to—I thought she was the one who—I—" He broke off and took a moment to slow his breathing. "I don't know what she did with the money. I assumed she handed in the receipt to the accountant. I trusted her to do that. I didn't check up on her. Like I said, Claudia was honest. She never lied. If that's what she said she was going to do, that's what she did. Maybe she gave it to a different charity."

Either he genuinely didn't know what had become of that thirty thousand dollars or he was lying. Josie's money was on the latter.

She took her phone out and brought up the photo she had found on Facebook. Turning the screen toward Beau, she said, "You told us that you were at the WYEP studio at the time that Claudia was being murdered."

He glanced at the photo but didn't take a good look. "I was. I told you, the security guard could verify what time I left."

Josie said, "You lied."

"No, I didn't! I—"

Noah cut him off. "Our colleagues, Detectives Palmer and Mettner, just spoke to that guard. He admitted that you paid him to lie about what time you left the studio."

"No, no. He's wrong. He's mistaken. There's been a misunderstanding—"

Interrupting him again, Noah said, "Mr. Collins, you were very clearly at the rec center next to the city park. Why?"

"I was—" He broke off, looking at the garbage bag Margot had left on the floor. Josie let the silence stretch out. A creaking sound came from the bathroom. Margot eavesdropping, most likely. Beau rubbed his eyes with the heels of his hands. "It was stupid. I was on my way home and I stopped..."

When he didn't finish the sentence, Noah said, "You were running late for your fifteenth anniversary dinner so you decided to stop at the rec center to watch a bunch of seven- and eight-year-olds play basketball?"

Another creak. The bathroom door opening a crack. Josie put her phone back into her pocket. Liam's words came back to her. Beau would never admit to anything even if confronted with hard evidence. "Mr. Collins," she said. "As you can see, we've got photos of you there. My colleagues are pulling footage from inside and out of the rec center. There are only two reasons I can think of for why you would lie about this: either you're involved in these murders, or you are hiding something very big. Something you don't want anyone to know. Something you definitely did not want Claudia to know."

Beau looked stricken. "I didn't have anything to do with any of this. If you can get me on camera, you will be able to see that I was at the rec center at the time that my wife was at home setting up. I got here right after Margot. She'll tell you."

"Why were you at the game?" asked Noah.

Beau didn't answer.

Josie said, "On Saturday, the killer left Eve's body inside

Lovers' Cave with your wife's wedding rings on her hand. Eve was your lover."

"I told you that I had broken things off. It was a mistake. A lapse—"

Josie interrupted him. "A lapse in judgment, yes. We know. On Monday, the killer texted and asked you about Claudia's biggest failures. You said it was not getting the job with the Pennsylvania Women's Alliance for Refuge and Assistance. Whether you answered correctly or not is immaterial. When Trudy Dawson was murdered, the killer staged her body with the application that you and Trudy took from the outgoing mail."

"I didn't tell Trudy to do that," he protested.

Josie held up a hand to silence him. "I don't care. I want you to listen to me. Your answer to the question was related to Trudy and Trudy's murder. Whether you told her to or not, Trudy took that application and made sure it was not mailed. Trudy was killed. Tell me you see where I'm going with this."

He gave her a blank look. Josie couldn't tell if it was genuine or not.

Noah said, "You went on air today and told everyone watching that Claudia's deepest regret was not having children."

Beau made a noise of exasperation. "According to some guy. A camera operator, evidently. I don't even remember seeing that guy before. You should check him out."

"We did," said Noah. "He's worked for WYEP for almost ten years. He moved from the news division to your show when it began airing."

"He was right, wasn't he?" asked Josie. "Claudia wanted children. You did not. When only one person in a marriage wants children, typically, you don't have children. Claudia stayed with you, but she regretted not becoming a mother."

"So what? Claudia made a choice. She chose to stay with me and to pursue our careers."

Noah said, "What happens if the killer thinks you got the answer wrong?"

Beau threw his hands in the air and let them fall to his lap, giving them a helpless look. "I don't know! I don't know what the hell this crazy monster is planning, what he's thinking."

"But we do," Josie said. "We can make an educated guess. He thought you got the first question wrong, so he killed the person who had knowledge of Claudia's bid for that position, the person who was directly involved in squashing Claudia's dreams and keeping your secret. If he thinks that 'having children' is not the correct answer now, who will he kill?"

Beau shook his head. "I honestly don't know."

"Why were you at that basketball game?" asked Josie.

"I told you, I just stopped—"

Footsteps padded across the carpet. Josie and Noah turned to see Margot approach. She muscled her way past Josie and Noah, surprisingly strong, and stepped in front of Beau. "What are they talking about?"

He didn't answer. Margot looked to Josie and then Noah. She held out a hand. "I want to see the picture."

Josie produced it for her. Margot stared at it for a long moment. "You said this was a game played by small children?"

Noah said, "Seven- and eight-year-olds."

Margot handed Josie back her phone and turned on Beau. "You son of a bitch. Seven or eight years old? That would have been—" She stopped, eyes lifting to the ceiling as if she were calculating something. "Right around prime childbearing age for Claudia. What did you do?"

Beau leapt to his feet, hands up in a defensive posture. "Margot, listen. It was a mistake, okay? I only saw her a few times. She wanted to keep the baby. It's not like I had a choice in the matter."

Before Josie or Noah could react, Margot flew at him, arms extended. She pushed him hard, and he fell back onto the couch. "You're so disgusting," she spat, standing over him. "I'm finished with this. I don't need to get to know you. I don't need this shitty job, and I'm not keeping any secrets for you anymore."

She stomped over to one of the wingback chairs and snatched up her purse.

Her hand was on the doorknob when Beau cried out, "Margot, please. Don't go. Without Claudia, I have no one. All those people—producers, agents, managers—they don't care about me. They care about making money. I need you."

Tears streamed down Margot's face. She hesitated, turned back, and took a few steps toward him. Then she stopped and studied him. Josie had to admit that he looked pathetic and broken. Apparently, Margot didn't buy it because she put her hands over her ears and screamed. Beau reared back, looking frightened, like he was in the room with a wild animal. Dropping her hands, she spat, "You don't need me. You never even cared about me until I showed up on your doorstep. You're so full of shit. I don't know why I thought— You know what? You deserve to suffer."

She spun on her heel and with a terse "I'm sorry" directed toward Josie and Noah, she left.

Beau watched her go, blinking back tears. Noah said, "You want to tell us what that was about? When we got here, you told us you weren't sleeping with Margot Huff. But she seems pretty upset to hear you've had a child with another woman."

Beau's face crumpled. "I'm not sleeping with Margot! She's my—she's—oh my God." He put his face between his knees, as if he might be sick. After taking in a few deep breaths, he sat upright again. "She's my daughter."

Even Josie had not seen that coming. Somehow, she managed to keep her surprise to herself.

Beau added, "It was before Claudia and I—well, I was young and in grad school. I wasn't ready to have children. Her mother said it was fine, that she could handle it. It was up to me whether or not I wanted to be in Margot's life. At first, I thought I'd pop in now and then but then I met Claudia and life got away from me. I never told her. She never knew. No one does. One day, Margot showed up at the studio. She said she was my daughter. All she wanted was to get to know me. I couldn't very well do that without drawing the wrong kind of attention, could I? So I hired her as my assistant. No one batted an eye to see us spending so much time together."

Josie wondered what else no one knew and how much of it had led to the horrific events of the last several days. For now, she had to focus on the immediate issue. She said, "You had an affair with a woman eight or nine years ago. Who was she?"

Beau's gaze remained fixed on his lap. "I'd rather not say."

"You do understand that the killer may target this woman—and your child."

Beau put a hand to his chest. "My son? No. He wouldn't."

"We don't know that," said Noah. "But we need to take precautions. Give us the name of his mother."

"You can't—you can't—I promised her I wouldn't bother her or confuse him. If she thinks they're in danger because of me or Claudia, she might... it wouldn't be good. Please."

Josie said, "I am sure that her concern for her son's safety will outweigh whatever anger she might have toward you. Just give us her name. Please. We need to make sure that they are safe. The sooner the better."

Noah added, "Last time, he killed Trudy almost immediately after the show. When is the last time you had contact with this woman?"

Beau's eyes widened. "I don't have contact with her at all. That's the arrangement. I'm only allowed to see a photo of Sam every now and then. That's all. If she even knew I was at that game, she would be furious. I pay for all of Sam's needs and stay out of their lives and in return, she won't tell anyone that I have a son. Not that she would want to. She hates me. Listen, there is no way this killer would know about her or Sam. I promise you. No one knows."

Josie said, "You'll excuse us if we don't believe you, Mr. Collins. You haven't exactly been forthcoming with us from the beginning. In fact, all you've really given us are lies on top of lies."

"They're safe," he insisted. "Please. I don't want anyone to know—"

Noah said, "If you don't tell us, we will talk to every mother of every boy on the teams that were playing that night until we find her. Either everyone who was at the rec center that night finds out that you have a secret son with another woman, or you tell us her name and we discreetly protect her and your son. Your choice."

For a long moment, Josie didn't think he was going to tell them. He slumped in the middle of the couch, shrinking down into its cushions. After what felt like an eternity, he said, "Jasmine. Jasmine Toselli."

FORTY-EIGHT

Jasmine Toselli lived across town in East Denton. Her home was well kept with the trappings of a seven-year-old strewn across the lawn and porch. Even so, her home could easily have fit inside the Collinses' living room. Josie thought about Beau's cavernous home, now a crime scene, sitting empty while here, only a few miles away, his son lived in a modest house, completely unaware of his father's identity or of the danger that now stalked him and his mother. Josie and Noah had called for the nearest units to go to the Toselli household for a welfare check immediately. When Josie and Noah arrived, there were two patrol cars parked out front.

Lights glowed from the windows, but the uniformed officers tromped around the house with their flashlights. One of them came down the porch steps as Josie and Noah got out of their vehicle. "Doesn't look like anyone is here," he said. "Lights are on, but no one answered when we knocked and rang the bell. Dispatch got her phone numbers—cell and home—but she's not answering. A window here in the front and one in the back gives us a limited view inside, but no one appears to be there."

Noah said, "They could be upstairs or in a room that's not

visible. We have to get inside. I don't think we should wait for dispatch to try to get this woman on the phone. In fact, have dispatch ping her phone right now."

"You got it," said one of the other officers. He walked off, head bent toward his radio.

Josie's stomach burned. She turned in a circle, taking in the quaint, quiet street. "Do we know what kind of vehicle Jasmine Toselli drives? Is it here? Maybe she's gone out."

The other officer pointed to a small Mitsubishi a couple of houses over. "That's her car."

Jasmine and Sam Toselli had come home. Why weren't they answering their door? Why wasn't Jasmine answering her phones?

Josie sprinted up the steps. "Let's go. We're going in. I don't want to waste any more time." She instructed the other officer to go to the back of the house and cover that entry point.

Noah joined her on the porch. "We can't force entry," he said gently.

"The hell we can't," Josie said.

"Josie, this is a welfare check. We can only go in if signs of a struggle or a body are visible. They're not."

"Noah," she said, feeling a vise tighten around her chest. "You know damn well this killer is after them. He may have already killed them."

"We can make some calls, try to get in touch with someone close to Jasmine Toselli. Maybe we can contact Sam's school and find out his emergency contact."

"We cannot wait," Josie said.

"The policy—"

Her words came out as a shout before she could stop them. "I don't give a damn about policy right now!" It was the first time she'd ever raised her voice to him. Noah stepped back. More quietly, she said, "This kid is Harris's age, Noah. He's seven years old. I'll go in there myself. You can step off this porch and I'll take responsibility for it. The Chief can fire me, for all I care. I won't be able to live with it if we hesitate and this boy dies. I—"

She stopped talking because Noah wasn't looking at her anymore. His gaze was locked on the door behind her, eyes cast downward at waist-level. "Josie," he croaked. "Look."

She turned toward the door. It was a screen door with glass panels. A large piece on the bottom and a smaller piece up top. At first all Josie saw was a child's greasy handprint on the lower glass panel. "I don't—" she began, but Noah moved closer. He took her shoulders and guided her over to where he had been standing.

"You can see it from this angle."

She looked back at the door. The vise squeezing her chest grew painfully tight. Noah was right. It wasn't visible unless you stood where the light hit the door just right. Left by the natural oils of the boy's finger was a crude drawing of a man's face. Just an oval, beady eyes, a slash for a nose, another slash for a mouth and wild scribbles for a beard. Next to that was what first appeared to be an arrow, but on closer examination, she realized it was meant to be a gun. Under both hastily drawn items were two words, scrawled in a seven-year-old's uncertain hand.

Bad Man.

Before Josie could react, Noah was in front of her, yanking the screen door open. His pistol was in his hands. He tried the front doorknob but it didn't budge. Stepping back, he lifted a booted foot and kicked at the area just next to the knob. It took three tries and then wood splintered and the door flew open.

He looked back at her. Somehow, her mind had gone on autopilot. Her pistol was in her hands, ready. Without thought, through muscle memory, they dropped into house-clearing mode. Noah took the lead.

As they stepped across the threshold, Noah swept the right side of the room while Josie swept the left. Her mind catalogued details as they went, filing them away for future use, if needed. A tiny foyer area was separated from the large living room by a waist-high wall. The carpet in the foyer was rumpled. In the living room, an iPad lay on the couch next to a crumpled blanket. A bowl of pretzels sat on the coffee table.

Next to it was a rectangular puzzle box.

"Noah," Josie choked out.

"I see it," he said. "Let's keep going."

She tore her eyes away from the box, trying to ignore the rush of blood in her ears, and process the rest of what she saw.

The television played a cartoon show that Harris watched so often that Josie could recite each episode from memory. Just on the other side of the half-wall, a dry-erase art easel lay on its side. Markers were scattered on the floor. A standing lamp lay broken in half nearby, a clump of curly brown hair tangled in its cord. Droplets of blood glimmered like rubies in the flickering light of the wrecked lamp.

There had been a struggle in this room. Jasmine Toselli had fought like hell.

Josie's heartbeat thundered painfully against her rib cage. She tried her best to tamp down her raging anxiety. It was hard not to think of Misty and Harris in this scenario. Imagining the terror that Jasmine and Sam must have felt gave Josie a visceral jolt.

They had to keep moving.

Next they moved into the kitchen, which was an open space that included a dining room set. Josie's throat almost closed up when she saw the fridge. Drawings of various animals and vehicles and a few dinosaurs covered half of it. The other half was wallpapered with photos of a woman and a young boy. Jasmine and Sam Toselli. At the zoo, at the city park, at a basketball game, at some kind of school awards assembly. Jasmine was younger than Josie had expected with curly brown hair and a wide, vibrant smile. Sam resembled her more than Beau, although Josie could see his resemblance to his father in his eyes and the shape of his jaw. He matched his mother's smile in every photo, his front tooth gap melting Josie's heart in the millisecond she took to study the photo. She had to force her attention away from the photos to keep her focus on the scene. A cell phone with a shattered screen lay near the doorway. A bowl of pasta had been dropped between the stove and the table, where two place settings waited. Beside one of them was a juice box.

After clearing the kitchen, they found a door to a basement. Josie was grateful that it was well-lit, having been converted to a home gym. Empty. They moved at a steady, measured pace up to the second floor. Two bedrooms and a bathroom, all undisturbed and empty. As they returned to the living room, Josie let out the breath she was holding, relieved that they hadn't found Jasmine or Sam already dead. But as soon as the thought passed through her mind, fear replaced it. If they weren't here, then the killer had them.

Noah stood in the middle of the living room. "She must have been in the kitchen when he showed up. Somehow, he got in. She panicked. He went into the kitchen and attacked her. The fight carried into here."

Josie tried to picture it. When had Sam had time to leave his message? Had he let the man in? Or had the front door been unlocked? Had Sam tried to run away when the killer confronted Jasmine in the kitchen and then froze? Perhaps he hadn't wanted to leave his mom. Had he watched from the door, scrawling his message, and tried to run back into the living room when the killer came out of the kitchen with Jasmine, leading to a second altercation? An even more chilling question flashed through Josie's mind. Did the blood in the living room belong to Sam or Jasmine? Or had one of them injured the killer badly enough to draw blood?

"We need to call Gretchen and Mett," she said. "And the ERT. We need to know what's in that box. Right now. This scene has to be processed. The street has to be canvassed. Footage from every single home that has cameras needs to be gathered. The 'bad man' in this drawing has a beard. Archie Gamble also has a beard. We need to check with the unit outside of his house."

Noah holstered his weapon and took out his phone. They went outside and assigned a uniformed officer to guard the scene until the ERT arrived.

Noah said, "I'm calling the state police. We need to get an Amber Alert out on Sam Toselli immediately."

Josie looked back toward the front door. "We need to prioritize getting that puzzle box open. It's possible that whatever is in it could help us find them before time runs out."

FORTY-NINE

"I can't just open it," said Hummel. "We have to process the scene. You know this."

Josie stood on Jasmine and Sam Toselli's front porch, facing off with him, hands on her hips. Noah was on the street, already on the phone with the state police working to get an Amber Alert out on Sam. "We don't have time for that, Hummel. Processing a crime scene takes hours. I need to know what's in that box right now. If there is something inside it that could help us find this mother and her son before they're murdered, we need to know."

Hummel sighed, straightened his skull cap, and paced a small circle in front of her.

Josie waved toward the front door. "Chan is in there right now taking photos. You can bring it out, dust it for latent prints right here using aluminum powder, and then open it."

"That's not how I usually like to do things," he said. "You know how these things go when we get to court. If there is even the slightest misstep, a defense attorney will have a field day with it."

Josie reached out and clamped a hand over his forearm,

stopping him in place. "We're talking about a seven-year-old boy, Hummel. We've got this killer's DNA from multiple other scenes already. If we can find Sam and Jasmine alive, the box won't matter so much. They'll be able to testify as witnesses. Please. I'm not asking you to compromise the entire scene. I'm asking you to open a box after it's been photographed."

Noah jogged up the steps. "Amber Alert is in the works. Gretchen and Mett will be here within the next sixty seconds. The officer stationed outside Gamble's house says he's there and has been all day. I've already got uniformed guys canvassing the neighbors to see if we can get anything—maybe someone saw this guy or they have cameras that will show a car." He stopped talking when he realized neither of them was paying attention. "What's going on?"

Josie didn't relinquish Hummel's arm. She kept her eyes locked with his. "Just open the box," she said quietly.

It felt like an eternity before he took his other hand and patted hers, sliding out of her grip. "Give me a few minutes."

Relief rushed through Josie as she watched him disappear into the house, calling for Officer Chan.

Before she could say anything to Noah, Gretchen and Mettner came running down the street. "We got here as soon as we could," said Mettner.

Josie and Noah joined them on the sidewalk, catching them up while Hummel processed the puzzle box and got it open. As they were talking, all of their phones blared an alarm simultaneously. It was the Amber Alert for Sam Toselli.

Josie closed it out on her phone and clicked on a text message that Chief Chitwood had sent to all of them. "Chief's going to do a press conference."

"Then we need to get him all the information we can," said Gretchen. "This is a pretty dense residential neighborhood. No way someone didn't see a car. This guy didn't kidnap a mother and child using his bicycle."

Noah said, "I've already got officers pulling any surveillance footage."

From the open hatch of the ERT's SUV, Hummel called, "Boss! I've got the box open!"

They ran over and crowded around Hummel. He'd laid down plastic sheeting in the back of the SUV so that he could dust the box for prints and then open it. A rubber mallet lay next to a few splintered pieces of the box. Directly in front of him, Hummel smoothed out a piece of newspaper that had been rolled up inside the box.

Mettner said, "Do they even print newspapers anymore?"

"It could be old," Gretchen pointed out.

Hummel said, "It doesn't have a date on it from what I can see."

"Is there any way to tell which newspaper it came from?" asked Noah.

Hummel turned it over, looking at the back, which appeared to be an ad for tree removal. "No, but you can probably find out given this article." He flipped it again and laid it out so they could read it. Josie's heart fluttered as she took in the words.

LENORE COUNTY WOMAN SUFFERS ANOXIC BRAIN INJURY IN TRAGIC CAR ACCIDENT

Lenore County resident, thirty-year-old Brooke Sullivan, suffered severe anoxic brain injuries after her vehicle crashed into Cedar Creek near Old Arch Bridge. Her vehicle was found Monday, suspended upside down from the bridge in what appears to be an accident. Only a broken part of the bridge and the branches of an encroaching tree near the creek bank kept the vehicle from plunging completely into the water. Sullivan was trapped inside the car by a malfunctioning seatbelt. Another Lenore County resident saw her vehicle as he

*drove past and called 911. By the time first responders got
there, more of the bridge had broken off, causing the vehicle to
fall even further down so that water from the creek entered it.
Mrs. Sullivan's head was submerged for an unknown amount
of time before first responders were able to cut her loose. Once
she was removed from the car, EMS workers were able to
revive her and transport her to Denton Memorial Hospital.*

*"She is in a persistent vegetative state," said the head of
neurology there. "She suffered injuries to her brain from lack of
oxygen when she was stuck inside the car with her head
submerged in water. We hope for the best in terms of her recovery, but we can't predict how much function, if any, she'll
regain."*

*Police do not know why Mrs. Sullivan crashed on the
bridge but have speculated that it could have been weather-
related, given that it was below freezing that day and the
bridge had iced over. They also advise that Mrs. Sullivan was
alone in the car, and they do not believe there were any other
vehicles involved in this accident.*

"Sullivan," Mettner said. "Why is that familiar?"

"Brooke is familiar as well," Noah added.

Gretchen said, "The social media guy for WYEP—his name
is Sullivan. Raffy Sullivan."

Josie said, "And he told us his ex-girlfriend's name was
Brooke."

"When we were there to talk about internet trolls, a woman
named Brooke kept calling him," Noah added.

Josie took out her phone and brought up her internet
browser, googling Brooke Sullivan. Only one source came up:
the article from the *Fairfield Review* in Lenore County. It was
the same article they'd just read. "She was in the accident five
years ago," said Josie. She found another database and ran a
quick check for Brooke Sullivan. "Apparently, she still lives in a

house in Lenore County—4342 Silver Springs Road in Fair-field. I'll check this on the MDT to make sure it's up to date, but I think it bears checking out."

Something about the address seemed familiar to Josie but she couldn't say why.

The sound of a cell phone ringing sent the rest of them searching for their devices. Noah held his out. "It's mine," he said. "The Eudora."

"Great," said Gretchen. "If Beau's there, tell them to keep him right where he is, we've got questions."

Noah answered, stepping away from them for a moment. Mettner said, "We didn't look into Raffy Sullivan's relationship status, only his background. He had no criminal record. No arrests. There was nothing concerning. So who is he? Why would the killer lead us to his ex-girlfriend—or I guess, his wife?"

Gretchen said, "They have the same last name. She could be his sister, although if he told Noah and Josie she was his ex-girlfriend then yeah, she's probably his wife or ex-wife. He was seeing Margot Huff. Maybe he didn't want her to know he was divorced."

"Or maybe he's still married to her," Mettner said.

Josie started running through the entire case in her mind once more. "This killer never intended to get away with all of this," she said.

"What do you mean?" said Mettner.

Gretchen studied Josie. "The boss is right. This case has always been about ruining Beau Collins's life."

"He wants revenge for something," Mettner said. "Seems like Beau Collins has a long list of sins to atone for, though."

The killer had started with Claudia, staging the murder scene on a night that the couple had intended to publicize in a huge way. He'd left behind a puzzle box that he'd likely ordered from the Collinses' website that contained a page from their book. A book about pursuit and playing games as a way to strengthen relationships. Even before the killer texted Margot from Eve's phone saying the game was on, it was apparent he was playing a game.

The object was not just to ruin Beau's life but to expose him. Expose all his secrets. The affair with Eve. The stolen job application. The secret family. Josie had long theorized that the killer was someone in Beau and Claudia's inner circle. It seemed as though no one fit the bill.

"Raffy Sullivan has had access to the Collinses' inner circle for months," Josie said. "Like Gretchen said, he's been dating Margot. When we met with him, she had even left her phone in his office, unattended, while she went to the restroom. She trusts him. He's in the station because he works there. He's got plenty of access."

Gretchen said, "You think Raffy Sullivan is the killer?"

"I don't know," said Josie.

Mettner said, "If he's the killer, why would he point us right at him? It doesn't make sense. The pattern is that the thing in the box leads to a secret that Beau was keeping. Brooke Sullivan has to be the secret. I don't think we have enough information to make the leap that Raffy is the killer. We don't know nearly enough about him or where he fits in. We need to track Raffy down and talk to him. I interviewed him the first day at the studio. I ran his background check. He rents an apartment not far from here. I can also call WYEP and see if he's there."

Noah stepped back into the circle. "He's not."

"What do you mean?" asked Josie.

Noah held up his phone even though the screen was black now. "That was Mr. Brown, the manager of the Eudora. A staff member reported that they saw Beau leaving the hotel through a rear service entrance with another man about twenty minutes ago. They're pulling the footage now but the man with Beau was described as approximately thirty-five to forty years old, tall with brown hair and a goatee."

"It sounds like that could be Raffy," said Gretchen.

Noah started to jog away, calling over his shoulder, "I'm going to go over there and look at the footage myself. I'll let you guys know."

"In the meantime," said Josie. "I think that someone needs to track down the bridge where this accident happened. Whether the killer is Raffy or not, he'll be staging Jasmine and Sam's murders at this bridge."

"What makes you say that?" asked Mettner.

"He killed Claudia at her anniversary dinner—in many ways, the Collinses' marriage was a sham. He killed Eve in Lovers' Cave—she was Beau's secret lover. He killed Trudy in the practice office—the site of Trudy and Beau's 'crime' against Claudia. This killer has been leading us the entire time. Leading us on a tour of Beau's secrets, indiscretions, and sins. Why would he leave this article at this scene if he didn't intend for it to expose some new secret or lead us to Sam and Jasmine's bodies? This article leads us to the bridge."

Gretchen touched Mettner's shoulder. "You stay here and work this scene. Get us anything you can. Witnesses, footage. You said Raffy's apartment isn't far from here? Send a unit there to knock on his door. While you're doing that, I'll head down to Lenore County, find this bridge, and check it out."

"I'll check on the last known address of Brooke Sullivan," Josie said.

Mettner said, "You're going there alone?"

"Of course not," she said. "The article says she's a Lenore County resident. I'll call the sheriff down there and ask for an assist. I'm sure someone will meet me there. If we're going into their territory, talking with Brooke and checking out the bridge, we've got to give them a heads-up."

"I'll make a call, too," said Gretchen.

As Josie watched her colleagues split off to work different leads, her phone trilled. She took it out and swiped answer. "Quinn."

Their desk sergeant, Dan Lamay, said, "Boss, I just hung up from a call with the officer assigned to Archie Gamble."

Dread was a brick in Josie's stomach. "What did he say?"

"Uh, Archie Gamble is gone."

"What?"

"He's not at his house and the officer cannot locate him."

"Are you sure?"

"Uh, yeah. Apparently, the officer on duty saw him leave his house on foot and go into the woods. He hasn't been seen since."

"How long ago?" asked Josie.

"About twenty minutes."

She sighed. "I'll handle it."

FIFTY

DIARY ENTRY, UNDATED

I know who it is now. My lover. Today, a woman came to our house. I don't see anyone besides my husband anymore other than when we go see the doctors. I know this because I write in this diary every day, so I'll remember what happened. I scoured all the entries since the accident. None mention people other than the doctors. When I heard a woman's voice coming from the kitchen, I knew I had heard it before. I had to see her face. Something might come back to me if I saw her. I only meant to peek into the room, but I fell. Since the accident, I fall a lot. They heard me. My husband took great pleasure in letting her see me. He asked questions I didn't know the answers to until I finally started crying. Each time I said I don't know or I don't remember, he seemed to get happier. It felt sadistic. The woman must have thought so, too, because she cried, too. After she left, I asked who she was. He said he would show me. He got out his laptop and put something on for me. A clip from a television show. It was called Couples' Corner With The Collinses. I recognized the woman who had just been to our house.

And the man. As soon as I saw him, I knew. He was the one.

The man I loved. And he is on television with his wife while I waste away here in this tiny circle of hell with a man who claims he is my husband but whose hatred for me seems to have no end.

FIFTY-ONE

Inside her vehicle, Josie blasted the heat. The chill that had taken hold of her the moment she saw Sam Toselli's drawing on the door wouldn't let go. She fired up the Mobile Data Terminal and took a moment to look up Brooke Sullivan. There wasn't much information. She'd never been arrested, much less convicted of any crime. Her driver's license had expired three years ago but the photo showed a young woman with long brown hair and a close-lipped smile. She looked as though she would be quite beautiful if only the weight of the world wasn't on her shoulders. Josie wondered what she had been dealing with when this photo was taken. If Raffy was a cold-blooded killer, it was doubtful he'd made a pleasant husband. Having heard the way he talked about both Brooke and Margot when he thought he and Noah were speaking privately, Josie wouldn't have been surprised if there was a history of abuse. She couldn't find any reports of domestic calls to their residence, but that meant little.

Next, she honed in on the address in Lenore County. Something about it nagged at the back of her brain still. The house was listed in Brooke's name only. She pulled it up on a map.

Zooming out, she saw it was a few miles down the road from Archie Gamble's ramshackle home. If Raffy was behind all this, it would have been easy for him to drive Eve Bowers's car to the state gameland adjacent to Gamble's house, abandon it and then take his own car home. He could easily have passed through Gamble's property. For all they knew, he could have used one of the many bicycles on Gamble's property to go back and forth to town, thereby throwing suspicion onto Gamble. Josie doubted that Gamble would notice if something had gone missing from the premises, especially if it was returned. There was also the possibility that the two were working together.

Since Gamble's house was on the way to the Sullivan home, she would stop there first. As she drove, she used the hands-free feature in her car to call the Lenore County Sheriff's office and explain the situation. Gretchen had already contacted them regarding the bridge. Their staff was stretched thin due to a bus accident on the interstate near their county seat, but they promised to dispatch a unit to meet Gretchen at the bridge and another to meet Josie at the Sullivan house. Josie's next call was to Luke. If Archie Gamble had left his home on foot, Blue would be able to follow the scent. Luke and Blue were already on another case in a neighboring county but promised to get to Denton as soon as possible.

A drop of sweat slid down her spine. She toggled the heating switch. She'd been so engrossed in the conversation that she hadn't noticed the heat becoming so intense. The air blasting through the vents fell to a soft, steady hum. Still, sweat gathered in Josie's armpits and along her hairline. She rolled down her window, letting in the crisp night air. A moment later, the cruiser assigned to Archie Gamble's house came into view, its lights flashing. Josie parked behind it and got out, jogging up to the door. The officer rolled his window down. Immediately, she recognized Brennan.

He wiped sweat from his brow with the back of his sleeve.

His face was flushed. "I called for more units," he told her. "No one's come yet."

"They're pretty busy," Josie replied.

Brennan motioned across the street toward Gamble's house. A single light glowed in the front window. "I went after him, but I got lost and turned around in the woods. Even with my flashlight. I couldn't find him. Once I found my way out, I figured I'd call in reinforcements, but no one has come."

"Luke Creighton and his dog are on their way," Josie said. "They'll be able to help, although I'm not sure that Archie Gamble is our biggest problem anymore."

"You sure?" said Brennan. "'Cause when he came out of his house, it looked like he had a weapon."

The dread in Josie's stomach expanded. "What kind of a weapon?"

Brennan shrugged. "Don't know. I was too far away. Something shiny, though. Could have been a knife, could have been a pistol. Hard to tell."

Josie swore. She had no idea what Gamble was up to or why he had finally chosen to leave the house at this precise time after so many days of inactivity. "Okay," she said. "You wait here for Luke and Blue. They shouldn't be much longer. I've got to head down the road and check something out. If I'm not back by the time Luke and Blue get here, just go on without me."

Moments later, she pulled into the driveway of the Sullivan home. It was located on a road similar to Archie Gamble's—dark, barely used, crowded with trees, with no neighbors nearby. That was where the similarities ended. While there were no adornments outside this house, it was clean and looked well-tended. It was a simple, single-level cottage. Josie saw no vehicles when she pulled into the gravel driveway, nor did she see any Lenore County Sheriff's cars. She made another call and received another promise that someone would be out to assist her shortly.

Then she weighed her options.

If Raffy was really the killer, would he have brought Sam and Jasmine here?

Josie called Noah. He answered on the second ring. "Hey," he said. "I was just getting ready to call you. We got something."

"At the hotel?" she asked.

"And on the street," he replied. "Mett said that none of the neighbors saw anything but one of their cameras picked up footage of a man forcing Jasmine and Sam into the trunk of a black sedan. It's grainy, from a bad angle, and far away, but that is what it shows."

Josie felt a flutter in her chest. "What about the hotel?" she asked.

"It's him," Noah said. "Brown has much better footage of Raffy going to Beau's hotel room door. He disappears inside for a few minutes and then they come out together. Down the back stairwell and out the service entrance. No gun, but Beau looks scared shitless. Beau's phone was left in the room. We're pulling the parking lot footage now. Now that we've got confirmation on Raffy, we're putting a BOLO out for the car. Where are you?"

"I'm sitting outside the Sullivan house waiting for a deputy to back me up here. Noah, what's the timeline?"

"Footage shows him abducting Jasmine and Sam at five fifty-three. Then at six forty-seven, he shows up at the hotel. He left with Beau at seven twenty-eight. Mett and I are going to try to follow the car on surveillance from here as soon as we've got it on camera outside."

It was after nine. If Raffy was bringing Beau and the Tosellis here to this house, he would have been here already. If he'd meant for police to find them all, he wouldn't have hidden his car. He wasn't here. Had enough time passed for him to get to the bridge? It appeared that way and yet, there hadn't been any word from Gretchen yet.

"All right," Josie said. "Keep me posted."

She got out and went to the front stoop. Standing under a circle of pale light, she unsnapped her holster. The fluttering in her chest grew more frenzied. Without warning, the front door swung open.

FIFTY-TWO

A woman who only vaguely resembled Brooke Sullivan stood before Josie, staring blankly. Her brown hair was past her waist, but it was matted in several places. Some of the knots had turned into full-blown clumps of hair. The skin of her face was so pale, it was almost translucent. Her eyes were sunken. She wore a T-shirt with a sweater over the top. The sweater's buttons had been fastened crooked. It didn't match her sweatpants. One of her socks was a different color than the other.

"Who are you?" she asked Josie.

Josie took out her credentials and turned them toward Brooke.

"The police?" she said. "Why are you here?"

"Are you Brooke Sullivan?" Josie asked.

She scratched at her temple, her wrist jerking in a repetitive movement. Instead of answering, she turned away and moved deeper into the house. Josie put her hand on the grip of her gun and followed Brooke inside. The house didn't have much in the way of furniture. In the living room, an old, sagging blue couch sat in front of an entertainment center. It held a small television that was turned off. There were no photos or even wall art anywhere in the room. The coffee table, instead of being in front of the couch, had been pushed across the room, up against a bare wall. Two lamps stood behind the couch, casting circles of light over its worn fabric. Josie followed Brooke.

In the kitchen doorway, she froze. Josie caught up to her and, peering over her shoulder, saw all the Post-it notes that had been stuck to almost every surface in the room. On the fridge, one read: *Close the door*. The kitchen faucet had two Post-its on the wall behind it, indicating which was hot and which was cold. The toaster and coffeemaker were labeled. All the cabinets had notes taped to them with a list of their contents. Brooke stopped walking when she came to an island countertop.

"Mrs. Sullivan," Josie said. "Is there anyone here with you?"

Brooke turned back to Josie, smiling uncertainly. "I stay here alone because I have to. He used to come sometimes but now he is never here. Unless I'm not remembering." Her chin dipped to her chest. When she lifted it again to meet Josie's gaze, her brow furrowed. "Who are you?"

Josie stepped forward and offered her credentials again. Brooke stared at Josie's ID but Josie got the distinct impression that she wasn't seeing it at all. "Brooke," Josie said. "Do you live here alone?"

"I have to," she said. "He said I have to live alone because of what I did."

"What did you do?"

Brooke pulled a stool out from under the countertop and sat on it. She spent several seconds balancing herself just right on the top of it before noticing Josie again. "Did you say you're with the police?"

"Yes," Josie said. "I wanted to ask you some questions."

"About the accident?"

"No," Josie said. "About Beau Collins. Do you remember him?"

Something passed over her face, a shadow, but she shook her head. "I'm not sure."

"Are you married?"

"I'm not sure. Wait. Yes, I think I am, except he doesn't come back as much now. Maybe I'm not."

Distress gnawed at Josie's insides. What was this woman doing out here in the middle of nowhere living by herself when she couldn't even remember if she was married or not? Josie touched a nearby Post-it that said *Eat at this table*. "Who puts these up for you?"

"They're so I remember not to burn the house down," Brooke explained.

"Whose house is this?" asked Josie.

"It's mine. It's always been mine. That's why he left instead of me. He said I could stay here because I got a... I got... a settlement! That's it!" She clapped her hands together triumphantly. "I remembered!"

"That's great," Josie said. "Do you know what a settlement is?"

Brooke frowned. Several seconds passed. "No. I don't. I only know he waited years and years for it so he would have enough to leave me here finally and go live... in town? I think that's what he said. I have a lot of trouble remembering since the accident. I'm sorry."

She had most likely received an insurance payout after her accident although, being the only driver involved, Josie wasn't sure how she had managed to get a settlement unless her attorney had been able to prove negligence on the part of the township in terms of de-icing the bridge, or some sort of defect in the bridge itself that had not been cured. But for Josie's purposes, it didn't matter. She asked, "Who takes care of you, Brooke?"

"I do everything now," Brooke said proudly. "I get dressed

myself and take a shower and I can even make some kinds of food now."

Sadness stabbed at Josie's heart. "Right, but who comes to this house and brings you food? Makes sure you're okay?"

"He does," Brooke said simply.

Josie swallowed down her frustration, wondering if Brooke even remembered Raffy's name. "Who is he?"

Brooke said, "My... I'm so sorry. I can see him in my mind. I know his face. I just can't—" She squinted as if light was being shone directly into her eyes.

Josie took her phone out to pull up a photo of Raffy but realized she didn't have a photo of him. He hadn't been a suspect up to this point in the investigation.

Brooke said, "Do you want to see my memory box?"

For the first time since Josie had entered the house, she felt a surge of hope. "What's your memory box?"

Brooke smiled. "It's exactly what it sounds like. The place I keep all my memories. The ones I can't hold onto since the accident. Usually, I forget where it is or he moves it but if I can find it, I can tell you the answers to your questions."

"Sure," said Josie.

She followed Brooke from room to room, watching her check various hiding places—inside cabinets and under furniture. There were only two bedrooms. One was empty. The other had a queen-sized bed and a single dresser. More Post-its announced the contents of each of its drawers. Finally, in the depths of the bathroom closet, at the back of a shelf marked *Pads and Tampons*, behind two boxes of feminine products, she found a shoebox. She went back to the living room, but rather than sitting on the couch, she sat cross-legged on the floor, cradling the box in her lap. Josie squatted beside her to get a better look at it. The name "Brooke" was scrawled across the front.

Again, sadness pricked at Josie like a thousand tiny bee stings.

Brooke pointed to the name. "This is my name. Brooke."

She carefully lifted the lid from the box. One by one, she took the contents out and placed them all around her on the floor. Photographs, a newspaper clipping, loose notes, and a diary. She tapped a finger against the newspaper article. Josie leaned in to see that it was the same one that had been left at the Toselli house.

"This is why I have trouble remembering," Brooke said. "I remember a lot about the accident, even though he thinks I don't. There's something about the accident that I need to remember, though. Something important. Oh wait! I know!"

She stood and went back into the kitchen. There was a commotion. Pots clanging, silverware clattering. Moments later, she returned with a brown paper bag with handles. She set it in front of Josie and cleared away takeout menus from the very top of it. Beneath that were stacks of hundred-dollar bills. "Where did you get this?" Josie asked.

"From the accident lady," Brooke said. "She came here—" She squeezed her eyes shut, face turned upward, pinched as though she had tasted something sour. After a few seconds, she opened them and said, "Twice!" She grinned triumphantly. "I remembered! The first time she came to talk to him, and I only saw her by mistake. That was a very bad day."

She frowned, her eyes taking on a faraway look. Josie wasn't sure if she was searching for the memory or if she'd found it—or fragments of it—and didn't like what was there.

"What about the second time?" Josie asked.

"The second time?"

"The second time that the accident lady came here," Josie reminded her.

"Right, right." Brooke knelt down again and touched the stacks of hundred-dollar bills, running her fingers across them as if they held some kind of Braille. She said, "She gave this to me. Because of the accident. I can keep it. I'm supposed to give it to him, but I didn't. He's... mean and cruel and I need to get away from him. Do you think this is enough?"

Josie could barely take in a breath. "Enough for what?"

"To get away from him?"

"Oh, Brooke," Josie said softly. "I can help you get away from him with or without money."

Fear flashed across Brooke's face. She looked back at the doorway. "Okay, but we have to be careful."

Josie stood and took a quick walk back to the front door. There was no movement outside. Returning to Brooke, she took her phone out and pulled up a photo of Claudia Collins. "Is this the accident lady?"

Brooke frowned. "I'm not sure."

Josie pointed to the stacks of bills inside the bag. "If I counted this, would there be thirty thousand dollars?"

"I don't know."

Josie turned her attention to the photographs. Her heart was pounding so hard in her chest, she was sure Brooke would hear it. She hadn't really needed confirmation since the pieces were all coming together in her head but there it was—if you looked hard enough. The man in the photos with a much younger, more kempt Brooke had thick glasses, long blond hair, and about a hundred extra pounds on his person. He looked very different now.

But his eyes were the same.

"Your husband is called Rafferty," Josie said. "People call him Raffy."

Brooke reached over and snatched up the photo of the two of them at their wedding. "This is him!" she said. "I am married. This is my husband."

"Yes," Josie said. "Do you know where he is right now?"

"No, I'm sorry, I don't know. But I told you, my memory is

bad." She picked up the diary and handed it to Josie. "That's why I keep this. I found it after the accident and started writing in it again so I don't forget so many things. You read it. Maybe it says where he goes when he's not here."

Josie took it and began to page through it. It was thick, with several entries, none of which were dated. She could tell the pre-accident entries from the post-accident entries because Brooke's handwriting had altered slightly. She moved toward the end of the entries, reading as quickly as she could. It didn't say much at all about Raffy other than how cruel and abusive he had always been. There were no clues to where he might have gone. The biggest revelation was that Brooke and Beau had been lovers. Josie was not surprised. There seemed no end to the women Beau had been involved with behind his wife's back. She kept going until the end, letting out a gasp as she read the final entry.

"Are you okay?" asked Brooke.

"Um, yes," said Josie.

"Did you find what you were looking for?"

"Not exactly." Josie put the diary back into the box and then brought up a photo of Beau Collins on her phone. She turned it toward Brooke. "Do you remember this man?"

Brooke tugged at a long, greasy shank of her hair. A deep sorrow pooled in her eyes. "He was my lover," she said. "It's one of the few things I can remember but I think it's only if I see his face. The more I see it, the more that comes back. I wish he would come and get me. My husband says he will never come back for me because he is a..." she took a moment to find the memory. "A lecherous liar."

The words hit Josie like a slap. The review. *Beau Collins is a lecherous liar who cannot be trusted. He is not a real therapist. He's not there to help you. He's there to steal your wife.*

"Brooke," Josie said. "This man's name is Beau Collins. Do

you remember you and your husband going to marriage counseling with him?"

Brooke looked down at her lap. "I did a bad thing and I have to pay."

Josie reached over and touched Brooke's hand gently to get her attention. The woman quickly clasped Josie's fingers, holding on tightly. "Brooke," Josie said. "I think you've paid enough."

Brooke nearly knocked Josie over as she sprang up from her haunches and threw her arms around Josie's neck. Still on her knees, it was a challenge to stay upright, but Josie accepted the hug and slowly returned it. Brooke smelled sour but Josie barely registered it. She wondered, when was the last time anyone had hugged this woman or shown her any affection at all? When was the last time she'd been out of this house? When was the last time she had seen anyone besides Raffy or Claudia Collins? What the hell had Claudia Collins been doing, giving the Sullivans thirty thousand dollars in cash?

Brooke was facing the front door. When her body went from relaxed to tense, Josie knew something was wrong. The floorboards creaked. Hanging onto Brooke, Josie turned both their bodies, pivoting on one of her kneecaps to see Archie Gamble flying toward both of them with something metal flashing in his hand.

FIFTY-THREE

The three seconds it took for Gamble to get from the door to looming over Josie and Brooke went by in slow motion. As Josie pulled Brooke onto her and rolled to the side, the flash of metal in Gamble's hand resolved into the shiny blunt end of a hammer. As he smashed the hammer down onto the place where Josie and Brooke had just been, Josie rolled again until they were clear of the couch and she was straddling a shocked Brooke. Frozen in place, both hands to her chest, Brooke stared up at Josie with wide, frightened eyes. There was no time to reassure her.

Josie brought her left leg up, foot flat, ready to stand as her right hand unholstered her pistol. Gamble pivoted from where he had stumbled into empty space, slicing the hammer downward, and came at her. Before Josie could call out and tell him to stop or even properly aim at him, he was on her, sweeping the hammer down and toward the side. It hit the pistol, ripping it from Josie's grip, and sending it somewhere into the corner of the room. Brooke shrieked.

Josie's body reacted without thought. As he wound up again to bring the hammer down on her head, she sprang up, away from Brooke's prone form, and charged at him, spinning as she came into contact with his body until her back was pressed against his chest. Both her hands followed the length of his sinewy arm, all the way to the hammer's long handle. His free hand found her face, clamping over her mouth. It tasted of cigarettes and dirt. His fingers dug into the scar on the side of her face, making it sting and bringing back memories of her six-year-old self, sliced open, bloodied, afraid.

Twenty-seven stitches.

When he yanked at her jaw, it only pissed her off more. She held fast to the handle of the hammer and bit down whatever hunk of flesh her teeth could find. He made a guttural noise deep in his chest. She felt the vibration against her back, and she held on, jaw clenching tighter until something hot and coppery filled her mouth. Flesh gave way. His grip on the hammer loosened just slightly. Josie used both her hands to yank the hammer from his grip. Staying in the tight circle of his arms, she spun again, away from the hand she'd just bitten, and used her body's momentum to bury the head of the hammer into his thigh. As she completed the turn, now facing him, he stumbled backward. Somehow, he managed to stop himself from falling all the way onto his back, instead falling onto his knees. He nearly buckled when his right knee hit the floor. His facial expression morphed from anger to shock to intense pain. Yet, when he looked up at her, Josie knew he was nowhere near finished with her.

She'd been in enough scuffles as both a woman and a police officer to know that most of the time, a devastating blow to certain parts of the body would knock an opponent down and either put them out of the fight or stun them long enough for you to subdue them, but every once in a while, the opposite happened. A blow like the one she'd just delivered to Gamble's leg sent a person's adrenaline into overdrive, numbing any pain they might be feeling and giving them the strength of two very pissed-off people.

Gamble was pissed.

Their eyes locked for a fleeting second. His lip curled upward in the sort of smile that told her that he was very much going to enjoy killing her in the most savage way possible.

Josie lifted her chin in acknowledgement and then spat out the hunk of his hand she'd torn off directly in front of him.

Then they flew at one another. She had a slight advantage since he was on his knees, but it didn't last long. He was bigger and stronger. Still, she stayed tight to his body so that he couldn't put much strength or momentum behind any of the blows that he rained down on her head and shoulders. She used her elbows on his rib cage to no avail. When she felt their bodies falling—her on the bottom—she reached down and, through his jeans, did her best to grab the biggest fistful of skin and muscle on his inner thigh that she possibly could, hoping she'd find the exact spot she'd hit him earlier.

She did.

He howled as he fell on top of her, but again, it only seemed to infuse him with more rage and energy. Straddling her, even with one mostly dead leg, he started throwing punches at her head. Josie dipped her chin to her chest, curled her hands into fists, and brought them up over her head, twisting from side to side so that her fists and forearms took the brunt of the onslaught. Her lower body worked to shimmy out from beneath him. When that didn't work, she pressed her feet flat to the floor and drew her knees up. She hooked a foot over one of his ankles and tried to roll, using her hips to throw him off balance. It stopped the punches for a brief, glorious second, but he stayed on top of her.

"You bitch!" he grunted. He had a few more choice words for her, but Josie's mind tuned them out, searching through every hand-to-hand combat tactic she knew to try to get out of this. A couple of punches made it past her defenses, glancing off her shoulder, her forehead, her collarbone. She put one foot flat and used her other knee to try to hit him in the kidney. Mostly, she hit his tailbone which only made him angrier.

Then, suddenly, he stopped. Disoriented, Josie lost the precious seconds between his last punch and his entire upper body suddenly pressing down on her. His chest pushed her fists into her face. His blood-covered T-shirt scraped over her forehead. For a moment, she thought he had simply decided to smother her but then the weight of him on her chest shifted back to her pelvis. He straightened his upper body, looking down at her with that menacing smile. In his hand was the hammer, claw edge pointed right at her. Blood dripped down the handle, snaking down his arm. He'd stopped to reach for it. He had seen it on the floor and stopped to reach for it.

Even if she used her forearms to block it, the hammer would shatter her bones. She had no chance against it. He'd kill her in moments.

For the first time, fear edged out Josie's anger and adrenaline.

She was going to die.

Time slowed. Everything around them seemed to stop, plunged into an ether with the consistency of molasses. Light glinted off the claw of the hammer as it began to descend. A breeze ruffled the hair near Josie's ear. She swore she heard her late grandmother's voice. It was just a whisper, but it sounded as clear as anything Josie had ever heard.

Not yet, dear.

The hammer's trajectory was suddenly knocked off course, jerking to the side. A large figure slammed into Archie Gamble's body. Josie was relieved of his weight. At first, she thought she was hallucinating. Then time sped up again and her senses returned. A dog started barking ferociously.

In a swirling heap beside her, Luke and Gamble struggled,

wrestling around on the floor. The hammer lay a few feet from them. Luke was bigger than Gamble, but his hands weren't equipped for fighting and Josie knew he hadn't been in a physical confrontation in almost a decade. Blue stood back, hackles raised, barking and snarling, long strings of saliva shooting from his mouth. Josie tried to stand up and fell. The fight had taken more out of her than she realized.

She looked around for Brooke but she was gone. Josie crawled around, looking for her pistol. Gamble managed to squirm away from Luke. He lunged for the hammer with his uninjured hand and grasped the handle. He was on his feet before Luke could recover. The leg that Josie had struck earlier buckled a little, but Gamble stayed upright. Even as her hands searched the floor for her pistol, Josie watched in horror as Luke's feet scrabbled, pushing his body until it hit the wall. He didn't try to get up. He couldn't.

The panic had him again.

Josie recognized it from the day outside of Gamble's house. It was the hammer, she realized. They'd never talked about it, but it was likely that a hammer had been used in the torture sessions that had shattered his hands. His eyes were locked on the blunt end of it, pointed down at him as Gamble loomed.

"Son," he said. "By the time I get done with you, there won't be anything left of those things you call hands for any doctor to put back together."

Josie called, "Luke!" but even if he'd been able to hear her over Blue's barking, he was too far gone to register her voice. She had to abandon the search for the pistol and go at Gamble again. Luke was defenseless. He wasn't going to come out of this. Josie staggered to her feet and charged at Gamble but before she could get there, Blue launched himself, barreling into Gamble and knocking him to the floor.

Blue was a blur, biting at Gamble, tearing flesh, making noises that Josie would never have imagined the sweet dog capable of making. Gamble squirmed and struggled under the dog, grunting.

Josie spotted her pistol near where Luke had fallen. She stumbled toward him, dropping to her knees again. The gun was right next to him. She cupped his cheeks and talked into his face, his unseeing eyes. "Luke, it's okay. This is almost over." She reached down next to him and touched her pistol. "My gun is right here. I've got this—"

Blue yelped. A sound that sent a wave of nausea and horror right through Josie. Now everything seemed to move at warp speed. There was a split second of silence. Gamble grunted. Blue yelped again. Luke blinked. Awareness flashed through his eyes. Josie felt his warm palm over hers.

Then the gun was gone from her grip. Luke pushed her aside. Josie said, "Luke!"

Blue had started to limp away from Gamble, whimper-snarling back at him as he went. Gamble got to his knees, hammer in hand. Blood flew from his various wounds with each movement. Blue had done a number on him.

Luke pointed the pistol at Gamble. "Don't touch my dog, you son of a bitch."

Then he fired a shot into Archie Gamble's chest.

FIFTY-FOUR

Outside of Brooke Sullivan's home, at least a half dozen emergency vehicles had amassed. Lenore County Sheriff's deputies, Denton cruisers, and ambulances. Brooke had been loaded into the back of an ambulance where EMTs were checking her over. Noah pulled up shortly after, as well as Chief Chitwood. Over their protests, Josie refused to be checked out by the EMTs until Blue was taken care of. Luke had stayed inside the house, sitting on the floor, cradling him and crying into his fur, just feet from Archie Gamble's body.

Noah gently took her face in his hands, grimacing. Gamble's blood was drying on her face, but she still tasted it in her mouth. "You're hurt."

"No," Josie said. "I'm fine. Not my blood. Please, we have to help Blue and Luke."

Noah found some water and a towel. Josie cleaned herself up as best she could while she, Noah and the Chief discussed the situation.

Once they had a plan in place, Noah walked Josie back inside. She knelt beside Luke and touched his shoulder. He flinched but relaxed when he looked up and saw it was her.

"Luke," she said. "Brennan is outside in one of our cruisers. He's going to take you and Blue back to Denton. I've already called our vet. Her name is Dr. Courtney Capone. She's the best there is, and she's waiting at the hospital for you two to get there."

Noah said, "Full lights and sirens."

Luke nodded wordlessly. Together, Josie and Noah helped him and Blue up and walked him out to where Brennan waited. Once they were gone, Noah took Josie by the shoulders and looked her over. At his touch, a tremor went through her. She had almost died. Would have died if it wasn't for Luke and Blue. Noah leaned in, pressing his forehead against hers. He snaked a hand around the back of her neck. They breathed into one another while Josie fought off a tidal wave of emotion. Raffy was still out there. Jasmine and Sam Toselli were still out there. Alive, hopefully.

"Ahem," Chief Chitwood coughed.

Josie and Noah parted and looked over at him. "I made the rounds here. Looks like Gamble left his house with his trusty hammer to come here. We have no idea why. Not sure who he was after—Brooke or Raffy—since he had no way of knowing Quinn would be here."

Josie touched a tender spot in the center of her forehead. Only now were all the sore places on her body starting to announce themselves. "He didn't exactly stop to ask questions."

"Seeing as he left his house with a hammer," said the Chief, "I think he was out for blood. Any blood. Luke and Blue tracked him here through the woods. Patrol units couldn't keep up with the dog."

"What the hell happened to my back-up unit from Lenore County?" Josie complained.

"He was late," the Chief said.

Noah said, "He was late, and it almost got Josie killed."

"No," said Josie. "I chose to go in there alone. There was no threat when I went inside. How the hell could I have known

Gamble would come here? How does he even know Brooke? Or Raffy?"

"Listen, Detectives, we don't have time for any of this right now," the Chief interjected. "We can hash out blame later if you want. Right now, what's most important is that Quinn is alive, Gamble is out of commission, and we still have a mother and son to find. Gretchen and Mettner went to the bridge from the article— Old Arch Bridge. Lenore County deputies were able to direct them there, but it's been closed since that accident. It was shut down years ago. It was too structurally damaged from when Brooke's car went through the guardrail. They closed it off. There's nothing there. No one. We pinged Raffy's phone and got nothing."

"What?" Josie said. She ran a finger the length of the scar on her face, feeling a brush burn where Gamble had damn near ripped her face off. "That can't be right. Why would he leave the article if he didn't mean for us to go to that bridge? That's where the accident took place."

Noah said, "Are you sure it has to be that bridge? You think he's trying to recreate the accident?"

"Yes," Josie said. "I think that he is. I think all of this is leading to that. He's taken huge risks committing all these murders. He was careful—using a bicycle, throwing suspicion onto Archie Gamble, and turning the phones off—but he was only being careful long enough to be able to see his plan all the way through."

"What's his plan?" asked the Chief.

Noah said, "To expose every single one of Beau Collins's secrets and destroy his life."

"And to leave Beau alive to endure the aftermath," Josie said. "This was always about making Beau suffer. Think about this: Raffy and Brooke went to Beau for help in their marriage. Beau had an affair with Brooke. According to the diary, she was going to leave Raffy."

"What diary?" Noah and the Chief said in unison.

Josie explained about Brooke's diary. "But once the accident happened," she continued, "Beau abandoned her. She was still married to Raffy. He was responsible for her, and she needed a lot of care—still needs a lot of care. Even if he could have gotten past the cheating—which he never would have, given that he was violent toward her to begin with—he isn't married to the same person anymore."

"But he still has to live with the aftermath," Noah said. "Caring for a wife who fully intended to leave him for their therapist, who no longer even remembers him, all while said therapist goes on to become rich and famous, living in a grand home with his wife, who is healthy and unscathed."

"He's been planning this for a long time," Josie said. "I don't know if he worked at WYEP before all this or if he got the job afterward but he lost weight, dyed his hair, changed his appearance and ingratiated himself into Beau and Claudia's inner circle at the TV station so that he could gain inside knowledge of their lives—find out all of Beau's sordid secrets. Brooke said she got a settlement from the accident and that's when Raffy left her to 'live in town.' He must have gotten his apartment with some of the money so that he could start dating Margot without her ever knowing he was still married or becoming suspicious of him. Claudia must have found out who he was somehow. She must have thought he was going to expose them just at the moment they were about to go national. She showed up here with money. Thirty thousand dollars in cash. Maybe she meant to pay Raffy off, but then alone with Brooke, she couldn't bring herself to do it?"

Noah said, "I don't think Raffy would have taken the money anyway. This was never about the money for him."

The Chief said, "Quinn, I know you just got your ass kicked in there, but I need you to focus. If this guy means to end it all tonight with Beau's secret child and the kid's mother, where would he do it?"

Josie looked around until she saw Brooke in the back of one of the ambulances, looking scared and confused. "It's a long shot, but she might know."

Noah and the Chief followed Josie over to the ambulance. They waited outside while she climbed in and sat on the bench beside the gurney. Brooke's brows furrowed as she studied Josie. A few seconds later, she smiled and said, "You're the police!"

Josie couldn't contain her own smile. "You remembered! That's great. Yes, I'm Detective Josie Quinn. We met earlier. We talked, and you told me about the accident you were in, how you have trouble remembering things. We talked about your husband and the 'accident lady.'"

Brooke nodded along, although Josie wasn't sure how much of the night she truly remembered.

Josie found her phone inside a coat pocket. Somehow, it had survived the attack by Archie Gamble. She pulled up the photo of Beau Collins, remembering what Brooke had said, that seeing his face sometimes helped her remember things. She handed the phone to Brooke. "I want you to hold that. Look at his face."

Brooke peered at it. Her face clouded, then realization flashed through her eyes. "That's him! My lover! He's on television and I'm here. My husband says he's a 'lecherous liar.'"

"Yes," Josie said. "That's what you told me earlier. Brooke, I know you use your diary to keep track of things you've forgotten. You remember how, in the diary, you wrote about your husband being abusive? How he hated Beau? This man." Josie tapped the screen.

"I—I think so, yes. I would have to see the diary again, but if you say that's exactly what I wrote, I believe you."

"Okay," Josie said. "I'm going to tell you something now that you didn't write because you didn't know about it. Your husband, Raffy, made a plan to hurt Beau and some people that Beau cared about."

"All this time, I thought Beau cared about me," Brooke said in a small voice.

"I know," Josie said. "I'm very sorry."

Brooke looked from the photo to Josie. "I deserve this though, after what I did."

Josie gave her wrist a light squeeze. "Brooke, I think you deserve much better than all of this."

"Thank you," said Brooke. "You're with the police, right?"

Outside the ambulance, the Chief made a noise. Josie shot him a glare and then turned back to Brooke. "Yes. That's right. You were helping me to figure out where your husband would take this man." Again, she tapped the screen. "If he was going to do something bad to him."

Brooke looked at Beau, a range of emotions flying across her face again. She stroked Beau's cheek. "We were so in love. We were going to be together. Then the accident happened. I thought he would come back for me. I couldn't leave the house anymore except to see doctors."

"Quinn," the Chief hissed. "This is a waste of time."

She ignored him. Brooke and Beau had had an affair. Both were married and the affair was even more taboo, given that Beau was the Sullivans' marriage counselor. They would have had to meet in secret to carry on together.

"Brooke," Josie said. "When you and Beau were together, where did you meet?"

Her brow furrowed. "I'm not sure. I think—"

"Was it the same bridge where you had your accident?"

"No," said Brooke. "No. That bridge—there was something wrong with it. I didn't want to drive on it, but we were fighting, and I took a wrong turn and we were fighting and—"

She broke off as tears spilled down her face. Josie found a

tissue and handed it to her. As she dabbed away her tears, she said, "He thinks I don't remember the accident, but I do."

"I know," Josie said. "I know you do. You took a wrong turn that day, you said. Where had you meant to go?"

"I only ever use the Candle Bridge to get back here. It takes longer but it's safer, and since it's farther away, he never thinks to look for us there."

Josie looked at Noah and the Chief. Noah's phone was already pressed to his ear.

"Thank you," Josie told Brooke. She held a hand out for her phone but Brooke didn't give it back.

"You're going to see them, aren't you?" she said.

"Yes," Josie replied.

Noah said, "There is no Candle Bridge."

The Chief said, "Quinn, I told you, this is a waste of time. Let's get the sheriff's dogs. A helicopter from the state police. We just have to do this the old-fashioned way and search. We'll start at the Old Arch Bridge and follow the creek."

Josie looked from the photo of Beau to Brooke. "Let's bring her with us," she said.

"Are you nuts?" said the Chief. "She needs to go to the hospital. Absolutely not."

"I think if we take her, if she sees the creek, she might remember."

"No," said the Chief. "Now let's go."

Josie said, "Do you remember that time you took me to your house and showed me your sister's cold case file?"

He bristled.

"Do you remember what you said to me?"

Josie would never forget it. *Quinn, listen good, because I'm not going to say this again, and I'm sure as shit not going to say it in front of anyone else. You're the best investigator I've ever seen.*

The Chief threw both hands in the air. "For the love of crap. Fine. Bring her. But you're keeping an eye on her."

FIFTY-FIVE

Josie drove her own vehicle with Brooke strapped safely into the passenger's seat. Brooke pressed a hand against the passenger's side window, face as close to the glass as she could get it without touching, watching the darkened scenery flash past. Every so often her breath clouded the pane, and she quickly wiped it away. "I never get to just take a ride," she told Josie. "We can only see doctors."

Behind them was a convoy of vehicles including Noah, the Chief, Gretchen, Mettner and two Lenore County Sheriff's cars. Even in the dark, with only the help of the headlights, Brooke started to remember some things by their third go-round in the area where the abandoned bridge sat. Road names and landmarks. Josie drove slowly, letting her talk until, almost subconsciously, she began to point out places where she and Beau had met. Behind an old barn on a farm that was no longer active. At the rear of a church cemetery. In the parking lot of a state park fishing area. Finally, the bank of a creek over which spanned a covered bridge, the trusses beneath its peaked roof open.

Not the Candle Bridge. The Cattail Bridge.

Josie parked along the bank, which was several feet below the bridge. As the vehicles behind them pulled in, headlights passed over the space between the base of the bridge and the rushing creek below. At first, she thought it was a trick of the light, but by the third time, she realized what she was seeing were two humans—one small and one bigger—suspended upside down from the bridge like cocoons.

Josie jumped out of her car and ran toward the edge of the water. Another set of headlights strobed past, and she caught a glimpse of the back of Jasmine Toselli's head, swinging gently. Then she saw Sam Toselli's tiny face. His hair hung down. His lips were turning blue. Raffy had wrapped them each in a plastic tarp, duct-taping their bodies inside of it. Both their feet had been bundled and secured with what looked like a seatbelt. Could that be right?

Sickness rolled through her. The webbing in the patterned injuries on Eve Bowers's and Trudy Dawson's necks. Now this. Brooke had been stuck inside her upside-down vehicle while it sank lower and lower into the creek water because her seatbelt malfunctioned. Raffy couldn't recreate the tragedy with a vehicle, but he had cut seatbelts out of cars—maybe even the car Brooke had had her accident in—and tied them together to fashion these death ropes.

From somewhere above them, a man shouted for help. His cries were quickly cut off.

Noah, Gretchen, and Mettner appeared beside Josie.

"Jesus," Mettner breathed. "This guy is crazier than we thought."

Josie said, "We need a team down here in case he decides to drop them into the water. We'll probably need someone downstream too. If he cuts them loose, they'll fall head first. We won't have much time before they drown—if they don't break their necks. The current is moving fast. Someone should be downstream to catch them in the event whoever is positioned here doesn't catch them."

Gretchen said, "The fastwater rescue team will never get here in time."

Josie turned and motioned toward the vehicles. "They've all got ropes inside them. Start tying them together. Anchor rope to the base of that tree—" She pointed to a large oak a few feet away. "And that one down there. Then tie it to whoever's going in the water. The trick will be catching them when they fall. People on the shore will be responsible for pulling you in."

Mettner said, "Good idea, boss." He tapped Gretchen's shoulder. "You a good swimmer?"

Noah said, "Not as strong as me. Gretchen, you go up top with Josie. We'll handle the scene down here."

As the other officers spilled from their vehicles, Josie and Gretchen jogged up and around to the entrance of the bridge, followed by two Lenore County Sheriff's deputies. Here the darkness was more complete. There were no lights on the bridge or around it. The glow of headlights from the bank below barely reached the bridge but soon, as Josie expected, the marked vehicles began to turn on their take-down lights, which were on the front and sides of their light bars, casting more of a glow on the path to the bridge. Next, spotlights flicked on. Each cruiser was equipped with one on the A-pillar of the driver's side. Their beams began to swivel, searching the creek and the trusses of the bridge.

They cast enough of a glow along the path to the bridge that Josie could make out Raffy's black sedan angled across the mouth of the bridge, blocking vehicles from passing. Beyond it, the spotlights reached parts of the bridge's ceiling but below it was darkness and shadow. The small flashlights that the sheriff's deputies pulled from their duty belts hardly made a dent. There was no way to tell if Raffy had blocked the entrance to the bridge on the other side, but Josie radioed the team on the bank and asked for units to check.

As they reached the sedan, a gunshot boomed. Josie, Gretchen and the two deputies scattered, taking cover along the side of the road, behind trees. Another shot. Then another.

Boom. Boom. Boom.

From where Josie stood, she could see down to the bank where spotlights had been pointed at Jasmine and Sam's dangling bodies. With each shot, Jasmine's body jerked. Josie's heart skipped a beat and then galloped into overdrive. At first, she thought he was shooting Jasmine, but then she realized that it was Jasmine reacting to the noise. She was still alive. Josie wasn't so sure about Sam. She hoped he was merely unconscious.

The shots ceased.

Josie called out, "Raffy Sullivan! This is Detective Josie Quinn with the Denton Police Department. We're here with the Lenore County Sheriff. Put down your weapon and come out with your hands where we can see them."

No response.

"Raffy!" Josie called again. "Rafferty Sullivan!" She repeated her earlier request.

More gunshots rang out, echoing in Josie's ears. She waited a few minutes, looking down at the team on the bank. Mettner had been tied to the rope nearest the bridge. He was in the middle of the creek, beneath where Sam's small body dangled. The water came to his chest. He couldn't reach the boy.

As Josie's hearing returned, she heard a wailing. From a tree nearby, came Gretchen's voice. "You think that's Beau Collins?"

"Probably. He'd want him to watch."

Josie called out his name again, gave the instructions.

Finally, a voice called back. "He's going to kill me. You have to come in here and shoot him. He's going to kill my son. Please. Help us."

Beau Collins.

Josie said, "Raffy, this is over. Let Mr. Collins go and come out. There's only one way this ends."

"You're right," Raffy shouted back. "With this piece of shit watching everything he ever cared about get destroyed."

Gretchen whispered. "He fired fifteen rounds. Odds are he's got a handgun. There aren't many that hold more than that."

Josie said, "He could have an extended magazine."

Gretchen replied, "I don't think he owns one of those."

"It's a risk," Josie said.

"I like risks."

Josie gestured toward the asphalt and then, in a low crouch, pistol at the ready, ran over to the car. Gretchen followed.

From somewhere beyond the darkness, Beau's voice pleaded. "You don't need to do this. You don't. You've already taken everything. I'm sorry, okay. I'm sorry."

"You're sorry for what you did to me? To my wife? Or are you just sorry that your life is ruined?"

The answer didn't come fast enough for Raffy. The sound of knuckles hitting flesh came next, then more cries from Beau.

Gretchen carefully poked her head up over the sedan's hood. A second later, she resumed her position beside Josie. "We need another light up here. A big one. Powerful. The way these spotlights are angled upward, I can only see the bridge ceiling. I can't see where Raffy or Collins are positioned. If we get a decent light, we can shine it in Raffy's eyes and we blind him. Rush in, take him down."

Josie said, "One of the cars will have something. Go get one. I'll stay here. The biggest flashlight you can get."

"Now," Raffy said. "I've got everyone's attention. The spotlight is literally on your secret mistress and bastard son. I'm going to make you watch this."

"Please don't," said Beau. "My son didn't do anything. He

doesn't even know who I am! If you want to hurt someone, hurt me. Throw me over. Shoot me. Strangle me. Stab me. I don't care. But let him go."

A female voice came from the shadows that Gretchen had disappeared into, disembodied but strong. "Husband?"

Silently, Josie cursed. Who had let Brooke Sullivan up here?

"Go back!" Josie hissed, as Brooke emerged from the darkness, walking unsteadily toward the car. "Brooke, go back."

"Brooke?" Raffy called.

"Stop this," she said. "Stop all of this."

"You, of all people, should not ask me to stop! He ruined you. Ruined us. He manipulated you, violated the sanctity of our marriage, and then when you asked him to leave his wife to be with you, he refused."

"No—" Brooke cried. Her legs wobbled and she fell.

"Stay down!" Josie told her. "He'll be able to see you. He's armed!"

Ignoring her, Brooke hauled herself back to her feet.

From inside the bridge, the sound of an impact came, followed by Beau yelping. "Tell her."

"That's not what happened," Beau cried. "That's not it. I just wanted some time to think about things."

Another blow, another yelp. Raffy said, "You're such a liar. You can't stop yourself. If you won't tell her the truth then I will. Brooke! He was in the car with you that day. The day of the accident. He was with you. You don't remember but after you woke up, you were lucid for a short while. You kept crying for him, wanting to know if he survived the accident. That's when I knew. He was with you, and he left you. He got out of the car, climbed to safety, and left you there, hanging, waiting to plummet to your death."

"No," Brooke called, taking another step. "No, that's not true."

"Brooke!" Josie pleaded. "Please go back!"

"Stop it," Beau cried. "Stop this now. Just shut up."

A thud silenced him.

Raffy went on. "It's true. He will never admit it, but I saw him right after the accident. I followed him. He was banged up. Bruised. He had been in the accident. I was going to confront him but then the hospital called because you coded. By the time I got there, they had brought you back again, but I knew the truth, and I realized with each day that passed and you not getting any better that he needed to pay."

"No," Brooke said. Through the shadows, Josie could see that she was almost to the car.

"Why won't you listen to me?" Raffy shrieked. "Why can't you ever admit the truth about this piece of garbage? He left you in the car that day. He left you to die. He never even called 911. That's how much he loved you, how much he cared about you."

Beau's sobs flooded the night. "That's not true. I did—I did love her. I—that's not how it happened."

"I said shut up! Now you're going to pay for running your mouth."

There was a sound like metal clanging, a brief sawing, and then a chorus of shouts from the riverbank. Something crashed into the water. More cries. Mettner's voice. "I lost her, I lost her!"

Jasmine, not Sam.

"Nooo! No! No!" Beau screamed.

"Watch it," Raffy shouted. "Watch. Hey!"

Noah's voice echoed up from the creek. "I've got her!"

Next, there was only the sound of grunts and thuds. Beau taking a beating. Every fiber in Josie's being wanted to flip on her cell phone flashlight and rush inside the bridge to confront Raffy. But it was too risky, especially with Brooke standing in the open.

"Stop!" Brooke screamed, now within Josie's reach. Brooke's

hands slapped against the hood of the car. "Stop! Stop hurting him!"

Josie tried to pull Brooke down into a crouched position, but she slapped Josie's hands away, using the car to keep her balance.

Raffy was out of breath but by the sound of it, he stopped. "You still care what happens to this asshole? Even after knowing the truth? How he left you to die? How he made you what you are now? A shell of a woman. A worthless twit who can't even remember my fucking name?"

Brooke slapped the hood again, her scream piercing the night, causing a momentary lull so silent that Josie could hear every nuance of the current below the bridge as well as footsteps padding toward them. Gretchen.

"You're wrong," Brooke said. "You're wrong about what happened. You think I don't remember anything. You think I'm worthless, but I remember the accident. You're right. Beau was there. He was in the car with me. He did try to get me out. He did everything he could. I told him to go get help."

"But he didn't!" Raffy screamed back.

Brooke's voice was so sad that Josie felt it in the depths of her soul. "But he did," she said. "He called the one person he always turned to in times of trouble."

"What?" Raffy said, voice now alert, almost afraid, "No."

"It's true," Brooke said. "When I saw her at the house I started to remember something. Her voice. It took a long time to come back. Then when I finally got it, I wrote it down in my diary. I've read it every day since then."

A chill shot through Josie's veins as she remembered the last entry in the diary.

Brooke continued, "He called his wife. Her name—her name—I can't remember it—"

"Claudia," Raffy supplied.

"Yes. Claudia. He called her. She came and he told her the truth. He told her everything. And she—she—"

Brooke broke off. Josie felt the pain radiating off her in waves. Gretchen sidled up to Josie on her other side, nudging a flashlight against Josie's shoulder. "I've got it. A big one. When you're ready."

Beau's voice came, thick and tortured. "Claudia told me that we had to leave her. We had to walk away. She didn't think that we would be able to get Brooke out. The way the car was suspended, it was all so precarious. Claudia said even if she survived, even if we got her out, the affair, the fact that I had slept with a patient, all of it would ruin us. Not just me but her, too. She reminded me how much she had given up for me. The career she wanted, children. She said if I didn't walk away from the car, from Brooke, that it was over, everything we'd worked for. The practice, the book, the show, the wealth."

"It was her," said Brooke softly. "It was her."

There was more silence. Then Raffy began shouting again. "Bullshit! Bullshit! So both of them are pieces of garbage. So what? They ruined our lives, Brooke. They ruined you!"

"Let's go," Josie said. "I'll go around. On three, hop up and flip on the light. Try to get it in his eyes."

Quietly, she radioed the other deputies nearby, letting them know that she and Gretchen were taking the lead. Raffy was still screeching as Josie ran, crouched down, around the car, under the roof of the bridge. A blinding light appeared, shining in his direction. Josie registered Raffy's face, red with fury, eyes squinted against the light. As he threw up an arm to block the light from his face, she saw a large hunting knife in one hand. Along the side of the bridge, a length of seatbelt was tied to the side of one of the Vs in the trusses.

Sam.

At Raffy's feet, Beau lay in a bloodied heap, his face purple and streaked with blood.

Gretchen kept the light on Raffy as Josie approached him, pistol pointed at his center mass. "Drop the knife," she told him. "Kick it toward me, and put your hands in the air where I can see them."

He thrashed his head, trying to get away from the light. Zigzagging inside the small space, he still couldn't get away from it. Josie shouted her instructions again, to no avail. Brooke ran onto the bridge and threw herself on top of Beau. Shielding his face with one arm, Raffy saw the two of them. He ran at them, knife above his head, poised to strike. The beam of Gretchen's flashlight bobbled as it tried to keep up with him. Josie tightened her grip on her weapon, trying to get a good line of sight. Her finger applied slight pressure to the trigger, ready to fire. Raffy ignored Beau and Brooke, instead making a beeline for the seatbelt. He brought the knife down on it and began sawing.

"Stop!" Josie shouted. "Stop or I'm going to shoot!"

But he was beyond reason now. When the sawing didn't work, he began hitting the frayed belt with the knife. Josie gave him one more warning as the flashlight beam steadied. When he didn't heed it, she took the shot, hitting his arm. It was enough for the knife to drop. Raffy staggered backward and fell, clutching at his arm, shock spreading across his face. Josie kicked the knife away. Gretchen was by her side then as they turned Raffy onto his stomach and zip-tied his wrists together. Gretchen shouted the all-clear so that the deputies could enter the bridge and get Raffy to the nearest ambulance.

Josie snatched up the flashlight and ran back to the wall of the bridge. Shouts came up from the water below. A creaking noise filled the air. The light illuminated the seatbelt just as the final thread gave way. The flashlight tumbled over and down into the water as Josie threw her body at the seatbelt. Her hands caught it, the edge of the wall slamming into her ribs. She teetered there, the strap holding Sam Toselli aloft in both hands.

Then the momentum took her, and she tumbled after him, into the darkness, plunging into the icy water.

The shock of the water pierced every cell of her body, stunning her heart, stopping time. Then her limbs began to work, to try to swim upward toward the surface. Except it was too dark to tell which way was upward. She tried not to panic but soon her lungs burned, aching for air. She heard Lisette's voice again. *Stop fighting, dear.*

She let go. Let her limbs go slack. Let her body float. Bob to the surface. Then a pair of familiar arms encircled her waist. She was dragged out of the water. Shouts replaced the stillness of what might have been her underwater grave. She heard only one. Noah.

"I've got her. I've got her."

She felt rocks beneath her. Noah's fingers pressed against her throat. Her eyes flew open. He smiled down at her though she could still see the vestiges of panic lining his face. "Hey," he said. "You're okay."

"Sam," she said. "Is he—"

Noah palmed her cheek. "Mett caught him. He's alive. Dehydrated, in shock, scared shitless, but okay. So's his mom."

Josie felt exhaustion seep through every inch of her body. She closed her eyes. "Get us some blankets, would you?"

FIFTY-SIX

ONE WEEK LATER

Josie and Noah rang Beau Collins's doorbell. From outside, she could hear the chime echo through the cavernous space inside. Soon after, Margot Huff opened the door. Fatigue had taken its toll. Large bags sat beneath her eyes. Her sweater and jeans hung loose on her. Still, she managed a wan smile for them. "Come on in, he's in the great room."

Josie and Noah walked into the foyer. Noah asked, "Does he know we're coming?"

Margot shook her head. "I didn't want to give him time to come up with a selection of lies to offer in response to whatever revelations you two are bringing with you today."

She held Josie's gaze for a beat, as if testing to see if Josie would disclose why they'd asked for the meeting, but the truth was, even Josie herself didn't know what all the evidence meant.

Margot shrugged and turned away, beckoning them to follow. Beau was seated in the middle of the couch that faced the wall of windows but paying no attention to the view. On the coffee table before him were a collection of trinkets that he was carefully rolling in bubble wrap and placing into a large box.

He offered Josie and Noah a small smile although it only

served to make him look more gruesome. Raffy had beaten him so badly that it would be a few weeks before all the swelling and bruising went away. The doctors in the Emergency Department had assured him that his face would, eventually, return to normal. "Officers," he said. "What can I do for you?"

Josie and Noah stood on the other side of the coffee table, looking down at him. Margot stayed off to the side, as if she were ready to flee out the front door at any moment. Josie had a feeling that if she could get the truth out of Beau, for real this time, Margot would wish she'd never walked through the doors.

"We just need to ask you some follow-up questions," Noah said.

Beau put a vase he'd been wrapping into the box and wiped his palms on his jeans. "How's Brooke?"

"She's well," Josie said. "We found her a spot at an assisted living facility. She's starting occupational therapy." She didn't mention that the last time she had seen Brooke, she asked for Beau to visit. Of all the things for poor Brooke to remember consistently, it had to be Beau Collins. Although, Josie supposed it could be worse. The greater percentage of her memories could be of Raffy. Regardless, Josie was hopeful that Brooke would make newer, better memories in her new place. She would never function at full capacity again but with consistent care and an environment where she felt cared for and safe, she might regain a lot.

"I'd like to see her," Beau said. "I've already set up a trust for her. It should help with her future care. It's the least I can do. How are Jasmine and Sam? She won't take my calls."

"We're not at liberty to say," Josie told him.

Sam and Jasmine Toselli were recovering well from their ordeal, but Jasmine had specifically asked them not to share any details with Beau Collins. At least, not yet.

He looked disappointed. "Oh, okay. Well, I've left messages for her. Maybe she'll reach out."

Josie moved around the coffee table and perched on the edge of it, facing him. Their knees touched. "Beau," she said. "We need to talk about some things but first, I'm going to have to read you your rights."

He laughed nervously. "My rights? What is this? A TV show?"

When he realized it was not a joke, he swallowed, looking at her soberly. "Okay, sure. Fine. Go ahead."

Josie read him his Miranda rights and when she asked whether or not he understood them, he said yes. She waited for him to ask for an attorney, but he didn't. Instead, he just looked at her expectantly.

Josie took in a breath. "We got the DNA results back from the crime scenes. Claudia. Eve. Trudy."

"Okay," he said.

"The DNA of two people were found on Claudia's person. Rafferty Sullivan and Archie Gamble."

At the mention of Gamble's name, a pallor appeared beneath his bruising.

"At the other two scenes, only one person's DNA was found," Josie went on. "Rafferty Sullivan."

He waited for her to continue, so she did. "We know why Rafferty Sullivan's DNA was here, in this house. He was planning an elaborate killing game in which he exposed all your secrets and killed everyone you loved. But Archie Gamble?"

She let the name hang in the air.

"I don't know him," Beau said. "I told you that."

Noah said, "He was following your wife for months. We have his records. He followed her to the studio. To the practice. To The Grotto, where she was having lunch with Liam Flint."

At this, Beau said, "Who?"

Margot piped up. "The camera operator from the show!"

"The guy with the glasses?" Beau said.

Josie didn't answer him, instead continuing, "Gamble even

followed her twice to Raffy Sullivan's home—the one he shared with Brooke in Lenore County. It took me a while to make the connection but Gamble took notes from when he followed her. One entry appeared twice: 4342SSRR. 4342 Silver Springs Road—Brooke and Raffy's home."

"I don't understand," said Beau.

"Neither did we," said Noah. "So we went back and looked at the timeline. You said that you'd never met Archie Gamble—"

"It's true! It's true. I never met the man."

Margot stepped forward, arms crossed over her chest. "You literally have no reason to lie right now, you know that, right?"

Josie knew exactly why he was lying but they had to get him to admit it. She said, "You and Gamble had an altercation at the DMV four months before Claudia's murder."

"So?" Beau said, trying a weak smile. "I meet lots of people all the time, everywhere. I don't remember it."

"Do you remember meeting the bartender at Leo's bar two weeks after the DMV incident?" asked Noah. "'Cause he remembers you. Quite well, actually. You didn't exactly fit in there."

Beau said nothing.

Josie said, "It was around that time that Margot overheard you and Claudia at WYEP arguing over a large amount of cash that had been withdrawn from one of your accounts. Thirty thousand dollars, to be exact."

"We already discussed this," Beau said. "I told you. Claudia took it out to give to some charity. Maybe it wasn't the one I thought it was, but that's what she said she was doing."

"As you know, the women's center never received it," Josie said. "She actually took that money and gave it to Raffy. Well, she gave it to Brooke, because only she was there that day."

"So what? I told you on the bridge. It was Claudia's idea to leave Brooke there. I thought Brooke had died. I never looked

back because it was too painful. I thought if either Brooke or
Raffy wanted to speak with me, they would get in touch. They
didn't."

Josie reached inside her coat and pulled out a folded piece
of paper. She placed it on the table and smoothed it out. "This is
a copy of the diary entry that Brooke wrote the day that Claudia
showed up on her doorstep with thirty thousand dollars in
cash."

When he made no move to read it, Margot strode over and
snatched it up. She read it out loud, her voice trembling as she
neared the end.

"*The accident lady was here again today. She brought all
this money. My husband was not home. She said it was for him
and I should give it to him. She said something like it was for
him to keep quiet at the station. I'm not sure what station she
means. Then she got upset and started crying. She said maybe I
should take it and get away from him, get out of here. I don't
know where I would go. She hugged me and it felt so wonderful.
I can't remember the last time that happened. But then she said
she was sorry for what she did to me. I didn't know what she
meant. Not then, at least. Even after she said that, I still didn't
want her to leave even though she kept crying. I asked her why
she was crying and she smiled and stroked my hair, like a
mother. It felt so good. She said her husband had withdrawn the
money and she caught him with it and she thought he was going
to do something very bad with it. To her. 'My days are
numbered, I think,' she told me. 'But maybe if you take the
money, we'll both make it out of this alive.' I didn't know what
that meant.*

"*I didn't even know who her husband was until I came to
write in this diary and I saw my last several entries. Her husband
is my lover. The one who hasn't come back. He's on television
with her, and now he's going to do something bad to her. Something to do with this money. I still don't understand any of it, but*

*the harder I thought about her, and about Beau, the memories
started coming back. About the accident."*

Margot stopped there. She knew about the revelations on
the bridge—how Beau had been in the car and unable to free
Brooke. How he had called Claudia for help, and she had
insisted they leave Brooke behind.

Her hand shook as she thrust the page in Beau's face. He
reared back so it didn't hit him. "What is this?" she asked.
"What does this mean?"

Again, he said nothing.

Josie waited a few beats and then she said, "You weren't
telling the truth about the money, were you? It wasn't Claudia
who took it out, it was you. When Margot asked you about the
argument, you lied to her. It wasn't you who was angry with
Claudia for taking the money, was it?"

He didn't answer.

Josie said, "It was Claudia who was upset with you. She
wanted to know what it was for. You made something up. Something she obviously didn't find believable. Either she took it or
you gave it to her. She had already figured out that Raffy was
working for WYEP, insinuating himself into your inner circle.
She had already gone to see him, to confront him."

"We know that's true," Noah said. "Because he told us. We
interviewed him in the hospital. He told us that Claudia figured
out that he was your former patient whose wife had been in the
accident with you. She went to his house to ask him why he was
working at WYEP. Why he was dating your assistant. That was
when he brought Brooke out, showed Claudia the damage that
had been inflicted by leaving her in that car. Claudia was
incredibly distraught. She left but later, at the station, she went
to him and asked him what he wanted, what his plan was, and
he refused to give her a straight answer."

"But she was worried about it," Josie said. "She told Liam
she had done something unforgivable but wouldn't tell him

what. We know now it was leaving Brooke to die—and knowing Brooke suffered a fate worse than death."

"So what?" Beau blurted out. "What does any of this have to do with anything? You caught Raffy. He's going to prison. It's over."

Josie said, "What was the money for, Beau?"

"This is ridiculous," he said, standing up.

Margot's hand shot out and pushed hard against his shoulder. He fell back onto the couch. "What was the money for, Dad?" She said the word "dad" with sarcasm. Beau flinched.

When he still refused to answer, Noah said, "The night that Sam and Jasmine were taken—the same night that Raffy came to the hotel to get you—you left your phone behind. It was part of a crime scene as far as we were concerned. We got a warrant for its contents in case it contained anything that might help us find where Raffy had taken you."

Josie picked up the thread. "After Raffy arrived, you made a phone call to Archie Gamble. It was shortly after that that Gamble was seen by one of our officers leaving his home with a weapon in hand. He went directly to Brooke and Raffy Sullivan's house. Why?"

Beau spread his hands in a helpless gesture. "How should I know?"

Noah asked, "What did you talk about when you called him?"

"I don't—I don't know. I mean, Raffy made me call him. I didn't know who he was. I was just doing what Raffy told me to do."

"Fine," Josie said even though she knew he was lying. "What did Raffy tell you to say to him?"

He hesitated. When he finally spoke, his voice was barely audible. "That I was going to be there. I would meet him there and I'd have the rest of the money he was owed."

"Who owed him money?" Noah asked.

Beau didn't answer.

"Why would Raffy tell you to say that to him?" Josie said.

"I don't know."

Josie said, "Raffy was stalking you—all of you—for years. Learning your routines, your secrets. He had always planned this game, it was just a matter of when to begin. After Claudia confronted him, he moved up his timetable. He admitted to being here the night she was murdered. He'd been spying on her closely for weeks. His intention was to abduct her, not to kill her. She was meant to be the prize in the game he wanted you to play. If you answered enough of his questions correctly, you might get Claudia back—but your life would be ruined."

Beau's fingers started to tremble. He laced them together in his lap.

Josie said, "He'd seen this older guy trailing Claudia a lot. He didn't know what to make of it. Then the night of your anniversary dinner, Raffy was out there, in the woods of the city park, watching the house through these very windows." Josie swept her hand back toward them. "Waiting for everyone to show up for the big dinner. Eve. Margot. Liam and the crew. You. He knew exactly what time everyone was due to appear because his girlfriend, Margot, had told him."

At this, a visible shudder worked its way through Margot's body.

"Imagine Raffy's surprise," Noah said. "When the only person who showed up was Archie Gamble."

"And instead of spying on Claudia, as usual," Josie said. "He walks right into the house."

"And right back out only minutes later," said Noah. "Covered in blood. He goes to his old truck, grabs a pair of overalls out of the bed, and throws them on. Then he leaves."

"I don't—I don't know what this has to do—"

Margot's eyes narrowed. "You know something. I know you know something. Just tell them!"

Josie said, "This is the question that's plagued us since day one of this investigation. How did the killer know that Claudia would be utterly alone for that half hour?"

She let the question hang in the air.

Margot pressed a fist to her mouth. From behind it came a muffled, "Oh my God." She fell onto the couch beside Beau and stared at him. He wouldn't look at her.

Josie and Noah let the silence do the work, waiting patiently, unmoving, eyes locked on Beau.

Margot said, "I know you never tell the truth. You're like, allergic to it, or whatever, but Beau, please. Look where all this lying has gotten you. It's literally destroyed your whole entire life. Your marriage. Your show. Your practice. Your publishing career, podcast, all of it. Everything. Even your mistress is dead. If you did what I think you did, I get that you don't want to go to prison. I really do. But without anyone in your life, who cares about that? Living alone as the most hated man in this city is a prison all its own."

His head swiveled in her direction. He took one of her hands. Josie expected her to snatch it away, but she didn't. "I have you."

"No," said Margot. "You don't. Not if you refuse to take responsibility for anything in your life, ever. What you did for Jasmine when Sam was born—providing for him but staying out of their lives because that's what she wanted, that was good. What you did for Brooke—establishing that trust, that was a start, but it's not enough."

"But Margot," he said, voice husky.

"Don't 'but' me," she said. "Here's the thing: I know there is some good inside you. Whether it comes from a place of actual virtue or from a place of self-preservation, I'm not sure yet, but I've always wanted to find out. All my life, I dreamed of who my dad might be. When I found out it was you, I was ecstatic. You were a superstar. You had it all, and on top of that, you were kind. Now I know none of that was true. You can never give that to me. There is only one thing that you can give to me, as my father, and that is to take responsibility for the worst thing you've ever done. If you do that, I promise to stay in your life, to be here when you get out. If you don't, I walk out this door today and you will never see me again. You will be alone forever, for the rest of your life, if you don't start taking responsibility now and telling the truth."

Slowly, Beau's resolve crumbled. His shoulders shook. He covered his face with his hands. Sobs erupted from his throat. No one spoke. They simply waited for him to collect himself. Then he said, "Okay. It was me. I called Archie Gamble the afternoon of Claudia's murder to tell him she would be alone until six thirty. I had made sure that everyone would be late."

Noah said, "Why would you do that?"

"Because I hired Archie Gamble to kill my wife."

Tears rolled down Margot's face, but she didn't leave.

Beau continued, "Things were never the same after she found out about Brooke. I had had lapses in judgment before that. I think she knew but she didn't care enough about them to say anything. I wasn't lying when I say that I cared for Brooke. I was genuinely considering leaving Claudia and trying to make a go of it with Brooke, but then the more I thought about it, about how disruptive it would be, how much it would cost— how much I would lose—I balked. The day of the accident, Claudia convinced me to walk away, to focus on our future together, and I did. But she was never happy. Not with the show or the book or the podcast or me. We were living two separate lives. In fact, I suspected she might be having an affair. I was so angry. We were about to go national. I was going to break it off with Eve, and Claudia seemed like she was going full throttle with someone else. She was going to ruin everything."

Noah said, "You didn't think that your wife, who hosted

your couples' show with you, being murdered would ruin everything?"

"I could have spun it," Beau said. "All the focus groups liked me better than Claudia anyway. I could have grown the show—from widowhood to finding love again. I had the star power to do that. She didn't. I couldn't see any other way out of it that wouldn't result in everything we had worked for going down the toilet permanently. If you get divorced, the audience will blame you. If your wife is killed, that's out of your control."

Josie had had an inkling of what they were going to hear from him if their interrogation was successful, but still, the loathing she felt for the man was hard to quell.

Noah said, "The thirty thousand dollars was for Gamble?"

"Yes, but Claudia caught me with it and confronted me. I made something up—about a charity—but she didn't buy it. She could always see right through me. She took it. She said she'd return it to our account, but she didn't. I didn't ask about it because I didn't want the subject coming up again. So I had to take out another thirty to pay him. Thirty to hire him. Another thirty when he completed the job. He followed her and at a certain point he told me that he was ready whenever I was, but I had to make sure she was alone. So I did. I didn't think that all of this would... happen."

Raffy had been waiting in the woods outside. He'd told them that after Gamble came and went, he'd come into the house to see what had happened and found Claudia dead. He was frustrated but it was as good a time as any to begin his game. He moved her and left the puzzle box.

Noah said, "After he killed Claudia, you owed him another thirty grand."

Beau nodded. "But then Eve was killed, and I didn't know what was going on. I had no chance to contact Gamble. The next thing I knew, you had his name. You knew his name. I was terrified. He called me on this 'burner' phone he'd given me to get in touch with him. He was so angry. He said he had nothing to do with Eve's murder. He just wanted his money. I told him I couldn't get it for him until the investigation was over. He wasn't happy. He threatened to kill me! I had no idea what was happening or who was behind the murders of Eve and Trudy—or who was leaving the puzzle boxes. Then Raffy came to the hotel. He told me the truth. I had no idea he was Brooke's husband. He looked so different. All those years he'd worked at the station, and I had no idea. He was with my daughter, for God's sake. I had no idea he had been tracking us, worming his way into our lives, and following Claudia. That was when he told me that he knew about Archie Gamble —not that I'd hired him but that he'd been following Claudia. He'd seen him come into this house and leave covered in blood. He knew Gamble had killed her—he just didn't know why."

"You lied to us a few minutes ago," Noah said. "It wasn't Raffy who told you to call Gamble from the hotel, was it?"

"No, it wasn't. It was my idea to call him. I was trying to buy time, distract Raffy."

"What do you mean?" asked Josie.

"Raffy wanted to know who he was and whether or not I knew that Gamble had been the one to kill Claudia. I told him I knew Archie Gamble, but I didn't say more than that. Raffy still didn't put the pieces together. He couldn't figure out how I knew Gamble or why Gamble had killed Claudia, but he wanted to know—badly. He felt one-upped by Gamble."

Josie knew this to be true. When she and Noah questioned Raffy in the hospital, he had told them the same thing. "Gamble had ruined his plan."

Beau shrugged. "Sort of. I guess. Anyway, yes, I lied before. Like I said, it was my idea to call Gamble. Raffy wanted me to leave the hotel with him. I didn't know why at first, but I knew it couldn't be good. I was sure he was going to kill me even though he seemed much more concerned about exposing all my secrets."

"Lies," Margot corrected.

Beau had the good grace to look sheepish. He cleared his throat. "Lies," he said, nearly choking on the word. "I convinced Raffy that if he really wanted to expose me, Gamble was the key. I told him what I knew about Archie Gamble was my biggest secret of all—bigger than Brooke or Jasmine and Sam. I didn't tell him that I had hired Gamble. I thought if I kept that to myself as long as I could, it would work as leverage. Keep Raffy from killing me. Raffy thought I was trying to trick him. I told him that if we could get Gamble to meet us somewhere, I'd prove that there was a connection, my secret would be revealed and Raffy would hold all the power once and for all. Raffy asked me how I could get Gamble to meet me. I said that I owed him money and he'd meet me anywhere I asked if it meant he could collect it. Raffy told me to call him and tell him I'd meet him at Raffy's house and that I'd have his money."

Noah said, "What did you think was going to happen once you got to the house?"

Beau looked at his lap, his voice lowering. "Gamble had already killed for me once, hadn't he? I thought if I just got the two of them in the same room, I could somehow convince Gamble to kill Raffy. It was in both of our best interests. It wasn't a perfect plan but it was all I could think of in the moment."

It was his desperate attempt at self-preservation. Above all else, Beau Collins would always choose to try to save himself, no matter what he had to do and no matter how risky the choice.

Beau added, "I had no idea Raffy was taking me to that bridge."

Gamble had shown up to Raffy and Brooke's address enraged, fully intending to kill Beau or anyone else who got between him and his money. Beau hadn't realized that Gamble would be out for blood. However, Gamble must have lost it after Beau failed to pay him his final payment, and then the police had shown up on his doorstep. Once again, Beau had set Gamble in motion, having no idea the destruction that would follow.

What a colossal mess. Josie could hardly stand to think of the damage to so many people left in Beau's wake all because of lies. Lie atop lie atop lie. With a sigh, Josie took out her handcuffs.

"Beau Collins," she said. "You're under arrest for conspiracy to commit murder."

FIFTY-SEVEN

TWO WEEKS LATER

Josie stood beside Luke on the pitcher's mound of one of the city park's softball fields and watched Harris run across the outfield, dragging a stick behind him. Hot on his trail, his easy lope turning to a full-blown run, was Blue, looking healthy and happy. Luckily, the injuries inflicted by Archie Gamble had been minor and he had recovered well and quickly. He caught up with Harris and grabbed the stick. The two played tug of war and then Harris let Blue have the stick. Blue sauntered off with it, making his way back to Luke. He dropped the stick at Luke's feet and looked up at him, panting, tongue lolling.

Luke bent and patted Blue's head. "Good boy."

He turned back to Josie and flashed her a smile. Harris ran over and grabbed the stick again, sprinting away with it. Blue shot to his feet and followed.

"I'm glad to see he's doing well," Josie said.

Luke smiled as he watched Blue chase Harris across the outfield again. "He's tough."

"He's not just tough," Josie said. "He's a total badass. Luke, I wanted to thank you. If it wasn't for you and Blue, I'd be dead. You saved my life."

Luke nodded. "Blue saved both of us. That's what he does."

She touched his hand. "How are you doing? Are you okay?"

He sighed and gave her a weak smile. "I'm working on it."

An awkward silence stretched between them, broken only by Harris's giggles as Blue took the stick from him and ran away with it again. Luke pointed toward boy and dog. "He's so big now."

"Yeah," Josie agreed. "It's gone so fast. Before we know it, he'll be driving."

Luke chuckled. "You and Noah, you two don't want kids?"

Josie's throat constricted. It was hard to push her answer out. The last time Luke had been in Denton was also the last time she and Noah had discussed children. Josie didn't want them. Hadn't ever wanted them. Not because she didn't love kids, but because after her horrific upbringing, she was terrified that she would turn out to be a terrible mother. How could she justify bringing a child into the world when her parenting example was someone who had literally murdered people? Noah had assured her she would be an excellent mother but had also said that if she never changed her mind, she'd be enough for him. They'd left it at that.

"Guess that's a no," Luke said. "It's okay. I know you don't like to talk about things. I was just making conversation. I'm not very good at it."

"No," she choked out. "It's fine. I—it's not that we don't want them. It's just that I'm afraid. My childhood wasn't exactly ideal. What do I know about being a mom?"

"Everything," Luke said easily. "You know what not to do—that's easy—and I've seen you with Harris. You're a natural."

"No," Josie said. "I'm not."

He met her eyes. "I know that's what you think, but you're wrong. Parents love and protect and they make difficult decisions. You already do those things for everyone you love, and Noah? He's a really good guy."

"Yeah," Josie breathed. "The best."

"I'd just hate to see you two short yourselves. You'd be really amazing parents. If you decide not to, it shouldn't be because of fear. That's all I'm saying. I know a lot about living from a place of fear."

Blue streaked past, stick in his mouth. Harris followed but stopped short when something behind them caught his eye. His eyes grew large and a grin lit up his face. "Uncle Noah!" he hollered. He took off toward home plate. Josie and Luke turned to see Noah walking onto the diamond, a coffee in hand. Harris slammed into him, hugging his leg with both hands. Noah kept walking with Harris attached to him.

Luke smiled at Josie. "You should go."

Josie nodded and jogged over to Noah. He handed her the coffee and gave Luke a mock salute. "Whose idea was it again to take a walk in February?"

Josie sipped the coffee. "We're walking through the park to the rec center for a basketball game," she said. "That hardly counts as a walk."

Harris tried to climb up Noah's body. Noah grabbed him under his armpits, lifting him easily and throwing him over his shoulder. Harris's body was arrow-straight across Noah's shoulder, his head and arms extended outward over Noah's back, legs pointed the other way. Noah held onto Harris's legs and spun him around, faster and faster. Harris giggled and shouted with joy.

Josie said, "Please stop. You're going to get dizzy and drop him."

"No, I'm not," Noah said with complete confidence. Somehow, without even putting Harris down, he managed to position the boy so that he was seated on the back of Noah's neck, his hands in Noah's thick, dark hair. Noah held onto his thin legs like they were backpack straps.

They waved to Luke as they left the field and headed to the rec center. Noah said, "They seem okay."

Josie was still worried about Luke, but the last few times she'd seen him and Blue, they did seem fine.

At the rec center, Noah lowered Harris to the ground, but not before performing more acrobatics that made Harris laugh with delight and Josie cringe. They saw him to the locker room and then went to take their seats. From the bottom of the bleachers, Jasmine Toselli waved a greeting and then turned back to watch Sam do practice drills.

"It doesn't get better than this, does it?" said Noah.

Josie took another sip of her coffee. "What's that?"

Noah smiled as Harris emerged from the locker room in his uniform and picked up a basketball. "Normalcy," he said.

A LETTER FROM LISA

Thank you so much for choosing to read *The Innocent Wife*. If you enjoyed the book and want to keep up to date with all my latest releases, just sign up at the following link. Your email address will never be shared, and you can unsubscribe at any time.

www.bookouture.com/lisa-regan

As always, I consider it a privilege to continue to bring you Josie Quinn books. It is a pleasure and a privilege to write these stories for you. As with all my books, I have done my best to make the police procedural elements as authentic as possible. Some things may have been modified for the sake of pacing and entertainment. As always, any errors or inaccuracies in the book are my own.

I feel so blessed to have such passionate and enthusiastic readers. I never get tired of hearing from you. You can get in touch with me through my website or any of the social media outlets below, as well as my Goodreads page. Also, I'd really appreciate it if you'd leave a review and perhaps recommend *The Innocent Wife* to other readers. Reviews and word-of-mouth recommendations go a long way in helping readers discover my books for the first time. Thank you so much for your loyalty and continued love for this series. Thank you for returning to Denton book after book, even though its crime rate is astronomical. I am so thankful! I hope you'll return for the next adventure!

Thanks,

Lisa Regan

www.lisaregan.com

 facebook.com/LisaReganCrimeAuthor
twitter.com/LisalRegan

ACKNOWLEDGMENTS

Amazing readers: thank you for joining Josie and the team on this new adventure. I say it all the time, but I don't feel as though I can say it enough: you are truly the best readers in the world! I am overwhelmed with gratitude for your love and loyalty to this series. There is nothing I would rather do than write more Josie stories for all of you!

Thank you, as always, to my husband, Fred, and my daughter, Morgan, for your unwavering support; your patience; your good humor; and for giving up so much time with me while I'm crime-fighting in a fictional town! Thank you to my first readers: Dana Mason, Katie Mettner, Nancy S. Thompson, and Torese Hummel. Thank you to Matty Dalrymple, Jane Kelly and Jane Gorman for helping me work out some tricky plot items. Thank you to my incredible friend and amazing assistant, Maureen Downey, for keeping me on track and coaching me through the panic stage of every single book. I'm not sure what I did to deserve you, but I sure am grateful that you're in my life and my corner. Thank you to my grandmothers: Helen Conlen and Marilyn House; my parents: Donna House, Joyce Regan, the late Billy Regan, Rusty House, and Julie House; my brothers and sisters-in-law: Sean and Cassie House, Kevin and Christine Brock and Andy Brock; as well as my lovely sisters: Ava McKittrick and Melissia McKittrick. Thank you as well to all of the usual suspects for spreading the word—Debbie Tralies, Jean and Dennis Regan, Tracy Dauphin, Claire Pacell, Jeanne Cassidy, Susan Sole, the Regans, the Conlens, the Houses, the

McDowells, the Kays, the Funks, the Bowmans, and the Bottingers! As always, thank you to all the fantastic bloggers and reviewers who read Josie's adventures every single time, as well as the ones who've only met Josie in this book. I appreciate your time and how generous you are with your support!

Thank you, as always, to Lt. Jason Jay for answering all of my never-ending questions, sometimes more than once. You are a saint. Thank you to Lee Lofland for answering my law enforcement-related questions and getting me in touch with experts whenever needed. Thank you to Stephanie Kelley, my incredible law enforcement consultant, who so generously and thoroughly answers my questions, reads my books and helps me get the details as close to right as fiction allows. Thank you to Leanne Kale Sparks and Laurie Roma for the help with HIPAA privacy laws. Thank you so much to Wade Walton and Aunyea Lachelle for answering all of my television studio questions! Thank you to the Drip N Scoop in Ocean City, New Jersey, where I wrote the first quarter of this book, for your space, Wi-Fi, lattes and delicious donuts!

Thank you to Jenny Geras, Noelle Holten, Kim Nash, and the entire team at Bookouture including my copy editor, Jennie, who is absolutely fabulous, as well as my proofreader. Last but never least, thank you to the best editor in the entire world, Jessie Botterill. Thank you for your patience and kindness and for generally being incredibly brilliant, as always. You just get me. You always manage to make everything okay and say exactly what I need to hear exactly when I need to hear it. I'm so incredibly grateful for everything you do for me, I'm not sure words will ever adequately express it.

Made in the USA
Middletown, DE
16 March 2023

26925616R00213